The Cowboy Gets His Girl

JANE POLLER

This book was written while bonding with my Dad over old Western movies—and while dealing with shit from my brother-in-law, who needed bailed out of jail again. Thanks for the inspiration. Life is weird sometimes, but it's all a learning opportunity.

Vinci Books

vinci-books.com

Published by Vinci Books Ltd in 2026

1

Copyright © Jane Poller 2024

The author has asserted their moral right to be identified as the author of this work in accordance with the Copyright, Designs and Patents Act 1988. This work is a work of fiction. Names, characters, places and incidents are the product of the author's imagination or are used fictitiously. Any resemblance to actual persons, living or dead, places and incidents is entirely coincidental.

All rights reserved. No part of this publication may be copied, reproduced, distributed, stored in any retrieval system, or transmitted in any form or by any means, including photocopying, recording, or other electronic or mechanical methods, nor used as a source for any form of machine learning including AI datasets, without the prior written permission of the publisher.

The publisher and the author have made every effort to obtain permissions for any third party material used in this book and to comply with copyright law. Any queries in this respect should be brought to the attention of the publisher and any omissions will be corrected in future editions.

A CIP catalogue record for this book is available from the British Library.

Paperback ISBN: 9781036707996

By Jane Poller

Crimson Creek

The Soldier Gets His Girl
The Sheriff Gets His Girl
The Songwriter Gets His Girl
The Surgeon Gets His Girl
The Mechanic Gets His Girl
The Ranger Gets His Girl
The Cowboy Gets His Girl
The Convict Gets His Girl

Chapter One

July

Hunter prowled the Electric Cowboy, sticking to the edges of the dance floor as he casually searched. He smiled at acquaintances as he passed, the music loud enough to make speaking difficult. That was fine by him. He wasn't much of a talker.

Actions were much better. Body language went a long way too. He'd spent the better part of fifteen years in and out of this little honky-tonk bar in Crimson Creek. He'd played drums in a band with his brothers, and their weekends were full, keeping them out of trouble in their early twenties.

Except someone had been missing. He looked around the dance floor, searching for his long-lost brother. Gunner and Landry had already gone home with their wives. His littlest brother, Parker, was dancing and laughing, grinding on some girl. But not Chase.

He walked past the bar and the mingling crowd to the

side room, pushing open the saloon doors. It was quieter here, but not by much. The crowd at one-thirty in the morning was mostly desperate drunks. He snorted. Or people like him, Parker, and Chase who had nothing to go home to.

As the oldest, it was his job to make sure everyone was taken care of. That included making sure his two bachelor brothers got home safely. Or at the very least, didn't drink and drive.

Couples were playing pool together, with one guy thrusting his hips into the ass of a woman bent over the pool table. Hunter knew her act. She liked to pretend to be an amateur pool player to get the guys to teach her, lean into her just like they were now. Then they'd end up in the parking lot or at the seedy motel on the outskirts of town.

He'd fallen for that trap a time or two in his youth. Different time, a different girl, but always the same result. *Nothing gold can stay.*

Several nodded and waved at him. To them, he was just a rough, quiet cowboy needing to escape a big family and a big ranch.

Maybe it was time to find a girlfriend. His family had long since stopped bugging him to bring a girl around. He hadn't dated in years, instead preferring to pick up a girl here once or twice a week.

Would a girlfriend help shake him out of this funk and get him back to normal? Two of his brothers were married with kids now, and sometimes he looked at them and wanted that acceptance and love. It wasn't quite outweighing the caution he'd felt since his last big breakup, though.

He wasn't sure there was a woman who could handle all of him. The itch was back, not that it ever really left. He needed to get outdoors and lose himself for days, but with their parents pushing him to take over more responsibility on the ranch, his ability to just disappear when he needed to get away was gone.

Plus, he had to help Chase.

He sighed and turned to walk through the back door to the fenced-in patio. Fire pits were burning even though it was a hot July night. This was where people were lounging at the outdoor bar and talking. All of them except Chase.

Chase leaned against the wall, arms crossed and feet wide apart, eyes wide, watchful, and wary. Tonight was his brother's first night at the Cowboy. It was a momentous occasion. Both of their married brothers and wives had come out to show their support too, but they'd long since left.

He stared at Chase as he walked. Hunter remembered that feeling of newness, the wide-eyed awe. The excitement of this place had first brought him here over a decade ago. It had been his home away from home, his oasis and sanctum. With all the expectations that came with being the eldest of five boys and running his parent's ranch, Hunter had needed the escape.

It'd been a long time since he'd felt anything like that. He'd gotten more and more depraved as time went on, but for almost a year now, he'd felt... lackluster about everything. Nothing changed, nothing made him feel alive anymore. It was just something he did, like checking the fences or washing dishes for Ma after Sunday dinner.

He was in a rut and didn't know how to get out of it.

Hunter joined Chase and leaned against the wall. Together, they gazed at the people around them.

It wasn't as loud out here, so he had no problem hearing

Chase as he said, "Hunter, I know you mean well, but can we go home now? It's too overwhelming."

Hunter sighed. "I know, but it was good for you to get out, Chase. The first six months, you were practically a recluse. You've been easing into life on the outside for the last year, right? You've been taking it slow and easy, but it's time to join the real world."

Chase shrugged. "I'm not like you, Hunter. I don't need to lose myself in a crowd. I just want to go home."

Hunter frowned but didn't say anything. He'd need to think about that. Did he love this place because he could lose himself for a while? He needed to mull that over.

Landry and Parker thrived with a crowd of people. That's why they were front and center in the band for all those years. They knew how to work the crowd. But Hunter preferred watching from the shadows, hanging back and observing.

Gunner was a chameleon. He could sit back and observe in the shadows, or he could step up to the mic and take charge like the sheriff he was. Chase was the closest to him, even after all the years away. He shook his head and smiled. Some things just never changed.

"You were in prison for fifteen years, Chase. So that's fifteen years plus the past year of freedom. I don't know how you kept your sanity all this time, but I'm glad you haven't changed too much."

Chase grimaced and shrugged. "I changed plenty. Prison makes you grow up quick." Chase's voice was gravelly and deep, hidden with things he'd not say yet. Hunter kept waiting for him to open up, but maybe his brother needed a softer touch. Lord knows his other brothers had gotten softer once they'd met and married their women.

Hunter smiled and shoved his hands into his pockets.

"Fair enough, but it's time to rejoin society and build a new life. Maybe even find a nice girl and take her home."

Chase snorted. "I'm not sure this is the right place to meet someone. It hasn't worked that great for you after all."

Hunter chuckled. With the way couples were cuddled up around the fire pits, he had to admit his brother was right.

His lips twisted in self-deprecation. "I guess you're right. Fine, let's head home."

Chase pushed off the wall, and Hunter led the way back inside, people-watching as they walked. It was much like watching the herd of horses on his parents' ranch.

Hunter's mind wandered, clinically noting Parker's moves on the dance floor and filing away tips he could offer later. His job as big bro never ended, even on his free nights.

He waved at Katie, the Electric Cowboy's owner. They'd grown up together. He'd even dated her way back when but had quickly realized they made better friends. Maybe that was why this was the one place where he'd been able to scratch the itch that was always under his skin.

He felt comfortable here. Safe and relaxed. Katie smiled and pointed to the dance floor with a lifted brow. Hunter glanced back as Parker stumbled on the edge of the crowd. He frowned and nodded at Katie, then caught Chase's eye and jerked his chin toward Parker.

Chase frowned and together they walked over to where he and a petite, curvy girl were drunkenly dancing together. Parker stumbled again, and Chase grabbed him, bumping into Parker's dance partner who was probably barely legal.

She spun on knee-high leather boots and jerked. Her sleeveless arms waved around in panic, and Hunter stepped in and caught her to his chest with a grunt.

The smell of strawberries rushed him. The feel of her

body flush against his seemed to stop time. His hands slid around her back in a hungry hello. Instinct made her clutch his biceps. Her back arched into him, pressing them closer as she gasped. The feel of her, the sound out of her mouth, the look of surprise... it all made the itch under his skin roar into a full-fledged need of hot desire.

Her head shot up, and she stared at him with bright green eyes. Her mouth was still open in surprise, and the ruby red lipstick made her plump and kissable lips beg for his attention. He pictured those red satin lips encircling his dick, and her dark green eyes looking up at him with just this look.

Her eyes widened in surprise. Her long black hair tickled his hands on her back. His hands tightened with the need to wrap her high, sleek ponytail in his fist.

Her features were sharp, but her face was round. It wasn't beautiful in the classical sense but arrested his attention in its uniqueness. Her button nose was a little too wide, but it matched her wide mouth.

Chase nudged him in the back and almost had to yell to be heard over the music. "Come on, man. Let's get him home. He's practically falling asleep."

"Take him outside. Let me get her sorted out."

Hunter shifted, his cock now painfully hard, and glanced down at the little woman in his arms. His heart was pounding in time to the music as he finally registered what he was seeing and feeling.

Shock made his fingers curl on her lower back.

Her strapless red dress had pulled down to her stomach when she tripped into his arms. And she was braless.

Her breasts were probably bigger than his hands. They were round and full and pressed against his chest. His mouth watered, and he wondered what color her nipples were. It was too dark on the dance floor to tell, with how she was pressed against him.

What would she taste like? Strawberries and cream? Salty popcorn?

Oh god, where had that thought come from? He was a gentleman. He juggled her in his arms and jerked her dress up as she giggled. Disappointment slithered along his spine as he wasn't able to see her nipples, and he refused to take advantage and cop a feel.

Her arms seemed to tighten on his biceps, and her smile got impossibly wider.

"It's not even our first date yet, and you're already to first base, slugger. How long will it take you to hit it out of the park?" She laughed at her own joke.

His heart seemed to stall at the sound. It vibrated through him, sparking life and something else deep in his soul. He wanted this woman with such intensity that it scared him. He felt like he was on a very high cliff, staring into her green eyes that begged him to jump.

He took a deep breath and the smell of stale beer and body odor from the dancers around him brought him back to reality. He shook his head and grinned. "Not sure you're in any condition to make that decision, sugar tits."

She laughed again, and he spun them slowly toward the bar. Every step was painfully tight in his pants. Hunter kept a careful eye on her chest to make sure her dress stayed up.

You sure that's the reason you're staring, son?

Hunter felt a pang in his chest at the ever-present voice in his head.

"Condition, decision. You're a poet!" Her voice wasn't as slurred as he'd expected, but she was definitely leaning on him and unsteady on her feet.

He grunted, "Maybe." He slid his arm around her back to keep her upright.

She wrapped an arm around his waist to walk by his side, not even questioning him leading her toward the bar. "Are you really? Don't joke around about it, for fuck's sake."

He shrugged. "Maybe I am, maybe I'm not. You'll never know."

She scowled. "What kind of answer is that? A home-run would've been *yes, I'm a poet. Can I read some to you?*" She said the last in a faux deep, mocking voice. She was witty for being drunk.

He barked a laugh as they stopped in front of Katie at the bar. Her brows rose in surprise as she asked, "What can I get you?"

Hunter nodded at the girl he loosely held against the bar. He was afraid if he let go, she'd fall down. "She needs some water."

The girl frowned up at him, opened her mouth to say something, then seemed to think better of it. "You know, I think you're right."

Katie slid a tall glass over, and said, "Why don't you let Hunter take you home?"

Hunter rolled his eyes at Katie and sighed.

The girl almost inhaled the water as she chugged. When she set it down with a thunk, she wiped her mouth with the back of her hand. "Are you sure that's a good idea? What if he's a serial killer or something? No, I think I'd better call a cab."

Hunter snorted. "No cabs out here, sugar tits. Did you drive?"

She nodded, "Yeah, but I'm not going to drive. I might be tipsy, but I'm not stupid. Don't worry." She squinted at Katie and leaned over the bar a little.

Hunter held his breath, waiting for her breasts to pop out of her dress again. He both desperately craved it and dreaded the thought of everyone else seeing her like that.

"Psst. Is he a good guy? If he takes me home, is he going to take advantage of me?"

Hunter scowled down at the back of her head, but Katie just waved a hand and chuckled.

"He's fine. He's a pretty good guy. He might look it, but he's not the take-advantage type."

The girl looked up at him with a squint. He wondered what she saw, and he shifted self-consciously, then she almost bent double. His hands immediately went to her waist to steady her.

He swallowed, finding his crotch pressed against her ass. Before he could register it, she was straightening and holding up her phone. She waved it around and grinned at him.

"Ah ha! Here we go. I'm going to text my friend and tell her you're taking me home, and if you try any funny business, you'll find yourself on the wrong side of the US Marshals. I know a guy."

Hunter rolled his eyes but stood still as she held up her phone and took pictures of him.

Katie chuckled. "You don't have to worry, sugar. His brother is the sheriff and isn't afraid to beat him up if he crosses the line."

Hunter pursed his lips. "Like he could ever take me." Katie laughed, but he continued, looking down at the little pint-sized bombshell. "But she's right. I'll get you home safe, and that's it. Nothing to worry about."

She glanced at him through her thick lashes and nodded before looking back down at her phone. When she finished, she grabbed his arm and lifted her leg to slide the phone back inside her boot.

Katie wiped the counter. "Y'all be safe."

"Thanks, Katie. See you next time," he said as he slid a hand along the girl's back and navigated them to the door.

They pushed into the hot, humid air, and he led her through the parking lot. "What's your name?"

She held out a hand, and he had to let her go to shake. She swayed but remained upright. "I'm Taylor, and I'm new to town. What's your name again?"

He smiled and hovered around her as she walked, gently holding her elbow as they talked. "Hunter."

She glanced up at him and smiled. "Ooh, are you going to hunt me down and eat me?"

It was his turn to stumble, and she giggled. They reached the Jeep, and he growled, "I'd love nothing better, sugar tits."

Chapter Two

Hunter grinned as she giggled, and he spied Chase and Parker on the passenger side, leaning against the vehicle. He squeezed her hip where her dress flared, falling to mid-thigh. Under his hand, he couldn't feel any underwear either. He swallowed past the lump in his throat and reached into his pocket for the keys.

And to adjust yourself like some green boy outta high school.

Taylor nodded like a bobble head, then held a hand to her cheek to force her head to stop. "It's been too long for me, personally, but like you said… I'm in no condition to make that decision."

She giggled again, and Hunter gritted his teeth to unlock the Jeep. He was still painfully hard. Chase got Parker in the backseat while Hunter helped the mystery woman.

"Where do you live, Taylor?" he asked as he flipped his drivers' seat up so she could climb into the back.

She put her knees on the floorboard, and her ass was waving almost in his face. Her red dress rode up to show cheek. Her bare thighs were ripe for the plucking. He wanted to flip her dress up and bite her ass.

Would her skin turn pink or red if he bit into it? How much could she take? Was she a screamer or a moaner? Either way, she'd be yelling by the time he was done with her, loving every moment. Was she as much of a glutton for it as he was?

She wiggled, and the lower curve of her ass peeked out from the bottom of her dress. He sucked in a breath and muttered, "Fuck me."

She wavered, her boot caught on the door frame. His hands were suddenly on both her hips to steady her.

Yeah right.

"I got you," he growled and unhooked her foot to help her crawl onto the seat. When she flopped onto the seat, her dress twisted and both tits popped out again. "Fucking hell."

"You alright back there? Need a hand?" Chase asked.

His fingers yearned to touch her, his mouth to taste her. Raw, wild need slid through his veins. He watched them sway, her nipples pebbling. Damn the light from the Jeep; he still couldn't tell what color they were.

"No, I've got two hands. I can handle it." His voice was choked. He knew exactly how he wanted to handle her. Rough, fast, and hard for starters.

She looked down at her bare, perky breasts and giggled again as she reached to pull up the dress. She struggled and yanked too hard, showing the crease in her leg where her thigh met her—

"Dear Lord, woman, get yourself under control," he said too harshly.

Her head popped up, and she froze with raised

eyebrows. She looked like a deer in the headlights, and a pang of guilt at the harsh words speared through him.

She frowned and stilled, putting her hands in her lap. "Yes, sir."

He stared into her green eyes for a beat too long, neither of them backing down. She was quick to listen, and the ideas spun in his head, teasing him and tempting him like he hadn't felt in a few years.

He reached for her seatbelt and buckled her in, thankful that her dress covered her tits again. The entire time, she stared wide-eyed at him, watching and waiting.

His voice was low and gruff as he felt for the belt buckle. It clicked into place, and he slowly moved his hands down her bare thighs before letting them drop to his side.

His mind felt dazed, drunk on the essence of her. He had to focus.

He cleared his throat and deliberately gentled his voice. "Taylor, if I'm going to take you home, I need to know where you live."

She nodded slowly and frowned. "I—I don't know exactly."

His brow furrowed. "What the hell does that mean?"

She flinched and seemed to shrink into herself. Then her spine straightened, and she leaned forward and reached into her boot. She pulled out her phone again and fumbled with it. Then she turned it around and showed him.

"I just moved into these apartments. Do you know where it is?" Her voice was much more slurred now, and he nodded as he slid his seat back to its normal position and climbed in beside Chase.

Hunter looked in the rear-view mirror as he shut the door and started the Jeep. Parker was out cold and leaning against the window. Chase sat with arms crossed, but a small smirk played on his lips.

"Don't start," Hunter grumbled, glancing at the goddess in the backseat.

He backed up and drove toward town. *Bruno Mars* blared on the radio, automatically connecting to his phone, and he started tapping his thumbs on the steering wheel.

Suddenly, she started singing softly from the back seat, her words slurred but keeping up well. He turned it up at the chorus, and they all sang almost at the top of their lungs.

Even Chase got into it, for once seeming to relax and smile as they sang. When the next song came on, she sang softly, but by the fourth song, she was quiet.

He pulled up in front of the apartment complex and parked. When he opened the door and flipped up his seat, she was out like a light. He frowned and unzipped her boot to find her phone, key, and a tiny wallet. He rifled through it, but none of it said which apartment was hers.

"What's the problem?" Chase asked.

Hunter explained and then shook her knee. "Taylor? Wake up, sugar. I need you to tell me which apartment."

She didn't move, just sighed and leaned her head back. She looked so peaceful in sleep, but he knew she was a dirty girl underneath that innocent exterior. He could feel it in his bones, had seen it in her eyes.

Chase said, "Check her phone? Any saved locations?"

Hunter used her thumbprint to unlock the phone, then he went to her map and searched for home. He sighed. "Thank God, it worked. Apartment 203."

He zipped her boot back up and tucked her phone and wallet into his back pocket. Then he gripped her key and eyed her.

The Cowboy Gets His Girl

"You're going to have to throw her over your shoulder, you know," Chase said.

Hunter sighed and nodded. He couldn't get her out of the back seat any other way. "Just avert your gaze. I don't want you staring at more of her than necessary."

Chase chuckled, but Hunter ignored the stab of jealousy that made him grind his teeth together. He grabbed her arm and eased her onto his shoulder. Then he slowly backed up and juggled until she was securely slung over his shoulder like a sack of potatoes.

His arm wrapped around her thighs, but he was afraid to tug down on her dress. He wasn't even sure if her breasts were still confined on his back. Hunter walked up the stairs to her apartment and unlocked the door, dropping the key on a table. He flicked the light and looked around.

Boxes were along every wall, but there was no big furniture to speak of. He went through one of the open doors to the single bedroom and flipped another light. A mattress lay on the floor, the headboard and frame still leaning against the wall.

He knelt and laid her down as best he could. Her legs landed on either side of his knees. She moaned, and the sound went straight through him. The tent in his pants hadn't gone down since he'd met her.

Her hands flopped to the side and her breasts popped free once more. He was on all fours with this gorgeous woman under him. He couldn't resist another look. Dusky nipples pebbled at the air. They were a mix between rose pink and strawberries.

He needed a taste. His mouth watered, and his hands clenched into the bedsheets to keep from reaching for her. He had to leave before he did something fucking stupid.

He went to push up, but then her arms were around his neck, pulling him down.

"Stay," she whispered, her lips raking along his jaw. "Don't leave me."

Her voice was like a dagger to the soul, and he ached to give her everything she desired. He'd never had such a visceral reaction to a woman's soft pleading whisper.

He groaned and let her pull him flush with her plump body. Her hips rose to meet his, and she ground herself on his dick.

"Shit, no, Taylor—you're not, I can't—damn it." He groaned and reached to untangle her hands. "Go to sleep, sugar."

She squeezed and resisted him, pressing her lips to his. He froze. Her lips were soft and plump and tasted like strawberries. He fucking loved strawberries. The scent flooded his nostrils, making his mouth water more.

But he had to be strong, for both of them. He pressed his lips to hers, but refused to open his mouth and dive into everything she was offering.

He pulled back, jerking her hands free and stumbling to his feet. She was sprawled on the bed, her dress bunched around her waist and barely hiding her lady bits.

She should've looked like a hot mess, but all he saw was the most gorgeous woman who didn't give two fucks what anyone else thought. He was mesmerized.

He adjusted himself and walked to the bathroom door. He rifled through a box and found a bottle of pain pills, then went to the kitchen and found a bottle of water in the fridge.

When he went back to her bedroom, she had turned onto her stomach and had one leg hiked to the side. Her bare ass made his mouth water, the thong barely visible.

But her gorgeous face was relaxed in sleep, one hand near her cheek and the other behind her. It took all his willpower to set both bottles on the side table near her bed, pull her boots off, cover her with a blanket, and high tail it out of there.

He was practically sweating by the time he got back to the Jeep. Chase stared at him when he climbed into the driver's seat. "You survived?"

Hunter slammed his door. "Barely."

Chase laughed, and Hunter drove them home, not even bothering to take Parker to his own apartment. Hunter was fucking done.

Tits and ass haunted him as he drove, but it was a magical laugh and big green eyes that flooded his dreams that night.

Chapter Three

Taylor woke up with a headache that put all others to shame. The pounding in her head wouldn't quit, and her eyes were glued shut.

She groaned, but the pounding continued, now with a muffled voice added to it. She lifted her hands and rubbed her eyes. God, what time was it?

She blinked and forced them open. Oh yeah, she'd moved. This was her new apartment. She really needed to get the curtains up. Light streamed through the window and across her bed.

She sat up and held her head. The pounding faded but a faint voice came through her open bedroom doorway.

"Tay? Are you here? You better be here or so help me God, I'll—"

She rubbed her eyes again before squinting at the door. "I'm here, I'm here," she grumbled as she climbed to her knees and stood up on wobbly legs.

Her best friend Lucy walked through the door with her

baby boy on her hip. She gasped, her cheeks immediately turning pink as her jaw dropped.

"Taylor Anne Grimes, you're naked!" Lucy nearly shouted.

The noise made Taylor squint, and she looked down. Her dress was bunched around her waist and her boobs flopped as she stumbled out of her dress and to a box in the corner.

She pulled out clean clothes, turning her back to Lucy, and mumbled, "I wasn't, but I am now. Who let you in?"

"I have a key, remember?"

"I believe your key is for emergencies. What if I had a guy in here?" Taylor glanced over as she walked to the adjoining bathroom.

Lucy rolled her eyes and turned back into the living room. Lucy's voice floated to her through the open doors. "It wouldn't be the first time I'd have walked in on you and a guy."

Lucy's voice droned on, but Taylor tuned her out. She turned on the shower and brushed her hair out while she waited for it to heat.

Her head pounded, and she looked around the bathroom for her bottle of aspirin. When she didn't find it, she went back to her bedroom where she found it next to her bed with a bottle of water.

She frowned and popped the pills. She didn't put the water there, so how did it… She was mid-drink when she froze, remembering parts of last night.

Fuzzy memories flowed through her head. There were some guys. Or one guy? Brown hair, hazel laughing eyes, and strong arms. She definitely remembered strong arms carrying her up the stairs.

"It's almost lunchtime, and I didn't even know if you'd

made it home. The last thing I got was a text with a blurry picture of one of the Williams' boys. Did he bring you home? What the hell happened after Mason and I left the bar last night?"

Taylor shook her head and said over her shoulder, "I'll tell you after the shower. I feel so gross."

She shut the bathroom door behind her, not in a mood to listen to Lucy yet. She loved her like a sister, but after six years of rooming together, she needed a few minutes to herself. Thankfully Lucy was used to her walking around naked.

She quickly braided her hair, loosely because her head still hurt. Then she stepped into the shower and leaned her head against the cool tiles. There'd been lots of drinking and dancing. The songs had changed after Lucy had left. That's when it all went downhill.

Then that man had shown up and rescued her from herself. What had Lucy said? A Williams' boy? She lathered up and scrubbed away hard, trying to wash away memories of her past like Lady Macbeth.

A thought made her frantically give a quick inspection, then she sighed in relief.

She might have woken up naked, but she wasn't covered in anything other than sweat. Even better news was that she wasn't sore between her legs, so nothing had happened.

Thank God. She had just turned twenty-four and had moved to this little town to escape her bad habits back in Denton. It wouldn't have been a good start for her to wake up to—

She shut down the thoughts. That wasn't who she was anymore. Grown up, graduated, and no longer living near campus, she had her own apartment and lived by herself. She was strong and could do this adulting thing.

She turned off the water and put on a clean pair of black leggings and a crop top before brushing her teeth and finally opening the door to face her bestie.

Lucy was in the kitchen pulling items out of boxes and putting them in drawers. The baby was playing on a blanket in the still empty living room. She didn't have a TV or a couch or even a coffee table.

Their apartment in Denton had been furnished except for their mattresses. Most of these boxes held things Lucy had collected when she'd moved out last year after graduation. A few were Taylor's mom's stuff finally pulled out of storage.

Those boxes remained stacked neatly against the living room wall. Taylor would happily wait years before opening those, but Lucy thought it was time.

Lucy glanced over and arched her brows, her brown hair pulled up in a bun. "Are you feeling more human? I've made coffee."

Taylor made a beeline for the coffee pot, then sank onto the floor, leaning against the wall as Lucy continued busying herself putting things away.

"We're still going to the resale shops, right? You need furniture. Mason is coming home at lunch, so he'll provide all the muscle. We just have to go pick the stuff out and wait for him in Denton."

Taylor nodded slowly, popping her neck and stretching. Harry crawled over to her and smiled. Taylor held her coffee up safely out of reach and played with him with her other hand. He sat back on his haunches and clapped and babbled.

She smiled at this sweet, innocent, precious little kid. His big blue eyes tugged on her heart and made her feel less alone.

Lucy picked him up and set him down on his hands and knees facing the other way. Then he took off crawling toward an overturned box.

Taylor chuckled. "Does he ever get tired?"

"Yep, that's why we need to get going to Denton. We have to time our trip so he naps in the car. Otherwise, it'll be a nightmare shopping with him. Are you ready?"

"Let me finish this cup?" Taylor asked as she took another sip of her coffee.

Lucy unpacked another box of mismatched plates and nodded. "That's fine. Where's your phone, by the way?"

Taylor shrugged and finished her coffee, one eye on Harry and mind reliving the events of last night.

Lucy went into her bedroom and returned, sitting in front of her and leaning an elbow on one knee as she stared at Taylor. "I don't see your phone anywhere and have called over and over. You lost it again, didn't you?"

Taylor closed her eyes and leaned her head back against the wall. "Oh god, I—I had it in that guy's Jeep, right? Did I text you then?"

"Yeah, Hunter Williams. Thankfully, you sent me the pictures. Your texts were just a bunch of letters that made no sense. I think his brothers were in the pictures too. Here."

Lucy took her phone from her back pocket and handed it over. Taylor opened her eyes and scrolled up. Most of the images were a blurry mess, but the more she looked, the more her memories returned.

She pulled her knees up, setting the empty coffee mug on the floor and burying her head in her knees as she handed the phone back over. Tears pricked her eyes and her stomach hurt.

"Tay, what happened last night?" Lucy asked softly, her hand patting Taylor's knee.

What happened? The tears fell silently down her cheek. She choked out, "Nothing. They just played some of Mom and Dad's songs."

"Oh hun, I'm so sorry." Lucy shifted, and Taylor felt her arms envelop her in a side hug.

Taylor squeezed her eyes harder, hoping to stop the flow. Stupid emotions that wouldn't stop. It must be the stress of moving and the new job getting to her.

"Have you heard from him lately?"

Taylor shook her head. Her dad only called when he needed bail money, so not hearing from him was a good thing. She wished he was still the man she'd grown up with.

The music had shifted to early eighties last night after her friends had left. It had thrown her into a serious mood. Normally she would've just gone home and read to escape.

But the guy she'd been dancing with had distracted her with drinks and laughs. He'd been competing with another guy for her attention. She didn't remember either of their names.

After a while, she'd stumbled into the Jeep guy. Hunter. A hazy memory made her gasp and her head shot up, eyes wide.

"What?" Lucy asked as she dropped her arms.

Taylor opened and closed her mouth before saying, "The guy who brought me home. Hunter? Oh god, I can't believe I did that."

"Did what? Did you hit on him?"

Taylor rubbed her temples, hoping the pills would kick in soon. "There were some seriously cheesy pickup lines, but that's not the worst part."

Lucy raised her brow skeptically, and Taylor waved her hands wide. "My boobs popped out on the dance floor!"

Lucy barked out a surprised laugh, making Taylor groan. Lucy laughed and Harry crawled over to see what the fuss was about. Lucy picked him up and kissed him, still chuckling.

Taylor frowned. "It's not funny. I was dancing with this other guy and fell into Hunter, and my dress practically fell to my waist."

Lucy's eyes sparkled as her laughter picked up again. Harry crawled away to a tipped over box and pulled clothes out. Taylor stood and righted the box, putting the clothes back in and handing him a random t-shirt to play with.

"I tried telling you not to wear that dress, didn't I? But noooo, you always know what's best." Lucy laughed again and gathered the coffee cup from the floor, then asked, "Weren't you most likely to live in a nudist colony? Why is this a problem?"

Taylor held her head with both hands and leaned against the kitchen counter. "Not in a public place like that. At least in a nudist colony, everyone else is doing it too, you know? Oh god."

Lucy shrugged, setting the cup in the sink. "What did he do when you ran into him with boobs flopping everywhere?"

Taylor rubbed her temples. "He pulled my dress back up, got me some water, and we went to his Jeep. My boobs popped out again, and he might've yelled at me."

"Yelled at you?" Lucy asked, brow arched.

Taylor nodded. "Told me to cover up and called me *woman*."

"Ugh, I know how much you love being called that." Lucy wrinkled her nose, and Taylor glared.

"Exactly. After that it all gets fuzzy, but he obviously brought me home. I remember him carrying me up the stairs, slung over his shoulder. I'm sure my boobs popped out then too and probably my ass. He definitely got more than an eye full."

Lucy giggled and followed her into the bedroom. "Based on your state of undress when I came in, I'd say so. Did y'all fool around?"

Taylor picked up her boots and felt inside with a frown. She shook her head. "No, I don't think so. I don't remember anything after the stairs. I got dizzy and must have blacked out. Damn it, my phone and wallet were in my boot, but now I can't find either of them."

Lucy glanced behind her to check on Harry. "I've told you to be careful about getting drunk in strange places, Tay."

"I know, I know. It's dangerous, but I did ask your boss, Katie, if I'd be safe with him taking me home. That's progress, right?" Katie owned the bar, but also worked at the salon where Lucy did nails.

Lucy sighed. "Yeah, it's a step in the right direction. I just worry about you."

Taylor smiled and pulled on her sneakers. "I know, and I appreciate it and love you so much, you have no idea."

Lucy tilted her head. "Why do I hear a but in there?"

Taylor grinned. "No buts. I wouldn't have moved to your little town if I didn't love you and hate the idea of being apart from you. After spending all that time on the cruise last month for your wedding, I just had to be closer to you. I've missed you this past year and a half."

Lucy's face softened, and she leaned against the bedroom door frame. "I've missed you too, Tay."

Taylor nodded and glanced around before going back

into the living room. "Great. Now that that's settled, we need to track down my phone. Let me pull up the find my phone app."

She found her tablet on the kitchen counter and turned it on. Her brows rose as Lucy looked over her shoulders.

"It's in the middle of nowhere."

Lucy chuckled behind her. "Not nowhere. I think that's Hunter's ranch. Looks like we're taking a detour to see a cowboy about a missing phone."

Taylor groaned and set the tablet down. "I must have dropped it on the floorboard of his Jeep last night. Great. This is just great. I have to face him so soon after I was practically naked."

Lucy's face scrunched in confusion. "You've been naked around plenty of guys. It's not that bad."

"Not that bad? The man practically tucked me in like a child, Lucy!" Taylor said, stomping to the tiny entrance table and grabbing her key. At least that had made it home.

Lucy picked up Harry and grabbed the diaper bag. "You just said practically twice back-to-back. He's really gotten to you, hasn't he?"

Taylor scowled and jerked the door open. "Wouldn't you be mortified if a stranger saw you like that?"

Lucy walked through the door and said, "Definitely, but I'm not you, remember? You're the badass who had the entire college boys track team bowing to you when they'd run into you—on a dare."

Taylor blushed and locked the door. "That was one time," she murmured, but Lucy kept talking as she started down the stairs, squirming Harry in her arm.

"Hunter's a rancher, an outdoorsman and responsible eldest brother. Mason and Ray have actually fished with Hunter a lot. Mason likes their family, and all the Williams' brothers are good people. You've got nothing to worry about with him."

Taylor locked it behind her and followed Lucy down the stairs. "That's great for him, but that doesn't mean I want him to know what I look like naked."

Her heart sank to her stomach as they walked to Lucy's car.

Lucy laughed. "No, I mean that he's always working at the ranch. You're living and working in town. After you get your stuff back, you'll probably never run into him again."

Taylor breathed a sigh of relief as they walked. She was trying to start over and needed to make a good impression with the town. She couldn't go to the bar anymore, last night had been a last hurrah kind of thing. She couldn't go home with pillars of the community like these Williams' boys. She couldn't do dumb shit like she was still a college kid.

It was high time she started acting like the librarian the mayor had hired her to be. It was time to grow up. And it started with facing the tall, dark, and handsome stranger from last night.

Chapter Four

The baby got fussy while they drove. By the time Lucy pulled through the gate, he was crying louder by the minute.

The noise distracted Taylor from the wide-open fields on either side of the long driveway. There were horses grazing, and they passed a dirt arena where a few ranch hands were gathered, three on horses but a few leaning against the fence.

Taylor watched as a small calf was released. Two of the ranchers started lassos swinging over their heads. They passed the scene before she could see the end of their run.

She had no idea she'd moved to the cowboy side of Texas. She'd always assumed that was further west. They were less than an hour to Fort Worth and only twenty minutes to Denton, but apparently it was already cowboy country.

Lucy reached a hand back to soothe Harry. "Sh, it's okay, it's okay. We're almost there."

The Cowboy Gets His Girl

Taylor felt her anxiety climb higher the closer they got to the now visible barn and house.

"Here, I got this," she said as she unbuckled and climbed over the center console to the back. Once safely in the backseat, she found a pacifier, but Harry just grabbed it and threw it.

Lucy parked in front of the house. Taylor shifted to her knees on the seat and reached for the pacifier under the car seat in the floorboard.

Lucy opened the door and got out. Taylor could hear voices but was too focused on reaching for the pacifier on the passenger side. Her fingers were almost there.

"Aha!" She sighed. The back seat driver's side door behind her was thrown open.

Taylor looked up and saw Lucy open the passenger side back door and reach for Harry, completely glued to her baby and unbuckling him, softly soothing him with calm words.

Taylor put the pacifier in his car seat and glanced behind her.

Her gaze traveled up dusty cowboy boots, jeans that revealed some massive thighs, and— her jaw dropped. It was him, the man who took her home. Aviator sunglasses hid his eyes, but his grin made her palms sweat and her heart race as she scrambled out backward, still on her knees.

"Hmm, this is a familiar view. I recognize that ass from last night. Taylor, right?" he chuckled and stepped back from the door.

She was an ungraceful, awkward mess, and her cheeks burned in embarrassment. She stood on wobbly legs and grabbed the top of the door tightly. She faced him and said in a rush, "Hello, yes, you're Hunter, right?"

He nodded, and her stomach felt like a million butterflies were turned loose. She couldn't blame it on a hangover either. Her brain finally caught up to what she was seeing.

He wore a blue and white pearl snap shirt, but it was completely unbuttoned with the sleeves ripped off. Sweat and dirt mixed on abs that were so defined, she gasped. And his biceps... hot damn, she jerked her gaze up before she was caught staring.

"I am. It's nice to officially meet you, sugar." He tipped a finger to his dusty cowboy hat and nodded his chin. Taylor's jaw went slack at the movement. People actually did that. She'd thought the tip of the hat was a myth of movies.

His jaw was clean shaven, his hair appearing black under the brim. She needed to get this over with before she started drooling and embarrassed herself further. She pushed her own sunglasses up on her nose and frowned, straightening her spine.

She took a shaky breath, nerves twisting her stomach. "It's nice to meet you too. Thanks for the ride home last night. I really appreciate it, but do you know where my phone and driver's license are? I can't find them."

Her words rushed out as she shifted from foot to foot in front of him. God, he was tall. She felt like a kid standing in front of him.

Dark brows rose above his glasses. "Ah yes. I have them." He glanced over the top of the car. "Lucy's gone into the house to say hello to Ma. You can join her while I grab them if you'd like."

He spun on his heels and strode with sure steps to a building she hadn't noticed before. The driveway continued around the barn to what appeared to be another single-story house.

She glanced at the big house behind her, and nerves

made her stomach flip. Go inside and meet his mother? She glanced down at her purple crop top and black leggings.

Yeah, this was a better the devil you know type of situation. She didn't want to face his mom and admit she'd gotten so drunk that she'd lost her phone and ID.

She took off after Hunter and caught up to him. He glanced down at her in surprise.

She shrugged, "If it's all the same to you, I'd rather not meet your mom right now. I'm sure she's lovely, but then I'd have to explain what all happened, and that's not the impression I want to give right now."

He chuckled and nodded, opening the door to the small house. She stepped inside and wrinkled her nose.

"It smells like feet in here," she mumbled as she looked around. There was a large sectional couch in front of a giant TV to the left. To the right was a small galley kitchen with barstools.

Hunter stepped around her and down a hallway as he replied. "I take it you've never been in a bunk house before?"

She shook her head. She'd never even been on a ranch before, much less in a bunk house.

"We have a lady come in and clean once a month, but yeah. We're a sweaty, stinky mess of testosterone."

He disappeared into a room down the hall, and she shifted on her feet again, nerves building inside her. Why did he have her so on edge? He stepped back into the hall and walked toward her.

He'd taken off his sunglasses. His hazel eyes captured hers. Smile lines fanned his eyes as he handed over her phone and wallet.

"Here you go. I had your phone on the charger," he said

softly. His hands were rough and calloused as she took her things.

"Thanks," her voice was soft and breathy.

He leaned forward, and she tipped her head up, her heart racing. She froze as he came closer. That look in his eye had her paralyzed. She saw the desire, and she was a sucker for anyone who showed an interest. She waited with bated breath for him to make a move.

Then he grabbed the door frame behind her and opened the door. He stepped back, holding the door for her with a smirk.

She felt her cheeks burn. What a fool she was. She ducked her head as she stepped onto the porch and flipped her long, loose braid over her shoulder. Nerves made her talkative.

"Thanks again for the lift last night. I can't believe I dropped these."

"It's not a problem," he said, his voice deeper. "I found them on the floorboard and carried them upstairs to your apartment, but by the time I got you settled in bed, I was so distracted I forgot to take them out of my pocket."

She stumbled, and his hand came out to steady her elbow. "Oh god, I did something to distract you, didn't I?"

He chuckled and turned to face her. "Let's just say, if you were sober, we both would've woken up in completely different states this morning."

She groaned and closed her eyes. "Oh god, I'm so sorry."

"For being so drunk? Yeah, me too," he chuckled again and tipped her chin up softly with a single finger.

She opened her eyes. Why hadn't they put their sunglasses back on? They stood in the shadows between the barn and the bunk house. He stepped closer, and she backed up a step, her back hitting the wall.

He placed his other hand over her head, palm flat against the wall. She whimpered, the sound loud between them. His brows rose as he traced her jaw with one finger, then down the side of her neck.

She licked her lips, and he glanced down. What had he said? "You—you're sorry I was so drunk?"

He nodded. "Absolutely. If you would've been in your right mind, I would've taken you up on your offer."

"My offer?" she whispered.

He leaned closer, and she felt his breath on her cheek. He smelled like a real man, his aftershave just barely there under the sweat.

"I dreamed of you spread out naked on that bed last night."

She shivered as a chill ran up her spine. He stepped back and put his sunglasses back on.

"However, you might want to get some help with the alcohol, sugar. It's not healthy, drinking that much in such a public place alone. If it'd been any other man who took you home, it would've been a much different outcome."

She scowled and put her own sunglasses on with a frown. There were certain consequences she was all too familiar with, and she'd learned how to prevent them for the most part. She straightened and took a deep breath, shaking off her disappointment at his distance and reprimand.

"I know that, but don't worry. It won't happen again."

He shrugged and strode back to the car as Lucy came out of the front door of the big house.

"There's a time and a place, but bad choices will haunt you if you get that drunk often."

"Bad choices?" she whispered as she stumbled to a halt,

pain spearing her heart. She was always the bad choice, the bad egg, the— no, she wouldn't think that. She *couldn't*. It would lead to a spiral that was too hard to climb out of.

She gritted her teeth and stomped after him. "Who do you think you are? You get off on judging others and being a martyr, taking drunks home so you can lord it over them the next day? It's a wonder you have any friends at all."

He glanced over his shoulder as they slowed near the car. "I get along just fine with everyone. You might be the first one to complain, actually."

He stopped, and she rounded his big frame and slammed her hands on her hips. He was tall and beefy, making feel small, but she would not be intimidated.

"Consider this a formal complaint. If I thought it'd help, I'd take it up with management."

He threw his head back and laughed. The sound disarmed her, making her pause as it eased some of her frustration.

She raised a finger and pointed it under his chin. "Don't you laugh at me."

He grabbed her finger between his and lowered it, raising his other hand to bop her on the nose with his forefinger. "How can I not laugh? You're an adorable little pipsqueak. Someday you'll grow up and know I'm right. See you around, sugar tits."

He waved at Lucy as she finished putting Harry in the car seat. "You have a great day now."

Taylor was still sputtering as he spun and walked away, touching the brim of his hat in goodbye. She watched the sway of his hips. It should be a crime to wear jeans that fit so good.

Lucy shut the back door and rounded the back of the car. "You alright?"

Taylor's hands fisted at her side as she gritted her teeth again. "Just peachy."

She stomped around to the passenger side and climbed in. It was silent until Lucy backed up, and they drove past the corral again.

This time Hunter leaned on the top rail of the fence, one foot resting on the bottom rung. He glanced over and lifted a hand in a wave. Taylor snorted and turned away, ignoring him.

Lucy chuckled. "What's that all about?"

"The man is insufferable. He chewed me out for being too drunk and putting myself in a dangerous situation."

Lucy glanced over and gave her the look. Taylor rolled her eyes and looked back out her window.

"I know, I know. You've said it for a while now too, but it hits differently when it comes from *him*. He's a stranger who knows nothing about me."

"Well, just think of it this way. You don't have to deal with him now you got your stuff back. I mean, I think I've only seen him in town a handful of times in the year and a half I've lived here. Most of the time I see him is on the bank of the river."

Taylor's shoulders relaxed as she leaned back in the seat. "That's comforting. I hope the rest of the town is nicer."

"Oh, they are. Hunter's nice too. Y'all just got off on the wrong foot."

Lucy's phone rang, and she hit the button to put the caller on speaker phone. She planned to meet Mason at the furniture store in Denton as they turned on the highway that would take them to town.

A few hours later, Taylor's headache was returning as she trudged up the stairs to her new apartment. Lucy's energy hadn't waned the entire time. Taylor thought first time mothers were supposed to need naps, but Lucy was like a woman on a mission.

A mission to furnish Taylor's apartment and make it livable. She followed Lucy up the stairs where she unlocked the door and stepped to the side.

Taylor sighed as she pushed through and set the heavy bags on the floor. "I'm rethinking living on the second floor. I don't think the stairs on campus were this tiring."

Lucy laughed as she arranged a few boxes into a semi-circle in the corner. "We're getting older, Tay. That's just part of it."

She took Harry out of the car seat and put him in the makeshift playpen of boxes. Lucy started to unpack the bags, but Taylor grabbed the bottle of painkillers and popped two more before heading back down to the car.

She pulled an armload of bags out of the trunk just as Mason pulled up in his big truck. She nodded but didn't wait for him. It was too hot, and she might have a pill stuck in her throat.

She paused inside and finished half a bottle of water. Mason opened the door and took in the state of her apartment. But when he stepped inside, he was quickly followed by three other big guys.

Taylor's eyes widened as each one came through the door looking more and more familiar. When the last one stepped in, she choked on her water. Fucking Hunter.

She turned and coughed. Lucy slapped her on the back, and she took another drink to push past it.

What the hell was he doing here? Were those his two brothers that were in the fuzzy pictures from last night's drive? Oh god, had they seen her half naked too?

She wiped her eyes and turned back in horror to see two more people stepping inside her now cramped apartment.

She glanced from the guys to the older man and woman, clearly their parents.

She patted her hair, trying to smooth the wisps of hair near her temples, and pasted on a smile through gritted teeth. "Ah, hello. Welcome to my home?"

She hated how unsure her voice was, wavering on the end.

Mason patted the closest man on the back. "I called in reinforcements for the heavier furniture. This is Parker, Chase, and Hunter, my poker buddies. And these are Bill and Ava Williams, their parents."

Ava stepped forward and set a casserole dish on the cluttered counter. She was almost as tall as her sons, at least a foot taller than Taylor. Taylor took a step back toward her bedroom door, grabbing the hem of her crop top and tugging it down to cover the thin line of skin.

"Don't mind us, dear. We're the first round of the welcoming committee."

"Welcoming committee?" Taylor whispered, glancing from one to the other with a frown.

Bill nodded, setting another casserole dish beside the first one. "Yeah, Ava is on the church's food train committee. Any excuse to take care of people, they make up a meal train. It's our way of saying welcome to town."

He wiped his hands on his jeans and stepped forward with a hand extended. "It's nice to meet you. We hope you'll join us at church sometime."

Ava tapped on the casserole dish. "You'll want to refrigerate these or even freeze them. The directions are on top along with my phone number if you ever need anything. I wanted to meet you earlier, but you didn't stop in the house. My door is always open though, so you stop by anytime. If I'm not in the house, look in the barn."

Taylor blinked, overwhelmed by the show of—of... what was this? She'd never had such a welcome before.

Ava smiled and looked around with a frown. "I see you're in the middle of moving in. Do you want a hand? I talked with Lucy earlier about it, and we have some time—"

"Oh no, I couldn't possibly," Taylor rushed, shaking her head.

Ava tilted her head, her brown eyes kind and curious. "Don't worry about it, dear. We're happy to help. Now where can we start?"

Taylor nodded, feeling her cheeks heat and her chest tighten. She couldn't get out of this. She took a shaky breath, looking around helplessly and trying to catch Lucy's gaze.

Chapter Five

Hunter saw the lost look on the cute girl's face and gave her an out. "We'll start bringing up the couch."

Her brows rose in surprise, and she nodded, looking to the living room. "We'll clear a space for it then."

Everyone jumped into action, and he ducked back out the door. Her tiny apartment wasn't made for a crowd, and the walls had threatened to close on him. Footsteps echoed behind him, and he knew it was his brothers without even turning to look.

"Poor girl," Parker said as they rounded the landing.

Chase replied, "Why?"

"She remembers a little from last night. Probably mortified. Plus, being hungover on moving day and having to face Ma? She didn't stand a chance." Parker tsked, making Chase chuckle.

Hunter frowned and ignored the urge to protect her from Ma's prying questions as he turned to Mason's truck.

"Let's just get this over with," he mumbled as he put the tailgate down. It was hot work since it was still the end of summer in Texas, but Mason and Bill soon joined them, making it go faster. They brought the couch upstairs just as Ava, Lucy, and Taylor got the area cleaned of boxes.

Taylor hovered in the bedroom door while they brought it in, her big, green eyes never leaving him. He could feel them burning into his skin.

He ignored her as best he could because every time he looked at her, he pictured her naked. That just made carrying the kitchen table up the stairs with a hard-on even more difficult to manage.

By the time they'd moved all the big furniture inside, he was sexually frustrated, hot, and bothered. She was skittish and wary, but his parents had run down the street and brought back a couple of pizzas.

The old table was sturdy with mismatched chairs, the Goodwill stickers still on them. Hunter and his brothers sat on the couch, waters on the new coffee table while Lucy, Taylor, and their parents sat at the table. Mason leaned against the counter near Lucy as they talked and ate pizza.

"I just can't believe you moved all the way out here for Lucy," Ava said.

"She's like a sister to me. Besides, I wouldn't be a good godmother if I weren't in Harry's life." Taylor's soft alto voice scratched at his skin. He felt like a dog, shaking his leg as her voice scratched behind his ears.

Hunter glanced over, the baby boy asleep on a pile of blankets in the corner.

"Y'all went to college together?" his dad asked.

"Yeah, Lucy and I were roommates all six years."

"Six years! Goodness, that's a long time for school," Ava said.

Lucy chuckled, "It sure was, but we both survived and

The Cowboy Gets His Girl

graduated. It was tough this past year living apart, but now that she's in Crimson Creek, it's going to be amazing."

Taylor added, "I start my new job on Monday, so I really appreciate your help. With the apartment settled, I'll actually be able to find my work clothes."

She laughed, and it seemed like the apartment brightened. The sun shone brighter through the living room window. Hunter got up and put his now empty paper plate in the trash can. He nodded to the window and finally turned to face Taylor.

"You have curtains?"

Her cheeks pinkened, and he wondered what she was thinking. He loved that blush on her tanned features. She'd been bold last night, and he hadn't pegged her as a blushing type.

She nodded and hopped up, stepping around the table and into her bedroom. He followed her to a box. She pulled out a bright purple fabric and spun around, but he was closer than she realized.

She gasped in surprise and stumbled back. He grabbed her by the arms and pulled her in close. Their bodies molded together, and he groaned. Before he knew it, his head had dipped down to hers and that fresh, fruity scent wafted over him.

It was intoxicating and made him question all of his plans. The need to kiss her made him feel weak, but he couldn't date locals.

He sucked in a breath and stepped back, holding her at arm's length as he looked down at her. Eyes wide, hair slightly disheveled and coming out of her braid after a long day of moving, she looked so kissable, he ached.

Without a word, he took the fabric from her hands and turned back to the doorway. He ignored the looks from everyone else as he hung her curtains. They were all done eating and his parents said goodbye.

"Hunter, I have to run to the gym. Bryce forgot his key again. Mason is going to take us. Taylor, it was so good to see you again. I hope I didn't make a complete fool of myself last night," Parker said as he took Taylor's hand in his own.

Taylor laughed and leaned into him, making Hunter's stomach tighten. "You think I remember last night? That's cute."

Parker grinned and leaned forward, kissing her on the cheek. Taylor didn't blush, though. She just grinned, offered her cheek for the kiss, and ran her hand on his arm before he stepped away to follow Mason out the door.

Chase followed them with a nod goodbye. Hunter looked at Lucy and Taylor. "If you'll show me where the last of the curtains are for the bedroom, I'll get those hung and out of your hair."

Taylor waved at her bedroom and avoided his eyes. "Same box as before. They're green."

He nodded and stepped into the room to get it done, needing to get out of there. The longer he stayed, the more likely he was to do something stupid.

Like notice that these curtains were almost the same color as her eyes.

He heard voices as he hung them, thankful that the apartment had the hardware already installed. He doubted she had a screwdriver.

He wouldn't mind being her screwdriver. Or her hammer. He could hammer or screw her all night long.

Damn it, no. It had been years since he'd dated someone from town, and he wasn't about to start with her. Sure, a girlfriend would be nice.

But not someone in Crimson Creek. His parents would get their hopes up. There'd be all kinds of pressure to be like his married brothers.

Then there was all the drama and chaos of a breakup. Everyone got hurt, and it wasn't worth the risk.

No, he couldn't date Taylor. Not anyone in town. No matter how constantly he'd been fantasizing about her in the past twenty-four hours.

He shook himself as he stepped away from the curtains and turned back to the living room. Taylor was putting kitchen things away in a drawer, but Lucy and Mason were gone.

He felt his stomach twist. "Where'd everyone go?"

Taylor looked up between dark lashes and blinked heavily. "Lucy had to get Harry home. Something about running out of diapers after being out all day."

He swallowed hard as he watched her turn and put something else away. He was rooted to the spot. What the hell? Why couldn't he move?

"I see. Well, I best get going then. Unless you need me for anything else?" He held his breath. Why had he asked? It wasn't a good idea, but if she offered herself up to him again, he wasn't sure he had the strength to turn her down a second time.

She turned back and avoided his gaze. "No, I'm good. I just need to put the bed frame together, but I'll get to that later this week. I need to iron my work clothes and settle in, so you're good."

He frowned and glanced back at her bed. "Do you even have a screwdriver?"

She shook her head, her braid falling over her shoulder again. "No, it's a weird L shaped tool thing. It doesn't need a screwdriver."

He sighed. "Fine, where's the Allen wrench? I'll put it together right quick while you deal with your clothes."

Her head shot up, and her eyes widened. He watched as she swallowed hard, and it made him think of how her plump lips would feel around his dick. His spine tingled as she licked her lips.

"It's in a baggie taped to the frame. Are you sure? You don't have—"

"I know," he said curtly, staring at her and soaking her up. He shrugged off the uncomfortable mixture of emotions. "I might have been rude earlier, and I want to apologize. So let me fix your bed, and we'll call it even?"

She frowned and tilted her head back. "Fine, but don't think this gives you permission to keep being rude."

His lips twitched but he kept a straight face as he nodded and said, "Yes ma'am."

Her eyes softened, but he spun back into the bedroom and found the tools. He heard her in the other room and soon music was playing softly.

He sat the mattress up against the wall and laid out the frame. When she came into the bedroom and began putting clothes into the new dresser in the corner, he kept sneaking glances.

He caught sight of black and pink lace as she placed clothes from a box into the top drawer. His damn thoughts immediately went to imagining her in skimpy lingerie and ripping it off her perfectly curvaceous body.

They softly hummed to the music as they worked in silence. Half an hour later, he placed the mattress on the metal bed frame. He fixed her sheets, comforter, and pillows as she came out of the closet.

"Oh, you don't have to do that. I'll take care of it," she said.

He looked up and stared at her over the big bed. "If I don't make the bed, I'm going to keep thinking of you naked between those purple sheets."

She gasped and looked away.

"Don't look away from me," he growled.

She looked back, and their eyes met. Hers begged him but he didn't know whether she wanted him to do something about this tension or back off and leave her alone.

He was too old to play these games, damn it.

"What do you want?" he asked. He swallowed hard and cleared his throat, trying to ignore the stab of insecurity and vulnerability within him.

She licked her lips and shook her head. "I—I don't know what you mean."

He clenched his hands into fists. "What do you want with me? You stare at me with those begging eyes and pouty lips. Do you want me to kiss you? Fuck you senseless? Because I've been thinking of nothing else all fucking day."

She opened and closed her mouth, then licked her lips again. "I—I... oh god. No, we can't. I just moved here. I swore I'd be good from now on. This is a new town, a new opportunity to be better, do better. I—I can't just sleep with you. I just, I can't."

Her voice lowered to a whisper as she trailed off, her eyes roving over his shoulders and down his body. Her words said one thing, but the heat in her gaze told a different story.

"You sure?" he growled, his dick uncomfortably hard.

She shifted on her feet and bit her lip. "Probably."

She seemed to catch herself because her eyes widened. "I mean, yes. I have to be. What kind of girl sleeps with a stranger?" She shook her head, and her eyes were suddenly sad.

"No, I can't be that girl anymore," she said softly, almost to herself.

But he heard her.

And he had so many questions. Who *was* this woman? What did she mean by *anymore*?

She straightened her spine and tipped her chin up as she focused on him again. "I'm good. I'm an adult, damn it, and I'm going to be responsible for once in my fucking life. So, thank you, but no thank you. On the sex offer."

He raised a brow. "And the kiss offer?"

She grinned, and the twinkle in her eyes made him want to leap over the bed, just to capture some of the magic that was her. "Let's put a rain check on it, shall we? I feel like that's a bad idea too."

He wasn't anyone's bad idea. There had to be some way to convince her. He had been a perfect gentleman last night, but the dreams of her…

It was like a burr got caught between his toes. He needed to pick at it until that sweet relief came, and he desperately wanted to come with her. Dating he wouldn't do, sex he was open to, but a kiss? That was a hell yeah.

He stepped around the end of the bed and stopped a few feet away from her, ready to pull out the big guns and his best lines. "But sometimes being bad is so good. Just a kiss? *Come, let us kiss, then you'll hear no more of me.*"

His voice was a deep rumble in his chest.

Her eyes widened as her grin went slack. "Oh god," she whispered. "Don't talk like that."

As she talked, she started walking toward him. Slowly at first, hesitantly.

"Like what?" Fuck yes, it worked. He'd hoped, based on her comments last night, that poetry was the way to go with her. He stayed still, waiting for her to come to him.

"Poetry?" she gasped, her eyes pleading with him. "Is that your pickup move, to recite obscure poems to girls and capture them in your spell?"

He grinned, happily surprised by the challenge in her eyes. "Maybe. Does it work?"

She groaned and took another step closer. "I'm a fucking librarian. Of course it works."

His gut twisted in anticipation, and he sucked in a breath. A librarian... she was the vision of every wet dream he'd ever had. He pictured her in a librarian's outfit. "Fuck me," he whispered.

She froze, her eyes widening. He had to do something to bring her closer. Just one kiss, just one fuck, then they could forget about this sexual tension. *"All things by a law divine, in one spirit meet and mingle. Why not I with thine?* Let us kiss and feel that delicious tingle."

She sucked in a breath, her lips pursing and her eyes widening. If she liked poetry, then he'd hit her with it until she begged for a kiss. It was justice for the torture she put him through last night.

He stepped closer, pressing his advantage. "As *the moonbeams kiss the sea, what is all this sweet work worth if you don't kiss me?* Come on, sugar. You know you want a kiss. Maybe it'll take the edge off. Or maybe it'll be a terrible kiss, and we can both forget about each other and sleep peacefully tonight."

She stopped in front of him, their bodies separated by inches. "You don't really think that."

He smiled and reached up to trace her jaw and down her neck once more. "No, I don't. I don't date locals, but a kiss isn't dating."

Her head tilted. "It's not mindless fucking either."

He heard the wavering in her voice, and his stomach

twisted in anticipation. "If you tell me to back away, I will. If you tell me no, I'll stop. One kiss is all I want. Is that too much to ask?"

She sucked in a breath, and it brought her breasts close enough to graze his chest through his t-shirt. Her hand settled on his waist, and she stared up at him with lips slightly parted.

His control snapped, and his hand on her neck went down her back, pressing her closer. His other hand wrapped around her, under her crop top to feel the soft skin of her back, and he dipped his head.

He gave her plenty of time to pull away. He even paused and hovered his lips over hers, not touching. Then she whimpered.

The sound tore through him, and he crushed her plump lips to his. She immediately opened her mouth, and his tongue swept inside to tango with hers. He deepened the kiss, wanting to devour her.

What made her so special, so enticing that he stayed up for hours thinking about her?

He angled his mouth to seek the answer and ravish her lips. The kiss was more satisfying than anything he could think of. How had he never kissed this woman before? If he'd known it would be this earth-shattering, he might have kissed her on the dance floor last night.

It was hot, demanding more and more. It was an impossible kiss, born from shared madness and unbridled desire. He nipped at her bottom lip, sucking it gently and making her gasp. Her small hands settled around his waist, and he dragged her closer, ready to dive into the kiss again.

But she turned her head with another gasp, and his lips met her neck. He nipped at it, sucking at the spot under her ear that made her moan. He didn't know how he knew she'd love that spot.

He'd always known her, always known what she liked. Like they were lost souls finding their way back to each other, he just knew her.

And that was the thought that scared him shitless. It was like a bucket of water to the face. He bit a little too deeply, and she shuddered in his arms.

He dropped his hands and stepped back, fisting them at his sides. His lips pulsed from their kiss, and he could still smell the strawberries.

Her eyes were wide and heavy with desire. She lifted a shaky hand to her lips as their ragged breathing slowed. She was the perfect woman for him, and it terrified him. Perfect body, perfect kiss, perfect lips.

Open mouth of my soul is utter gladness, the eyes of my soul see perfection. I do not see one imperfection in the universe on her face or in my arms.

He raked a hand through his hair and growled, "Yeah, you were right. That was a bad idea."

Her jaw dropped in surprise and the hurt in her eyes gutted him. Without another word, he spun on his heel and went straight out the front door. Shit, he didn't need this right now.

Life was good. They were in the middle of foaling season, and the training of the next set of horses was going well.

He didn't need a local woman messing with his head. Marriage was great for his brothers, and a girlfriend might be nice, but not one as distracting as her. Not a local who would get attached to his big family and be in his pocket all day every day.

He stomped down the stairs and fled to his Jeep.

Chapter Six

Taylor's sleep was fitful. She'd hoped that moving all day with a hangover would've driven her to a deep sleep, but she kept feeling the pulsing between her legs in time with his kiss. She dreamed of him and woke up aching and frustrated.

If she was still back in Denton, she'd scratch that itch with a few swipes on her phone. Some faceless college kid would show up, and that would be that.

Or better yet, she would've just slept with Hunter after everyone left and been done with it. She could've moved on and left him behind.

But if she was going to be serious about this adulting thing and grow up, then she'd made the right choice. That's what she told herself as she tossed and turned throughout the night. She finally sighed and turned onto her back to stare at the ceiling.

Being a grown up came with its own set of disappointments, one of which was the need to invest in some new battery-operated friends. Too bad none of the stores would be open on a Sunday.

She threw back the covers and dove into cleaning and unpacking one room at a time. She worked on her bedroom first, organizing her work clothes. By the time it was all sorted and put away, it was almost lunchtime.

She changed into shorts and a sports bra, threw on a loose tank top and sneakers, grabbed her sunglasses and headphones, and was out the door. No time like the present to map out her new town. A quick glance at the map while she stretched, then she started a slow jog down the street.

The music rolled through her as she looked around. Lucy had said she wouldn't see Hunter again, but he'd shown up to help her move. Hopefully that was the end of that because the way that man kissed…

He was dangerous. Even when she was in college, she'd stayed clear of guys like him. The strong, silent type rarely did it for her. She preferred the fun, outgoing ones whom she could party with.

His brother Parker was much more her type. But after kissing Hunter, she couldn't bark up that tree. Parker was hot in that suave, sports jock way, with a quick grin that made any girl want to drop her panties.

Hell, he was who she'd been dancing with at the bar on Friday night. She knew exactly what she was getting with someone like him. No mess, no fuss. Just a wham, bam, thank you ma'am, and that was that.

Shit. She was repeating herself now. That was that? This town was already making her feel like an uneducated country bumpkin.

She reached an intersection and turned down Main Street. She'd been here a few times to visit Lucy over the past year, but she had yet to stop by the Diner.

The bell rang as she pushed the glass door open and walked in. The place was packed, and several of the patrons turned and stared at her. She froze, her hand still on her sunglasses.

Did she want to stay or leave? She could jog over to the grocery store and grab something there. She did need groceries anyway.

A cute little waitress finished pouring coffee at a table to her right and smiled. "Hello there, welcome to the Diner. There are a few seats at the counter. It could be ten to twenty minutes for a table. What would you like?"

Taylor swallowed hard and tilted her chin up. She didn't need to hide. This was her town now, and she had to face it like a big girl. She took her sunglasses off and smiled, resisting the urge to tug down the hem of her top.

"Counter is fine. Thanks," she said as the waitress nodded and walked behind the bar area.

Taylor sat down at the second to last seat. A couple of old guys on her right were deep in conversation. They were pointing and arguing at something in the paper that was laid between them on the counter.

She tried to tune them out, but they were really loud. After the waitress introduced herself and took her order, Taylor pulled her phone out of her shorts pocket and started to scroll. A shadow fell on her from near the window to her left, and someone sat on the stool next to her.

She glanced over, and her eyes widened. Damn it, Lucy was a fucking liar.

Hunter's brows rose as he did the chin nod and set his cowboy hat on the end of the counter. "Afternoon."

His smirk made her grind her teeth and her cheeks heated. Their kiss replayed in her mind. She took a drink of

The Cowboy Gets His Girl

her water and nodded hello, turning back to look at her phone.

"Out for a run?" he asked.

She nodded again and ignored him, embarrassment and nerves warring within her as she drained her drink.

The guys on the other side of her tapped the paper with a pen furiously.

Hunter leaned in to whisper, "Don't mind them. They argue over the paper every Sunday."

The scent of him drew her in, the musty smell of leather, sweat, and dirt. It made her relax somewhat, and she fought herself not to lean closer.

"But why?" she whispered back, nodding a thanks to the waitress for refilling her drink. She could almost feel his breath on her ear, and goosebumps raked along her arms.

"Could be anything, really. Today it sounds like they're arguing over the comics."

She shook her head. "That doesn't make sense."

Hunter chuckled, and the sound settled deep into her bones. "I know. Welcome to Crimson Creek and all the little idiosyncrasies you never knew you needed in your life."

She grinned, and the waitress set her chicken wrap on the counter. She glanced at Hunter, then at the people around them.

"Is it always this packed?" She took a bite of her food. It was delicious, and she barely chewed before she took another.

"Only on Sundays. As this is only one of three restaurants in town, it's normally pretty crowded when church lets out."

She winced, realizing what the stares had been when she'd walked in with a tank top and tight biker shorts. She definitely didn't fit in with the church crowd with her workout clothes.

She tried to distract herself. "What's the other restaurants?"

"The pizza place and the Old Mill." His voice trailed off as she ate. She took a drink of water and glanced over at him. He was just staring at her intensely with a slight frown.

"What?" she asked as she took another bite.

He shook his head and leaned forward again to whisper. "Nothing. Just wondering what it'd feel like if you ate my cock like that chicken wrap."

She choked on her food. Hunter laughed and slapped her on the back as he leaned away. She grabbed her water and chugged it, finally pushing the food down. Her throat felt all scratchy now, and her cheeks burned.

"Hunter," she finally scolded, frowning.

He grinned and wiggled his eyebrows, his eyes mischievous and the laugh lines deepening. "What? I can't help it. You were going to town on that chicken wrap. It's already almost gone. You devoured it, and I enjoyed watching every minute of it."

He shifted so that he was mostly facing her, his right leg extending behind her stool. He leaned on the counter, relaxed and grinning like the cat who ate the canary.

She wanted to wipe that grin off his face by sitting on it.

No. Oh god, *no*. She blinked hard to erase that image from her head.

"Damn it, Hunter. Don't go there. You *left* last night. You agreed that we can't, remember?"

He nodded. "I remember you saying something about not being that kind of girl anymore. What kind of girl were you, though? I'm dying of curiosity here. Stayed up all night wondering. Put me out of my misery."

"No, you'll use the information against me. Just let it go and leave me alone."

She flagged down the waitress and pulled her debit card from her shorts. When the waitress left, Hunter was still in his relaxed pose, but his eyes had sharpened. He reminded her of a hawk looking at prey.

His voice was soft as he said, "Or if you tell me, I'll actually leave you be. If you don't, I'll just keep asking."

She rolled her eyes. "Yeah right. Lucy says you're at the ranch all the time. When would we ever see each other for you to keep being an ass about it?"

He shrugged and sat up, leaning toward her again. "Who knows? In a town this small, it's bound to happen."

That's what she was afraid of. Whatever this was between them felt inevitable. There was an edge to their flirting that she'd never experienced before. The waitress came back with the receipt and a pen. She quickly scrawled on it and spun on the stool to face him.

The way he was sitting, she quickly realized her mistake. Both her knees were within his spread legs. Goosebumps broke out again, this time all over, at how near he was.

She leaned forward, flirting with fire, but kept control of her sanity with her words. "Hunter, I'm trying to grow up. This is my first time living alone and being responsible. I don't need a fuck buddy."

He leaned forward, his hazel eyes sharp as he glanced down at her lips and back up to meet her gaze.

"That doesn't answer my question."

"What question?"

"Why not?"

Her breath was growing shallower. "Because I'm not that person anymore."

"That's what you said before, but that's not an answer."

"And that's not a real question."

"What kind of person were you?"

She took a ragged breath and leaned back. When had she gotten so close to him? She shook her head. "What's in the past doesn't matter, Hunter. All that matters is the future."

"And why can't the future be filled with great sex?"

She smirked and leaned closer to him. "It can be."

His eyes widened, and he licked his lips. She continued, "But not as a fuck buddy. I'm tired of being the girl everyone wants to have at a party, but no one wants to settle down with. I want to be treated like I'm worth spending time and effort on. I want a *relationship*, Hunter. Is that something you can give?"

He frowned and leaned back. "What do you mean?"

She shrugged and glanced away, not liking exposing her deepest desires like this, but it was probably the best way to get him to back off. Didn't the thought of a relationship scare away more decent guys?

"Sex is great, but now that I'm older, I want the whole package, Hunter." She looked at him again, staring into his hazel eyes as if searching for the answers to the universe.

He smirked, his eyes sparkling. "Good, I've got a big package you can have anytime."

She chuckled and laid a hand on his knee, the one away from the crowd and hidden under the counter. "I want to be courted. I'm twenty-four and haven't had a boyfriend since middle school. I want dates to nice places, flowers, kisses on the front step that don't demand follow-up sex. I want to be wined and dined, Hunter."

He scowled and crossed his arms. "I didn't peg you as that kind of girl."

She raised her brows, the hair on the back of her neck standing up. "What kind of girl?"

"The kind who wants fancy things. I guess a city girl like you would be used to that kind of thing, huh?"

She narrowed her eyes, the stab of pain in her chest making her almost wheeze. "I might be a city girl, but that's exactly why I want to be courted, Hunter. I've never been on a proper date."

His eyes narrowed. "Ever?"

She shook her head slowly, her anger and frustration boiling under her skin. "It's not about fancy things. It's about wanting to feel like more than a fun lay. I'm not someone's *bad choice* or one night stand. Never again anyway. I want to feel like I'm worth the effort, and I want that long term."

His jaw clenched as he frowned. "Well, I can't do that. Sorry, but I don't date local girls. It's a personal policy."

Taylor didn't think she'd gotten her hopes up, but his words definitely made her feel like she'd been thrown off a bicycle. Disappointment stabbed through her almost as sharp as the pain of rejection. She took another drink of water and hopped off the stool with an overly bright smile.

"Well then. I guess we're done here. See you around, Hunter."

She walked away with her head high, ignoring the looks and whispers from those she passed. When she made it outside, she slammed her sunglasses onto her head and turned toward the park at the end of the block.

She didn't start running again, not with her meal still digesting or people in the Diner still looking at her. Instead, she strolled along the tree-lined path until she came to a gazebo next to a man-made pond. She leaned on the railing and stared at the water.

She was still disappointed, but this might've been the first time she'd put it all into words. She'd never even voiced all that to Lucy, and she told Lucy nearly everything.

Did she really want the white picket fence and a long-term relationship? For so long, she'd been afraid of making the same mistakes as her parents. That route led to pain and death.

She'd avoided every chance at so-called love in a desperate attempt at self-preservation, but seeing how happy Lucy and Mason were, seeing them grow closer together and having Harry…

She really was growing up. Her grandma would be proud of her. She smiled and turned back to the path.

The rest of the day flew by with unpacking and prepping for her work. She did her meal prep and filled her fridge for the week. When her head hit the pillow, she was out like a light.

And when her alarm went off the next morning, she jumped out of bed ready for her first day of work. She was buzzing with excitement and got ready in record time. For her first day as a full librarian at her own library, she wanted to look the part.

She put her hair up in a high bun. Purple pencil skirt with a gold silk tank top blouse made her feel like a real grown up. She found her most comfortable pair of black pumps and nodded at the mirror. This was it. The start of her life as a grown up.

Chapter Seven

Taylor drove to the library and parked in the back. It was across the street from the park, a block from Main. Another vehicle was already there, so she knocked on the back door and waited.

It opened to Lucy's grandma, Helen. She grinned and threw her arms around Taylor.

"You're finally here. Welcome, welcome. I'm so glad we finally convinced you to move to town," Helen said.

Taylor breathed in a floral scent that reminded her of her mother, and some nerves in her stomach settled. She'd known Helen for seven years now since she and Lucy had moved into the dorm together on campus. Last month, she'd gotten to know Helen on the cruise to Hawaii when Lucy had gotten married. They had a lot in common, including a love of English literature.

"I'm so happy to be here," she said as they ended the hug, and Helen pulled her into the back storage room. Helen had given her a tour after the cruise when they'd done the official interview, but she'd been hanging around this library since last October when Lucy had released her novel and had her first book signing.

The storage room had a large desk in the center for in-processing new books. Both the left and the back wall by the back door were full of shelves haphazardly stacked with books and supplies. To the right, a small office with barely enough room for a desk against the wall and a chair kept the main server and the cash box.

Mayor Ruby was on the phone, pacing in front of the office door. She waved and stepped into the office, shutting it behind her.

Directly in front of them was a swinging door to the public area of the library and a large window to see who was coming in or leaving the large oak front door. The window was one-sided, so the public couldn't see into the messy storage area.

"Let's get you caught up to speed, shall we?" Helen asked. She led Taylor into the public area to give a brief tour of the sections, but it was all standard practice. There was a seating area in the kids' section with bean bags, which she knew she'd have to keep an eye on. The opposite side of the building housed the adult fiction and non-fiction sections with a couple of couches separating them.

In front of the storage room was the main librarian's desk, which monitored the three public computers they had available as well as their physical Dewey cards. Helen sat her down at the main desk's computer and before she knew it, an hour had passed while she learned the ins and outs of where their files and programs were.

She laid down her pen and cracked her knuckles as Mayor Ruby came through the swinging door behind them.

She smiled tensely. "Sorry for the delay. There was an

emergency that couldn't wait. It's nice to see you again, Taylor. Lucy has talked and talked about you all year long."

Taylor chuckled and stood to shake her hand. "It's a wonder you decided to hire me at all, then."

Ruby laughed, and Helen tsked. "You know Lucy sings your praises. You've been her rock for the past seven years when she needed it most. It was hard on her to lose her mom like that."

Taylor touched Helen's arm. "It was hard on you too, to lose your daughter."

Helen's eyes misted as she nodded.

Mayor Ruby shifted and cleared her throat. "Either way you look at it, we're glad you're here. Helen was just part time until Regina retired and moved to Florida. It's been hard on her the past few months of running this all by herself."

Helen wiped her eyes and chuckled. "You've got that right. It's funny how once you retire, it's harder to go back to work. I'm looking forward to going back to part-time here. It's perfect timing, Taylor. We're at the end of our summer reading program, so I'll be able to show you how we're driving up interest."

Taylor nodded. "I was wondering what the summer schedule was. It has to be hard to get kids in here during the hottest part of the summer when they'd rather be at the pool."

Ruby perked up. "And this is why we're glad you're here. You can appeal to the younger crowd."

Taylor frowned. "I'm not that much younger than you."

Ruby laughed. "A decade is still plenty younger, trust me. You'll know what I mean when you hit your thirties."

Taylor shrugged. Twenty-four didn't feel that different from the years before it. She still felt like she was trying to keep her head above water, and her stress management and coping mechanisms were still absolute garbage.

"Anyway, I need to head to City Hall for a working lunch. Helen will show you around the office. Oh, and be sure to let me know if there are questions as far as budgeting, procedures, and things like that go. Whatever you need, I'm happy to help," Ruby said.

They shook hands again before she left.

Then Helen said, "Right, so let's hop onto the office computer, and I can show you around the back end of the computer system. I'm sure it's similar to the college library, but not as fancy."

Taylor smiled and followed her. Now that she was here, it felt like she was doing what she was always meant to do. She'd worked on campus for years, and the library had been her haven when the stress had piled on. Lucy had done yoga and written her stories, but Taylor had had a lot of sex and hidden inside book after book.

When Helen went to grab lunch with her husband, Ray, Taylor was left at the library by herself. In researching the job, she knew that the library's website was ancient, and they didn't have any social media presence at all, so she dove into setting something up.

The bell rang, and she looked up from behind the desk. A tall, lanky man in dusty jeans and a black t-shirt held the door for two adorable little girls. They were night and day, though. One wore a Cinderella dress-up costume and tiara. The other had a hole in the knees of her red leggings and a dinosaur shirt. Both had their brown hair up in pigtails.

"Well, hello there. You have to be the coolest kids to come into the library so far today. Welcome," Taylor said with a smile, finally looking at the dad.

The Cowboy Gets His Girl

He was hott, H-O-T-T with capital letters spelled out in fireworks.

He had a well-worn baseball hat on that said Texas Rangers, but when he took his aviator sunglasses off, brown eyes smiled down at her. He was lean but well-defined in that athletic way that made her sigh.

"What do you say to the pretty lady, girls?" he said, the deep timbre of his voice giving her goosebumps.

"Thank you," they said in unison. Then they took off to the kids' section, the princess skipping and holding her dress.

Taylor chuckled. "Looks like they know what they're looking for."

He nodded and held his hand out. "Yeah, we come in every Monday. You must be the new librarian. I'm Scott."

Taylor stood and shook his hand. "Hi Scott. It's nice to meet you, I'm Taylor. Since you've obviously been here way more than me, can you let me know if something seems off, out of place, or amiss?"

He grinned and nodded. "Sure thing. That's not a problem."

"You a Rangers fan?" she asked, nodding to his hat.

He grinned and lifted a dark brow. "Since I used to play for them, I'd say so."

Her jaw dropped. "For real?"

He chuckled and crossed his arms. "For real. Center field for eight years. Do you play?"

She shrugged. "I played through high school, but it's been years. But as short as I am, I couldn't do outfield."

He chuckled and glanced her up and down. "Little pint-sized pixie like you probably played third base. Am I right?"

She laughed and nodded. "Is it that obvious?"

He grinned and leaned against the front of the desk.

"Probably just to me. You have the build for it, and I can definitely see you body checking someone trying to round third."

She grinned, her cheeks hurting from smiling so wide. "Oh, that was the best part."

"Daddy, look what I found," the dinosaur girl came running around the corner with her arms full. She stumbled and went sprawling. Taylor and the dad both rushed to her side as she started sniffling.

He gathered her into his arms and checked her over while Taylor gathered the books.

"Are you ok, baby girl?"

Taylor sucked in a breath and glanced up through her lashes as she stacked them neatly with spines all turned in the same direction. The girl nodded and held up her palms.

"My hands hurt. Kiss it."

"Of course, baby girl. Magic kisses coming right up." He kissed each palm, then her cheeks.

She giggled and patted his cheek before hopping up and jumping from foot to foot. "That tickled, Daddy. All better. Now about my books."

Taylor looked at her and smiled. "You like Pete the Cat?"

The girl nodded and put her hands on her hips. "Yes, and these are new. I want them all."

The man reached out a hand to Taylor's elbow and helped her to her feet. He was incredibly close and smelled like freshly cut grass. She looked up into his brown eyes. She was definitely attracted to him, although not as weak in the knees as when she was this close to Hunter.

She blinked, her brain automatically comparing the two. Hunter was a little taller and bulkier whereas Scott was lean and athletic. Hunter didn't talk a lot and secrets hid behind his eyes.

This guy was more open, his face friendly and easy going. He had kind eyes, and his kids seemed to like him. She smiled, and he rubbed his thumb on the inside of her elbow before stepping back and releasing her.

He looked down at his daughter. "You know the rule, munchkin. Seven books for seven days. You can check out the others next week."

"But they might not be here next week. What if someone else swoops in and swipes them?"

The dad sighed, and Taylor rounded the desk and laid out the stack of books. "Here, let's decide on the seven, shall we? Which one are you most excited about?"

The girl pointed, and while she worked with her, the dad went around the corner to his other daughter. The girl amazingly enough didn't throw a fit about putting the others back, which Taylor had been worried about.

When the dad came back holding the hand of the princess, Taylor sighed. This was a nice, happy family. This was what she wanted, right? Something like Lucy and Mason were building. A family that reads and a dad who protects and helps his kids.

She turned her mind back to her customers. The princess had some of the thinner Geronimo Stilton books, which Taylor was surprised by. She was engrossed in reading one, and their dad just set four others on the desk when they stopped.

Taylor nodded to her. "Those are some big books for her age, aren't they?"

The dad beamed. "Yeah, she's reading above grade level. Paige is a good reader, but doesn't have the patience yet for the longer chapter books, isn't that right, Paige?"

The dinosaur girl nodded. "I like to read, but there's too much to do to read long books. Piper will be done with that one by the time we get home, though."

The dad chuckled as he pulled out their library card.

"What grades are you two in?" Taylor asked as she began checking them into the system. The princess didn't even glance up once, just turned the page and kept reading.

"I'm in kinder but Piper's in first."

"You and your wife must be so proud of them both."

Piper and Paige both looked at their dad and watched him with similar wary expressions. Taylor looked up and met the blinking gaze of the dad. He looked like he'd been punched.

He drew a deep breath and seemed to finally focus back on her. "She's gone. It's just me."

Paige wrapped her arm around his leg, and Piper took his hand. It melted Taylor's heart. Where had their mom gone? Or had she died? Oh dear, those poor little babies.

"I'm so sorry," she said softly, not breaking his stare.

He nodded. "You couldn't have known. You're new."

Piper jutted her chin out. "Daddy's the best. He taught us to read and homeschools us."

Paige added, "When he's not rescuing cats and saving burning houses."

Scott's nose wrinkled as he shrugged. "Firefighter. We have a lot to do on the farm today though, so we'd best get back to it."

Taylor mental jaw dropped as her eyes widened. He was a hero too? My lanta, he was the whole package. As she scanned the last book and pushed each stack across the desk, she wondered if he was single and looking for someone special.

She smiled at the girls. "You're all set then. It was nice meeting y'all."

"You too," he said. "Tell Miss Taylor bye, girls."

"Bye Miss Taylor," they said in unison as they took their books and turned to the door. He opened the door for them, waved, and then they were gone.

Helen pushed open the swinging door behind her. "Did I miss Scott and the girls? Darn it, I love those precious babies."

Taylor nodded, going to the window next to the door and peering out the curtain as he helped them buckle into his truck. "They just left. What happened to their mom?"

Helen fiddled with the desk, but Taylor didn't look away from the familial scene outside.

"She ran off with another baseball player, then died in a car accident. The youngest was just six months old."

"Oh, that's terrible. Those poor girls." Taylor's mind spun. She knew how losing her mom had impacted her. She couldn't imagine being that young and not even remembering her mom.

"Did you eat lunch?" Helen asked. Taylor nodded absently. "Great, then let's go over the summer reading program. I want to show you what we've been doing, then see if you have any ideas to get more kids involved. It seems like it's a slower summer each year."

Taylor followed Helen to the display case that served as the half wall to the adult side of the stacks.

Chapter Eight

Hunter crooned to Maribell as the vet checked on her progress.

"All seems good here. She has a week or two left, I think. You've timed them all well this year," Gemma said.

Hunter released a breath he didn't know he was holding. This was the first year that his mom had let him be completely in charge of the breeding program. As one of the top rodeo quarter horse breeders in the US, they were in demand and had to walk a fine line with their breeding program.

Good genes would bring in a lot of money, but good training was just as vital. Hunter had been focused on the training side for the past decade, but the older he got, the more he knew it was only a matter of time before he had to learn the ropes of the whole operation. Dad had been hinting at him taking over more in the office, so they'd started Money Monday talks.

Hunter had taken his lunch break to go around with Gemma and Ma to check on their pregnant mares. Half their ranch hands were dedicated to making sure all went well during their pregnancies and births.

Gemma patted Maribell's hindquarters and stepped out of the stall. She pulled off her gloves and turned them inside out.

"Hunter, I wanted to talk to you about Jewel."

His stomach tightened as he closed the stall's door. "What about her?"

Gemma sighed and grabbed her backpack. "She's moving back now that she's graduated and finished with her internship."

"Took her long enough," he said, some of his anger bleeding into his voice. It'd been fifteen years, and he thought he was over it by now. He sighed and turned away so she wouldn't be able to read anything in his expression.

Gemma followed him out of the barn. "She took as long as she needed. Look, there are some things you need to know, but I can't tell you. Will you just talk with Jewel already?"

"What's there to talk about?"

Gemma grabbed his arm, and he turned to face her. She looked so much like Jewel, but he thought he'd gotten used to it.

She frowned. "Are you going to be ok if Jewel is the one who comes out here to check the herd? Or do I need to keep you two separated? I don't want a repeat of what happened at the Christmas church program."

He pushed the door open and stepped into the sun. "It was too fresh then but it's fine now. Nothing to worry about. All water under the bridge."

She followed him and shut the door behind her. "Are you sure? She shouldn't be over here often. Only in emergencies if I'm out of town or she's on call."

He put his sunglasses back on and walked her to her truck. "That's fine. I appreciate the heads up, but I'll be civil if she will."

Gemma opened her door and climbed in. "She will. Dad's already talked to her. Just let me know if it's too much, okay?"

He nodded as she shut the door, started the truck, and rolled the window down. He grabbed the windowsill and pursed his lips. Just thinking about her sent his emotions into overdrive. All the pain, fear, and anxiety flooded him, and it bled over into his voice.

"She might not even want to come over, Gem." When he noticed his hands tight on the frame, he pulled them away and slid them into his pockets.

Gemma looked at him, unblinking, before snorting and putting her sunglasses on. "Right, but she needs to. You both need to talk things out. See ya later, Hunter."

He nodded and walked back to the house as she pulled away and left. It had been miles and years ago. They were both dumb kids with high hormones and tempers. He'd known she'd move back. He'd known this day would come. He'd prepared himself.

It'd be fine.

He pushed the front door open and walked to the office. Dad had changed it by adding a desk and computer for Hunter. He appreciated it, but computer work would never be his preference.

He sank into the computer chair and spun to face dad.

"All good with Gemma?"

Hunter nodded and waited, unable to talk past the lump of memories choking him.

Bill waved to his laptop. "We have an offer on Buzzer and another on Daisy Mae. I've cleared and replied to the rest of the emails, but it's the beginning of the month. We need to do inventory on supplies. Feed, hay, groceries for feeding the ranch hands. Here, let me show you the spreadsheet."

Hunter groaned and sank in his chair. "Not another spreadsheet, Dad. Come on."

"Hunter, you have to learn this if you're going to take over the ranch someday. And what about come September?" He stared pointedly, and Hunter sighed.

Dad leaned back in the chair. "When your grandpa died, I was wholly unprepared. You're thirty-seven now. It's time to learn the ropes. This is my legacy. I don't want you to have all the problems I did."

Hunter rubbed his temples. "I know, I know."

They'd been over this when they'd started Money Monday meetings. It was like he was back in school again. It made his skin itch and his foot bounce. He didn't want to be here; he wanted to be outside.

He rolled his chair beside Bill and waved his hand. Bill began explaining how they track the supplies and the daily and weekly tasks that made sure it didn't pile up and become overwhelming.

It made sense when he talked, but when Hunter looked at the screen, it was just a jumbled mess. Before long, he had a headache, and was second-guessing his plan to take over the ranch.

Chase came in from outside. Ma normally cooked breakfast and lunch for everyone, ranch hands included, but dinner was just for family.

"Dinner's ready," Chase said, glancing at the computer as Hunter rubbed his temples.

Bill stretched and walked out the door. "Finally, I'm starving."

Chase leaned on the back of Bill's chair, staring at the computer monitor. "You good?" Chase asked.

Hunter grunted. "Yeah, it's just not my cup of tea."

Chase cocked his head to the side and looked at the screen. "How so?"

Hunter pointed and explained the spreadsheet, then said, "It just feels like I'm back in school again. I barely survived that, and I'm just afraid of fucking it all up."

Chase slapped him on the back. "You'll be fine. You've always been the more cautious of all of us. Because of that, you'll take your time and do it right, instead of jumping in without a plan and messing it up. You're doing great, Hunter."

Hunter sighed and stood, following Chase out the door and down the hall. "Thanks, that means a lot."

They joined their parents at the table, each of them sitting in the seats they'd claimed as children. For too long, Chase's chair had been empty. They talked about local politics and chit-chatted. It was soothing and helped calm him somewhat.

After, he washed the dishes, and Ava put them up. Chase and Bill had disappeared into the office, and he was humming a random tune when Ava spoke.

"I hear Jewel is back in town."

He groaned and closed his eyes. He really did not want to have this conversation with her right now. Or ever. "That's what I hear too. Gemma might've mentioned it today," he said.

"Is there going to be another blow up like what happened at church or are you two going to be okay?" she asked matter-of-factly. She wasn't one to beat around the bush.

He sighed. "We'll be fine, Ma. I was a little hotheaded—"

"A little?" she snorted.

He grinned and handed her another dish to dry. "I've had years to calm down, so I'll be fine. Whether she's still pissed or not is another matter entirely."

Ava nodded and reached for another plate. "I understand that, but you can't hold on to the bitterness. It'll eat you up inside."

"Who said I was? I'm fairly certain I've let it go."

She snorted again. "I call bullshit on that."

"Ma!" he said, surprised to hear her cuss.

She shrugged. "What? I call it how I see it, and you're still raw about what happened between you two. Isn't that why you haven't had a decent girlfriend in all these years?"

His shoulders tensed as he scrubbed the pot harder. "Maybe."

It didn't matter if she was the reason or not. The logic was valid. He wasn't the only one who'd gotten his heart broken back then. His parents had been devastated that they'd broken up.

Jewel had been the little girl his parents had never had. She and Gemma both had hung around their ranch all the time, checking on animals with their dad the vet. It had been so effortless when they'd hit the teenage years and started dating.

But then they'd fought like cats and dogs her senior year of high school. She'd wanted him to go to college with her in Houston. There was no way he'd make it in the city, much less put himself through even more school. He'd barely survived that hell, and she knew it.

They'd tried to make a long-distance relationship work,

but then she'd come home for Christmas, and true hell had broken loose.

Ava leaned against the counter and crossed her arms. "Did I ever tell you about when your grandpa went out west to work the oil fields?"

Hunter grunted and continued scrubbing the pot.

"He was actually dating Melinda May back then. He was probably nineteen at the time? We'd just joined World War II, and he'd tried to join the Army. They'd told him he was too scrawny and unhealthy to make it as a soldier, so he packed up and went to the oil fields to build strength until they'd take him."

Hunter rinsed the pot and listened. It wasn't often that she talked about her dad. He'd died before Hunter had met him.

"You remind me a lot of him. If someone told him something wouldn't work, he'd make it work. He was stubborn to a fault, my daddy."

Hunter looked at her and arched a brow. She arched one right back and said, "What? Do you deny it? You've spent your whole life trying to prove yourself. You're still trying."

"What's the point of this conversation, Ma?" he asked. He didn't like beating around the bush any more than she did.

She shrugged and took the pot to dry it. "One of these days, you're going to meet someone who you won't have to try so hard with. It'll be like the puzzle pieces just click into place. You'll be able to be you, and she'll love you like no other. I just hope you're able to recognize it before you blow up at her, lose your temper, and burn all your bridges."

Hunter sighed and dried his hands. He knew she was talking about Jewel and their Christmas fiasco, but his mind went to Taylor. The way she made him feel, the way he was drawn to her like a ship to a safe port in a storm.

With Jewel, it'd been like he was sailing into the storm. It'd been exciting and exhilarating. But Taylor had him more terrified than the darkest, deepest ocean.

The storm had brewed for years in the cauldron of the fates. But now the gods had sent him an angel from on high, a slutty angel who made his dick weep with need. She both fired the flame of his soul and calmed the raging storm within.

He shook his thoughts off, not wanting to sink into his fantasies with his mom around. "I think I've chilled out with age though, don't you?" he asked.

She put the pot up and smiled. "Of course you have, but you've a long way to go before you're ready for the love of a good woman."

And miles to go before I sleep.

Taylor had demanded to be courted, but that wasn't something he could give her. It was too confusing, too new, too overwhelming. He needed to clear his head and think. Did he even want love? He'd just barely come around to the idea of having a girlfriend.

He and Jewel had declared love for each other all those years ago, but that was completely different to Taylor. He knew nothing about her except how she made him feel. Maybe he should get to know her before deciding whether he could or could not date her?

He needed to analyze all the possibilities first, and to do that he needed to be alone. He smiled and hugged Ma, then stepped away as he said, "I'll be in the barn for a bit if you need me."

"Night, son," she said behind him as he opened the door. The hot, humid air hit him, and he breathed deep of the fresh cut hay as he walked.

Chapter Nine

It was the end of the Saturday, and Taylor smiled as she cleaned up the library. She's made it almost a full week at her new job and absolutely loved it. She hadn't run into Hunter again, so she'd started to relax.

She was off work on Tuesday and Wednesday, so she'd straightened her apartment more and babysat Harry. Then she'd gone with Lucy to yoga on Thursday night and met some new friends. Mayor Ruby had been there, so she'd sat between her and Lucy.

She'd finished setting up the social media for the library and had advertised story time. Helen had encouraged her to jump right in, so she'd ordered some cookies from the bakery on Main Street for the Saturday event.

There had only been a half dozen kids but Lucy had said it was a good test run. It'd been short notice, so Taylor considered it a success. It would just grow from there. She waved as the last family went through the door. Story time had ended two hours ago, but many of them had simply hung around, chatting as their kids searched for books and read on the floor.

The bathroom door opened, and Scott stepped out followed by his two little girls. He smiled easily and reached for the empty box of cookies in her hand.

"Here, let me help. What else do you need?"

She smiled but didn't tell him no. "Thanks. Did y'all have fun? I didn't have time to ask earlier."

The girls nodded, Piper's face buried in a book again and Paige shifting on her feet.

"Sorry we were late. We don't normally come to town on the weekends, but the girls heard about story time from their grandparents and didn't want to miss out."

She smiled as he tossed the trash. "That's okay. I'm just glad y'all had a chance to stop by. I was really nervous about this first story time event."

Paige's eyes widened. "You were? I didn't think adults got nervous."

Taylor grasped her hands and held them in front of her. "Oh yes, we absolutely do. I was sweating so much, I'm sure I smell terrible right now. Don't get too close."

Paige giggled but Scott's brow lifted. "Really?" He leaned in closer, and Taylor froze. His head was near her ear, and he made a dramatic showing of sniffing her. Paige laughed out loud, but Taylor turned her head and met his eyes.

His brown eyes were shining with mirth, but his voice was deep and low. "I don't think you smell bad at all. Kinda nice, actually. Like refreshing strawberries."

Taylor felt a little flutter in her stomach at his nearness. She wanted to fan the flames because he was the perfect guy. A family man, loved his kids, was hot as sin, and a responsible adult. She was so afraid she was going to blow it, though.

Taylor saw Paige run off out of the corner of her eye as he straightened. He cleared his throat and shifted on his feet, still closer than normal.

"I actually wanted to bring the girls in today to return their books and stock up for the week. We won't be in on Monday as we're going on our annual camping trip."

Taylor felt a stab of disappointment. "Oh, that's going to be so much fun for y'all."

"I hope so. Last year we only lasted a few days before the rain sent us home early. We really needed it though, with that heat wave."

She nodded but didn't say anything else. She didn't know how to do this. She was great at flirting and making a move, and she was great at small talk and getting to know people. It was the in between that made her nervous.

Was it too soon to make a move? Would that be too forward? She didn't want to be that kind of girl anymore. She took a deep breath and waited for him. She'd follow his lead.

He shifted on his feet again and smiled. "We get back on Friday and my folks are taking the girls for the weekend. Could I take you out to dinner Saturday night?"

Taylor breathed deep and smiled, pushing past her nerves. "I'd love that."

His face lit up as he grinned. "Great, I'm looking forward to it."

"Daddy," Paige said, holding a stack of books. "I'm ready now."

Scott rolled his eyes and grinned. "You have seven? Awesome. Let me grab your sister while you check out."

Taylor went to the counter and chatted about the

camping trip with Paige while she scanned each book. Then it was Piper's turn. When the girls walked out, Scott held the door open and looked back at her.

"I'll see you next weekend. Wish me luck!"

She grinned. "Good luck!" She sat back in her chair and sighed as she stared at the ceiling. She had been asked on a date. A *real* date with a proper man, a good man who wasn't after just a quick lay.

What was she going to do? She'd never been on a real date before. Even in high school, she'd developed the reputation for always being down for a good fuck. She'd spent many years in college in therapy trying to analyze why she was like this, why she'd developed these bad habits.

And she was finally in a place where she could break them. She didn't want to start back down that destructive path again. She picked up her phone and did a quick search. She'd met a counselor at yoga who might talk her through this.

"Hello, this is Cool Counseling. How can I help you?"

"Yes, is this Tasha?"

"Yes, may I ask who's calling?"

"This is Taylor, Lucy's friend? We met at yoga on Thursday?"

"Oh, hey, how are you? Sorry, I didn't recognize your voice."

"That's okay. I was wondering if you had any appointments in the next few days. I have some things I need to bounce off someone."

"Sure, I'm free for the next two hours, then I have some openings on Monday."

Taylor bit her lip and said, "Tonight is fine. I'll swing by after I close up the library?"

"Sounds great. See you soon."

Taylor turned on the music on her phone and sang *What's Up* at the top of her lungs as she went to clean the bathrooms at the library. She had just started singing the chorus when her phone rang. She swiped to answer.

"Hello?"

"Are you closing up for the day?" Lucy asked.

Taylor replied and washed her hands. "Yep, just doing the last cleaning, then I'm locking the doors and heading home. Did Harry finish his nap?"

"Yeah, we're going to Nana's for dinner tonight, so I wanted to invite you."

"Aw, that's sweet, but I think I'm going to pass. I've got a good book calling my name and a bottle of wine ready to celebrate the end of my first week."

She didn't want to worry Lucy by talking about counseling. And once she worked through this anxiety about the date, she'd be fine.

Lucy asked, "Are you sure? What about tomorrow? We're going fishing, and you should join us."

Taylor wrinkled her nose. "Ew, no thanks."

Lucy chuckled, "Okay, but I was kind of hoping you could suntan on the bank while watching Harry."

Taylor inspected the bathroom and hummed. The sunshine would probably do her good. God knows her old therapist had always tried to get her outside. "Fine, I will brave the wilds for that little boy."

Lucy laughed, "That's the spirit! You're the best godmother ever."

"Yeah, yeah. You say that now, but just wait until tomorrow when I'm sunburned and swatting mosquitoes and scaring off all the fish."

Taylor grinned as they chatted, and she closed up the library. When they hung up, she headed home. The sun didn't set until almost eight this time of year, so she had plenty of daylight left to run home, change into jogging clothes, and head for a run.

Soon, she jogged to the counseling door and pushed it open. A small bell rang overhead and the brunette on the couch looked up over her laptop with a smile. She pushed up the glasses on her nose and set her laptop down on the coffee table.

"Taylor, it's so good to see you again. Welcome, welcome. Do you want water? Did you jog here from the library?"

"No, from my apartment. It's in between here and the library. And yes, water sounds great. I didn't keep you waiting, did I?"

Tasha grabbed a bottle from the fridge along one wall and handed it over. "Not at all. I was just working on a little project for the school. Have a seat when you're ready and tell me what brings you by."

Taylor chugged her water and wiped her mouth. She didn't want to sit, so she started pacing behind the couch. There were actually two couches in the middle of the room facing each other.

She told Tasha about her past—the short version—and about her upcoming date. "But I'm nervous and anxious and scared. What if I say the wrong thing? Or what if I'm too forward? The man's a widower. I'm not sure what his sex life is like, but what if he's been celibate since her death five years ago? Or—"

Tasha chuckled, and Taylor stopped, turning to face her. "Deep breaths, Taylor, deep breaths. It's going to be all right. Breathe with me now, that's it, and exhale. Better now?"

Taylor sighed and nodded, sinking onto the couch and

leaning her head back to stare at the ceiling.

Tasha continued. "You're putting a lot of pressure on yourself about this one date. But that's all it is, just one date. You have two options. You can worry about it for the next week, or you can rip off the band-aid."

Taylor frowned and sat up. "What do you mean? How do I rip off the band-aid?"

Tasha shrugged. "You're a gorgeous woman, and it's a Saturday afternoon. You've plenty of time to go find a date this weekend."

Taylor shook her head. "What? No, I can't—"

"Let me ask you this. Are you more nervous about the date with Scott because it's your first real date or because it's with Scott?"

Taylor frowned, thinking it over. "Definitely because it's my first real date ever."

Tasha nodded. "Then that's the band-aid. You just need a real first date. Get that out of the way this weekend so when you go out with Scott next weekend, you're free to enjoy it without all this pressure about it being your first."

Taylor pursed her lips and took another drink of her water, the idea marinating in her head. "Maybe you're right. I'm just so afraid of falling back into my old patterns. I want a family. I want the white picket fence and stability and love."

"And you won't get that by sleeping with everyone who's interested?" Tasha asked softly. Taylor felt tears prickle, and she looked up at the ceiling again, refusing to let them drop.

"Exactly," she said, her voice scratchy. "I want a family, but I don't want to start one with just anyone. It needs to be with the right one."

Tasha chuckled. "You and me both, sista."

Taylor grinned and finished her water. "Thanks for

squeezing me in today. I really appreciate it. How much do I owe you?"

Tasha waved a hand. "First one's free." She winked, then said, "But I do expect a follow-up appointment. I need to know if you rip off the band-aid and how the date with Scott goes."

Taylor laughed and tossed her empty bottle of water into the trash. "Fair enough. I have Tuesdays off work. You have room for me then?"

Tasha typed on her laptop, and they made the appointment, then Taylor was out the door and jogging home. Perhaps Tasha was right, and she just needed to rip off the band-aid.

She'd built up this real date into some major thing in her head. It was the anxiety leading up to it that was driving her crazy. If she had a test date with someone else, maybe she could get all the jitters and awkwardness out of the way.

She'd go home and scroll through her dating apps in the bathtub to see if she could meet anyone in Denton for a real date.

Chapter Ten

The next day, Taylor drove with Lucy and Harry to the fishing spot. She had chatted with a few potential dates last night, but none of them had given her a warm and fuzzy feeling, so she hadn't tried to meet up with anyone. She was trying not to think about her date next weekend and decided to just set the problem aside.

For now, she had to tackle the problem of getting on a river for the first time. She bit her lip and asked, "Do you really think this is going to work out?"

Lucy parked and nodded. "Yep, we're going to have a lot of fun. The two hours are going to fly by, just watch and see."

Lucy hopped out, and Taylor sighed. She mentally girded her loins and opened her own door.

Ray and Helen were already waiting by the truck, four canoes already in the water. Taylor stood back and held Harry while Lucy loaded a few bags into Helen's. Then Lucy took Harry and put his life vest on.

Taylor looked around, shifting uncomfortably on her

feet. She wasn't sure she could do this. She'd always taken the bull by the horns, but that was mostly when dealing with people. This was *nature*. It was an entirely different ball game, and she had no idea what to do.

Ray slid over to her, his thick white hair blowing in the breeze and making him look a little bit like Einstein.

"This is your first canoeing experience, is it?"

Taylor winced. "Is it that obvious?"

Ray shrugged. "No, Lucy mentioned it. Have you ever been in a canoe?"

She shook her head, and he pulled his thumbs into his belt loops. "Well, there are a few pointers you might want to know."

He showed her different things and Helen showed her how to get in and out of the little boat. Then Helen pushed off and waited for Lucy and Harry. When they were both on the water, Ray pointed and explained how to use the paddle.

Then she was sitting on her very own canoe and holding on tight to the paddle as he pushed her into the water. The thing tilted, and she gasped as it wobbled. Ray shouted instructions, but she couldn't hear him over the rushing sound in her ears.

The boat settled, and Ray slid through the water beside her in his own canoe. "You okay? You makin' it?"

She took a deep breath and grinned. "I'm doing it! I'm on the water!"

He chuckled and held up his paddle. "Ready to find your rhythm?"

She nodded, excitement coursing through her. She'd never done anything like this in her life, and it was a completely different challenge. She mimicked his movements, realizing what he meant by the rhythm of rowing.

It reflected her life, though. She was one week into a new town, new job, new life, and she was finding her rhythm. She was growing into a better person, one not so flighty who could be an adult and make good decisions.

She was trying new things too. This week, she'd cooked two meals instead of eating out. That was progress too, along with the meal prepping her breakfasts and lunches. She'd always eaten out or grabbed junk food in college, since cooking reminded her too much of her mom and grandma.

She shook her head and dug her paddle into the water harder. They rounded a bend, and she saw two men walking to the water through a field. Ray turned to the sandy area that sloped up to the grass. Helen was already out and tying her canoe to a tree.

Lucy sat in hers and waited for Helen to pick up Harry. Ray tied up his little boat, then waved for Taylor to come closer. She dipped her paddle and pushed too hard, making her jerk as it hit the sandy bottom.

Ray grabbed the front and took the rope. "Good job. You're a natural. What did you think?"

Taylor grinned and set her paddle down, turning to carefully get out of the canoe. "I loved it! I always wanted to go to this outdoor camp as a kid, but never could. I told myself that I didn't miss anything special, but now I know the truth. It would've been amazing. I could've learned to do that years ago."

Ray grinned and waded around the boats to the shore. She grabbed her backpack and followed him, her sundress getting wet. She didn't care, though. It was a beautiful, sunny day, and she'd just conquered the river. What else could she conquer?

She followed Ray to where Lucy and Helen had settled

in. Lucy had laid out a large beach blanket, and Harry sat with a variety of toys around him. He babbled while Taylor set out her own beach towel and took her sun dress off, adjusting the straps of her bikini. She sat and dug into her bag looking for sunscreen.

"Hello, beautiful day for fishing, isn't it? Can we join you?"

Taylor's head shot up to look behind her. She groaned and pushed her sunglasses up on her nose. It was Hunter and one of his brothers. What was his name?

"Hunter, Chase, what great timing!" Ray said as he fiddled with his fishing rod. "We're just getting started. How's your ma and pa?"

Hunter nodded and smiled. His sunglasses hid his eyes, but she felt the heat of his gaze. She lathered on the sunscreen and turned away as he answered.

She didn't hear what he said because Lucy turned to her with the diaper bag. "He should be fine for the next few hours, but I'll take him in around the two-hour mark. He'll need food in an hour. Just make sure he doesn't eat anything he shouldn't, like all these rocks."

Taylor smiled and put the sunscreen back in her bag. "Don't worry, Luce. I'll keep him alive. Go relax and fish."

Taylor had gagged when Lucy had told her about going fishing last summer with Ray and Helen, but she had to admit, it was rather peaceful here. She laid back, propping her head up on her bag so she could keep an eye on Harry and pulling out her kindle to dive back into her book.

If she ignored Hunter, maybe he wouldn't talk to her. She bit her lip and peeked at where he'd set up to fish. He'd taken his shirt off and now stood in just khaki cargo shorts. His muscles rippled as he pulled back and then let the lure fly across the water.

His back and shoulders were covered in tattoos, but he was too far away for her to make out what they were. He was inked with muscles, had that mischievous, bad boy smirk, and kissed like a god. Was it any wonder he set her on fire and made her stomach churn? When she was around him, she felt out of breath. Her heart raced like she'd pushed herself too hard on a run. Sometimes she even felt like she was going to throw up.

It was completely different with Scott. With him, the sexual tension wasn't as intense. It wasn't fair to compare them. It was like comparing apples to oranges. Fireworks in Dallas to fireworks in Fort Worth. Chocolate-covered pecans and chocolate-covered strawberries.

They were both good, but one was a tad more addicting than the other. It all came down to preference.

Knowing her, she always gravitated toward the bad boys. She glanced at Chase as Harry crawled on the blanket. He was the one who'd gone to prison, yet she had no feelings for him. Hunter was a down-home country boy. He didn't fit the bad-boy mold at all.

Yet those were the vibes she got from him. He had secrets. Every time she looked at him, she knew he hid a shit-ton of naughty thoughts. It was evident in the way he moved, that smirk of a smile when he looked into her eyes.

He made her mouth water just thinking about him, but now that he was here. In person, he made her nipples pebble and her core ache.

She took a drink of water as Harry babbled. Taylor turned back to him, pulling some rocks out of his hand and tossing them off the blanket.

"There, there. None of those nasty rocks. Doesn't this toy taste better? Go on, try it," she said to him.

It seemed like only a few minutes had passed when

The Cowboy Gets His Girl

Harry began to scoot off the blanket. Now that he was crawling, she was surprised he'd lasted this long without venturing off.

She set her kindle aside and straightened the blanket, following Harry and making sure he didn't get into too much trouble. She was on her hands and knees, one arm around Harry to pull him back to the blanket when Hunter's voice groaned from behind her.

"Damn girl, you're trying to kill me with that ass, aren't you?"

She squeaked and turned, setting Harry in her lap like a shield for protection. She looked up to where Hunter stood, hands on hips staring down at her.

"Why do you always show up when my ass is hanging out?" she asked, annoyed and embarrassed.

He grinned and sank onto the blanket beside them. "Like a moth to a flame, sugar. Your ass has the power to move mountains."

Her lips twitched, but she refused to encourage him. Instead, she hand Harry a toy as he struggled in her lap. "Is that why you came over here? To talk about my ass?"

She didn't know whether to be mad at him or flattered that he noticed. Now that he was closer, she could see birds tattooed on his chest, flying toward trees on his bicep. Harry lunged off her lap and to his busy book on the blanket.

"Of course not. I actually came to borrow some sunscreen."

She leaned over and dug in her bag, tossing it to him. He sat on the blanket and turned his back to her, holding the sunscreen out.

"Actually, can you rub it between my shoulder blades? I can't ever reach that spot."

She swallowed hard and looked at Harry. He was lying

on his back playing with a soft, crinkly book, so she sat on her knees behind Hunter.

She cleared her throat and squeezed the white goo on her palm, then slowly rubbed it into his warm skin. The tattoos on the back continued the wilderness theme. There was a bear next to a stream on one shoulder blade and a forest scene on the other shoulder blade depicting a lone man fishing with a tent in the background.

"You like the outdoors?"

"Hm?" he asked. She began to knead his back, and he groaned.

"Your tattoos. They're a lot of outdoor scenes. Why?" Her voice was softer than she'd thought it'd be. She looked at Harry to make sure he was still good, then got more sunscreen and began to rub it over one bulging bicep.

Damn, the man had arm porn. She didn't care about abs, but biceps knocked her flat on her back every time. Hunter was built like a brick house, tall and stocky. She wanted to climb him like a tree.

She snorted. She'd never climbed a tree in her life.

"It's peaceful outside. Fewer people, less noise among the trees and gurgling stream. *The heavens are closer under the open sky, among the fields and falling twilight, over the hills and in the valleys, I find the same peace with a wee lassie.*"

She gasped and squeezed his bicep. "There you go with the poetry again. Although I don't recognize that one. Who wrote it?"

He shrugged, making his skin ripple. "That was an original."

Her hands froze. "Holy hell, you *are* a poet."

He glanced to the side as she lathered on the other bicep. "Wouldn't classify myself quite that way, but I have read a lot of the great poets though. Some of it must've rubbed off."

She turned to Harry and moved him from the edge of the blanket. "Who's your favorite?"

He shrugged, and the movement drew her hands. She knew she was just rubbing his back now. She hadn't even added more sunscreen, but he didn't stop her.

"Whitman, Frost, Emerson—all the greats that talk about the outdoors," he chuckled.

She wanted to lean into him. The scent of leather drew her in, and she sat up on her knees. Her boobs grazed his back, and they both sucked in a breath and froze. She barely breathed, just feeling her body against his.

He growled, "If you don't want me to rip that bikini off and have my way with you in front of Harry and everyone else, then you need to back away right now."

The tone of his voice made her gasp and jerk back. The voice of sin, the growl of a predator, and the demand of a master sent tingles up her spine. Her cheeks flamed, and she reached for Harry as he was gnawing on the book.

He squirmed in her arms, but it helped to distract herself from Hunter. He was dangerous, and she couldn't play with fire anymore.

She avoided his stare as she reached for the container of baby food and spoon in the diaper bag. She could feel Hunter's gaze on her now that he'd turned back to face her. He took the sunscreen and rubbed it on his chest.

She stared, frozen as she held Harry with one hand and the food with the other. His pectorals rippled, making his tattoos move. It was like the outdoor scene came to life. She couldn't look away, but Harry wouldn't let her stay mesmerized for long.

Chapter Eleven

Hunter watched her twist open the jar of baby food and juggle Harry with one arm and the spoon in the other. She was good with him—he'd been watching her for an hour—but it was hard to feed a baby with one hand.

He'd seen his brothers struggle with it a time or two. He sighed and reached for Harry, holding him on his lap. "I'll hold him. You feed him. Deal?"

"Deal," she said softly, brows raised in surprise. "And thanks for the help." She took a deep breath and nodded, her lips relaxing a little.

"No problem," he said, clapping Harry's hands together as she scooped another bite. Taylor sat cross-legged on the sand, a small towel across her lap that she used to wipe the kid's face. She cooed and made silly faces as she spooned food to him, her sun-kissed skin glowing in the summer heat. Hunter admired her distracting beauty, but she didn't talk to him. She might not have enjoyed their kiss, might have gotten him out of her system. He didn't think this attraction was one sided, but more than the physical, he wondered what she was thinking about.

He longed to ask her about her interests, her opinions on books and music, but he knew better than to start anything with a local girl. As she wiped the boy's face with the towel, the strings of her bright orange bikini stretched taut against her lush curves, and Hunter could only imagine peeling them off like the rind of an orange to reveal the juicy fruit inside.

As she turned her head, the sunlight glinted off of her sunglasses, obscuring her eyes. But he could sense her gaze on him, the weight of it like a physical touch, sending a shiver down his spine.

He thought of all the things he could say to her, but in the end just kept quiet. That was always how it was with him. He mulled over the perfect words until it was too late to say anything.

She eventually broke the silence for him, though. "Do you have experience with kids? You look pretty relaxed around him."

Hunter shifted into a more comfortable position and nodded. "Yeah, I have some nieces and a nephew. You?"

She shook her head and frowned. "No, I'm an only child. Once Harry was born, I fell in love though and had to move here to be more present in his life. I got to babysit twice this week."

She sounded so proud, like it was a major accomplishment. He smiled and asked, "How did the first week at work go?"

She lit up, a wide smile on her face as she said, "It was great. I loved everything about it."

He smiled and clapped Harry's hands. "You're at the library in town?"

She looked up at him again, then back to Harry as she fed him another bite. "Yeah, it's the cutest little library I've seen, and there's a lot of cool stuff I've already got planned for it."

His chest tightened as he imagined her in her element. "I bet you're an amazing librarian. Do you wear reading glasses by chance?"

His mind splintered at all the possibilities. He pictured her bent over the librarian's desk in town. His mouth watered, and he wanted to see her like that. All put together and proper just waiting for him to come in and wreck her.

She grinned and tilted her head in a flirting manner. "You're picturing me with glasses, aren't ya? You should see this ass in a tight pencil skirt, hair in a bun, silk button up blouse just ready to be ripped open."

He groaned and leaned his head on the back of Harry's. "See? I told ya you're killing me."

She laughed, and the sound made him feel warm all over. "This is fun," she said with a soft smile as she wiped Harry's mouth.

He nodded. She was right. Who knew hanging out with a hot babe and a baby could be an enjoyable way to spend a lazy Sunday afternoon?

She bit her lip and frowned. "Maybe... Do you remember how I said I'd never been on a real date?"

He breathed in slowly and nodded. The twisting pain in his chest brought a wave of warning over him. Surely, she wasn't going to—

"Will you go on a date with me sometime this week?"

Damn, she did. She didn't pin him with her deep green eyes, and for that he was grateful. He remembered Jewel and all the other women he'd dated in the past decade.

He had to say no and disappoint her. Then he'd have to avoid her until she let the idea go.

"Why?" He frowned, not sure why he'd even asked. He had opened his mouth to turn her down, not dig deeper into it.

She bit her lip and took Harry, cradling him and giving him a bottle. Something in his chest twisted at the sight, adding to the lonely ache inside.

"I have a date next weekend with a guy I like, but I'm afraid I'm going to fuck it up, since I've never been on a date before. I thought maybe you could help me out."

"Like a practice date?" he asked, his brows rising. His temper flared. He wasn't anyone's second best, and he sure as hell wasn't a practice run. He was a motorcycle, not a bicycle with training wheels.

She tucked her hair behind her ear, some of it coming out of her messy bun in the breeze. "Yeah, a practice date. Since you already know it's my first, you can call me out when I'm getting too flirty. I don't want to come across as a floozy or be too forward."

He scowled, "Like when I took you home and you threw yourself at me?"

Her cheeks turned red, and she nodded, looking down and rocking Harry gently. "Exactly. I'm a one-night stand kinda girl, not a girlfriend kind of girl. Not yet anyway. But I want to be. Can you help?"

He choked on his frustration, some of his anger ebbing because this wasn't about him. It was about her being confident instead of just faking it. Her vulnerability brought out the bear in him, and he wanted to haul her over his shoulder and take her away to protect her from all that worried her.

He breathed deeper, trying to calm the beast within.

But then his brain caught up to what she'd originally said. She had a date next weekend. *With another man.*

He clenched his teeth as his vision blurred, his emotions spiking again. He breathed deeply, in and out, forcing himself to slow down and take a few minutes. Most people thought he was the strong silent type, but sometimes he was just trying to get a handle on his anger.

There is never jealousy where there is not strong regard. He cared for her? He blinked, breathing and processing.

It didn't make any sense to have this strong of a reaction to a stranger, a woman he'd only met four times. Of course, she could date whomever she wanted.

He recited various poems in his head to try to understand his feelings for this woman.

Lucy came over and smiled as she took Harry gently from Taylor. "He's almost out, isn't he? Well, we'd better get him home. Are you coming with me, Tay, or are you staying here a while?"

Taylor bit her lip and glanced at him, her cheeks pink again. She stood and dusted sand off her knees. "I'm coming with you. Let me just grab our stuff and pack up. You can take him upriver to the car. I'll be right behind you."

Lucy nodded and walked toward Helen and Ray, burping Harry as she went.

Taylor grabbed her sun dress and jerked it over her head, then she started putting away Harry's toys into the diaper bag. He grabbed one and handed it to her. She snatched it from him, her movements jerky as she mumbled, "Thanks."

She grabbed the corner of the bright, striped beach towel he was sitting on and pulled hard. He groaned as he slowly stood up, feeling every one of his thirty-seven years.

Clearly peeved, she snatched the towel away and snapped it in frustration.

"Oops, sorry," she said with a smirk.

As he coughed and sputtered from the sand, he brushed himself off and rolled his eyes. "I thought you were trying to grow up? But here you are giving me the silent treatment and throwing sand on me like a child."

He raked a hand through his hair, dislodging more sand. She made an adorable growl and shoved things into a bag, ignoring him. He didn't like disappointing her, and despite his reservations and the need to protect himself, he wanted to do this small thing to make her happy.

Stepping closer, he took the large towel and folded it. "Look, Taylor, I'm sorry. You're not a child. I was just taken by surprise by all this, and it usually takes me a few minutes to think through things. How about tomorrow night?"

She hesitated, and he could almost see her eyes through her sunglasses. "I thought you didn't date locals." Her attitude and bratty tone of voice made his body hum in anticipation.

"Just one date won't hurt, especially if we go out of town."

She frowned and pursed her lips as she stared him down. "So you're embarrassed by me." She said it so matter-of-factly, and it annoyed him.

He bent and grabbed the diaper bag and her backpack, leaving her holding the folded towel. "I'd never be embarrassed by you, sugar tits. I just don't want to start any rumors in town and Lord knows my mom has had matchmaking on her brain ever since my other two brothers got hitched and started having babies. Can we go somewhere in Fort Worth or Denton?"

Slowly a smile spread across her wide lips, and she

bounced on her feet, her breasts jiggling in her sun dress. "Oh, that will work, I think!"

He swallowed hard and followed her to the canoe like a leashed puppy.

She nodded, her grin dimming somewhat as she leaned closer to whisper, "And don't worry, I won't tell a soul. Do you want to meet me at the library or on the edge of town somewhere, so no one sees us?"

He frowned and stiffened as she put the towel into her canoe. He added the bags, securing the straps.

"No, that won't work. This is supposed to show you what a proper date is like, right? I need to pick you up at your door. I'll be there at six tomorrow. Will that work?"

She nodded as she gently sat on the canoe seat and swung her legs in. "That works for me," she said as she grabbed the paddle.

He untied her from the tree and waded into the water, not wanting to let her go yet. She grinned at him and sat awkwardly on the seat as she glanced around.

"Um, can you point me in the right direction? I'm not sure how to turn this thing around."

The tension between them was palpable as he spun her around in the canoe slowly. It definitely wasn't one sided, and while he knew this was just a practice date for her and he couldn't—shouldn't—act on it, he wasn't sure he could resist. Pushing her away hurt her, but she set the boundaries and he'd honor them.

But damn him if he didn't clearly explain his thoughts on the matter.

He let the canoe pass him and grazed her thigh, leaning forward to whisper in her ear, "I don't know how to do a proper date and leave you at the door with just a kiss, but I'll try if that's what you want. It sounds like torture though because all I want to do is fuck you until you can't even remember this other guy's name."

She gasped, but then he was pushing her into the river. She gripped the paddle and side of the canoe, sitting stiffly as she floated away. He wanted their date to end with her legs wrapped around him, and he couldn't let her leave thinking otherwise.

He wanted her, like the grass wanted a spring breeze, gentle showers, and sunshine.

If his time outdoors had taught him anything, it was how to play the long game and be patient. *Patience is bitter, but its fruit is sweet.*

This was supposed to be a proper date with no expectations of sex at the end. She wanted to take things slow and for someone to take the effort to date her instead of just being a quick lay, which was ridiculous. She'd never be a quick lay and whoever she'd been with before were nothing but morons.

One kiss and he'd been able to think of nothing else for days. He was already half addicted to her, standing in the shallows and watching as she paddled up the river.

He'd make this the most perfect date anyone had ever been on. He'd do every step right, including leaving her at the door with just a kiss. It might lead to a long night with no sleep, but it'd be worth it. When they finally fucked—and he had no doubt now that they would eventually—it'd go all night. Maybe even for days, so great was their connection.

It defied reason, but here he was. Illogical brute who could barely read, standing in a river trying to cool off a raging hard-on as he stared at her drifting away around the bend.

Chase joined him and handed him a pole. "Didn't we come here to fish, big brother?"

The teasing tone made Hunter's brows rise, and he grinned. "Maybe I am fishing."

Chase snorted and cast his lure. "Fishing for pussy doesn't count. We're here for… why *are* we here?"

Hunter shrugged and checked his hook. "Tradition? Trying to recapture what was lost? Just spending time together because I missed you?"

Chase made a humming noise and an easy silence descended between them. Hunter cast his rod, sending the hook flying across the water.

Tomorrow night might be the best Monday night of his life. He was excited, but he couldn't take this too far. It was just one date so she could practice for that fucking dude next weekend.

He cast his lure with an extra snap of the wrist, his nostrils flaring with emotion.

Chapter Twelve

Taylor went to work on Monday with a pep in her step. She had *two* dates this week, and she was on top of the world. She went through the inventory in the back storage room while she listened to an audio book.

The door dinged, and she went out into the main room to find a delivery man. He peered around a giant bouquet of orange roses and white lilies.

"What in the—"

"Are you Taylor?" the young man asked. She nodded as he set the arrangement on the desk. If she made a circle with her arms, she wouldn't be able to wrap them around the flowers.

"Yes, but I wasn't expecting a delivery," she said.

The young man grinned. "That's the best part about getting flowers, isn't it?"

She laughed and turned the arrangement, looking for the card as the young man left.

White lilies for rebirth of purity. This is the start of the new you.
Orange roses for the passionate fascination between us.
Can't wait to see you tonight. —*H*

Her cheeks burned as she laughed and did a little dance. He'd gotten her flowers! She hadn't expected so much. She bent her head and breathed in the sweet aroma, her chest feeling tight as tears threatened to spill.

No one had ever given her flowers before. In school, all the other kids had gotten flowers for Valentine's Day. She'd received some candy, especially suckers in high school from some boys she'd been with who were looking for another good time.

But flowers?

She wondered how their date would go, if he was sending her flowers too. Was he going to pull out all the stops and go over the top? Or would they just enjoy a nice evening and get to know each other?

She was walking on cloud nine until lunch when her phone rang.

"Hello?" she said, sliding a book onto the shelf.

"Baby girl! How are you?"

Her phone fell along with the book in her hand. She cursed and picked them up with shaky hands, a feeling of dread in her stomach.

She cradled the phone to her ear and frowned. "Dad? What do you want?"

He tsked. "Can't a father just call his daughter on a random Monday and say hello?"

She sank onto the couch and tilted her head back with a sigh. "No, you can't. What do you want, Dad?"

A heavy pause made her stomach twist, then he said,

"Well, I was wondering if you had any rent money. I'm a little behind and my roommates are getting testy about it."

She rubbed her temples and gritted her teeth. "I don't think so, Dad. I just don't have it right now, not with moving costs and the new job—"

"You moved? Where to?"

She snorted. "I'm not telling you that."

"Aw, don't do me like that, Tay. But congratulations on the new job, baby girl. I'm so proud of you."

Her eyes burned as she squeezed them tight against the tears. "If you were so proud, why didn't you come to my graduation? Any of them? You always do this, Dad. You always call and ask for money, and I'm just so tired of it."

This was part of the new her. She wouldn't act as his enabler anymore. If she had to grow up, so did he.

"Ah, I'm sorry about that. I didn't have the gas money—"

"Then you could've taken the bus," she said bitterly.

He sighed and his voice dropped. "Taylor, I would've loved to have been there, but I was working, remember?"

She felt a tear roll down her cheek and sighed. "Yeah, you'd started at the Miller plant right before my high school graduation. Then when Mom died, you got fired and went to the Coca Cola factory. Then it was the Walmart warehouse, then Amazon, then—well, I lost track after that."

Her dad's voice turned hard and brittle. "Look, I don't have to explain myself to you. Will you help with rent or not? It's just a few hundred dollars."

She felt the tears rolling down her cheeks as she ground out. "What's the name of the apartment complex? I'll pay them directly, but I'm not sending you any more money through PayPal."

"What about Venmo? I have that now too."

She laughed, but there was no mirth in it. "I'm sure it's to pay your drug dealer, isn't it?"

There was another pause on the line, then he said softly, "Willowby Apartments in Fort Worth. The lease is under Dave for apartment 705. Thanks, baby girl. I'll see you around."

She snorted. "Hopefully not. Bye, Dad."

She clicked end before he could reply. She couldn't bear to hear him say he loved her when his actions clearly said he didn't.

That was the entire reason he kept calling her. He knew she loved him. Whether she had the money or not, she'd pay what she could for his rent. She could go back to living on Ramen for a while.

Damn it, love hurt. Why did she put herself through this for him?

It made her question her entire life's trajectory. If she kept falling into the same trap with her dad, what made her think she could ever reach for the stars and find someone to love her, date her, and marry her?

Would loving a man be as painful as loving her dad? If falling in love meant this kind of pain and heartache, it would be so much easier to just keep being the town slut and not get close to anyone.

She curled onto her side on the couch in the fiction section and squeezed her eyes closed again. If she went back to whoring around, she wouldn't ever have someone to hold her when she hurt like this either. She'd never have her own little boy like Harry, never have a house of her own, never see the look of wonder on her kid's face when they saw the ocean for the first time.

She wanted her kids to grow up with Lucy's kids, be best

friends, maybe marry each other. They'd dreamed about it for so long.

But whoever she married would have to put up with her dad. She choked on a sob, afraid no man would ever love her enough to deal with him.

At five-thirty, Lucy called while she was trying to get ready for her date. She changed into five different outfits before Lucy stopped talking about Harry and said, "Tay, what's going on? You sound frazzled."

Taylor stepped away from her clothes and into the bathroom. She stood in her underwear and put on her makeup while she explained about her dates and her dad calling.

"Why didn't you tell me about the dates yesterday on our way back from fishing?" Lucy asked softly.

Taylor released a sigh of relief that she didn't want to dive into analyzing her dad's call. She couldn't think about him right now, not when she was already anxious.

Taylor switched her makeup brush and replied, "Because he doesn't want to start any rumors in town or get his mom's hopes up. And it's fine with me, honestly, because it's just a practice date."

"But you're still nervous."

Taylor snorted. "Yes, thank you, Captain Obvious."

Lucy chuckled. "Why?"

Taylor paused as she put on her makeup. "I guess I'm tired of being the girl who's always down for a good time. I want to be more than that. I don't want to let guys treat me like some piece of meat, even though it's fun. I want to be courted, like I'm settling-down material." She shrugged, pushing off the heavy emotions.

There was a reason why she loved having fun, and avoiding her deeper emotions was one of them. She was growing up, but she still had a long way to go.

Taylor shifted the topic before Lucy could react. "I'm going to video chat you so you can show me your outfit."

They hung up, and Taylor clicked to turn on her video. Lucy shrieked and pushed the phone away, "Uh, Tay, put some underwear on."

Taylor laughed and changed the angle on the phone. "I have underwear on, don't get your panties in a twist."

"I don't think nipple stickers and a thong counts as underwear."

Taylor laughed again and leaned forward to peer into the mirror with her mascara wand. "Just let me finish this eye, and I'll show you the outfits I've already tried on."

Twenty minutes later, she stood in front of her mirror and turned this way and that. The black dress was simple with a square neckline and wide straps at the shoulder. But the way it hugged her curves and ruffled just under her butt in a cute little flounce made her feel confident and sexy.

"Yes, that one. With the bright red heels you love so much," Lucy said.

Taylor felt a thrill when she put on the heels. They were her lucky fuck-me shoes and always delivered. She bit her lip, then checked that her lipstick didn't smudge.

"I don't know, Luce. These shoes always end in sex, and that's not really the point of this date."

Lucy changed positions on her bed and leaned on an elbow. "Why not though? Are you planning on having sex with this Scott guy?"

Taylor frowned and shook her head. "No, I want to do this right and take my time. He has kids, so I know he's not going to rush into anything."

Lucy arched her brow. "Aren't you always the one who's telling me what a great stress reliever sex is?"

Taylor put on extra deodorant and nodded. "Yeah, what's your point?"

"The point is, if this is a practice date and you've already kissed him, don't beat yourself up if you do end up sleeping with him. Just let it all flow naturally, okay? Maybe you need that stress relief before the big date with Scott."

Taylor frowned and picked up the phone, holding it close to her face. She narrowed her eyes at Lucy. "That's some weird logic that somehow makes sense, but who are you and where have you taken my best friend?"

Lucy laughed, and Taylor moved the phone to a normal distance so she could see. "Seriously, that doesn't sound like you at all, Luce. I never thought I'd hear you say I should just sleep with someone. You were always harping at me to slow down. Now I am, and you're telling me to speed up?"

Lucy rolled her eyes and grinned. "What can I say? Now that I have access to good lovin' regularly, I know what all the fuss is about. Besides, a girl can change her mind. The only real question tonight is—do you *want* to sleep with Hunter?"

Taylor opened her mouth to answer, but there was a knock at the door. Her stomach twisted with nerves, as she said, "I gotta go. He's here."

Lucy squealed, "Good luck." Then they hung up. Nerves assaulted her as she walked toward the door.

Chapter Thirteen

Taylor slipped her phone into her little red clutch purse as she walked and called out, "I'm coming."

She heard him chuckle on the other side of the door, and when she opened it, he said, "Not yet, but I sure hope you will at some point tonight."

He grinned, and she giggled with nerves. Of course, she wanted to sleep with him. What red-blooded woman wouldn't? He made all her dreams come true. Tall, rugged, and handsome with a panty-melting smile.

But that wasn't the type of woman she wanted to be anymore.

She sighed and looked him up and down. "You clean up nice," she said.

His jeans were freshly ironed, and his boots gleamed under the fluorescent lights of the apartment. His simple black pearl-snap shirt, sleeves rolled up to reveal strong forearms, was understated but fit him like a glove. In his hands, he held a small bouquet of bright orange roses and a signature black cowboy hat, ready to sweep her off her feet. His grin, tipped higher on one side, partnered with his dark intentionally messy hair sent a thrill down her spine. She was in so much trouble with this one, and she wasn't even upset about it.

Instead, anticipation filled her as he handed over the roses.

She breathed in the aroma, melting inside. "More flowers? Hunter…"

Her voice trailed off as it choked with emotion. She blinked rapidly and turned on her heel to find something to put them in, pushing the emotions down.

She set them on the kitchen table next to the big bouquet as he cleared his throat. She turned in time to see a flash of vulnerability on his face as he asked, "I hope you like them."

With a shaky breath, she approached him and placed her hand flat against his chest, feeling his steady heartbeat beneath her palm.

When she looked up into his hazel eyes, she smiled. "They're perfect. No one's ever given me flowers before."

He frowned and placed his hand over hers. "No one?"

She shook her head as sadness swept through her. "No one until you. You will never know how much that means to me, Hunter."

She reached up on her tiptoes and kissed his cheek softly. His hand settled on her back as she pulled away.

They were on a precipice, about to fall over the edge into unknown territory. Her heart raced with excitement. The way he held her close, the hidden promises in his eyes—they made her want to lean even closer. The scent of leather flooded her nose, and he glanced down at her lips.

He growled, "I swore I'd make this the perfect first date for you, but damn it, sugar, you could tempt a priest."

She grinned and tilted her head back, breaking the intensity of the moment. "I know, I'm too hot to handle."

He cupped her cheek and growled, "Not for me, you're not."

Heat stole over her cheeks. She wanted to drag him into her bedroom, but she straightened her spine and stepped out of his embrace. Taking a deep breath, she grabbed her key and opened the front door.

"Where are we going?" she asked, locking it behind him.

He held her elbow as they walked down the stairs. "I thought we'd drive down to Fort Worth. Do you like Mexican food?"

She nodded, her stomach flipping. She hadn't eaten lunch, too anxious about her dad's phone call to even attempt it. "Mexican sounds amazing."

He chuckled and opened the door to his Jeep for her. "Then I think we'll go to Joe T. Garcia's. It shouldn't be too packed on a Monday night."

She pulled at the edge of her dress as he shut the door and rounded the front to open his own door. He started the engine and off they went. Her hands began to sweat as he tapped on the steering wheel in time to the music.

"What do we talk about? Or what do normal people talk about on dates?"

He chuckled and glanced at her. The late summer sun was still out, so she could clearly see him. "What do you normally do when you meet a guy you like?"

She shrugged and looked out the window, shifting uncomfortably on the seat. A wave of embarrassment made her cheeks heat and guilt gnawed on her stomach.

He grabbed her hand and linked their fingers. "Ignore that. You don't have to answer. Let's play twenty questions

The Cowboy Gets His Girl

or we can go through a list of favorites. Your choice, sugar."

She felt warmth rushing up her arm from his touch. It'd been a long time since anyone but Lucy had offered her comfort. She could get used to this.

The grassy hay fields waved in the wind as they drove past. She couldn't get used to this, to him. He was just the practice run. She had to remind them both of why they were there.

A glance at him had her saying softly, "You knew that question made me uncomfortable. I'm impressed. Guys rarely pick up on my emotions like that. Normally it's very straight forward. I'll be dancing or at a party and get to flirting. The innuendos start flying, then a guy will shift a little closer. Place a hand on my back or something, a little touch to say he's interested. Next thing I know, we're doing the dirty."

She shrugged and looked back out the window.

He said gruffly, "You didn't have to tell me."

"I know," she said, biting her lip and glancing at him out of the corner of her eye. "But I wanted to let you know more about what I'm trying to move away from. I don't want to be that mindless drunk girl anymore. Last weekend when we met... I hope that's the last time I lose my head like that. Any other guy, and I would've woken up in a completely different state. Thanks for not being like them."

He turned onto the freeway and squeezed her hand. "Don't mention it. It was the right thing to do. Besides, I used to get drunk a lot at your age too. I think it's a normal part of growing up, a phase of sorts. It's very mature of you to have such self-awareness."

She narrowed her eyes at him. "How old do you think I am? I just turned twenty-four and am well into adulthood."

He groaned and gripped the steering wheel tight. "Jesus, now I feel ancient, and I'm only thirty-seven."

She laughed, a thrill going through her. "No, you're not. There's no way."

She'd never admit how many older guys she'd obsessed over in the past six years of college, but if he thought it was a deterrent, he didn't know her at all.

He pursed his lips and nodded. "Thirty-eight in October."

"Wow, you really are ancient. I hope I have all my shit together by the time I'm your age."

He laughed, and the sound made her grin. "Ha ha, very funny. I'll remind you of that and rub it in when the time comes."

Her stomach twisted, and she suddenly imagined them sitting on a boat on her thirty-eighth birthday, blowing out candles before kids jumped into the lake to swim. She blinked and the image disappeared. Sadness flooded her, making her sigh.

"My birthday was a few weeks ago in June."

He let go of her hand to focus on the Fort Worth traffic, and she felt cold without his touch. They talked about birthdays from their childhood, their most memorable parties. Well, for him anyway. She hadn't ever had any parties.

"Seriously? You've never had a birthday party?"

She shrugged. "Lucy took me to a restaurant with our college friends when I turned twenty-one, then we went dancing. She's taken me out for dinner every birthday since. We had a cool girls' day at a spa in Hawaii last month to celebrate my birthday and her wedding, which was nice. Growing up, everyone was always out of town and starting their summer breaks."

"What about your parents? Surely, they celebrated you at home."

She looked out the window and leaned her head on the glass. "They weren't those kinds of parents. My grandma was cool, though. She'd send me a card every year with twenty dollars, which my dad would take before I even got the card."

The music crooned in the background, then he said gruffly, "That's shit. You should've been woken up with breakfast in bed, had flowers and a birthday lunch, then taken out somewhere to party for dinner."

She laughed, trying to steer the conversation away from her depressing parents. "Is that what birthdays mean to you? Food, food, and more food?"

He grinned as they parked in the parking lot and shrugged. "It used to be. Now that I'm an adult, it also involves sex, sex, and more sex."

She laughed again as he opened the door and came around to help her out of the Jeep. He took her hand and tucked it into the crook of his arm as they walked across the street to the restaurant.

"You might've had a different childhood than me, but I still think you turned out amazing. You're actively working to change into a better person. By the time some people hit their twenties, they think they've already figured out life and know it all."

She felt heat spread on her cheeks at his words. She wasn't sure about all that, as it was mostly therapy that was helping her open her mind and realize some of her destructive behaviors.

She leaned closer to him. "Hell, I think that happens when people hit the teenage years. At least, a lot of the teenagers that come into the libraries think they know it all."

He chuckled as they were led to a table.

"Making adult decisions, living on my own, growing up… it's harder than I thought it'd be."

He pulled out her chair and asked, "In what way?"

"I still have this itch to let loose," she said softly. He paused behind her chai, then reached out and brushed the hair over her shoulder to fall down her back. The trail of his fingertips left goosebumps in their wake.

"Like last weekend when you got drunk?" he asked as he sat.

"No, it's more than that." She ignored her feelings for him and tried to stay on topic as the hostess left.

He stared at her, patiently waiting for her to talk. It was a new feeling since most guys didn't want to *talk* to her much less listen. She struggled to put her feelings into words.

"When I was in college, I would go wild because I was searching for something. I guess I'm still searching for it, just in a completely different way."

"How so?" he asked.

She glanced around the outdoor seating area and shifted on her seat, frowning as she thought about why she did the things she did. Some of it was too raw, and she couldn't say. But at the core of her, she wanted to be loved.

He reached across the table and took her hand, calming her nervous twisting of the napkin. "What do you search for, Taylor?" he asked softly.

She relaxed into his touch and met his eyes. They probed her soul, searching for answers that she didn't want to admit out loud.

"I want to be wanted. To have someone look at me and

know they're thinking of nothing but me at that exact moment makes me feel..."

"Desired?"

She chuckled and nodded. "Yeah, my therapist says I have daddy issues, and she's right, but I'm working on it."

Hunter kissed her palm. "Do you want to talk about it?"

She smiled, unsure of how she felt to even be talking about this with him. "No, I want to ignore it for now. I'm fairly sure I shouldn't talk about daddy issues on a first date, right? Doesn't that scare them away?"

She didn't want to ruin their night with depressing talk of her dad.

He chuckled and released her hand, sitting back and resting his hands on his meaty thighs. "You won't scare me, sugar tits. I think we've established that I'm not like other guys. But to be fair, at this point on a first date, you'd probably talk about your jobs, family, living situations, and hobbies. With that in mind, tell me about the library."

Her shoulders relaxed as she launched into a more detailed explanation of her first week at work, her plans for the children's program, and the back-to-school events she wanted to run.

The waitress finally came, and they placed their orders. She got a big margarita, and asked, "Tell me about the ranch. Did you just fall into it, or do you love it?"

Chapter Fourteen

Hunter sipped his beer and shrugged, enjoying their date so far. "I've always loved ranching. There's something freeing and peaceful about being outside, working with nature day in and day out. It's the inside stuff that I don't like."

"Like what?"

"My parents are going on a surprise vacation in September—don't tell my mom or anyone else. Dad's planning it, and they're leaving me in charge. I'm fine with that part. I already act as the Foreman anyway and run the day-to-day operations, but Dad is trying to teach me the business side of it too, and that's just not my wheelhouse."

She nodded, "I can understand that. It's like this dating thing, right? I feel completely out of my depth. It's scary, and I'm not sure I can do it."

He ate a chip and salsa while she talked, then said, "Yeah, it's like that. Except you can do anything, remember?"

He shifted on the seat, needing to shift the conversation back to her. He didn't want to get into all the difficulties of the ranch on their first date. It always made him feel less than, and that wasn't how he was going to win this war.

He blinked as the waitress delivered their food. What war? The battle between him and her other date? There was no war, nothing to win. She wasn't some prize, and he wasn't a Neanderthal. Their food was delivered, and he shifted to talking about his brothers. He told her about the time he had helped his mom babysit all three of his nieces and nephew, including the poop incident.

She laughed, "Oh, I can just picture it now. Your face must've been so shocked."

He snorted, playing up the story just to see her laugh. "That's an understatement. I'd never seen so much come out of such a tiny thing, and I deal with horses all the time! Babies are terrifying."

She laughed again. "Oh, they're not so bad. When Lucy first found out she was pregnant, I moved in with her for a while. That was before she and Mason worked things out. I was afraid I wouldn't be able to hold him or take care of him. It was terrifying until I saw him smile. After that, I couldn't get enough of him. Still can't, I suppose."

Her voice turned wistful, and he took a bite of his food. "I suppose if you're going to date that means you want to get married and have a baby of your own?"

She nodded, her eyes falling to her plate as she looked down and frowned.

"Yeah, Lucy and I always swore we'd raise our kids together," she said softly. "But first, I need a good man. I see the way Mason treats her, and I want that. Someone to be there for me when I need them. Someone to hold me when I get scared. Someone reliable who will make a great dad. I didn't have any of that growing up. Just once, I'd like to experience that kind of love."

His chest burned for her. The beast within him roared that *he* was that man, that *he* would love her like that.

But his mind knew better. She was better off with someone else, someone who wasn't haunted by the pain of rejection.

"Love is overrated," he said harshly, the memory hitting him. Her eyes snapped up at his tone, and he gentled his voice. "Love hurts. One minute, you're flying through the sky like a bird in flight. The next you're falling like a rock, buffeted on all sides by the storms of life."

She blinked, her eyes thoughtful like she was trying to analyze him. Needing to distract her from his weakness and vulnerability, he fiddled with his drink and fell back on the comfort of poetry.

"You left me boundaries of pain, capacious as the sea, between eternity and time, your consciousness and me."

Her eyes glittered as she asked, "Who said that?"

He shrugged, shifting uncomfortably. "Dickinson, but that's not the point. Sure, some people get it right. My brothers, my parents, Lucy and Mason. But for some people, it's just not meant to be."

"You don't believe in one true love for everyone, a soulmate?"

He shook his head and wiped his mouth with his napkin. "I do believe everyone has one true love, but whether we find that person is a completely different thing. Who's to say that my forever person isn't in Taiwan right now? How am I supposed to meet her in the middle of Texas?"

He sighed and leaned back in his chair, pushing his plate away. "No, some people are just destined to stay single."

She frowned. "Do you think I'm doomed to stay single?

Do you think that's why I haven't had a proper date before?"

"No," he said, then thought about how he could explain it. He took too long to answer though, because she pursed her lips and pushed away from the table. She stood up and grabbed her clutch. "Excuse me, I'm going to the restroom."

He sighed and watched her walk away. Damn it, why did he always put his foot in his mouth? The waitress brought the check, and he passed over his card. He was just signing the receipt when Taylor came back.

He stood and asked, "Ready to go?"

She nodded, looking around. "Did you pay? What do I owe you?"

He placed a hand on her back as they wove through the outdoor tables to the gate. "Nothing, sugar. A proper date will see the man take care of the woman."

He felt her stiffen beside him, but he rushed on, determined not to make a fool of himself completely.

"Not that you can't take care of yourself. You absolutely can, but I want to take care of you too, and that starts with paying for dinner."

They stopped on the sidewalk as a car passed. She turned to face him, her eyes wide and that dark green drawing him in. "You—*you* want to take care of me?"

He pulled back and looked away, checking the traffic. Panic clawed at him. He hadn't actually said that, had he? That was a rookie mistake, and he was supposed to be the older, wiser guy helping her out. He ignored her hopeful expression and redirected the conversation.

"You want someone who will take care of you. That starts with paying for dinner, opening the door, protecting you as you walk through a crowd, that kind of thing." He waved to the street and kept his hand on her back as they crossed.

She was silent as he opened the Jeep's door and helped her inside, and he took his time walking around to open his own. She was confusing him, with her big doe eyes and vulnerability.

He needed time to think about her, but there was no time left. He opened his door and climbed inside, sticking to the plan. "Want to go dancing?"

She shrugged, looking out the window away from him. He hadn't meant to put a damper on the night. He wanted to see her happy.

He grabbed her hand and squeezed, trying to get her to look at him. "Taylor, you're a gorgeous, young woman with plenty of time to settle down. Of course, you'll find your true love, the one who will take care of you and love you all the rest of your days."

She kept her face turned down, and her other hand picked at the hem of her dress. "But you're probably right. There're a billion guys out there, and I'm supposed to find *the one*? It's improbable."

"But not impossible," he said. "Give yourself time, okay? Don't just jump into a relationship because it's new and exciting. If the guy doesn't treat you right, dump him. Take me for example. If I were you, I'd ask to be taken home right now because we clearly have two different goals in life. You want a family and kids, but I don't."

She finally looked at him, her expression hesitant and wary. "You don't want kids? But the way you talked about your nieces and nephew—"

He nodded, and it was his turn to stare out the window. "I know, and I do have fun with them. I just don't think that life's for me."

She sighed and looked out the window. "Fair enough, so are you going to take me home?"

He grinned and leaned over the seat to kiss her cheek. She inhaled quickly as he leaned back and reached for the gear shifter. "Nope, I'm taking you dancing. We're going to have the time of our lives tonight and give you that perfect date. Minus me putting my foot in my mouth a few more times."

She chuckled as they drove the few blocks to Billy Bob's. She sat forward when they parked. "Oh, I love this place! We came here the night of my college graduation. It was pretty chaotic that night and not fun."

He shut off the engine. "Do you want to give it another chance or go somewhere else?"

She nodded and smiled, reaching for her handle. He released the breath he didn't know he was holding and hopped out of the Jeep. He quickly helped her down and led her inside, paying the cover charge.

It was way bigger than the Electric Cowboy, with a bigger dancing area, more flashing lights, and a party vibe. She pulled a gold chain out of her clutch and then draped her purse over her shoulder to hang at her hip.

She grabbed his hand and pulled him onto the crowded dance floor, smiling as they swayed to the twang of classic country music. Her red heels tapped against the wooden planks as she laughed and spun around him fearlessly, her short dress flaring out.

He matched her infectious energy, holding her close and then smoothly dipping her back before pulling her back up again to spin across the floor. They seamlessly moved together, taking turns leading and following, and he got lost in her smile, the effortless fun and pure joy of being with her. After several dances, she gestured towards the bar with a playful smirk on her lips, and he chuckled and nodded in agreement before escorting her off the dance floor.

He nodded and took her hand, leading her to the bar. They could barely be heard, but both of them chugged their drinks. The amount of people in here drove up the heat, and his head already pounded in time to the beat.

She slammed her empty glass onto the bar top, and her lips tipped up in a mischievous grin. He glanced at the bartender and slid his glass over, then his cowboy hat disappeared.

He turned to see Taylor sliding his hat onto her head. He spun her in his arms, pulling her close to growl into her ear.

"You know what that means, sugar?"

She leaned back, her eyes sparkling and her lips quivering in a mischievous smile. "Maybe I do, maybe I don't. The world will never know."

If she was going to start dating, she needed to know the rules. If she takes a man's cowboy hat, it means they're going to fuck. His dick knew the rules and was very excited by her move. His heart raced, and the flirty look in her eyes held him captivated.

Kissing her felt like coming home, like the world and time had fused together to create this very moment, this very kiss.

She pressed herself against him, clutching at his shirt, fisting handfuls of the fabric. Her heart thumped against his chest, or was it his own? Her strawberry flavor invaded his senses, a concoction of sunshine and warm honey that intoxicated him to his core. Heat flooded every vein in his body, igniting a blaze that started in the pit of his stomach and traveled upwards to engulf him whole.

His arms wrapped around her waist, drawing her even

closer, as if they'd always been destined to fit together like the missing pieces of a puzzle. The way she sighed against his mouth sent shivers down his spine, tingles dancing along his skin like fireflies on a summer's eve.

Peace flooded his soul even as the fire of her burned him, adrenaline pumping through his veins with a rush he'd never experienced before. It wasn't the thrill of the chase but something more potent, more intoxicating that made him both want to savor and remember this moment forever.

He ravaged her mouth in slow, wet, coaxing motions that let her know exactly what he wanted to do with her. The kiss made his head swim like the smoothest whiskey, and he had to stop before he drowned in her.

As they broke apart for air, his chest heaving and hers rising and falling in sync with his own, their eyes locked in a silent promise neither dared to break. Slowly, he put the hat back on his head and cleared his throat.

"If you take my hat again, you might not be dropped off at your door like we'd planned, sugar. Now come on. This is a good song."

He took her hand and tugged her to the dance floor to distract them both. The next hour of dancing was painful, his dick hard as he swirled her around and around and his mind refused to stop thinking about the promise of her kiss. Their bodies crashed into each other like waves on the sand then parted again like the tides.

Finally, her cheeks flushed, she indicated she was ready to leave. They swung by the bathroom, then she hung onto his arm and laughed as they walked through the parking lot.

"Oh, that was so much fun. Did you see that girl's face when you refused to dance with her?"

His brows rose. "No, I was too busy trying to fight off that guy who kept trying to cut in."

She laughed and nudged him with her shoulder. "You got a little jealous there, didn't ya?"

He opened her door and echoed her words from earlier, "Maybe I did, maybe I didn't. The world will never know."

She laughed as he shut the door behind her. By the time they made it to the outskirts of Fort Worth, she took his hand, a small gesture that held so much weight for them both. He had been reaching for her hand all night, but now she was the one who wanted the connection. It felt right, and a rush of contentment rose within him as he kissed the back of her fingers, placing their joined hands back down on his thigh.

After another song, she let go and slid her palm over his thigh. He sucked in a breath and gripped the steering wheel with both hands.

"What are you doing, sugar?"

She shifted closer, but the Jeep had bucket seats. For the first time, he cursed his love of Jeeps.

Her voice was deep and sultry. "I had a great time tonight. Let me show you how much."

He tensed under her hand as she caressed his thigh. "You don't have to do that, sugar. We talked about it, remember? I'm going to walk you to your door and kiss you on the doorstep. No sex on the first date."

Her hand stilled on his leg, but she didn't remove it. He felt her touch like a furnace. He burned for her, wanted nothing more than to pull over and fuck her senseless, but she'd set the boundaries and expectations.

She squeezed his leg and leaned over the console to whisper in his ear. "I'm not drunk like when we met. This was the perfect first date, Hunter, except for one thing..."

He struggled to breathe, the scent of strawberries teasing him as he tried to focus on the road. They were still ten minutes from town and would soon be passing his parents' ranch.

"What?" he ground out, her scent, her words, her hand driving him wild with want.

"The perfect ending to this date would be a happy ending, don't you think?"

He groaned, squeezing the steering wheel. "I'd love nothing more, sugar, but I think I need to take you home and stick to the plan."

"Plans are overrated. What was it you said? I believe you wanted to fuck me senseless, yet now you're backing down. I think you're chicken shit, scared senseless that sex won't actually live up to your expectations." She sighed, sliding back fully onto her seat and taking her hands with her. "And I'll be honest, you're probably right. It can't possibly be as good as I think it will. It never is."

He felt empty and cold without her hand, but lava still flowed through his veins. The back and forth from the past week had reached its peak. He'd wanted to kiss her and had practically begged her for it before he'd backed off. Then *she* was asking for a date and telling him she was down to fuck. She was practically daring him to fuck her.

Enough was enough. Far be it from him to deny a lady in need. He came upon the turnoff to his parents' place, and his instincts kicked in.

He slowed and turned with a sigh. "Fucking hell, sugar tits. If that's what you want and you're in your right mind, then here we go."

"Go where?" she asked as they passed the corral and his parents' house. They kept going around the bunk house and barn until they couldn't see it anymore.

"The sale barn." The big building rose ahead, and he smiled. "This is where we have parties and auctions, but it's empty at the moment. Come on. I'll show you my favorite spot."

He was one of the strongest men on the ranch, but around her, he was weak. It seemed like he'd give her anything she wanted. It didn't bother him like he thought it would. He wanted to spoil her.

He parked and hopped out, grabbing some bottles of water and the spare blanket from under the back seat. Then he opened her door and helped her out. Her heels sunk into the dirt, but she didn't seem to mind as he led her to the back and opened the storage room door.

He flipped a switch and the single overhead light bulb flickered on. Bridles and supplies hung from the walls of the little room, but he pointed to the ladder on the back.

He growled, "Start climbing."

Chapter Fifteen

Taylor felt a rush of adrenaline at his commanding tone of voice. With a grin, she hurried to the ladder and scrambled up. His hands slid along her calves and up her thighs as she climbed, sending goosebumps along her skin.

When she reached the top, she stumbled to her feet, but his hands quickly found her waist and steadied her. The moon shone through a floor to ceiling glass window. It was so big, it almost took up the entire back wall.

The pale light revealed plain wood planking and another storage room. Two walls had nothing but boxes neatly stacked and labeled. The third wall had a twin bed on an old, rusted metal frame. At the foot of it was a small fridge with a microwave on top next to a cabinet of some sort.

Hunter stepped around her and bounced on the bed, disrupting the neatly made old handmade blanket as he kicked off his boots. He put one arm behind his head and reached for a metal cord that hung from the ceiling with the other.

"Come join me, sugar. You gotta see this."

She bit her lip. She was such a flake. She's told him no, then yes, then no, then yes again. She'd made a move when they'd first met, then he'd come onto her, and now she was coming onto him again.

A deep breath pulled in the scent of leather, wood, and dust. It was comforting and made her think of her grandpa's workshop. He looked at her expectantly, and something seemed to click in her chest.

The two of them were inevitable, so she might as well enjoy the ride. She smiled and walked to the bed, kicking her heels off on the worn woven rug and laying down next to him.

It was a tight fit for two adults to lay side by side on a twin bed, but it felt right, like they were in a cocoon away from the world and none of the bad could reach them.

He tugged on the cord and a whirring sound echoed. The ceiling began to shift, a wooden rectangle sliding back to reveal a skylight above.

She gasped at the stars shining brighter than she'd ever seen. "What—how did you—"

"I get overwhelmed by life sometimes," he said softly. "I used to come here to hide away from the world. My grandpa found me one too many times and helped me rig all this up years ago. He was a jack of all trades. My brother Landry took over his handyman business when our grandpa died."

She frowned. "I thought Landry was a big-time songwriter for some country stars in Nashville."

Hunter nodded and moved his other hand to cup the back of his head too. She had somehow snuggled down so her head was next to his chest. When she turned her head to look up at him, the scent of his deodorant mixed with that unique leather smell that was all him.

"He is. He does both and makes pretty good money for himself too. We're all proud of him." Hunter's voice trailed off as he stared at the stars above.

She looked up, feeling the now cool summer evening breeze through the open skylight. It wasn't glass but open air, and she liked that. She could see why Hunter did too, if he was such an outdoorsman like she thought.

"Do you have any hobbies like that? I assume Landry started off with songwriting as a hobby and turned it into a career."

He shifted, turning his body to face hers a little, his hands still behind his head as he bent at the knee, placing his foot on the bed.

"Not really. I'm a pretty simple man. I like to hunt, fish, and camp. A few times a year, I'll load up my Jeep and just drive to a camping spot. I'll spend days in the middle of nowhere, just fishing and swimming. One time, I decided to stay a day extra and Ma about had a heart attack."

"Why?" she asked.

"I don't even turn on my cell phone when I'm out there. She was just worried about me."

Taylor wondered what that must be like, for someone to worry about you so much that they make themselves sick. Her parents had never cared one way or another and had barely been home. She was the quintessential latch key kid, fending for herself from a young age.

It was why she'd gone wild in middle and high school. She'd been trying to get their attention.

Hunter shifted again, turning onto his side and propping his head on his hand with elbow bent. With his other hand, he brushed her loose hair off her shoulder. She sucked in a breath, her eyes shifting to him.

It wasn't light enough to see into his eyes, but she could see him staring at his fingers as he traced down her shoulder.

"I've never brought anyone here before," he said huskily. "But I'm glad I'm sharing it with you."

"Why me?" she asked, her heart racing. She was just a flaky, sex-crazed librarian trying to make it on her own in the world. *Looking for love in all the wrong places* had been stuck in her head since the bar.

He looked back into her eyes as he pushed one of her shoulder straps off her shoulder. "Because you're special."

She snorted, the mood ruined. She tried to get up, but his hand settled on her chest. He didn't press down, but she was pinned either way. A thrill went through her as she settled back on the bed and looked up at him with a frown.

"You are," he grumbled. "You're special in every way. When I met you at the Cowboy, you didn't give two fucks who saw your tits. You just laughed and enjoyed the moment. I've never met anyone who embraced life so wholeheartedly."

Tears pricked her eyes as his hand caressed down her shoulder to her hand. He lifted it and kissed her knuckles.

"I think that's just called being drunk," she said.

He shook his head and nuzzled his cheek against her hand. She turned it and cupped his face, her body naturally turning to his until they almost faced each other on the tiny bed. He smiled, sending a thrill up her spine once more.

"No, it was more than that. You trusted me, and I want to honor that trust. I want to fuck you senseless, sugar tits, that hasn't changed... but if that's not what you want, say the word, and we'll take you home."

Her breath caught in her throat as he stared down at her, his eyes holding so many secrets that she wanted to reveal. "You really are a gentleman, aren't you."

Her world didn't have a lot of those, and she wasn't sure how to handle it or what to say.

He paused, and his hand fell to his side until they weren't touching, leaving her cold. "I'd never put you in an uncomfortable position, Taylor. If you want to stay, if you want me too, then it's game on, and I won't let you go for a long time."

Taylor could still back out. No one else had ever given her an out before. Most guys just rolled with it and pounced. Actually, most guys would've already finished, and she'd be on her way home with a load of regret.

Hunter was deeper than she'd thought. There was something about him that drew her in. She trusted him, had talked about things she'd not even told Lucy.

The more time she spent with him, the more he opened up. She'd thought Scott was an open book, friendly and jovial.

But she'd learned more about Hunter in just a few hours than she'd ever expected. Plus, she desperately wanted him with every fiber of her being. Her core ached, but maybe that was just because this was the longest she'd ever gone without sex. It'd been months.

She smiled slowly. There was only one way to find out. She raked her palm against his five o'clock shadow and slowly pulled him down to kiss her.

"Well, it's a good thing the library is closed tomorrow then, isn't it? Time to put your money where your mouth is, cowboy."

Chapter Sixteen

Hunter growled and crushed his mouth to hers in a brazen kiss that held nothing back. When their lips touched, her body came alive. It was like she had been swimming underwater and now could finally breathe.

Taylor sucked in a breath, flooding her senses with the intoxicating scent of leather and Hunter. Her mouth opened, and his tongue swept inside like an inferno. It scorched her, burning away the thoughts and memories of all who'd come before.

Their tongues slicked together, and she tugged him closer. His knee settled between her legs, and she ground on it with a moan. All the while, his mouth possessed hers with the best kiss of her life.

That was when she realized he was making her toes curl. Fucking hell, it was straight out of a movie. Except no movie on the planet would air something this hot. It was about to get explicitly graphic, and she was so here for it.

The ache inside deepened, clawing at her with a need to be released. She gripped his collar and pulled. It snapped apart, and she ran her hands over his chest, the muscles rippling under her touch.

Thank God for pearl snap shirts. Her hands explored, and his knee ground against her. She moaned, her breath coming in soft pants as he broke the kiss. He peppered kisses down her jaw to the sweet spot on her neck.

She raked her nails down his chest as he nipped and bit softly, making her squirm beneath him. His hand slid up her thigh, and she ground up against him, trying to ease the ache between her legs.

He let go of her neck and sat up on his knees, pulling his shirt off and tossing it to the floor. "Take your dress off. Are you on birth control? Are you clean?"

She blushed at the questions but tugged the dress up and over her head. He stood, kicking off his socks and shimmying his jeans down.

"Yeah," she panted, sitting up and taking off her nipple stickers. "I'm good. I had everything checked before I moved here."

She laid back down and tugged her thong off, dropping it on the floor. He grabbed her knees and spread them wide, making her gasp.

"Do you want a rubber or not?" he asked, his voice breathless and deep. He settled between her thighs, his hands on her knees the only part of them that touched. He stared at her with a fire in his eyes that made her spine tingle.

She went up on her elbow to get a good look at him in the faint light. She gasped at the size of him. "Good God, you're a monster."

A shiver of anticipation went through her, making her nipples pebble. She wanted him to be a monster. She wanted him to fuck her like no tomorrow, like a beast who couldn't keep his paws off her.

He chuckled and fisted his cock, stroking it slowly until a bead of pre-cum came out of the tip. "I'm just me, Taylor. Take me or leave me."

She reached down, rubbed her finger around the tip, then licked the pad of her finger. The tangy sweetness of it made her moan as she caught his gaze with her own.

He groaned.

She loved the feeling of power. She may be on her back, but this man was at her mercy. She smiled like the Cheshire cat and spread her legs wider.

"Oh, I'll take you. I'll take it all. As for the rubber…" She bit her lip and took a deep breath. "I've never done this without one. Is it different?"

She'd been sexually active for a long time, but she'd been smart about it. She'd always insisted on a condom, actually. Perhaps it was the stress and pressure of being such a grown-up about everything, trying to be the perfect small-town librarian and a mature adult… Adulting on her own for so many months without any reckless decisions was exhausting. Perhaps that was why she'd been leaning more and more into Lucy's thinking as the date wore on. What was the harm in sleeping with him? Perhaps taking the risk, just this once without a condom, would be enough of letting loose for her to not feel so restricted and bound by expectations.

He leaned forward, one hand on the bed beside her, the other guiding his cock to rub up and down her clit. "God, yes. I'd be honored to pop your bareback cherry."

She gasped, her hands falling to the bed as she gripped the blanket, her knees already shaking as she thrust up slightly. "Oh my God, that feels so good."

He teased her folds, but she was ready for him. "Sugar, don't do that unless you want to skip to the foreplay." He coated himself with her wetness and found her opening, teasing slightly.

She gasped and thrust again. "Fuck foreplay. Give me that monster."

He chuckled and pushed, slow and steady until she opened up. Her eyes widened at the incredibly full feeling, and he went impossibly deeper.

After what felt like hours, he stopped and held himself still. He panted with shallow breaths. "How's... that?"

She shifted, lifting her hips slightly. He twinged inside, making her squeeze around him. They both moaned. She'd thought he'd be too big, but it was perfect. He stretched her completely.

"That's... so fucking good," she said, ending on a rush of air.

Then he began to move inside her.

She half gasped and half screamed, arching her back as she stretched and melted around him. He settled his elbows next to her head and kissed her temple. She reached up, grabbing his biceps and holding on like handlebars.

Hard, rough strokes rocked her body. She lifted her hips to meet him. His mouth found hers, this kiss desperate with need. He made hungry sounds in the back of his throat, and it drove her mad with desire.

Body to body, mouth to mouth, they moved in unison, a collision of two stars in the night. She bit back a whimper as he sank into her aching wet heat over and over. His hips slammed into hers, his strokes hard, possessive, and relentless. Each thrust sent her reeling, her mind fracturing bit by bit.

He hammered into her, demanding more and more of

her soul, and a rush of hot need filled her. She needed this man who was too good to be true. His mouth clashed with hers, nipping at her lips and biting hard enough to make her cry out and clench around him. He swallowed the sound and changed the angle slightly to rub his pelvis against her clit, soothing her lip with his.

She hurled through space like a love-streaked comet, thrashing against him as her entire body shuddered with white-hot heat. The force of the orgasm shook her, tearing her in two. She writhed beneath him, soaking up his groan as he tensed.

She felt the warmth spread as he flooded her, each pump continuing her orgasm. They came hard, each fueling the other's climax with the heat of the sun. Their bodies fused in one shared hot, sticky release, and the stretching and filling of her pussy made her doubly glad to be free of the condom.

They broke the kiss, and he dipped his head into the crook of her neck. Hard loving became heavy breathing in an afterglow more intense than any she'd ever had before.

She stared up at the stars above and caressed his back gently. Her body slowly descended from heaven, and with it, she expected the doubts and self-recrimination like all the others before.

But they didn't come. Instead, she was filled with such contentment and peace. The euphoria sweeping through her couldn't be explained by just a quickie. This was something more. Perhaps getting to know him first brought an added level of release to sex. Perhaps that's why people swore that sex with someone you love was just so much better.

He leaned onto his elbows and kissed her softly. She

didn't love him, but there was something about him that made everything she felt so much more intense.

He broke the kiss and brushed the hair back from her face. "Are you alright?" he asked.

Her heart melted at his concern. He was a country boy, a bad boy, but also a sweetheart. There was something else, something she hadn't been able to put her finger on, that made her think once again that he was too good to be true.

She smiled lazily and nodded. "I'm fucking fantastic. Thanks for asking."

He chuckled and kissed her softly once more before pulling himself off. When he slid out, she felt an overwhelming sense of loss. She lay there with her knees bent and watched him as he walked to the cabinet by the fridge at the foot of the bed.

She felt his cum leaking out, so she dipped her fingers down and scooped it up. She didn't want to waste it, and she definitely didn't want to make a mess. There was only one thing she could do.

He turned back to her with a container of wet wipes in his hand in time to see her stick her fingers into her mouth.

He stopped in surprise. His cock jumped slightly so she opened her mouth to show him the sticky goo, then swallowed and opened her mouth again to show him it was gone.

He gripped the metal bed frame with one hand and said, "Damn, sugar tits, that's the hottest thing I've ever seen. Guess you don't need this to clean up with?"

She grinned and scooped her fingers back inside. "Sorry, I didn't know you were supposed to clean up with a wet wipe. All the others have always just tossed their condom and that was that."

She hummed as she licked her fingers once more. He

chuckled and set the wet wipe on the edge of the bed anyway, then opened the fridge, handing her a bottle of water.

"Fair enough. Want to watch a movie before the next round? I can stream on my phone."

Another round? She nodded and took the water, guzzling it down. Her heart leaped at the chance to spend more time with him. Normally, she was the first one out the door or the guy would already be gone, but the itch to escape and get out of there hadn't hit her yet.

She scooted to the side of the bed, and he spooned her, pulling up a movie with one hand. It was a naked domesticated setting that she never expected to find herself in.

But wasn't that part of the adventure of growing up? Learning new things and experiencing something different than normal?

Maybe part of being a mature adult meant taking calculated risks, like sleeping with Hunter barebacked or doing it multiple rounds. She was going to love this adulting phase of her life.

Chapter Seventeen

Hunter laid in bed, unable to move and his mind whirling. Taylor had fallen asleep halfway through the movie, so he'd turned the sound down and finished it, hoping she'd wake up.

He wanted to spend every moment with her. Their time was limited, though. Once this practice date was over, she'd go back to work and then to her real date and forget all about him.

That was the way he wanted it, wasn't it? That question played in a loop in his brain as he stroked her hair.

She lay on his chest, curled up on her side while he laid on his back, staring at the stars overhead. She nuzzled him in her sleep, drawing closer, so he pulled the blanket over her shoulders.

He tried to remember the last time he'd laid in bed cuddling a woman. There had to have been someone since Jewel had left. His mind drew a blank, though.

The ladies in the past fifteen years were mostly faceless.

He'd dated a few from out of town for a month or two, but they never lasted.

His phone buzzed with a message, and he glanced at it.

We should probably talk on our own terms before we run into each other at the ranch or in town, right?

She hadn't changed her number. And he hadn't deleted it, so what did that say about him?

The pressure on his chest tightened. He put the phone down, not replying since it was already after midnight. He didn't know what they had to talk about. The past was in the past.

He pulled Taylor closer and breathed in the strawberries from her hair, some of his tension relaxing from his shoulders. He didn't want to think about Jewel, not when he had Taylor in his arms. He gently rolled her onto her back and tugged the blanket down.

His eyes settled on her breasts, so round and full. They were like beacons calling to him in the night. The moon had now risen overhead and shone down on her as if casting an ethereal glow on a goddess. He bent his head to worship her, caressing the side of her breast with his nose until he found her dusky rose nipple.

He licked, then blew softly until it pebbled. She shifted slightly, turning her head toward him, but still didn't wake. He dipped his head and drew the perfect nipple into his mouth.

He swirled his tongue around, then sucked and tugged. Her breathing changed, and he moved to reach the other with his mouth. His hand rolled the now wet nipple between his fingers as he teased the other, suckling until she gasped beneath him.

The beast within him roared in pride as she squirmed.

"Wha—Hunter?" she asked groggily as she came awake.

He tugged harder on her nipple, and her back bowed as she whimpered. The sound speared him like Cupid's arrow. He sat up and took her other breast into his hand. They filled his palms, and he plucked at the ripe berries of her nipples.

Then he twisted, testing her. She gasped, her back bowing again as she fisted the bed sheets. A slow smile spread across his face.

"Do you like that, sugar tits?"

She whimpered and nodded, her eyes heavy with desire and sleep as she looked at him. He twisted the other direction, and she shifted, rubbing her legs together. She was so beautifully responsive. He smiled and slid his hands down her stomach, pushing the blanket off further.

He followed his hands and knelt between her thick thighs, pressing her knees up as he took a deep breath. She smelled like heaven, of woman and raw, untamed nights. He nuzzled the inside of her thigh, moving his fingers and mouth ever closer to the ambrosia that awaited him.

Two fingers touched the crease of her leg and traced upward then over, finding her slippery nub and lightly circling around it. He kissed the inside of her thigh until she sucked a breath and tilted her hips up, seeking more friction.

Then he moved his fingers down. His tongue settled on her clit as his fingers slid inside, and she bucked against him. His other arm wrapped around her thigh and settled on her lower stomach, holding her down as he lost himself in the stroking, licking, and sucking. He curled his fingers and stroked deep and slow, all the while setting up a rhythm with his tongue that had her thrusting up against him.

He felt her start to clench around his fingers, and she whimpered and moaned. He wanted to test her, push her boundaries.

When he teased her asshole with a finger, she splintered beneath him. She screamed and thrashed so much he was thankful he was holding her down. He drank as she came on his tongue, lapping at the nectar that he craved.

She spasmed around him, the tension making her stomach hard beneath his hand as she shuddered. All too soon, her body went limp, and the spasms grew farther apart. He pulled his fingers out and pressed her thighs impossibly wide, then bent to lap at her with a flat tongue.

He licked up all the juices. He'd always loved this part of sex, had a craving for pussy that was probably more than healthy. But the scent of her, the taste… it all combined to overload his senses. He had to have more. He had to have all of her.

He teased her ass again while dipping his tongue into her wet core. She gasped, her hands coming to rake through his hair. "Hunter, what are you doing?"

He eased back and slid a finger through her wetness then back to her ass. "What's it feel like, sugar?"

She gasped and fisted his hair. "Ass play, but I've never done that before."

He arched his brow. "Are you telling me that with all your experience in college, you've never had anal?"

Her shoulders tilted in, and he could barely make out a faint blush. She shook her head. "No, it was more of a wham, bam, thank you ma'am type situation. How—how does it work?"

A flash of heat shot through him in anticipation. He

The Cowboy Gets His Girl

wanted to show her all the pleasures that she'd apparently been missing out on.

He needed her with a ferocity that scared him, but he refused to give in to the fear of it. Instead, he eased up her body, gripping his dick and teasing her folds.

"We'll need to build up to that, sugar. As much as I want to fuck you in the ass, I don't have any lube, and I don't want to hurt you."

He slid his cock inside slowly, her pussy tightening around him as he stretched her. She gasped, grabbing his arms and digging her nails in as she arched her back. "Oh god, I don't think it'll work at all. You're impossibly big. What are you, ten inches?"

He grinned and lifted on his knees, draping her thighs over his arms at the elbows. He eased out and shook his head, "Not quite but it's the thickness you like, isn't it, sugar?"

He slammed back inside, and her eyes fluttered closed. She was impossibly tight and wrapped around him like a vise. He closed his eyes against the sensation and took a deep breath.

"Yeah, I love how you stretch me, fill me, fuck me," she whimpered as he eased out and slammed back.

"Hell yeah," he said between clenched teeth, still kneeling on his haunches, loving her dirty mouth. Then he set up a bruising tempo. He wanted to see her flesh turn red and purple, wanted to see a bruise on the inside of her thighs from his hips.

"Fuck me," she gasped. "Fuck me, fuck me, fuck me."

He rammed himself home, his body hard and primal against her. He used her thighs as reins, and all she could do was lay there and grip the metal frame of the bed at her head.

"My dirty little slut. You take my dick so well." His heart stopped but his body didn't miss a beat. His mouth was going to get him in trouble again, and he didn't want to ruin the moment. So many women over the years had noped out when he talked like that.

But she gasped and her pussy clenched at the words. Her eyes widened in surprise, and she hissed out, "Yes, I'm your dirty slut. Fuck me harder."

Fuck, she liked the dirty talk. This woman was everything he'd ever wanted.

He drove into her with an animal fierceness, the pounding need and driving hunger pushing him to claim her and keep her forever. He wanted to fuck her so hard she couldn't think of anyone else. He surged inside her, her body welcoming the beast as he roared.

"You like that dick, slut? You want to be my cum princess?"

"Yes," she gasped, cupping her own breasts and rolling her nipples.

"That's it. Play with yourself. Time to come. Are you ready? Come with me, sugar."

He thrust harder, his balls tightening as his rhythm went wild. He pistoned harder, his shaft slicking in and out with the sounds of their dance. His body ached for release, but he wouldn't give in without her.

She slid a hand down her stomach and found her clit, taking control of her pleasure. One hand on her breast, the other swaying with every thrust, it was the most beautiful sight he'd ever seen.

Then she screamed and clamped down on him as her back bowed. Sensation ripped through him as she choked the life out of his dick. Every muscle tensed as he teetered on the brink, squeezing her thighs and soaking up the feel of her spasms.

He thrust forward one more time and threw his head back in a roar, exploding and filling her with lava-like spurts until his roar eased into grunts of pure animal satisfaction.

He opened his eyes and looked down, needing the emotional connection. Hers were still closed as her body shook. He eased down, pinning her hips beneath his as he claimed her lips.

This time, the kiss was soft and spoke of promises that were not meant to be. Her mouth was tender, opening to him without hesitation. He kissed away all his doubts and thoughts of tomorrow, and just focused on living in the moment, on enjoying every second he had with her.

He gave her lower lip a hungry nibble, then explored her mouth slowly and thoroughly. She whimpered, and the sound went straight to his dick. He began to move in and out once more.

She broke the kiss, her eyes wide. "Are you—are you getting hard again?"

He grinned and kissed the corner of her mouth. "What can I say? I can't get enough of you, Taylor."

Her eyes glistened as he rocked deeply, his dick growing harder and harder. She ran her hands up his back and smiled. "I'm glad."

This time, their loving was slow and steady. He trailed kisses down her cheek, then he rolled them, so she was on top.

She gasped, her hands falling to his chest and making her breasts press together. He grinned and shifted his hands to cup her breasts.

"Ride me, slut. Fuck me like you want me to fuck you. Hard and unrelenting," he growled and twisted her nipples.

She whimpered and slammed down onto his cock. He closed his eyes, seeing stars as their hips ground together. Her damp heat stroked him, holding him prisoner to her charms.

When she started to lose the rhythm, he opened his eyes and used her breasts like reins, tugging on her nipples until she whimpered and ground her clit onto his pubic bone. Then he started to slam his hips up, helping her find the rhythm again.

"That's it, sugar. Ride that dick. Take all you want. Take it all."

Their eyes locked as she lifted her hips and slammed back down. There was a world of emotions in those eyes, and he couldn't look away.

The slapping of flesh on flesh filled the room, but neither of them broke eye contact. Neither of them made a sound. It was a challenge to see who would last the longest, and he was determined to win. He thrust up into her velvet heat.

She rode him as well as any stallion. Heart pounding, they moved as one as the tension built. Then she slowed and shook her head.

"I—I need something more," she said, biting her lip. He arched a brow and flipped them, making her squeal as she slammed into the bed on her back.

He kissed her hard and deep until she was on the edge, then pulled out and stood. Her eyes fluttered open along with her mouth, surprise etching her beautiful face.

Then he took another risk, saying, "Tell me to stop if I get too much, sugar." Without waiting, he grabbed her by the hair and pulled her around until her ass was in the air, her knees on the edge of the bed.

She gasped, not telling him to stop but whimpering in

The Cowboy Gets His Girl

need. His dick jumped at the sound, and he licked his lips in anticipation.

He stood behind her and palmed her big ass. "Hm, maybe you need a bit more to stay in the moment, eh? I think I can accommodate."

He spanked her ass, and she jerked, which made her hair tug in his hand.

"Ouch, oh god."

He spanked her again, then rubbed the flesh to take away the sting. "I figure if we only have this one night, I'd better make it count, right? I should show you what you're missing by going out with this other guy."

He spanked her again and teased her entrance with his dick. She spasmed around the head, and he groaned. "God, tell me if you like it or not. Tell me to stop or keep going."

He was taking a chance with the rougher play. He didn't want to hurt her, but there was so much they could explore together, if she'd take a chance with him.

She buried her head in the mattress and mumbled. He spanked her again.

"I can't hear you, sugar. What do you say? Keep going or stop?"

She turned her head and fisted the blanket. "Harder. I said fuck me harder. Treat me like a dirty little slut."

He exhaled a breath. Halle-fucking-lujah, she wanted more! He reared back and spanked her harder, thrusting deep at the same time.

She screamed and clenched, then gasped, "Again."

He withdrew, twisting her hair and bringing her head up off the bed. "Say please."

She whimpered and pushed her ass back toward him. "Please, fuck me like an animal."

He slammed into her and spanked her again. "That's

right. I'm an animal. There's no escape. I'm going to fuck you until you see stars, slut."

She moaned. "God, yes, please, fuck me like a beast."

He spanked her again and drove back in. He pistoned harder, his body aching as he slammed into her roughly. He rubbed the warm spot on her ass, then moved his thumb to tease her asshole.

She whimpered, clenching her pussy around him.

He growled. "I won't fuck you in the ass tonight, but someday..." He trailed off, pushing aside his hopes for another night with her. Disappointment threatened to distract him, knowing it would never happen.

Instead, he spit and rubbed his thumb around before easing it into her tightest hole.

She flailed beneath him with a gasp, squeezing him impossibly tight. He thrust faster and harder, his fingers digging into the flesh of her ass as his thumb was buried to the hilt.

Chapter Eighteen

"Oh god, that feels so good," Taylor moaned, shifting back to drive him deeper. He had filled her up from the other positions, but from behind she swore he was bigger, wider, fuller.

And the thumb... how had she been missing out on this for so long? He thrust harder, his hands tugging on her hair.

"Yes, yes, yes," she gasped, squeezing her eyes closed as she splintered apart. Convulsive waves gripped her, and she screamed. Her toes curled as the waves washed over her, sweeping her off her feet and battering her soul.

Her orgasm ripped through every cell and every nerve ending quivered. Her body clenched around him, and he roared like a bear. With a hot rush, he erupted inside her, squeezing her ass with his fingers so hard, she knew it'd leave bruises.

She milked his release with a savage grunt, and he released her hair. She fell forward on her stomach, dislodging him.

He kneaded her ass, his thumb easing out. Then she felt

kisses and nips on her ass too. She squirmed and heard a soft chuckle as he moved away.

She fell onto her side as the box of wet wipes landed on the bed beside her.

"Just in case you're not hungry," he grinned, kissing her with a quick peck on the lips.

She yawned, now wide awake. "Thanks, but I don't normally eat snacks in the middle of the night."

He chuckled and pulled on his boxers and then shoes. "I don't know about you, but I need to use the bathroom. Normally, I'd just open the window and let loose, but I don't want you to think I'm some country bumpkin."

She grinned and sat up, wadding the now dirty wipe in her hand. "There's a bathroom in this barn?"

He took her elbow and helped her stand on wobbly legs. "Yeah, but we have to go outside. Do you want to wear my shirt?"

He offered her the shirt, but she shook her head with a mischievous grin. "No thanks. I like walking around naked."

An answering smile tugged on his lips. "You little slut. You just want to tempt me more, don't you?"

She traced her fingers up his arm and leaned her breasts on him. "Obviously. Call me a slut again, and I might not make it downstairs before I jump you."

He burst out laughing and pulled her into a hug. "God, where have you been my whole life?"

She tensed in his arms as he held her, his hands hot on her back. Somehow, this hug, his statement was more intimate than anything they'd done thus far. Her heart melted, and her throat closed, choking off her smart-ass reply. She knew this night was more than just a physical release of tension, and it scared her.

He nuzzled her neck and pulled back. "I would test that

theory, but I really do need to use the bathroom. You probably won't get cold walking around down there naked—it's still eighty outside—but you might want to slip on your shoes."

He dropped his hands as she walked to her shoes and groaned. "Fine, but they aren't the most comfortable."

She slipped them on while he asked, "Then why wear them?"

She felt her cheeks heat as she stood, still only reaching to his shoulder. She stood in just her heels, lifting her head in defiance at her nakedness.

Under the moonlight, she met his distracted gaze and smirked, "To impress you. I didn't want you to think I was a country bumpkin."

He laughed and turned to the ladder. "Not at all. Had you pegged as a city slicker, actually."

She followed him down the ladder. "I'm that obvious, eh? And here I thought I had you fooled with how expertly I maneuvered that canoe."

"I wasn't even paying attention to how you handled it. All the blood had rushed to my dick the moment I saw you in that bikini."

She felt a thrill at his words. Knowing she was the object of his attention made her heat with a different warmth.

His boots hit the wooden floor, then he whistled. "Damn, this view."

She wiggled her ass as she went down. As soon as she was close enough, his hands palmed her ass. She took another step, then his hand pressed her against the ladder, stopping her progress.

"Wait," he growled, hiking one of her legs up before he buried his mouth in her pussy from behind and licked her clit until her knees threatened to buckle.

She closed her eyes and leaned her head on a rung of the ladder. "Damn it, Hunter, you really are a beast, aren't you?"

He pulled back and gripped her waist, swinging her down to the ground. She gasped, finding his shoulders as he set her feet on the floor. His mouth met hers, leaving her mind still spinning, the taste of the both of them mingling on their tongues.

This man had made her feel things she'd never felt before. He made her feel special, like she was the only woman in the world that he wanted to be with. His kisses made her see stars and feel more alive than anything she'd ever experienced. For the first time, she didn't feel cheap and used after sex.

He pulled back and grinned under the single light above. "Come on. I'll show you the barn. Our next party is Halloween. Imagine this…"

His voice was smooth as butter but deep as the ocean. It sent a tingle up her spine, but that could also be the way he easily held her hand. Fingers laced together, they walked outside and around to another side door.

He led them into a cavernous room with a built-in bar on one side and a stage in the corner. In the half of the building to their left were rows and rows of hay. They went right to a small hallway and found the bathroom.

She thought it'd be awkward to pee with him outside the door. She hated people listening to her use the bathroom, but the thought didn't even cross her mind until she was washing her hands at the sink.

Thankfully when she walked out the door and down the little hallway, he was leaning against the wall. He probably hadn't heard her, but all concerns fled when he looked up and smiled as she approached.

He linked their hands together as they walked back outside. She shivered and looked at the dark field, barely visible from the moonlight. He was right, it wasn't cold. But the open air... it made her feel reckless and wild. It was a similar feeling to being at the bar or a frat party, but this was a quieter wildness that spoke to her soul.

"You alright? Are you rethinking coming down here naked?"

She shook her head and gripped his bicep, holding on tight to his hand as she stepped closer to him. "No, it's fine. I'm not cold, and I actually like being naked. I like doing something naughty, getting that thrill of bucking expectations and going against the grain of society."

He stopped beside the door to the attic space and pressed her up against the wall, caging her in with his big arms. He nuzzled her neck.

"An exhibitionist, eh? Do you have any idea how hot it is to see you naked under the stars? I want to see you naked under the sun too. On the bank of the river where we fished. Under the tree in the north pasture. Bent over the fence by the north woods, your perfect ass turning red from my handprints and the sun."

She gasped, arching her neck closer to his lips. "I don't know that I'd be classified as an exhibitionist if this is the only time I've been naked outside."

He chuckled, "I love that I'm the only one who's seen you like this and felt you raw."

She grabbed his hair and moaned as he kissed up the side of her neck. "Oh god, how do you get me so revved up so fast?"

He shifted his boxers, freeing his monster before grabbing her ass, lifting her enough that she wrapped her legs around his waist. "Good to know, sugar, because I need you wet and ready for me always."

He sank deep inside, and she groaned, closing her eyes. White flashes hit the back of her eyelids like fireworks. Her nails bit into his head and shoulders as he set up a thunderous pace. It was fast and furious, deep and rough just like she liked it.

Her back rubbed raw on the wood siding behind her, but she didn't care. It hurt so good, the pain of how wide he stretched her combined with his bruising hands on her ass. It was more than she could take.

She splintered apart with a cry, her body squeezing around him as he pounded even harder. His pace slowed and he ground deep once, twice. On the third, he roared, his head thrown back and eyes closed.

He looked like a bear, roaring in the wild. He was an animal, and she was slightly obsessed with how he made her feel. If this was dating, she didn't want to ever stop.

The pulsing of his dick subsided with her own orgasm, and he slowly slid from her. She stood in her heels, and he cupped her dripping pussy, making her gasp at the touch.

"Oo, watch it. I'm so sensitive now," she whispered.

He chuckled and pulled his fingers away, holding them up to her. "I just thought you'd want a snack, since we left the wipes upstairs."

She grinned and licked his hand, her eyes never leaving his. His other hand slammed into the wall above her head, and his body swayed as she sucked his fingers into her mouth.

"Damn it straight to hell, you're such a good little cum slut, princess."

She grinned and slid from his arms and into the room.

The mouth on this man made her weak in the knees. She looked over her shoulder as she went to the ladder.

"Oh yeah, tell me more dirty things like that, you beast. But first, you'll have to catch me," she laughed as she raced up the ladder. His laughter and steps on the rungs followed her, driving her heart rate up even more.

He tackled her to the bed, and she squealed at the bounce. They ended up rutting like animals, scratching and clawing and biting and screaming. It seemed to last forever before she screamed so much with her orgasm, she blacked out.

Sun was streaming through the window when she blinked awake. She stretched and looked around. Hunter was gone, but a note was on the microwave.

Gone for coffee and better food. I'll be back before 7.
—HW

She looked at her phone and smiled, tucking herself deeper into the warm blankets. She had at least twenty minutes before he'd be back. Her bladder wouldn't wait, though.

She found an old plaid button-down shirt and put it on before going down the ladder. She didn't mind being naked outdoors, but if Hunter wasn't here, she just didn't see the point.

Her mind twisted that puzzle as she used the bathroom and washed her face. She wished she had toothpaste, but maybe he had some upstairs. She came out of the side door just as his Jeep rumbled around the corner. She leaned against the barn and crossed her arms as she waited for him.

He stepped out wearing jeans and a t-shirt, sunglasses

already on against the blinding morning light of summer. He grinned and waved before reaching across the seat and picking up a bag and a travel coffee mug.

Then he was slamming his door and striding toward her on his impossibly long legs. "Mornin', sugar tits. How'd you sleep?" he asked.

She felt her cheeks heat as he stopped in front of her, kissing her softly on the cheek. It was such a sweet, innocent gesture, but it wasn't something she was used to.

She smiled and straightened, walking beside him to the door of the barn. They fell into step together as she replied.

"It was the best sleep I've had in a while. How about you?"

He held the door open for her, his grin widening. "Same for me. I haven't slept that good in a long time. I brought breakfast. Are you hungry?"

She shook her head, but her stomach growled, contradicting her. He laughed, so she shrugged and went up the ladder. "Okay, maybe a little."

His hand on her ass gave a little squeeze as she scurried up. She kicked off the heels and sat crisscross on the bed as he pulled out a to-go food container. She sniffed, her eyes widening as she saw heaping portions of eggs, bacon, hash browns, biscuits, and gravy.

"Where did you get all this?" she asked, taking the fork he offered.

He sat on the other side of the container and grabbed a piece of bacon. "Ma makes breakfast for all the ranch hands every weekday."

She blinked in surprise. No wonder he didn't want to date locally. It's a wonder he wanted to date at all. They said a man who loves his mom will end up marrying someone just like her. She was probably the opposite of his mom, though. Short versus tall. Bookish versus outdoorsy. She never cooked versus his mom feeding an army of ranch hands multiple times a day.

Sadness swept through her as she took a drink. It was probably for the best. They said girls married versions of their dads too, right? And her dad was a strung-out loser who couldn't keep a job.

She had to be smart about her dating life. Hunter wasn't anything like her dad, but she didn't even kid herself with him. This was all they'd have. This one fake date and a wild night that she couldn't bring herself to regret.

She asked how many ranch hands they had and what they did all day. Their conversation was easy as they ate, although the coffee was too bitter for her. They were just finishing up when her phone rang.

"Hello?"

"Would you like to accept a collect call from—"

She hit the end button, her ears ringing. He couldn't be back in jail, could he?

"Wrong number?" Hunter asked, gathering their trash. She nodded absently, staring at the phone.

She looked up, pasting on a smile as she worried about her dad. "Yeah, spammers. They're fucking annoying. Anyway, will you take me home?"

He frowned and looked down at her. "I thought we could hang out all day today, since you're not working."

She picked at the hem of her shirt and saw her dress on the metal frame headboard. She reached for it and shook her head. "I'd love to hang out, but I desperately need a shower. I'm sticky all over."

He chuckled and took her wrist, drawing her to her feet. He tipped her chin up with a finger, and she looked at him. He was so handsome with his brown hair and hazel eyes.

He could be a model for Renaissance sculptors with his chiseled jaw and wide grin.

"We can head to the river and go skinny dipping. That'll get you clean and let me keep you naked for a while longer."

She felt a twinge in her chest. "It sounds like a great, lazy day off, but I actually need to run and check on my dad. Plus, I'm pretty sore. I think my pussy needs a break."

He laughed, and her heart soared at the sound, to know that he wasn't mad about being turned down. Then he kissed her softly on the lips, the most perfect, sweetest kiss they'd had.

"Fair enough. I guess I shouldn't be greedy then, huh? Let me know when you're ready, and we'll head out."

He let her go, and she felt cold as she turned her back to him. She took off the plaid shirt and quickly slipped her dress over her head. She was half-surprised he didn't take advantage of her naked state, but he let her dress in peace.

When she turned back around, he had a small bag of trash in hand. He was staring at her with a wistful expression that defied his rough, tough, bad boy cowboy persona. Then he smiled, a mask seeming to come over him as he waved to the ladder.

"Ready?"

She nodded, unable to answer him past the knot in her throat. They drove to her apartment with only the music on the radio. He tapped on the steering wheel and hummed while she stared out the window.

He didn't reach for her hand again, which made her sad, but he still opened her door and walked her up the stairs. His hand on her back made her feel a little easier. When she unlocked her door, he grabbed her wrist and spun her into his arms.

He wrapped her in a tight embrace and dug his head in the crook of her neck. "I had a great night, sugar. I hope it's not our only one together."

Then his mouth devoured hers in a bruising kiss. His tongue swept inside to conquer hers in a sneak attack that left her breathless, but all too soon he was stepping back with a sad smile and walking to the stairs.

She watched him walk away, unsure of how she felt about the past twenty-four hours. Yesterday, things had seemed so simple, but now they were anything but.

Chapter Nineteen

Taylor stepped out of the shower and grabbed her phone. "Hello?"

"Would you like to accept a collect call from Chris Grimes? Press one for yes, two for no."

Taylor sighed and pressed one. A few seconds later, her dad came on the phone.

"Baby girl, there you are! I was getting worried."

She wrapped the towel around her and walked to her bed, curling up on her side. "What are you doing in jail, Dad?"

He paused for a second, then cleared his throat. "Well, it's those roommates of mine. They set me up. I need you to bail me out so I can get away from them for good."

She clenched her eyes closed and felt her chest tighten. "No, Dad. I can't. I spent the last of my savings on your rent, remember?"

"Don't you have a credit card?"

She shook her head and tears spilled onto her cheek. "My credit card is still maxed out from the last time I bailed you out. I have nothing left, Dad. You're going to have to stay there."

"I can't. Come on, baby girl. You gotta help me out. You're my only chance to get back on my feet. I have an interview tomorrow that I can't miss. Once I get that job, I'll pay you back, I swear."

"Sorry, Dad," she said softly, her throat threatening to close. "I just can't. I love you, but I can't."

His voice turned brittle. "Look, I'm in county lockup, and the bail bondsman here is Jeffrey on 28th Street. Can you just call and talk to him? It's only five hundred dollars. Then I can get out and go to work."

An automated message said, "You have one minute remaining."

She swallowed hard. "Sorry, Dad, but you're going to have to figure this out on your own."

"Baby girl, don't do this. Your mom would want you to take care of your old man, wouldn't she? She's gone, and now it's up to you to take care of me."

She sat up, anger threatening to choke her. "No Dad, it's time for you to fucking grow up and learn to adult. If I can, then so can you."

He sneered, and she could just picture his face through the phone. "Don't you talk to me like that, baby girl. You wouldn't even be here if it weren't for me."

"You have thirty seconds remaining."

She gripped her towel. "Time to go, Dad. I don't get paid for another week at my new job. Sorry, but there's nothing I can do. You've wrung me dry. I have nothing more to give."

He started to say something, but she clicked end and hung up. She choked on a sob, burying her head in her hands.

She was such a hypocrite. She'd told him to grow up, but she hadn't made much progress. She'd had one date with Hunter last night and how had that ended? With her on her back. It was exactly what she'd said she wouldn't do anymore.

She couldn't help Dad. She couldn't even help herself. She sobbed until her body was too tired to cry anymore.

She awoke to another phone call. She rubbed her eyes and glanced at the time as she answered it. Hell, hours had passed and now it was early afternoon.

"Hello?"

"I thought I'd have heard from you by now," Lucy said.

Taylor sat up and rubbed her eyes. "What?"

Lucy sighed. "I thought you would've called me first thing this morning and told me how your date with Hunter went."

"It wasn't—"

She stopped, cutting herself off with a sigh. It wasn't a date, but it was. She groaned and sank back onto her bed. She heard Harry in the background babbling.

"It wasn't what?" Lucy asked, water turning on and banging coming through the line.

"Are you doing the dishes?"

"Yeah, Mason has to work tonight. Do you want to come over for dinner and tell me all about the date?"

Taylor looked at the clock and winced. "Yeah, give me a few hours to get ready. I have a therapy appointment, then I'll be over."

Lucy paused at news of the therapy, but didn't say anything, which Taylor was grateful for. "Great. Afterward can we go to a yoga class together?"

"Yeah, that's fine."

They hung up, and Taylor finally got dressed for her

appointment. Her hair was a tangled mess and took the most time to brush out. She finally just braided it and tossed it over her shoulder. She glanced in the mirror and bit her lip.

A crop top with short jean shorts didn't exactly scream respectable town librarian. She wanted to grow up, but she didn't want to lose who she was. Where was that line of what she could and couldn't do? Why didn't adulting come with a fucking manual?

She sighed and brushed her teeth, then grabbed her keys, purse, and phone and went down to her little beat-up car. A few minutes later, she pulled up to Tasha's office.

The door rang as she pushed it open. Tasha was sitting on the couch at her laptop, her bare feet propped up on the coffee table in front of her. She smiled and pushed up her glasses on her nose.

"Hey girl, you're right on time. How are you today?" Tasha asked. "Can I get you anything? Water, soda?"

Taylor shook her head and went around the other couch, sitting to face Tasha and propping her own feet up. "No, I'm good. Thank you, though."

Tasha nodded and tilted her head. "Want to tell me why your eyes are red and puffy?"

Taylor smiled and sighed. "Nothing gets past you, does it?"

Tasha grinned. "You have no idea. Now, out with it, missy. What's going on?"

She leaned her head back and closed her eyes. "Two things. The ripping the band-aid off date and my dad. Which one do you want to start with?"

"Which one made you cry?"

Taylor laughed, feeling more tears threaten to spill. She

closed her eyes and sighed. "Well, my dad, but some of it is self-recrimination too."

"In what way?"

She explained about her past with her parents, her mom's death, her dad's neediness from the past few years, and her dad calling for rent and bail money.

"I was really proud of how I stood up to him, but it was like it went in one ear and out the other. I think he still believes I'll call the bail bondsman and get him out, even though I said no."

"Are you going to?"

She shook her head, squeezing her eyes closed. "I can't."

"Would you if you had the money?"

Taylor got up and began to pace behind the couch. "I honestly don't know. I told him on the phone that he has to grow up and figure it out himself, that I can't keep doing this."

Tasha nodded. "It's classic co-dependency."

Taylor rubbed her temples. "I know. I'm a smart woman. I've read thousands of books and know in my brain that it's not healthy. But my emotions get the best of me sometimes and are so irrational. It's stupid."

"It's not stupid. We're emotional beings, and the fact that you're able to even recognize how the behaviors are affecting you is great news, actually."

Taylor nodded. "See, I know that in my head, but my heart aches. Every time something happens with Dad, I make stupid decisions. I just want to handle the stress he puts me through better."

"What decisions do you consider stupid?"

Taylor laughed and looked Tasha in the eyes. "I'm a slut. I sleep around like you wouldn't believe."

Tasha's head tilted to the side. Her eyes were still open and curious, not judgmental like she expected. "Based on your tone of voice and your previous comment of bad decisions, you're not happy with sleeping around?"

Taylor shrugged. "I just want someone steady, one person to love, one person to sleep with who knows me inside and out. Someone who can fuck me senseless and knows exactly how I like it, but cares for me and treats me like I'm worth the effort to be with day in and day out. I'm tired of being random fucktoys for silly boys who tend to disappoint in every category. I love having sex, but it has to be good sex, ya know? I don't think it's healthy to keep searching over and over hoping that good sex will turn into a decent relationship, do you?"

Tasha arched a brow. "Does it matter what I think? It's your life. What do you think?"

Taylor turned and stared out the front window at the small town, knowing that no one could see in. Some people passed on the sidewalk, others drove by and waved at the pedestrians. It was a quaint little town and should be drama free.

She shouldn't have brought all her baggage to this cute little place.

Tasha asked, "Let's take another tactic. You said that when you sleep around, you keep searching over and over. What are you searching for?"

Taylor snorted. "I keep searching for something better, something stable, something permanent even though I'm afraid of it."

"Ah, now we're onto something. Are you self-sabotaging? Last week, you said you wanted a family, a white picket fence, stability, and love. Did you go on a date this weekend and search for love?"

Taylor crossed her arms. "Yeah, my life is basically that Johnny Lee song, *Looking for Love in All the Wrong Places.*"

Tasha chuckled but gave her the look. "That goes back to your daddy issues. If you would've had a stable father figure, maybe you wouldn't be searching for love through sex."

Taylor winced. "Yeah, that sounds about right."

Tasha's gaze softened. "But there's nothing you can do about your dad being unreliable in your life. Your search for love is not going to replace the feelings your dad's absence and abandonment brought you."

"I know, I know. But talking about my dad is going to need a whole different appointment."

Tasha pursed her lips and sat back in her seat. "I see. Well, let's go back to sex then. Sleeping around is important to you because it's part of your search for love. It's not the only thing you should look for in a relationship, but it sounds like you're using it as a type of screening process."

Taylor tilted her head. "I guess you're right. Other girls will date first and then sleep with someone. But I do the opposite. I'll sleep with them, then I want to get to know them. In the past, once the guy gets what he wants, he's gone. Then there's no way of really getting to know them."

"That's why you've never really dated before, right?" Tasha asked. Taylor nodded, so Tasha continued. "Based on your phrasing, did you go on a date this weekend? Sleep with someone or get to know him first? How'd that go?"

Taylor smiled and turned back to the couch. "Yes, I had a date last night actually, and it was pretty amazing. We went down to a Mexican place in Fort Worth, then we went dancing at Billy Bob's. If I had to choose the perfect first date, I'd have to say that was it."

"Really?" Tasha's brows rose. "What made it perfect?"

Taylor leaned back and looked at the ceiling as she thought. "Lots of things. The food. The company. The excitement. The sex."

Tasha nodded, tapping her pencil to her lip. "Interesting. Tell me more."

"Well, I told him I wasn't going to sleep with him. I wanted to practice having a real first date, and he agreed to help. But when we were on the way home... I don't know." Taylor shrugged. "I really like him. I wanted to sleep with him. So we did."

"Is this where self-recrimination comes in?" Tasha asked.

"I didn't feel any shame at all until after I talked to my dad and second guessed myself." Taylor blinked and tugged on the hem of her crop top. "If I separate last night from my past, I don't regret sleeping with him. I—I don't think I've ever been so turned on in my life. Of all the guys I've slept with, this guy put them all to shame. The way he talked, the way he made me feel..."

Her voice trailed off, but Tasha didn't break into her thoughts. She thought back to how her heart raced, the thrill up her spine at his touch. Her shoulders relaxed as she remembered the look in his eyes as he stared down at her.

"I never once felt like I was doing something I shouldn't. With him, it just felt natural, like it was meant to be." Taylor cringed and laughed. "God, did I just say that?"

Tasha smirked and nodded. "Yep, but was it that good because the perfect date was before it? Or was it really because of this man?"

Taylor frowned. "I'm not sure. I guess I'll find out in a few days. My date with Scott is on Saturday."

"How do you feel about it? Are you still nervous?"

Taylor thought, then shook her head. "Actually, I'm

okay for now. I was mostly upset about my dad today, but I don't want to talk about him anymore. Even though I enjoyed myself last night, I need to move on and focus on seeing Scott in a few days. I do feel much better talking with you though. I'm glad I kept the appointment."

Tasha nodded. "Me too. I take all digital payments and cash too."

Taylor laughed and pulled out her phone to send payment. Then she was out the door and on her way to Lucy's. Harry was screaming when she pushed open the door.

Lucy looked over with a harried expression on her face, stirring something in a bowl.

"Oh hey, thank God you're here. Can you change him for me? He's not a fan of sitting in a mess."

Taylor scooped him up from the play pen and blew strawberries on his cheek. "Is my little man cranky today? Hm? Let's get you changed and find a snack, shall we?"

Taylor told him a story of a cranky little bear while she changed him. She really should write some of these stories down, but that was more Lucy's wheelhouse. Taylor loved reading books but didn't actually want to write any herself.

She had him laughing when they finally went into the kitchen. Lucy was doing the dishes as some casserole cooked in the oven.

"There's Mama, see? Show her how happy you are now," Taylor said, nuzzling him on the neck to get him to laugh again.

Lucy grinned. "Thank God he's back to being happy. I think he's cutting a new tooth. He's been fussy all day and barely slept last night."

She put Harry in his highchair and cut up half a banana for him. "Well, let's see if we can wear him out.

Why didn't you call me earlier? I could've watched him while you got some sleep."

Lucy sighed and scrubbed a pan. "I thought about it, but I didn't know if you'd stayed over with Hunter or not and didn't want to interrupt."

Taylor stood up and wrapped an arm around her shoulders, steering her to the kitchen table. "That should never factor into anything, Luce. If you need me, I'll be here. No matter what. Next time, call me, okay?"

Lucy nodded and sank to the table. Taylor fixed her a cup of sweet tea and then turned to finish the dishes.

"Thanks, Tay. I—I'm sorry I didn't call earlier."

"It's fine, Luce. I'm here now. Do you want me to stay the night? What time is Mason getting home?"

Lucy shook her head and rubbed her temples. "I don't know. Could be tonight. Could be in the morning."

Taylor nodded as the oven timer went off. "That settles it then. I'll stay the night. Now let's see what's smelling so yummy."

She took the food out of the oven and scooped a small bowl of pot pie for Harry. She put it into the fridge to cool before she served up two plates, putting one in front of Lucy.

Lucy picked at her plate, and Taylor glanced at her watch. "You know what? I don't feel like going to yoga tonight. Let's stay in and veg on the couch. I'll play with Harry while you take a nice, long bubble bath. What do you think?"

Lucy smiled and finally took a bite of food. "That sounds heavenly. You know I love a good bubble bath."

Taylor smiled and grabbed Harry's bowl from the fridge, grabbing a baby spoon to feed him.

Chapter Twenty

As the week went on, Hunter worked harder and harder on the ranch. He stayed out from sunup to sundown in the blistering summer heat fixing fences, moving horses from one pen to another, and all the other million and one tasks that needed done.

On Friday, he found himself on the wrong end of a constipated horse who finally let loose all over him. The water hose had cleaned as much as it could, but he needed a long, hot shower to get rid of the rest of the shit.

He walked to the bunkhouse as Chase was leaving, dressed in his pressed jeans and tight black t-shirt.

"Whoa, brother, where'd all the shit come from?"

Hunter glared, his eyes narrow. "Minerva. The meds Gemma gave her finally worked, and she had a massive blow out."

Chase gave him a wide berth as they passed each other, but he stopped, his eyes narrowing.

"You're working harder than normal. Are you nervous about the new foals due next week?"

Hunter shook his head and continued to the front porch of the bunkhouse. "No, they'll be fine."

He pushed open the door as Chase called, "Work through how to talk to me, because you need to get something off your chest. Are you going to poker night?"

Hunter closed his eyes and threw his head back. "Shit, I forgot. Okay, I'll be there later."

He didn't wait for Chase's reply. Instead, he went inside and scrubbed as hard as he could. Three times.

He hoped it was enough, but he couldn't tell anymore. A lot of aftershave and cologne later, and he hopped in his Jeep and drove to Landry's. They'd been having poker night there for years, before Landry had even met his wife, Holly, or had their twins.

For a while, they'd moved it to Kendall's house, but now they were back at Landry's. He parked with a frown, not remembering why they'd moved it from Tuesday to Friday. He was a few minutes early, but there were no other vehicles in the drive or on the street.

He knocked on the door and opened it. "Hello?" he called out.

Holly came around the corner of the kitchen and smiled. "Oh hey, Hunter. Are you looking for the guys? They went to Parker's tonight. Eddi is cutting a tooth and cranky. Did you not get the text?"

Hunter shrugged and raked a hand through his hair. "You know me. I'm not the best with text."

Holly wiped her hands on a dish towel and walked toward him, a gleam in her eyes. "You know, I met a new girl at yoga this week. I think y'all have history?"

Hunter's shoulders tensed as he froze. Did Taylor go to yoga and talk about him? He both dreaded the idea and felt pride at it. He wanted to gloat and lay claim to her.

He frowned. She wouldn't do that and jeopardize her date this weekend, though.

"Jewel is just as sweet as Gemma. It's no wonder you've waited so long for her to come home," Holly said with a smile.

Hunter blinked in surprise. She'd met Jewel? "Right," he said, thinking of what else to say.

Holly grinned wide but a kid started crying upstairs. She sighed, distracted as she went to the stairs. "Tell everyone I said hi." She took a few steps up while he turned to the door.

"Oh, and Hunter?"

He turned back, meeting her soft smile. "I'm happy you waited. She's amazing. Good luck."

His gut twisted as he shut the door and jumped in his Jeep. There was no way in hell he was going to date Jewel again. They were just too volatile together. He drove to Parker's new house. Really, it was Kendall's house that he'd sold to Parker when Kendall moved in with Lola.

His mind circled back to Jewel like a scab that he just couldn't leave alone. It put him in an even worse mood to think about how he'd been left behind.

After their very public breakup, she'd not come back home. Everyone had given him the stink eye for months. Hell, it'd been touch and go there for a while with her dad. Ma had had to do some fancy sweet talking to convince him to keep them on as customers.

And thank God for that because the ranch might not've survived with any other veterinarian. When Gemma had come home from college, he'd expected her to say something about Jewel, but she never had.

He'd just put up with all the nasty looks from the townspeople and the silent treatment from Gemma and her dad.

He'd been the one still here, so he'd been the one blamed for it all.

By the time he pulled up at Parker's, he was simmering. He slammed the door and stomped up the steps.

Laughter echoed inside as he pushed open the front door. Parker saw him and said, "Hey, you finally made it!"

Hunter glared. "No one told me it was here. I went to Landry's."

Landry rolled his eyes and handed him a beer. "I texted you earlier, but obviously you didn't read it."

Hunter drank the beer, trying to get a handle on his emotions. His skin itched, and Landry waved to the platter of chicken.

"You better eat so you can cure that hanger."

Hunter growled, "I'm not hangry."

"Then what's the problem?" Parker asked, fixing a plate. The rest of the guys were on the back patio already, based on the voices and laughter.

Hunter shrugged his shoulders as Chase came from outside. "There you are. I was wondering if you could get all the shit off."

Landry wrinkled his nose. "*That's* what that smell is!"

"I don't smell," Hunter grumbled, stabbing food onto a plate. "And I don't have a problem."

Chase crossed his arms and widened his stance. "You've gotta be kidding me. You've been storming around the ranch all week. Ever since you stayed out all night on Monday, actually."

Hunter glared at him but didn't say anything.

"Oh, the plot thickens," Parker said, rubbing his hands together.

Landry grinned. "Did you finally run into Jewel?"

The emotions swarmed him, and he exploded with

hands thrown wide. "Why is everyone fucking focused on Jewel? Why can't anyone just leave it alone?"

Landry took a drink of his beer, and Parker crossed his arms, eerily matching Chase's stance as he said, "We weren't born yesterday, Hunter. We know you were out, and Jewel just got back in town. It stands to reason you two would hook up. You've been waiting for her forever, after all."

He blinked. Where had everyone gotten this idea that he was waiting around for Jewel?

The back door opened, and Kendall poked his head inside. "Y'all going to talk all night or join us? We're ready to deal."

Parker picked up his plate and went outside without a word. Landry opened the door for him and gave Hunter one more glance before he shut the door behind him.

"They didn't do anything wrong," Chase said softly.

Hunter looked at him. He was stony silent with a thunderous expression, but he didn't move. Instead, he focused on his breathing, trying to calm the boiling rage inside.

Hunter took another drink and finished fixing his plate. "I know. That's just the way they are."

"So don't fucking take it out on them," Chase said.

Hunter leaned his hands on the table and closed his eyes, taking deep breaths. Rage made his skin itch, clawing him from the inside to get out.

"I'm trying not to, brother, but watch your tone. I'm already on edge and don't want to lose it on you too," Hunter ground out, his nails digging into the table.

He breathed deeply as Chase opened the front door. "Come on," he said.

Hunter looked up and frowned. "Where?"

Chase held the door. "We're going to settle this right here, right now."

Hunter felt a thrill and followed him out the door. It banged shut behind him as Chase stepped off the front porch and onto the grassy lawn.

"What are we settling?" Hunter asked, staying on the porch. He battled with himself, trying to regain his cool. He'd long since learned that fighting when he was this emotional and angry never ended well.

Chase stretched his arms and popped his knuckles. "You've been on edge since you came in Tuesday afternoon. But you were all smiles and chilled out at breakfast. So either you tell me what pissed you off all week or we throw down."

Hunter snorted. "Violence never solved anything. Don't you remember Ma telling us that?"

Chase grinned and widened his feet. "Ma didn't go to prison. Violence solves plenty."

Hunter winced. "I didn't either, Chase."

Chase shrugged. "Are you going to tell me what happened?"

Hunter shook his head. "Not a chance."

"Were you with Jewel?" Chase's tone was hard and angry.

Hunter's hands fisted at his side, and his spine straightened. "Why does everyone assume I'm getting back together with Jewel? She fucking ripped my heart out."

Chase nodded, stepping closer, his steps wary even as he held out a palm. His fingers bent in a come-hither motion.

Hunter didn't go looking for trouble, but somehow it always found him. Isn't that how he ended up taking Taylor home in the first place? Seeing her naked ass and feeling her in his arms?

Hunter stepped to the grass, welcoming trouble with open arms. The way he was prowling, he didn't want to get too close to Chase yet. He needed to wait for his opening. It was like his wrestling days in high school all over again, but with more emotion.

Chase snorted, "So that's why you're pissy? Everyone's reminding you of that heart break?"

"Not everyone," Hunter said. "At the moment, just you."

"So, you don't think she'll want you back, is that it? No, that can't be it since you were clearly with *someone* Monday night. It must've been Jewel though because she didn't answer my call. Is she as good of a lay now as she was back then?"

Hunter froze, his blood turning cold in his veins and the words echoing in his ears. "What did you say?"

Chase shrugged. "You didn't know? I thought that's why y'all had that blow up at Christmas. She was my first, you know, so of course I wasn't anything to write home about. But that second and third time? Man, she could scream, couldn't she?"

Hunter saw red and lunged. Chase shifted, and Hunter's stomach slammed into his shoulder. Hunter landed in the grass with a thump and a groan, but his past kicked in and he rolled.

He sent a fist into Chase's ribs, and then it was on. Fists flew and Hunter's vision swirled with red and white bursts of color. He clawed at Chase, ripping his arm away and flinging it as he brought up a right hook. He blocked with his left arm, and Chase rolled them again.

They grunted, and Chase landed a solid hit to his face.

Chase laughed, "What a pussy. Who knew she'd prefer me to my perfect older bro?"

Hunter roared, determined to win and confused and angry to hear his brother talk like that. He hated losing and would not let his little brother off easily just because he felt sorry for him for going to prison.

"You slept with Jewel," Hunter grunted, hitting harder, reminding himself why he was so pissed. Chase groaned and jerked at the renewed vigor of the attack.

"I know. Hit me harder, pussy," Chase grunted, begging for the beating. His tone broke pushed a crack into Hunter's angry haze, and he realized Chase was angry at himself.

Hunter landed another blow and hooked his knee around Chase's, twisting to pin him in place. "No, just fucking apologize. This is shit, Chase."

"No, fucking hit me harder!" Chase roared.

Hunter reared back and slammed his fist into Chase's stomach. With it, the haze of anger broke in half and floated away. Hunter rolled away and to his knees.

They both panted, and Hunter felt his ribs, fist, and face burning like hell. Chase laid on his back, blinking up at the night sky.

"You slept with Jewel." Hunter processed the information, his brain whirling as he thought through the meaning. He needed all the facts first though.

Chase let out an exhale. "Yeah."

"And you tried to call her? Recently?" Hunter asked.

Chase nodded, his words heavy with disappointment and hurt. It was clear that the rejection from Jewel had deeply affected him. "She doesn't want anything to do with me. She still wants you."

Hunter felt a thrill, knowing he wasn't second best. Then he frowned, all the memories and emotions flooding back. He didn't want Jewel, hadn't been waiting on her.

Chase's tone of voice soaked into his brain, making him remember.

He laid on his back next to Chase and counted the stars. "When she came home for Christmas break, she had that jerk with her."

Chase nodded beside him. "Kevin."

Hunter snorted. "Little twig of a man. I thought she just brought him home to make me jealous enough to move to Houston with her."

Chase didn't say anything, and Hunter swallowed the question he didn't want to ask. Crickets and cicadas made music around them even though they were in a little neighborhood.

Hunter took a deep breath, his head finally clearing. Maybe Chase was onto something about violence helping because he actually felt better than before.

"What the hell happened." He didn't ask, just wondered out loud in confusion.

Chase's voice was deep and rough. "The summer she graduated... I was always flirting with her, practicing my skills because I knew it was safe. She was with you, and it was just harmless flirting. Or so I thought. Then she found me in the barn one day when I was hauling in hay. I'd stopped to use the bathroom and when I came out, there she was."

Hunter nodded, his throat closing on the betrayal.

"Can you forgive me?" Chase demanded. It wasn't a question. His tone brooked no argument and was almost its own challenge.

Hunter nodded, but still couldn't say anything. He'd lost Chase for fifteen years. He didn't want to lose any more time with him. Time was precious, and he refused to let some girl from the past get between them.

The door opened and Landry poked his head out. "Uh, what are you two doing?"

Hunter waved a hand. "Star gazing. Andromeda is beautiful tonight, don't you think?"

Landry snorted. "Whatever, we're going to start without you." The door shut behind him, and they laid in silence for a few more minutes.

Hunter rolled to his stomach and did a push up to get to his knees. His ribs ached and everything else pulsed. He offered a hand to Chase. When they stood, Hunter slapped him on the back.

"We good?" Hunter asked.

Chase shrugged, refusing to look at him. "It's up to you." His vulnerability reminded him of when they'd been kids and Chase had fallen off a horse. He'd laughed and pretended to be fine, but secretly had bled through his jeans and had a broken shin.

Hunter looked up at the stars and put his hands in his pockets. "You're my brother. Of course I forgive you. It hurts like hell to find out now, but back then, I was already hurting from Jewel bringing that Kevin dude home while we were still dating. What's one more guy thrown in the mix?"

"Except I'm not just one more guy. I'm your brother."

Hunter nodded, his chest tight with emotion. "I know, but bros before hos and all that."

Chase snorted and shook his head, wincing as he rubbed his jaw.

Hunter continued, "A word of warning, though. If you're wise, you'll not call her back. I haven't called her because I don't need that kind of drama in my life."

"How do you know that you've actually moved on, then?" Chase asked.

Hunter stared at the stars, his mind clear and his body

aching. That's a good point. I guess we do need to talk about how things ended, about you."

Chase winced and rubbed the back of his neck. "Same. I need to talk to her about that."

Hunter shook his head. "Don't fall for her tricks, Chase. Find someone who'll be faithful. You deserve someone better, someone who'll love you."

Chase snorted and kicked at the dirt. "I'm the bottom of the barrel, Hunter. A convict. Love isn't really in the stars right now."

Hunter looked up, a flare of hope shooting through the sky. "Maybe not tonight but someday. Just don't settle for less than love, okay?"

Chase looked up at him with narrowed eyes. "This from the man who was just trying to get me laid two weeks ago?"

Hunter laughed and slapped him on the back again. "Yeah, yeah. If you're just looking to get laid, by all means, call Jewel. Just don't give her your heart. I don't want to see you go through the heartache I did, alright? I kinda love you and shit."

Chase grinned and together they walked to the front door. "I love you too," he said softly, barely heard over the crickets.

Hunter held the door and together they went into the house. He wasn't sure about Chase, but he certainly felt lighter. Despite what everyone thought, he hadn't been cranky because Jewel was back in town. No, he had no idea what he was going to do about Taylor. He'd felt off all week since telling her bye.

He didn't even know if her date was Friday or Saturday night. He wanted to know, needed to talk to her, but it probably wasn't the best idea. He didn't want to send the wrong message after all.

Questions swirled within his head, questions about who was in her bed. *He'd drive himself crazy if he couldn't find the truth, but he should be the only one to suck her boobs.*

He snorted, his own poem making him wince at the corniness. God, she was messing with his head. He'd not made dumb poems like that since middle school.

No, he wouldn't talk to Taylor. But maybe he should talk to Jewel and hash out all their past. Maybe it'd make him feel freer like the way hashing things out with Chase on the lawn did.

Chapter Twenty-One

A hand shook Hunter's shoulder. "Hunter, wake up."

He groaned and opened one eye. His whole body still ached from the fight with Chase two nights ago.

Speak of the devil…

Chase sat on his bed across the room and tugged on his boots. "Ma came in. Maribell is foaling but it's not going well."

Hunter threw back the covers and grabbed his jeans from the end of the bed frame, tugging them on and ignoring the aches in his body. Less than two minutes later, they were both pushing open the screen door of the bunk house and running to the barn.

Ma was already inside soothing Maribell. Hunter felt her flank and crooned as he felt her body tense with a contraction. Dad came around the stall door, wiping his hands on a rag.

"Pandora and Raven are also in labor, but theirs seem to be going smoothly. How's she doing?"

Ava rattled off the details. "She started this morning, but it was all normal until I checked on her an hour ago."

Hunter picked up her tone. If she was worried, then they didn't have a moment to spare. He looked up at Chase.

"Call Gemma."

Chase nodded and took off to the house. Hunter felt her stomach and frowned.

"Do you feel it?" Ava asked.

Hunter nodded. "Yeah, have you checked her?"

Ava shook her head. "No, I've been walking her up and down the barn. She's too antsy, like she knows something's wrong. I'm afraid she's going to throw herself against the stall and try to knock this foal out the hard way. She's a stubborn girl."

Hunter nodded, stepping out and grabbing the hand sanitizer from the wall. He checked Maribell and rubbed her flank, his arm buried inside.

He frowned, "How close is Gemma? I see a red bag."

Ava squeezed her eyes shut, and Bill cursed. He didn't tell them that he couldn't feel the foal's head. It must be turned around.

They worked hard for the next half hour to keep the mare calm, but they were fighting the clock. Hunter crooned and held her neck, his worry for both mare and foal going up with each passing minute. A noise at the door drew his attention, and he turned his head.

His already tight stomach twisted. Jewel strode down the aisle with purpose, her hair pulled into a messy bun. She had filled out in the fifteen years since he'd seen her. She'd always been cute as a button—and had hated when he'd told her that too.

Her eyes met his, and her steps faltered. He felt a lump in his throat, and the knot in his stomach twisted even more.

She stepped into the stall and reached for Maribell, speaking softly as the horse side stepped.

"There, there, girl. It's going to be okay. I'm here, and we're going to get you through this." She asked questions, and Ava answered as Jewel went through the motions of checking the progress.

Hunter took a deep breath, and Chase stepped into the doorway of the stall.

"Hunter, can you come help Dad with Raven?" Chase asked.

Hunter looked to Ava and Jewel. Jewel met his gaze once more as she eased behind Maribell for an internal check.

"Is she—will you—" he took a deep breath, unable to think enough to process what he even wanted to ask.

"We'll be fine here. Let me know if you need me there though," Jewel said, her eyes going unfocused as she felt inside Maribell.

Hunter patted the horse's neck and stepped into the aisle to follow Chase to the other end of the barn. Several of the other mares who were close to foaling were already in stalls, but they seemed oblivious to the activity around them.

Bill stood behind Raven, sweat glistening on his forehead as he pulled. "I can't get the angle right, and she needs out," he said.

Hunter hustled to help, Chase patting Raven's neck and speaking softly to her while they worked. They tugged, and Hunter grunted as the foal finally slipped free onto the hay covered floor.

Raven shuddered and snorted but seemed alright. They all sighed and stepped back. Bill wiped his forehead and leaned against the wall. "I'll stay with her and help with the after birth. Go check on Pandora."

Hunter and Chase didn't argue. They'd done this hundreds of times growing up. Pandora wasn't as far along, so Chase said, "I'll stay with her and call if I need to. Go check on Maribell."

Neither of them mentioned Jewel. Honestly, Hunter was too worried about the horses to even care about Jewel and Chase and the whole mess.

It wasn't until he was sitting on the front porch of his parents' house with a cup of coffee in hand watching the sunrise that he stopped to think about them. The horses were all fine now, even with the stressful birth.

Ma was inside making breakfast, and Dad was still in the barn with Jewel. Chase pushed open the screen door to the house and sat on the top step of the porch with a sigh.

They watched the sunrise in silence, neither addressing the elephant in the room. There was something about watching the sun and helping the horses that made their relationship squabbles seem insignificant. It reminded him that they were just a blip in the universe and what happened in the past was just that.

It was in the past. *The sun rose and set on their backs drenched in sweat. Always toiling, always boiling. The Texas heat beat down, but which was more renown? The past that melted their hearts and souls, or the blood, sweat, and tears that went into the ranch as a whole?*

The poetry flooded his head, but still he rocked, basking in the moment, the stillness and beauty of it all.

Jewel came out of the barn and wiped her forehead, turning on the water spigot and washing her hands and arms as best she could. Hunter watched absently. She was still cute, but he didn't feel any of the familiar rush of attraction when he looked at her.

He didn't feel any of the familiar anger, either. Perhaps

he was too tired to feel it. She strode toward them, and he waited for any emotions to flare, but they didn't.

She stopped at the bottom of the stairs and looked up at them. Her eyes were red rimmed from lack of sleep. Her cheeks turned redder the longer the silence stretched.

"Hey," she said softly.

Chase grunted, but Hunter didn't say anything.

She tipped her chin up and said professionally, "They're good now. Pandora should foal this afternoon, but just let us know if you need help. Dad is working today while Gemma is in the city for training."

Hunter nodded and sipped his coffee. The screen door screeched open beside him, and Ava poked her head out.

"Jewel, come have some breakfast, sweetheart. Biscuits will be out in five minutes."

Jewel smiled tightly. "Yes, ma'am. I'd be lying if I said I hadn't missed your breakfast. Can you give us a few minutes?"

Ava paused and nodded. "Sure thing. Chase, come help set the table."

"Actually," Jewel interrupted, "I'd like to speak with him too. With them both, if you don't mind."

The screen door shut softly behind her, leaving a heavy silence. Still, Hunter felt nothing.

Jewel looked down and scuffed her boots in the dirt. "Did Chase tell you what happened?"

Hunter felt the hair on the back of his neck stand up as the Texas breeze teased him, and he nodded. "Thursday actually, thus my black eye and sore ribs."

Jewel peered at them both with a frown.

Chase shrugged. "It was bound to happen. You knew that."

Jewel sighed and leaned on the porch railing. "I guess I

thought y'all would've settled it long ago. Either way, I owe you both an apology. Hunter, when Chase and I—"

"I don't want details," Hunter said wearily, sipping his coffee.

"No, you need to hear this. That first time in the barn, I actually thought he was you. It was an accident—"

Hunter snorted, but she took two steps up, coming closer to him than she had in years.

"It's true. It was dark, and I'd been waiting for you. It wasn't until we were already in the middle of it that I realized—"

"For fuck's sake, Jewel, you expect me to believe that?" Hunter asked, sitting forward on the rocking chair as shock coursed through him.

She waved her hands wide. "It's true, I swear. I never meant to sleep with him."

Chase's voice was deeper than Hunter had ever heard it when he growled, "What about the second and third time?"

His tone was accusatory, and Hunter nodded, taking a deep breath to calm down as the anger built. Chase had been a horny teenager, and it would've been right before the accident that sent him to prison.

Jewel turned to Chase on the steps and sank to sit beside him, facing them both. Her voice softened when she looked at him.

"That was different."

They stared at each other, and Hunter felt like a third wheel. Hunter cleared his throat, and Jewel looked up at him.

"And the guy from college?" he asked.

She rolled her eyes and sighed. "He was gay, Hunter. He had nowhere else to go for the holiday, which is why I invited him home with me. But you didn't let me talk. You just assumed and talked over me at church, and we had that huge fight in front of everyone."

Hunter felt acid in his throat. "I knew you were seeing someone else. I could tell by how you acted. He was the logical conclusion because I never would've guessed—"

Her eyes widened, and she glanced at Chase, but Chase just crossed his arms and stared darkly, not offering an ounce of help.

She swallowed hard and nodded, looking down. "That summer with Chase—you started acting jealous before I went to college. The phone calls, the paranoid questions and needing to know who I was with at all hours."

Hunter shrugged. "I knew something was wrong. I just couldn't figure out what."

She took a deep breath, wiping her eyes. She rubbed at a blood stain on her dirty jeans and let the silence linger.

Hunter drained his now cool coffee, choking down the bitterness. "It doesn't matter now. It's all in the past. Like I told Gemma, it's all water under the bridge."

"Not quite," Jewel said, taking a deep breath and glancing between them. "The thing is, I have a daughter."

She waited, but neither of them said anything. There was only one reason she'd mention a daughter now. Hunter's lip began to sweat as he narrowed his eyes against the now fully risen sun.

Jewel eyed them both warily. "She's almost fifteen and is at summer camp. She'll be home in a few weeks. She'll want to meet you both."

Hunter croaked, "Both?"

He had to hear it. Dread filled him, somehow knowing what she was going to say.

"Both because one of you is the father," Jewel said,

biting her lip and picking at her jeans again. She couldn't look either of them in the face.

Chase looked up at Hunter, and Hunter stared at him with the same bewildered look on his face. Holy shit.

He blinked, stunned. "Fifteen years..." he trailed off.

Chase growled, swinging back to stare at her. "Why didn't you say anything earlier? Say, when you first got pregnant?"

Jewel shrugged. "I was going to at Christmas until it all went to shit."

"Why didn't you come home? After our fight, you left and never came back," Hunter said.

Jewel's jaw lifted, and she stared at the barn and the sun, her eyes unfocused. "I needed to prove I could do it on my own. I was going to come home that spring once the baby was born so we could do a paternity test, but that was when Chase was on trial. I didn't want to add to that stress on your family."

Silence stretched, each of them lost in thoughts of the past. Finally, Chase cleared his throat.

"I think we should do the paternity test before we meet her. That way we can start off on the right foot and not confuse the poor girl. What have you told her?"

Jewel sighed, her shoulders drooping. "That her dad lives here. She knows he's here somewhere but doesn't know who. It won't take her long to ask around and find out that Hunter was my boyfriend back then."

Hunter nodded. "I don't think we should mention this to Ma or Dad or anyone else until we figure out who's the dad, either."

Jewel rubbed her temples and nodded. "I—I know. Gemma and Dad already assume it's you, Hunter. Honestly, it'd be so much easier if it was..."

Her voice trailed off to a whisper, and Chase and Hunter looked at each other. Chase's jaw was clenched, but Hunter just gripped the coffee cup tight.

"How long have Gemma and your dad known about her?"

Jewel wiped her eyes. "From the beginning."

Hunter took a deep breath. "They've known this whole time and not said a word?"

Jewel nodded. "I asked them not to."

Hunter shook his head and stood up. "I need some time to think about this," he said as he threw the screen door open and went inside.

His breathing was ragged as he stomped to the kitchen and put his mug in the sink. Ava shut the oven and put the biscuits on the stove. His entire world had shifted in the five minutes it'd taken for the damn biscuits to finish.

"What's going on out there?"

His stomach rolled and he shook his head at Ava's concerned face. "Not now, Ma. I just—I can't. Give me time. I need to think."

He went upstairs to his old bedroom and curled up on his bed, wrapping his arms around a ragged stuffed horse. He faced the other twin bed where Gunner had slept and clenched his eyes shut.

What the hell had just happened? He might be a dad? *Him*? Voices echoed downstairs, but he blocked them out. He needed to think and process.

He'd helped baby-sit his nieces and nephews, but what did he know about teenagers? He might have a daughter, who would have her own style, her own personality, her own—

Shit, what was her name? He didn't even know. What a shit dad he already was.

Did she think he'd known about her this whole time and just hadn't done the right thing by her? Did she feel abandoned?

God, it ate at him, making his stomach lurch and his muscles tense. He was going to need another wrestling match or something at this rate, regardless of how sore he was.

Chapter Twenty-Two

Taylor's leg bobbed nervously as she watched the clock at work on Saturday. The kids had kept her busy for story time that morning, but time seemed to drag by that afternoon. Finally, it was three, and she closed up.

She'd spent the rest of the week trying to push away all thoughts of Hunter, all worries about her dad, and all anxiety about her upcoming date. She had ripped off the band-aid like Tasha had suggested, and it had helped to an extent. She wasn't nearly as nervous as before, but she also wasn't as excited as she'd been.

Other than her sleepover at Lucy's on Tuesday night, she'd gone straight home after work and devoured some books from her to-be-read list. The distraction had worked to keep her mind off her date with Hunter and how he'd made her feel, and it kept her from worrying about her upcoming date with Scott.

She went home after work and changed, then went for a late afternoon jog. The morning thunderstorm had cooled off the temperatures so she wouldn't get too hot.

All she needed was twenty minutes. She didn't have the time to lose herself in another book, but the physical activity would hopefully get her nerves under control before her first date with Scott.

She came to a stop on Main Street, glancing around. Her side spasmed as she squinted into the gym beside the yoga studio. Her eyes focused on the people inside, and her chest grew tight.

Hunter was inside with one of his brothers, boxing in a ring. She bit her lip, drawn to him like a fish on a line. His muscles rippled, and she pushed the door open, shivering at the cool, air-conditioned breeze.

A guy lifting weights eyed her, then set down his weights and came over. He was big and bulky, the typical gym rat, but she barely gave him a smile before she turned back to Hunter in the ring.

"Haven't seen you in here before. I'm Nick. Do you want me to show you around?" He had the high and tight haircut of a military man, and she finally took her gaze off Hunter.

She smiled at Nick and nodded. "That'd be great, thanks. I'm new in town. Taylor."

They shook hands, and he held hers a little longer than necessary. She automatically deepened her smile, flattered by the attention, and he turned to wave at the weights.

"These are the free weights. Then there's the boxing ring, which is a new addition. The treadmills are on that side, and if you go through that door, it'll take you to the yoga studio."

"I've been there few times," she said, following him.

"Holly's great, right? There are more bathrooms in the yoga studio and the female locker room there is so much nicer than what we have here."

Taylor smirked, "Been in the female locker room a lot, have you?"

Nick laughed and put his hand on the small of her back, walking her toward the back of the gym. "Not at all, but if you invite me in there, I'll be able to confirm my suspicions."

"Uh huh, you sure all you want to do is look around and see how much nicer the girls' room is?" she asked, her brow arching.

He laughed again, stopping at the entrance to a hallway. "Well, if you're offering, I won't turn ya down."

She grinned and shook her head. "Sorry, hot rod. I'm just looking around today."

"Well, let me know when you're done shopping and are ready for a purchase. I might know a guy." He hooked a thumb to point to himself.

She laughed and shook her head. The flirting thrill was as familiar as walking, and she slipped into it easily, relaxing into the verbal repartee.

He shrugged and grinned. "You can't blame a guy for trying."

With a nod down the hall, he said, "The guy's locker room is on the left and the girls' is on the right. Go see for yourself which one's better. No one else is in there, and I won't follow without an invitation, promise."

She laughed and half-turned, keeping one eye on Hunter as he boxed. "That's okay, I'll take your word for it. I can't stay long, but I did want to ask about the cost."

Nick jerked a thumb to the ring. "Parker can explain the gym prices if you want to join, but it's pretty straightforward. Just a flat fee to use as many times a month as you want or you can pay per day use."

Taylor nodded. "Thanks. I'll hang around and ask him about it then. Don't let me keep you from your workout."

Nick gave a half-hearted salute and grinned. "Whatever you say, little lady. Let me know if you need anything. It was nice meeting you."

"You too," she said, not even watching him walk away. Hunter glanced over and his hands dropped as he frowned in confusion. Parker swung at his jaw, and Hunter grunted at the impact, doubling over.

Taylor gasped and clenched her own fists, but Hunter shoved Parker and walked toward her, stretching his jaw.

He ducked between the rings and pulled the gloves off. "What are you doing here?" he asked breathlessly.

She arched her brow and cocked a hip. "Stopped by to check it out while on my run. What are you doing here? Looks like your face already got a beating."

Parker wrapped an arm around Hunter's shoulders and grinned. "The face wasn't me. That was Chase at poker night. They got into it over Hunter's girlfriend."

Her blood turned to ice in her veins, and she shivered again. "Your girlfriend?" Oh god, he was dating someone else. She had to get out of here.

Hunter shook his head and shrugged Parker's arm off. "Ex-girlfriend. How'd your date go?"

Taylor glanced at the clock and pursed her lips, needing the escape. "It's in a few hours. I was trying to run off the last of the nerves. I'd better get back to it. See y'all around."

Parker nodded his head, but it was Hunter's piercing gaze she felt on her back as she walked out the door. The summer sun beat down, and she took a deep breath before she started jogging back to her apartment.

Be rational. He'd said ex, right? Of course, he had an ex-girlfriend. Taylor wondered what she was like. She should've asked what the girl's name was. Why was he fighting over her? Did he still have feelings for her?

As she showered, she replayed the nagging doubts about Hunter, but there were so many unspoken questions. She took extra care with her makeup and hair, trying to look effortlessly beautiful. After changing outfits twice, she finally settled on a cute sundress and sandals. As she finished doing the dishes, the doorbell rang. She quickly turned off the water and dried her hands before answering it. Scott stood with a bright smile dressed in perfectly pressed khaki pants and a blue polo shirt. His brown hair was styled just right, and he held out a bouquet of vibrant wildflowers as his brows rose.

He looked her up and down, and she felt the heat of his stare, but it wasn't the same intensity as Hunter's gaze. Scott's look didn't send shivers down her spine or make the hairs on the back of her neck stand up. It left her wondering what that meant for their relationship.

"Wow, you're gorgeous. I forget how beautiful you are until I see you, then you take my breath away again."

She laughed as she took the flowers and opened the door wider. "Well, thank you. You're not so bad yourself, handsome. Let me put these in water, and then I'm ready to go."

Scott stepped inside, saying, "Nice place you have here."

She smiled and filled a vase. "Thanks. I've only been in a few weeks, thus the boxes behind the couch. I'll get to them eventually."

Scott put his hands in his pockets. "I moved into our house six years ago, and I still have boxes that need unpacked. I totally get it."

She nodded absently as she put the flowers on the coffee

table. Hunter's roses were still on the kitchen table and the flowers from their date were beside her bed.

"It's been so long since I've dated, I'm not sure what to say now," Scott said.

She chuckled, grabbing her purse from the table and was even more grateful to Hunter for coaching her in date etiquette. "Now I don't feel so bad for the awkward silence. Let's start with the basics. Where are we going?"

He shrugged. "There's a pizza place in town that has a pretty good evening buffet. Or we can run over to Denton for a nicer restaurant. What do you want to do?"

He opened the front door, and she stepped through, locking it behind them. "Pizza is fine with me. I haven't eaten there yet, but I hear it's decent."

They walked down the stairs. "Oh yeah, the girls love it."

He talked about his daughters as they drove the few minutes to the restaurant. It was a hole in the wall place with dim lighting and red booths. They sat in a corner, and the waiter stopped for their drink order.

The food was decent, and the conversation flowed easily, but it was mostly about his girls, baseball, the fire station, and his farm. After they ate, he asked about work at the library and college.

Before she knew it, the date was over, and they were walking out the door. His hand on the small of her back was warm, and he was such a gentleman. He even opened her door and helped her into his truck.

They drove back to her apartment, talking about funny stories from her college and his baseball days. When she unlocked her front door and turned to face him, her stomach knotted in nerves for the first time that night.

"I had a great time tonight," she said softly.

He smiled and took her hands in his. "Me too. I don't date a lot, and this was nice. Can I take you out next weekend too? Friday night this time?"

Her smile widened. "I'd like that."

He leaned in, and she tipped up her chin. His lips were warm and soft, hesitating before she felt his tongue. She opened her mouth, and their tongues danced.

In the back of her mind, she knew it was a good kiss. It could lead to a fun time, even if it didn't sweep her off her feet. Her stomach knotted, not able to put her finger on what the problem was.

He pulled back, ending the kiss with a soft peck on her lips, as if he didn't want to pull away. He squeezed her hands, then stepped back with a smile.

"I'll see you Monday with the girls at the library?"

She felt her lips and nodded before he walked back down the stairs. In a fog, she went inside, shutting and locking the door behind her before going to her bedroom, kicking her shoes off as she went. Her mind shied away from analyzing the date and comparing his with Hunter's.

Damn, it was only nine-thirty. She looked at her phone and saw a text from Lucy.

Hope the date goes well and is everything you wanted.

It was perfectly lovely. A week ago, it would've been everything she wanted from a first date.

She set her phone on the charger and went to the bathroom. After washing her face and brushing her teeth, she climbed into bed on her back and stared wide-eyed. She wanted to see the stars above her, feel that peace from the barn. What was wrong with her?

She'd had a perfectly lovely date, her first *real* date, and it was just... boring. She still had that itch under her skin, that feeling that something wasn't quite right.

Scott was great. He was the total package, a built-in family, a good father, a sexy firefighter, responsible and stable, and did she mention sexy? What did it say about her that she wasn't as excited about him as she should be?

He was a gentleman, bringing her flowers and kissing her at the door. His kiss was one of the better ones she'd had in her short life.

But he wasn't Hunter.

She sighed and groaned. Fucking hell. Was *that* what was wrong with her? She'd had a great night, a mature adult date, and she was aching for the bad cowboy who made her heart race and her body sing.

Thoughts of Hunter's bruised face made her catch her breath, and she imagined him growling above her, looking all dark and dangerous. The frustration from feeling slightly off about the whole date tonight combined with thoughts of Hunter had her reaching for the bedside table drawer.

She turned on her biggest vibrating wand—still not as big as Hunter—and slid it over her nipples, then down her stomach. Images of their night together in the barn flew through her mind. The way he'd spanked her. The way he'd called her a filthy slut.

Her orgasm built quickly, and her eyes fluttered in anticipation.

Then the doorbell rang.

She groaned and turned it off, tossing it onto the bed. Maybe it was a nosy neighbor? With a fling of the covers, she padded barefoot to the door and looked in the peephole.

Her heart raced and her jaw dropped, throwing open the door.

"Hunter? What—"

He eyed her hungrily, his black eye making him appear even more the bad boy.

"How'd the date go?" he asked as he strode inside like he owned the place.

She shut the door softly behind him, tugging her crop top down to cover more of her body. Why was she so nervous he was here? Why was he even here at all?

He sat at the kitchen table and bent to tug off his sneaker.

She frowned. "It went alright. What are you doing?"

The first shoe thumped to the floor, and he looked up, his eyes burning. "I saw you."

He leaned back over to tug off the other shoe.

She rubbed her temples, not sure she was ready for whatever this confrontation was. "Saw what? Hunter, I don't know what—"

He stood up in his socks, still in the gym shorts from earlier but now with a blue t-shirt too. He stalked toward her, pinning her to the front door with his hands on either side of her head. Her heart raced at his nearness.

"I saw you kissing him. I didn't like it," he growled.

Her eyes widened at the implications of his jealousy. "You were watching?"

He nodded, his eyes dipping to her lips. "I couldn't stop thinking about you on that damn date. After I finished beating both Parker and Nick up, I drove around until I couldn't stand it anymore. I watched him walk you up the stairs and kiss you. I prayed that you wouldn't invite him in."

She licked her lips. "I—I told you I wasn't going to. No fucking on the first date. That's what good girls do, and I'm turning over a new leaf, remember?"

He nodded, nestling his head into the crook of her neck. She felt her nipples pebble and goosebumps spread on her skin. Still, they weren't even touching, and she could feel her core aching for him.

"Yes, but you're not a good girl, are you? You're a dirty little slut, my little cum princess. Say it."

She whimpered. Fucking hell, what was this man doing to her? She'd agree to murder if it meant keeping this man forever.

"Fuck yes, I'm your little cum princess. Your dirty little slut. Whatever you want."

Chapter Twenty-Three

Taylor's heart raced as he picked her up, his calloused hands digging into her ass as she wrapped her arms and legs around him.

A last sliver of self-preservation made her murmur, "Hunter, I don't know if this is a good idea."

He grinned down at her and carried her into the bedroom. "Probably not, but can you tell me you don't want this?"

He tossed her on the bed, and she bounced with a squeal. When she settled, he was pulling his shirt over his head.

Her eyes drank in the sight of him in just his shorts, the play of shadows on his stomach mixing with the tattoos and bruised ribs made her lick her lips.

He smirked and shoved his shorts to the floor. "I'm waiting, Taylor. What do you want?"

He palmed his dick and stroked slowly. It was like a dam broke inside her, and her core flooded for him. Her heart raced, and she tugged her crop top over her head and tossed it aside.

"I want you." The truth of her statement reverberated through her body like a plucked guitar string. Vulnerability swept through her when she asked, "What do you want?"

His gaze raked hungrily down her bare breasts, growing darker in the dim light. "What I want is a taste of my favorite pot of honey. Shorts off, slut."

She gasped, loving the dirty talk and how he made her want to throw caution to the wind. With a quick shove, her booty shorts off were tossed to the floor as he knelt on the bed.

He leaned over and held up her wand with a grin. "What's this, princess?"

Heat rushed to her face as she tried to snatch it from his hand. He held it up, just out of reach, and her breasts to hit him in the shoulder before she crawled onto her knees.

She'd use her breasts to distract him, then take it back. God, how embarrassing. She arched closer to him, a nipple close to his lips as she reached for the vibrator.

"You dirty slut," he growled before he grabbed her hips and slid her to straddle his lap. His mouth latched onto her nipple, tugging and teasing. She gasped and grabbed his head, pulling him closer.

Her plan didn't work. She was the one distracted, not him. He bent her over, holding her back with one hand as he licked her nipple. Her back arched, and he laid her on the bed.

The movement brought his dick to her wet core. She planted her feet on the bed and bucked her hips, trying to get him closer, her nails raking down his back.

He sat up and grabbed her wrists, pinning them above her

head and holding them with one hand. His dick teased her entrance, and she licked her lips. "Now, now, my little honey pot needs to just sit back and take it like a good little slut."

She moaned at his words, her eyes flickering closed until the wand turned on. He pressed it straight to her clit, and she screamed, bucking her hips. His dick slid in slowly, stretching her impossibly wide and making her gasp.

Her pussy clenched around him, the wand vibrating constantly and not letting up. He crushed it between their bodies, holding it in place on her clit as he withdrew, then plunged back in.

He set up a furious tempo that had her gripping her pillow, struggling slightly against his grasp on her wrists. She had no idea how he knew exactly what her body and soul needed, but she wasn't going to look a gift horse in the mouth. She moaned, her breathing growing impossibly shallow as he fucked her so hard, she saw stars. The pressure built too fast, and she exploded with a scream.

The hand on her wrists moved, his palm covering her mouth. He kept fucking her hard through her orgasm. "That's my dirty little slut. Come for the beast."

His hand over her mouth pressed her into the pillow, and she felt another wave sweeping over her, her lashes fluttering. Another orgasm went over the first one, not giving her a break between. She clenched around his dick and screamed into his hand, her whole body convulsing.

This time he slowed to a stop and groaned as she squeezed him. When her spasms slowed, he pulled back and moved the wand, finally turning it off. She hissed in relief, and her muscles went slack.

He eased out and sat on the edge of the bed, opening her bedside table drawer. "Hm, interesting. I think we need to do some shopping because you're sorely missing out on lube and butt plugs. I'm going to the bathroom. When I come back, I want you on your hands and knees with two pillows under your hips and a blindfold on. Got it, princess?"

She panted and nodded as he went to the bathroom, aftershocks still echoing through her. She tried to control her breathing and make sense of what was happening. He'd said he couldn't date locals. Was she just a fuck buddy, then? She'd had a few of those in college, but it had been nothing like this.

She heard the toilet flush and flipped over, tugging two pillows under her. She grabbed her eye mask from under her pillow and waited. It seemed to take him forever to come back, but when he did, she felt goosebumps over her body.

His hands slid up her thighs, making her twitch. Her nipples ached, and she palmed their heaviness under her.

He hissed, "Yes, touch yourself. That's it."

She felt something cold slide inside, and she gasped.

"Is this your favorite dildo, princess? It can't possibly fill you up like I do. It's barely the size of a carrot."

She shook her head and whimpered. He turned on the vibrator and pressed it to her clit, making her legs jerk.

"Hold the wand where you like it, you dirty slut."

She took the wand and pressed it into the pillow, moaning. Then she felt something teasing her asshole. She gasped, automatically clenching.

"Easy, princess. Do you still want to try this? Yes or not?"

She licked her lips, her senses heightened behind the mask. Her inner muscles clenched on the dildo, and the vibrator was steadily pushing her toward another climax. Through it all, she knew she'd never trusted someone enough to try this. He knew so many of her darkest secrets, and she felt... safe enough to explore them. With him.

"Taylor?" He pressed against her asshole but didn't try to penetrate.

The waiting was driving her insane, and she nodded. "Yes, I—I want to try."

He groaned, and his need—the fact that he needed her—made her clench in response. "Good girl, now let's loosen you up and get you nice and relaxed."

A squirt, then his finger was back at her ass. It was wet and cold, but she ground back on it. His finger slid in past her sphincter, and she clenched again, pressing the wand to her clit and shuddering at the feeling.

"Oh god, that feels—that feels…"

She couldn't describe it. She had no words. It was incredible, the fullness was unlike anything she'd ever felt.

"God, I need to fuck that pussy again. Sorry, princess. You'll have to wait a little longer."

He slid the dildo out of her pussy and plunged his big dick in, making her scream into the pillow. She gripped the wand, the vibrations rocking her with his deep thrusts. Every thrust made his finger in her ass go deeper.

It was slow and deliberate, unlike the fast and furious pace earlier. When he removed his finger, she felt something else pressing against her asshole. She whimpered, forcing herself to remain relaxed.

He had it halfway in before she realized it was the smallest dildo. The tip finally went past her muscles as he thrust his big dick inside her pussy.

She pounded the bed with a fist. "Ow, ow, ow."

He slowed to a stop and held still before reaching around and pressing the wand to her clit. The vibrations distracted her from the pain in her ass, making her clench and grind down on it.

He leaned over her back and kissed her shoulder. "That's it, sugar. Open up for me. Feel how full you are? God, you're going to come so hard, you dirty little slut. Tell me when you're alright or if you want to stop."

He held still as she panted, her eyes closed as spots danced. She nodded, not trusting her voice. She didn't want to stop. No, something was already building inside her, and she wanted more.

"Gonna need the words, sugar."

Her body hummed, and she wiggled, gasping at the sensation of the thin dildo combined with his dick. "I— don't you dare stop."

He chuckled, "That's my girl." Her pussy clenched at his words, and he began to rock gently, each time making the dildo go deeper in her ass. He pressed the wand on her clit. The vibrations, the incredible fullness, it made her see stars.

She groaned as he rocked. He had been impossibly huge before, but with the dildo... oh god, it hurt so good. She widened her hips, wanting to take him into her soul and never let go. She stretched and melted around him and the dildo.

He groaned. "God, that's it. You took it all. Such a good little cum princess. Now it's an easy ride from here on."

His words made the waves rise higher. Her heart raced with each deep penetration. His hand ran over her ass, alternating between gentle caresses and sharp slaps that sent tingling sensations through her body.

Heat streaked through her as he thrust into her slowly, filling her to the brim and making her walls clench around him. He hit all the right spots within her, stretching her to the limit and making her back arch in pleasure. His grasp on her hip tightened as he continued to claim her with slow, possessive strokes.

She had no doubt he was claiming her, and she surrendered to the sensation, losing herself in the feeling of his touch, the movement of their bodies. Every nerve ending was on fire, and she pushed back against him, wanting more, needing him with an intensity that scared her. She whimpered as she neared the peak.

"Yes, that's it. So tight for a fucking dirty slut."

She clenched and gasped at his words. An orgasm slammed into her like a train, stealing her breath. Her teeth clenched and toes curled as it hit full force. Her body spasmed around him, convulsing like a madwoman as she screamed into the pillow.

He groaned behind her, burying to the hilt as he tensed. "Fuck yes," he hissed, spilling into her with a swelling heat that made her moan. Every pulse sent her clenching around him, and her body milked him with an animal satisfaction that left her sated and replete.

The aftershocks rippled through her, making her squeeze and gasp. His arm around her moved the wand, and she sank to the bed with jelly in her veins. It dislodged him, but she didn't care. She couldn't move, could barely breathe.

She felt him clean her and remove the dildo. She sighed in relief, but still didn't move, didn't even care when he went back to the bathroom and cleaned her everywhere—even her ass—with a warm washcloth. She was safe, even in this, and just soaked up his care and attention. When he returned, pulling her into his arms and turning them on their sides to spoon, she sighed in contentment.

Her mind lazily came back to earth, but she was too

exhausted from the roller coaster of being with him to talk. He'd shown up all growly and possessive, and she'd just laid there and taken that dick like the slut she really was.

She wanted to feel guilty but couldn't gather the strength for it. Instead, her mind turned to what him showing up really meant. Did he want to date her now? Was that what the jealousy meant? Did he have feelings for her too, or was it all just one-sided?

She blinked, a trip in her breathing. Oh fuck, she had feelings for him! Of course she did. To most, he was a wholesome, family-oriented cowboy—but underneath he had a wild, bad-boy streak as wide as the Red River.

Falling for him felt inevitable, but a frisson of worry ate at her gut. What if she *was* just a fuck buddy, a convenience because she was here? What if he was trying to use her to get back at his ex-girlfriend? What if he was just trying to make his ex jealous?

She sighed, her bones still practically liquid from the mind-numbing orgasms. What if this was all they had? Just this great sex?

Her mind finally settled into sleep, but her dreams were filled with being abandoned in a field of bluebonnets, Hunter walking away. No matter how much she chased him, he never looked back and never got closer.

Chapter Twenty-Four

Hunter stared out Taylor's window, unable to see anything in the darkness outside through the curtains. He was an idiot. His life was about to take a major turn, what with Jewel and possibly being a dad.

And what did he do? Show up and fuck Taylor's brains out.

He couldn't drag her down with him. Why had he even come here? He was a mess, and she had a good thing going with her date. She should see that guy again and move on. Get married, have babies and the white picket fence.

The pressure on his chest tightened at the thought.

What would she gain by even being with Hunter? He had nothing to offer. He didn't have a house of his own. He lived in the fucking bunk house. His mama still cooked all his meals, for fuck's sake.

As he carefully extracted his arm from under her slumbering form, she shifted onto her side, tucking a hand under her cheek and pulling one leg up. He palmed her ass, and she hummed in contentment in her sleep.

The drape of the sheet, her position... it reminded him of the night they'd first met. When he'd dropped her off after the bar and she'd been half-naked, it had rocked his world. He was still reeling, trying to pick up the pieces of his formerly well-ordered life. Was that only two weeks ago? Fuck.

He tugged on his shorts and searched for his socks. Finally, he gave up and slipped on his shoes without them. He couldn't find his shirt either but didn't want to turn on a light and risk waking her.

He walked out the door, locking it behind him. Each step down the stairs rang in his ears like a hammer on a coffin. His focus had to be on Jewel, his maybe daughter, and the ranch. He couldn't keep doing this dance with Taylor. She deserved better.

The thin light of dawn was just lightening the sky to a soft gray when he arrived back on the ranch. He didn't even bother going to the bunk house. Instead, he went straight to the barn and checked on the mares and foals.

All was fine, but he started on the morning chores anyway. There was something therapeutic in cleaning out the stalls. It helped clear his mind and made his muscles burn.

By the time breakfast was ready and other hands were showing up, he'd finished nearly everything. He went to the bunk house for a shower, scrubbing twice and trying to keep his mind clear.

But thoughts of the mysterious daughter kept warring with Taylor. He went to church that morning with his brain in a fog and a twitch in his eye.

He walked around the pews to the stage and sat behind the drums, exhaustion licking at his heels. Eventually Landry and Gunner showed up with their families. When

Landry took the microphone to start worship, Hunter picked up the drumsticks.

Absentmindedly, he looked at the list Landry had left on the drums, and they began to sing and play the first song. His mind wandered throughout it as people slowly took their seats. Stragglers came through the door.

Including Jewel, Gemma, and their dad. Jewel's daughter—he couldn't bring himself to claim the kid yet—was still out of town. Jewel looked good in her wrap dress and sandals. She'd matured into a stunning woman much like Gemma.

But Hunter's hand remained steady along with his heart. She just didn't do it for him anymore. The song ended, and he looked slowly over the congregation as Landry talked.

His gaze paused on Lucy and Helen's row because there at the end sat Taylor. His heart seemed to slow, but then Landry looked at him.

Hunter took a quick breath and began the next song, his eyes going from Taylor to Jewel and back again.

Taylor's black hair sat in a high, sleek ponytail. Her black sundress had yellow sunflowers on it and hugged all her curves, the v accentuating her full breasts. She stared at him with a soft smile on her face, and he frowned, looking away as he missed a beat.

He stared at Jewel, and his hand steadied. His anger was mostly gone this morning, but maybe he was just too tired to care about all she'd done.

She'd stolen fifteen years of his life with his daughter. He thought about all the firsts he'd missed with her, imagining his toddler nieces and nephew.

All he felt now was sadness at the missed years and

apprehension about meeting the girl. He needed to ask Jewel what her name was, what she was like.

The song ended, and Landry led them straight into another. It was more upbeat and kept his attention more, which he was grateful for.

He deliberately avoided looking at Taylor again. When the worship service was over, he went to the opposite side of the church to sit in his family's row. He stayed on the end, beating Chase to the coveted spot by the aisle.

Chase rolled his eyes and sat beside him. They both stretched out their legs, Hunter sticking one in the aisle and almost reaching the wall. He could feel eyes on him, but he stared straight ahead.

They would be watching him to see how he talked to Jewel. He had no idea how he could avoid it, but he had to be cordial. He would have to greet her and her family just to show the rest of the old biddies in church that they had all moved on. They were mature adults who weren't worth gossiping about.

The pastor spoke about forgiveness, and the woman at the well. Hunter felt his lips turning into a smirk by the end of the sermon, and he caught Chase's laughing eyes, his grin wide. Hunter snorted and shrugged.

They'd agreed not to talk about the daughter thing or the possibility of Chase being the dad for the time being. Not to their family or to anyone else.

When the pastor closed the service, Hunter went back on stage with his brothers for the final song. He kept his gaze straight, looking over everyone's heads as they finished.

He finally set the drumsticks down and stalled on stage. Did he really have to talk to Jewel publicly?

He looked at the side door then saw Ma waiting at the

bottom of the stage, her arms crossed and foot tapping, staring at him impatiently.

He sighed, and Parker finished unplugging his guitar. He looked from Hunter to Ava and back again, then grinned.

"Looks like someone's in trouble," he said in a sing-song voice.

"Shut it," Hunter grumbled as he stepped down the couple of steps to their mom.

She smiled with tight lips. "There you are. You need to put all the rumors to rest. Everyone's waiting for you and Jewel to have another big fight, so play nice."

He ducked his head and sighed. "Yes, ma'am."

He followed her down the aisle, frustration mounting. It'd been fifteen years, and they couldn't let it go? Jeez, they needed to—

Well, he was probably preaching to the choir. He needed to let it go too, didn't he?

Ava turned and wove through the mingling crowd to the front of the church foyer. Jewel shook the pastor's hand in front of the open door, but behind her was Taylor.

They three of them were talking animatedly, and Hunter's stomach flipped. He felt like each step was lead weights around his ankles.

Jewel moved outside, and Taylor shook the pastor's hand before going outside too. Hunter avoided the pastor and followed them.

At the bottom of the church steps, people mingled and chatted. Several gave him the side-eye before looking away. He hated being the center of attention, but there was only one way to conquer his nerves. He had to do what he had to do.

The Cowboy Gets His Girl

Jewel spied him over Taylor's shoulder and smiled. He walked over to join them and nodded with a frown.

"Jewel, Taylor."

Jewel's brows rose. "Oh, you two know each other? I wasn't sure. I was about to introduce you." She laughed nervously.

Hunter met Taylor's deep green eyes. The soft smile on her lips was secretive. She was a mischievous little minx and based on her arched brow, he had a pretty good idea of what she was thinking about.

Taylor said, "Oh yes, we met a few weeks ago at the Electric Cowboy. He took me home."

"Oh," Jewel said, her face falling.

Taylor frowned, looking at Jewel. "How do y'all know each other? I assume you grew up here with everyone else?"

Jewel nodded and put her hand on Hunter's forearm, stepping closer. "Yeah, we dated for five years before I went to college."

Taylor's eyes widened, and she took a half-step back. "Oh, I see. And now you're back in town."

It wasn't a question, but Jewel nodded anyway, a smile on her face as she started talking about joining her dad in his vet practice.

Hunter tried to swallow past the knot in his throat. His feet were glued to the ground, and he couldn't pull away. Jewel's hand on his arm was burning like a brand, but he couldn't move no matter how much he shouted poems at himself.

Taylor's expression seemed to close, and she folded her hands demurely in front of her. The soft summer breeze ruffled the hem of her dress at her knees, and she shifted on her feet.

"That's so exciting. I'm kinda jealous that you have such an amazing dad and sister to work with," Taylor said.

Lucy called her name, and Taylor looked over her shoulder. She waved and turned back to them with a smile. "I've gotta go. My ride is calling. It was so nice to meet you, Jewel. And Hunter... it was good seeing you again."

The flash of vulnerability on her face was so quick, Hunter wasn't sure it'd been real. Then she was turning on her heels to cross the parking lot to Lucy's car. *His chest ached as she turned to go, and with her, all his hope faded to a dull glow.*

"She's so sweet. I'm glad I'm not the only new girl in town," Jewel said with a forced chuckle.

When Taylor shut the car door, he seemed to come awake and finally pulled away, turning to face Jewel with a frown.

"You're not new," he said.

She shrugged. "Fifteen years is a long time to be gone."

Hunter nodded, spying Chase loitering on the edge of the crowd. No one talked to him, many of them still afraid simply because he'd gone to prison. No matter that he grew up in this church. No matter that many of the old ladies had changed his diaper and taught him Sunday School.

Jewel looked over to where Hunter was staring, and her voice softened, "We can't just let him be left out. Come on."

Hunter snorted as they started to walk. "Is that how it went? You felt sorry for him being left out?"

Jewel gritted her teeth and smiled as they passed a group of people. She lowered her voice to whisper, "I told you. It was an accident and just happened."

Hunter didn't even bother to reply. It was ridiculous.

Jewel smiled brightly at his brother when they approached. "Hey Chase."

"Hey," he replied, his sunglasses keeping his stony expression hidden.

They stood in awkward silence for a few minutes, then Jewel sighed. "Well, so much for breaking the ice and learning to get along again."

Hunter snorted. "Did you think this was going to be easy?"

"No, but I didn't think it'd be this hard. We were best friends for five years."

Hunter looked down at her. "We were more than that."

Chase nodded behind her. "Your dad's coming this way."

Jewel turned and smiled, her lips wobbly now.

Henry was a balding, gruff man who reminded Hunter of his mom. They were both abrupt, brutally honest people who didn't have time for lallygagging or gossiping.

"Boys," he said. "We're going to your place for lunch. Wanted to give you a heads up."

Hunter and Chase both nodded, but Jewel frowned. "Is that a good idea?"

Henry shrugged. "How should I know? This is your shit show, dear. You made your bed, and now you gotta lie in it."

He turned to Hunter. "I hear she finally told you about Destini."

Hunter took a deep breath, his heart jumping again with an irregular rhythm he was all too familiar with. He nodded, ignoring the panic clawing at him.

At least he finally had a name. "Yes, sir."

"I expect you to do the right thing, son. Including back child support."

Hunter frowned, his throat closing up again. All he could do was nod.

Henry nodded too. "Good. That's that then. Destini is a

good kid with a good head on her shoulders. You'll like her once she moves to town. I'm going to round up Gemma though. I'm hungry."

He walked off, and Jewel turned back to the two of them, her eyes shining in the sun.

"I didn't tell him about Chase. I didn't tell Gemma either."

Chase's crossed arms dropped to his sides. "No one knows she might be mine?"

Jewel shook her head, looking down at the ground.

Hunter swallowed hard. "I guess we'll just keep acting like she's mine? Since it's what you want anyway and what everyone in town expects."

Jewel bit her lip. "Yeah, but I don't expect you to pay child support, despite what he says. Don't even worry about that yet."

Hunter raked a hand on his jaw, the stubble abrasive. "Do we even need the paternity test, then?"

Chase's hands fisted at his sides. "Yes, we do. I need to know."

Jewel finally looked up at Chase, her eyes sad. She sighed, putting on her sunglasses. "That's fine then. We'll do the test when she comes back from camp, and then we'll know. I guess Dad will say something to your folks now about Destini."

Hunter nodded, and Henry called for Jewel. She gave one last sad smile and walked to his truck.

Chase crossed his arms again, saying belligerently, "If she's mine, I need to know."

Hunter clapped him on the back. "I know, but you know I'm right. It'll be easier if she's mine."

Chase didn't say anything, and together they went to his Jeep to drive back to the ranch.

Chapter Twenty-Five

Hunter slammed the door on the Jeep and jumped out. They'd beat Henry so he went inside to help Ma. He pushed the front door open, and the smell of garlic bread hit his nose.

His stomach growled, reminding him that he'd not eaten breakfast. He joined his mom in the kitchen. She closed the oven, a hot baking sheet in her hand, and turned to set it on the counter.

"Finish the dishes for me? The spaghetti is simmering now, so we're just waiting on the noodles to boil."

He opened the dishwasher and started putting things away. He cleared his throat, the need to confess to her pressing on him.

"Ma, there's something you should know before they get here." He pulled out a glass baking pan and bent to put it in the cabinet.

"Is it that Jewel has a teenager, and she's probably yours?"

Hunter almost dropped the pan, then took a deep

breath and put it up. "Yeah," he said gruffly. "I didn't know about her though, I swear."

"I know you didn't. I had my suspicions and asked Henry about it when I saw him last week. He told me about her. How are you taking it?"

Hunter shrugged, putting up the silverware. "About as you'd expect."

She chuckled as she stirred the pot on the stove. "That bad, eh? Well, can't say I don't blame you. I'm proud of how you talked with her at church. That was an important step for you two."

Hunter turned on the water to scrub the dirty dishes from breakfast. "I know, but Ma, please don't push us together again. That ship has sailed."

"But you make such a good couple," she said. "And if you have a kid together—"

"Ma, it's not going to work," he growled.

"But why not? You haven't even tried yet."

"We're two completely different people than we were fifteen years ago, Ma. Two people who aren't meant to be."

"Psh, what do you know? You haven't even spent two minutes in her company since she's been back."

He didn't respond, instead putting the dishes in the dishwasher. She might not listen to him until the paternity test, and what was the point in arguing with her anyway? Perhaps she just needed to see the two of them together to see there were no sparks left.

Ava sighed as Henry's truck pulled up outside. "You owe it to your daughter to try, Hunter. If she can have a two-parent household, wouldn't that be best for her?"

Hunter cleaned the sink, his brain too tired to process her words quickly. He supposed there was a kernel of truth to it, but he had no interest in starting things up with Jewel again.

The front door opened, and Henry came inside, followed by Gemma and Jewel. Ava went to welcome them, Chase came down the stairs, and Bill came out of the den. It was loud and chaotic as they all talked over one another.

Hunter turned and stirred the spaghetti, ignoring them all and trying to think. He honestly hadn't thought about what Destini might need at all. He was such a shitty dad already.

Ava came back, bustling around and encouraging everyone to line up as she pulled down plates and set them on the counter.

"Henry, will you say grace? Then we can eat," she said, turning off the stove.

They bowed their heads.

"Thank you, God, for this meal and the cooks who prepared it. Let it nourish our bodies. Thank you for family and friends and laughter. Let it nourish our hearts. And thank you for sweet tea and caffeine. Let it nourish our minds and keep us sharp. Amen."

They all laughed, and talk resumed as each grabbed a plate and loaded it with food. Somehow Jewel ended up sitting between him and Chase.

He didn't say anything, just dug into his food and ate like it was his last meal. What was he supposed to say? Talk revolved mostly around the ranch and the new foals.

"You did a great job with the breeding program this year," Henry said.

Ava nodded at Hunter. "It was mostly Hunter this year. I'm working hard on relaxing more."

Jewel cocked her head. "I don't think those are supposed to go together. Working hard and relaxing?"

Ava chuckled and took a bite of food, but Bill cut in. "Doctor's orders. She twisted an ankle last year, and it took longer to heal than he liked. If she would've stayed off it like she was supposed to, it would've been fine."

Ava scowled at Bill across the table, but he just winked at her as she replied. "I did what I had to do. We were busy, and life doesn't stop just because I had to hobble around."

"What's this I hear about a camping trip out here somewhere for the kids at the school?" Henry asked.

Gemma's face lit up. "It's going to be so cool. Parker and the school counselor thought it'd be a great opportunity to get more teenagers outside. It's supposed to help with bonding without screens."

Ava nodded. "Parker's really excited about it, but he's been working with Hunter to set it all up."

Hunter looked up, freezing to see all eyes on him. "Um, it's still in the planning phase. We don't have all the details yet."

Bill pursed his lips. "Well, you better get to talking with Parker because it's in October."

Ava continued, "Then there's the Halloween party to organize as well as sorting next year's breeding plan and starting training for the two-year-olds."

Hunter nodded, taking a bite of bread to keep from having to reply. It was a lot to manage, but he had most of it all in his head already. It was too bad most of what they needed was on the computer.

Chase cleared his throat. "I can help with that."

Bill and Ava shared a look and shook their heads. Bill smiled and dipped his bread in the sauce on his plate. "That'd be great, but you don't have to. We'll get it handled. Besides, I don't think you can be involved with the kids camping trip."

Chase clenched the napkin in his hand. "You mean with my prison record?"

"Chase," Ava chided.

Chase shrugged, leaning back in his chair. "What? Not talking about it isn't going to make it go away, Mom."

Ava sighed, but it was Henry who snorted. "Got that right. I feel like that with the whole Destini thing."

"Dad!" Jewel hissed.

Henry shrugged. "Like he said. Not talking about it isn't going to make it go away. Camp ends in a few weeks, doesn't it? She'll need to get registered for school."

Jewel bit her lip and nodded, looking down at her plate and pushing her noodles around.

"What grade will she be in?" Hunter asked, surprising even himself with the question.

"Tenth grade."

Silverware scraped and clanged as the conversation paused. No one said anything, but he felt their eyes. Hunter asked, "What's she like?"

Jewel twisted her noodles on her fork absently. "She loves soccer. Parker's going to be impressed when he sees her at try-outs. Good kid. Average grades except she's a math and science whiz. She's already finished all her math requirements for high school and wants to take some college math classes in the fall. I told her maybe in the spring after she gets used to the new school."

Jewel's words were rushed, and her cheeks were pink as she talked. But the more she talked about her, the more Hunter relaxed.

"Do you have any pictures?" Ava asked.

Jewel reached for her phone and swiped. "Of course, I didn't even think. I'm so sorry. This is us a few weeks ago at the water park in Houston. And this is at NASA. She loves the stars. That's where she's at, the NASA summer camp."

She turned the phone to show Ava, tilting it so that Chase could see too.

Hunter's stomach rolled at the information overload. If she was such a good student, maybe she was Chase's kid after all. Lord knows she'd barely read if she was his kid. Chase was the genius of the family, not him.

But then again, he did love studying the stars. The phone turned, and he caught his first glimpse of her. She had big, beautiful eyes that twinkled with laughter. It reminded him of Jewel as a kid.

Except her eyes were the same hazel as his, all his brothers, and his dad. She had their jaw and wide nose, too.

She had Jewel's hair though, all wild and curly. She wore a bright pink crop top with a green alien wearing a cowboy hat and black skinny jeans.

A knock on the door led to one of the ranch hands opening it and sticking his head around the corner.

"Sorry to bother y'all at dinner, but Medusa is foaling. It's going well, but I thought you'd want to know."

They all stood up, but Ava laughed. "No, let's finish eating. Hunter, you and Jewel go check on her. Let us know if you need a hand."

Hunter met Jewel's gaze, and she blushed. He pushed back his chair and wiped his mouth with his napkin. Then he nodded and walked out without a word.

Jewel caught the door after him, and Trent waited at the foot of the porch stairs.

Hunter asked, "How long has she been foaling?" He thought back to this morning. He'd been distracted, but she had shown no signs when he'd checked. Then again, this was her second foal, so maybe it was going faster than expected.

Trent shrugged. "Not long. Just a few hours, but she's getting restless."

Together the three of them strode across the yard to the barn. Trent held the door for them, and he strode down the aisle.

Hunter looked around, but Trent said, "She's in the corral. I didn't think she needed to be cooped up yet."

They walked to the opposite end and pushed open the door to the corral. Medusa was a brown and red mare who was prancing and throwing her head.

Jewel started crooning to her, walking slow and steady.

Hunter turned and pointed to the right. "You go right, I'll go left. Let's see if she'll let us touch her and get her calmed down."

Trent nodded and went right. Hunter circled the edge of the corral, keeping his eyes on the horse the entire time. Jewel got close, but Medusa just pranced away. It took time, but the horse didn't want Jewel. Hunter didn't blame her. Jewel was a stranger.

He started singing softly, and Medusa's head swiveled toward him.

"That's it, girl. I'm right here. You're doing so good. Such a good girl, aren't you? Will you let me hold you?"

The horse shook her head, and he chuckled. "I promise to make it worth your while."

Jewel snorted, and Trent grinned.

"Come on, girl. You'll feel better if you let me hold you. That's it. Remember last time? You know you're gonna be a mama again, don't ya? This is going to be so much easier than last time. Trust me. You're older and wiser now. Come here, girl. Let's get this show on the road."

He eased closer, and Medusa kept shaking her head and prancing, but she let him get close and touch her neck. He rubbed her softly, singing as Jewel came up behind him.

"This is my friend, Jewel. She's going to help make this easier. You'll like that, won't ya, girl?"

She finally let Jewel touch her as Hunter walked with her slowly around the corral. It reminded him of when she'd been a foal herself. He'd focused on the training aspect back then.

"Has she always had anxiety?" Jewel asked, feeling a contraction ripple through Medusa.

Hunter nodded. "Yeah, she's always been spirited and testy. One reason we kept her instead of selling her. She's too jumpy."

"She's still got a few hours to go, maybe not even until tomorrow, but I can give her something for anxiety. Helping her relax might help the birth go smoother. Then again, it also might draw it out longer. It's up to you."

Hunter frowned. "Is there a time limit on when you'd need to give it to her?"

Jewel shook her head, so he said, "Let's just wait then and see how she does."

An hour passed with a blur. Both Henry and Gemma came and checked on the progress before they left. Gemma brought the vet bag and left it inside the barn.

Jewel and Hunter talked about old times and kept Medusa outside until the thunder rolled in. Then Jewel gave her the shot for anxiety before they led her into a stall inside. The storm hit like the bottom of the clouds had been ripped open. Rain pelted the barn, but inside they were focused on helping Medusa.

The more they talked about old times, the easier it began to feel like his friend had returned. Gunner was two years younger than him, and his earliest memories were of playing outside with Gemma and Jewel. They were the best of friends, before their hormones got in the way.

He didn't feel as tense around her and his emotions calmed down.

Of course, most of that was because he was focusing on Medusa and their conversation was about happier times. There weren't expectations for him to say the right thing or do the right thing because he wasn't focused on Jewel.

Eventually Chase came into the barn, drenched from the rain and carrying a tray of food.

"Ma sent y'all dinner. Are you in a good spot to eat?"

Jewel stepped out of the stall and grabbed some hand sanitizer, nodding. "Yeah, I think so. She's resting now from the anxiety medicine. She might even get a few hours of sleep before the next stage of labor kicks in."

Chase set the tray on a bale of hay outside the row of stalls, and Jewel walked down the aisle to him. Hunter stayed with Medusa. Chase and Jewel were just a few feet away, but their voices were soft and hushed compared to the pounding rain outside.

He had no desire to hear them. They had some shit to work out too. There was no jealousy, and the only feeling he had was to worry that Chase might get hurt. Hunter wanted to protect his little brother, like always. He crooned to Medusa and let them have their time together.

Chapter Twenty-Six

"Are you sure you're up for this? I mean, you only moved to town a few weeks ago," Helen asked, leaning against the librarian's desk.

Taylor sat behind it, clicking on the computer and writing notes with her favorite pen.

Taylor smiled tightly and nodded. "I'm sure. This will be awesome, and a great way to get kids reading, don't you think?"

Helen crossed her arms and waved a hand. "That's true. They need to get off their phones."

Taylor picked up her phone for the hundredth time that week, hoping for a message from Hunter. He'd acted like they meant nothing to each other at church on Sunday.

And it was fine. It really was. Hadn't they said it was just a practice date? That's what she'd told herself all afternoon on Sunday.

But it didn't make sense. Why had he really come over on Saturday night? Why was he so jealous of Scott?

Monday, she'd finally broken down and texted him to

ask if he wanted to hang out on her day off on Tuesday or Wednesday. He hadn't responded.

She'd had her appointment with Tasha on Tuesday, and she'd helped her process the fact that Hunter had not texted her back or called her. But not even Tasha could tell her why he'd come over on Saturday night and broken their one and done agreement.

It was bullshit, but she wasn't sure why the radio silence hurt so much. She knew it was going to happen. This is why she hadn't dated anyone before, right? This was exactly why she wanted to stop sleeping around so much and have a proper relationship. She was so tired of feeling used afterwards. It just hurt too much. Although... most of the time, she was using them too.

She'd thought it had been different with Hunter. She'd caught feelings for him so fast. Too bad he obviously hadn't reciprocated. She pushed thoughts of him away, ignoring the pain and focusing on the man who *did* want her.

She scrolled to her texts and smiled at Scott's latest message.

Can't wait for our date tonight.

The bright spot of her week had been seeing him and the girls on Monday. They flirted and laughed. It had been simple and uncomplicated. When he'd texted her later that day, he'd said he wanted to kiss her but didn't feel comfortable doing that in front of the girls.

Lucy said it was standard for dates to text or call two days after. He was right on time.

She'd talked to Tasha about him too. Maybe love was supposed to grow on you, like planting a flower or tree or something. Maybe it wasn't supposed to be this grand passion that sweeps her off her feet. Maybe it was supposed to be simple and uncomplicated.

Now it was Friday, date night, but she wasn't nervous at all.

The phone vibrated in her hand, the caller ID staring her in the face. Damn it, she'd gotten another call from the jail, which she ignored. She was more emotional and on edge from her dad's drama than from the Hunter and Scott side of life.

She looked up, seeing Lucy and Helen looking at her expectantly. What had they been talking about? She looked back at the computer screen and remembered what she'd been doing.

Lucy bounced Harry on her hip and frowned. "You've never been camping before. It's a disaster in the making, Tay. You have no idea what you're signing up for."

Taylor paused and leaned back in her seat, tapping her pen against her lip.

"Not roughing it camping, but all those years at Girl Scout camp should count for something, right? Besides, Tasha and Parker have worked out all the details. I'm really just there to chaperone, talk about books, and get the kids excited about reading."

Helen held out her arms, and Harry practically leaped into them. "Well, at least you have some time to prepare for it. We can take you to the fishing spot on the river more over the next few weeks so at least you know how to handle the mosquitoes and bugs."

Taylor nodded. "That'd be great. Thanks for looking out for me."

Helen smiled, cooing at Harry. "Don't mention it, dear. Smells like you need a diaper change, little man."

Helen walked away, and Taylor sniffed.

Lucy narrowed her eyes. "What? He didn't smell that bad."

Taylor shrugged, putting her phone down and ignoring another call. "It's not him. It's just y'all are the best. Like the family I never had."

Lucy leaned on the desk and crossed her arms almost mirroring Helen's pose from earlier. "What's going on? Why are you tearing up?" Lucy asked softly.

Taylor wiped an eye and clicked on the computer, compiling her list from their records. "It's nothing. Just feeling emotional today."

"Why? You're not the emotional type."

She knew Lucy wouldn't let it go. She was laser focused, and the way she was staring so intently...

Taylor sighed and leaned back, knowing she couldn't distract her friend anymore. "My dad called from jail a few days ago. And again just now. I'm just worried about him, I guess. It's stressing me out."

Lucy sighed, and there was a wealth of understanding in that sound. It told Taylor that she wasn't surprised. She knew how much it would eat at Taylor.

"Do you want to go visit him?"

Taylor shook her head, wiping her eye. "No, absolutely not. That's a disaster waiting to happen. If I did, I'd spiral."

"Are you going to bail him out?"

"Can't. I'm out of money from moving and paying his rent a few weeks ago."

Lucy winced but didn't say anything, and Taylor knew exactly what she meant by that silence too. But instead of berating her like Taylor expected, Lucy wrapped her arms around her back in an awkward side hug.

Taylor's shoulders fell from the weight of responsibility. She used to want her dad to take care of her like a parent should, but now she just wanted him to take care of himself like a real adult. She didn't want to take care of her dad.

Life meant not always getting what you wanted though. She'd thought about blocking the number from jail for good, but she couldn't quite bring herself to do it.

That made her even more upset. Was it so wrong to want him to just stop mooching off her? She turned back to the computer, and Lucy pulled away. She couldn't give in to tears, not with her date tonight.

"There's nothing I can do right now. I'll just keep ignoring his calls. In other news, I have a second date with Scott tonight."

Lucy didn't say anything, and Taylor looked up at her. Lucy's brow was arched, but Taylor pursed her lips, staring her down and refusing to look away.

Finally, Lucy sighed. "Fine, we'll change topics, but this isn't over, Tay. I'm here for you, okay?"

Taylor nodded and turned back to the computer.

"As for the date tonight, what are your plans?" Lucy asked.

"What do you mean?"

"What are you going to wear? Where are you going? A second date is a big deal for you. Are you going to put out?"

Taylor shifted on the chair and leaned back again, tapping her chin with her pen.

"I'm going to wear a mini skirt and heels. I don't know where we're going. And I don't know."

"Really? The girl who puts out to thank a guy for a drink doesn't know if a second date will lead to sex?"

Taylor scowled. "That was one time, and he was smokin' hot."

Lucy laughed, and Taylor relaxed. "I read somewhere about a baseball strategy for dates. First date is a kiss, second is above the clothes, third is under the clothes fooling around, and fourth date is the homerun full-on sex, so we'll see."

Lucy snorted. "Think you'll hold out that long?"

Taylor shrugged and leaned back in the chair. "Honestly, I have no idea. I've been going to Tasha for counseling. I talked to her about sleeping around and wanting to become a better person. I don't want to be that person anymore, regardless of how fun it was. I want a family, stability, and unconditional love. I want what you and Mason have, Luce."

Lucy tilted her head. "What about with Hunter?"

Taylor picked at her nails and frowned. "It's complicated."

"How so?"

She rubbed her forehead. "So last Saturday, Scott and I kissed, but I didn't really feel that much. Sure, I probably could've slept with him and had fun, but I wasn't overwhelmed with passion. My heart didn't flutter or jump. I didn't get hot and flushed, just a nice hum of contentment."

"I hear a but in there," Lucy said.

Taylor frowned and rocked in the chair, her mind thinking about last weekend. "Well, after the date with Scott, Hunter showed up."

Lucy gasped. "What? Why?"

Taylor's cheeks heated, and her leg bounced with nerves. "He was jealous. He'd seen me kiss Scott on the doorstep of my apartment. When Scott left, Hunter came up and one thing led to another."

She shrugged. She wasn't going to beat herself up over enjoying another night with Hunter, even if it did complicate things.

Lucy frowned. "That was Saturday night. We went to

church on Sunday, but you said Hunter had acted like your date hadn't happened."

Taylor nodded.

"God, Tay, why didn't you say anything to me on Sunday?"

Taylor shrugged again. "Mason was home. You needed the time with him, what with him working so much lately and Harry teething."

Lucy put her hand on Taylor's shoulder. "That doesn't mean you don't get to tell me stuff."

Taylor arched a brow. "That's a double negative. Who are you, and where's Lucy?"

Lucy laughed, making Taylor smile. "I'm just saying that there are no secrets between us. You just said we're family, and family talks to each other. Don't wait to tell me what's going on, Tay. I'm here for you no matter the mommy brain fog, the tiredness, or whatever else I've got going on, okay?"

Taylor felt tears threaten again, and she nodded. "Fine," she leaned her head back and closed her eyes.

Lucy prodded her shoulder. "Now back to Hunter…"

Taylor sighed, but otherwise didn't move. "Hunter ignored me at church after fucking my brains out the night before. He actually snuck out while I was still asleep. He hasn't texted me, so I texted him. He hasn't responded."

Taylor paused, but Lucy didn't interrupt. She took a deep breath, trying to get a handle on the facts. It was easier to push the emotions down if she just focused on the facts.

"He acted pretty chummy with his ex-girlfriend, Jewel. She seems sweet, but I haven't heard one way or another if he's getting back together with her. Scott, on the other hand, *has* texted. He's sweet, funny, and we had a great time last weekend on our date."

The Cowboy Gets His Girl

"But none of the feels?" Lucy asked softly.

Taylor looked up at her friend. "Right, there's not a lot of chemistry there. I can't stop thinking about Hunter, but I feel like that's a lost cause, so now I'm going to focus on my date tonight, ignore my feelings for Hunter, and not think or worry about my dad."

Helen came back with Harry, who was rubbing his eyes. "He's all cleaned up but might be getting tired."

Lucy held her hands out, and Harry tried to jump into them. Taylor smiled, wondering what it'd be like to have her own kid someday. She'd not spent a lot of time with babies, not until Harry, but she wouldn't mind having a few someday. She tried to picture herself with Scott, but it was like a blank wall. She couldn't picture his home life or what a life with him would be like day in and day out.

She just didn't know him well enough. She pursed her lips. It was just a second date, not a lifetime commitment. She might have to date dozens of guys before finding someone to settle down with.

Someone to love.

Lucy picked up the diaper bag at the end of the desk. "Alright, we're going to head home for a nap. But you better call me first thing tomorrow morning, alright? I want to hear all the details of your date this time. No more waiting days to spill it, okay?"

Taylor chuckled and nodded. "Deal. Love ya."

Lucy walked to the door, saying over her shoulder, "Love y'all too."

When she was gone, Helen looked at the clock. "We have a few hours left. What's your plan?"

Taylor nodded to the computer, sitting up and grabbing her pen again. "I'm going to finish planning out this camping trip. I've settled on a theme based on what Tasha has said about the kids who've been invited. What are you going to do?"

Helen walked toward the back. "I'll inventory the new books that came in, then I'll dust the shelves."

Taylor nodded and scrolled on the computer.

Chapter Twenty-Seven

Taylor put the finishing touches on her lipstick as the doorbell rang. She stepped back, looking at herself in the mirror.

Black mini-skirt, dark purple plunging tank top, and black wedge sandals. Hair braided down her back with some wisps of hair framing her face, she was as ready as she'd ever be.

She walked to the front door and opened it with a smile.

Scott stood on the other side with a handful of wildflowers. He fit the khaki pants and green polo shirt well, his biceps bulging tight just the way she liked them. He handed over the flowers.

"Beautiful flowers for a beautiful lady. The girls picked these for you. I hope you don't mind that I told them we were going on a date," he said with a smile, looking her up and down.

She took them, sniffing. "They're lovely. And it's fine. I wasn't sure how you felt about them knowing, other than the texts earlier this week."

She turned to put the flowers in water, and he stepped inside, shutting the door behind him.

"You're the first person I've dated officially since their mom died. I've gone on dates, but none of them have ever met the girls before. I wasn't sure if I wanted the girls to know or not, but it was the easiest thing in the world to tell them. They were really excited."

"Aww, that's so sweet. I'm glad they approve. Not going to lie, that had me nervous," she said with an awkward chuckle.

She arranged the flowers and pushed them to the center of the kitchen table. When she turned around, Scott stood closer than he ever had before.

Her heart jumped in surprise, and she looked up to meet his serious gaze. He took her hands in his, his thumb raking over her skin.

"I was nervous too. Because of the situation I'm in—single dad and all that—I want to lay it all on the table. I'm not just looking for a good time. The girls need a mother. I'd like to have more kids someday. If you're not interested in having a family, you should probably tell me now. I don't want to get the girls' hopes up. Or mine."

He smiled ruefully, and Taylor felt her heart melt. He was a good man, a great dad, handsome and sexy. He was the whole package. Maybe she just needed to get to know him better.

She squeezed his hands. "I want a family someday, yes. Lucy and I always swore we'd raise our kids together. She's my best friend. Your girls are so sweet and amazing. Anyone would be blessed to be their mother."

He sighed in relief, then leaned down and pressed his lips to hers. She froze, surprised even though they'd been standing so close together. She closed her eyes and tilted her head.

His lips were soft and gentle. He coaxed the seam of her lips with his tongue. She opened, and their tongues dueled.

Her heart didn't race. Her core didn't ache to fuck him, but it was a good kiss, one of promise and hope.

He broke the kiss and pulled back, his eyes clearer as he smiled. "You look amazing. I've wanted to kiss you since you opened the door."

She grinned and tipped up her chin. "Right back at ya, slugger."

He laughed and moved to the side, waving her to the door. "Shall we go to dinner now? I was thinking about this little Italian place in Denton if you're up for the drive."

She grabbed her purse and keys from beside the door and nodded as he opened it. "Yeah, that sounds great, and it's only twenty minutes. It's not that far."

He shut the door behind them, and she locked it.

"I know," he said, "But even a twenty-minute drive seems like forever when you have two precocious kids in the back seat."

She chuckled as they went down the stairs. "I bet. Have they always had such different personalities?"

He nodded, launching into anecdotes of each of the girls as babies. The conversation flowed all the way to the restaurant on the square in Denton.

His hand on the small of her back was warm and comfortable. Being with him was like snuggling up with her favorite blanket. The hostess led them through the restaurant to an outdoor bistro table.

When she sat down, she looked around. Her gaze landed on a couple sitting by the wall at a table for two, and her heart skipped a beat. The breath seemed to get stuck in her chest, and she coughed, breathing deep to settle her sudden nerves.

Scott looked at her, then looked to where she was staring.

"Well, I guess that settles the million-dollar question, doesn't it?"

"Hm?"

"I guess they're back together. Have you met Hunter and Jewel?"

She swallowed hard and nodded, her heart beating too heavy in her chest. "Yeah, Hunter took me home from the Electric Cowboy a few weeks ago. Nice guy."

Scott nodded, placing his napkin on his leg. "He is. Good family, although it's a shame what happened to Chase. Do you go to the Electric Cowboy often?"

She forced her gaze away from Hunter to Scott, forcing a smile to her face. "No, it's not really my thing anymore. I used to go to the clubs and bars a lot in college. Lucy works with Katie, the owner of the Electric Cowboy, and convinced her to start a trivia night. I've only been to the Electric Cowboy to join in on the game half a dozen times or so since Lucy moved here."

He sat back and nodded thoughtfully. "I went a lot when I was younger and first moved here. Elaina loved the party scene."

He grew quiet and the waitress came to take their drink order. When she left, Taylor asked, "Was that her name? You've not actually talked about her before."

He swallowed hard, looking down. "Yeah, I thought she hung the moon. I didn't think she was a ball bunny when we met."

"How did you meet?"

He launched into their story, and she put her elbow on

the table to help her pay attention and to keep from sneaking glances at Hunter.

She totally felt the melancholy as his story continued. She hadn't been married or had kids, but the feeling of betrayal was fresh in her mind as she easily picked up on what Scott wasn't saying as much as what he was.

Betrayal was hard to come back from. She glanced at Hunter, then jerked her head back to Scott. Hunter had made it clear they would not date. He didn't date locals, yet here he was at dinner with his ex-girlfriend, a local. She shouldn't feel betrayed.

Their food was delivered, and the topic shifted to their parents. She talked mostly about her mom and grandparents and growing up in the city.

"You're a city girl, huh?"

She nodded, taking a drink. "Yep, through and through. I never thought I'd move to a small town, but I don't miss the city as much as I thought I would. To be fair, I've only been in town for a few weeks, though."

He grinned. "Well, that's good news at least. The girls have grand ideas about the city. They've never been to Dallas, and as much as I tell them Denton and Fort Worth are cities, they just don't believe me."

"They're not missing anything in Dallas," she said, putting her fork down. "It's not the safest place to raise kids, which is why Lucy wanted to move back. I don't blame her at all."

"Do you want to learn all the country ways or move even more rural? Or are you happy in town?"

She pursed her lips and took a drink as she thought. "I don't know, to be honest. I've always read books about the country. Camping under the stars, cowboys and horses and all the outdoor things. I like to experience new things, so I told Tasha and Parker that I'd join them on the camping trip for the school in October."

His brows rose. "That's a big step for a city girl. Are you nervous?"

She shook her head with a grin. "Nope, I'm so excited even if I have no idea what I'm doing."

He laughed and reached for her hand, linking their fingers together. "Well, maybe you can come to the house next weekend? I can cook dinner and show you around. You can get a taste of the rural lifestyle, maybe I can help build up your stamina for camping."

She smiled, squeezing his hand. "That sounds great. The girls can show me their rooms."

He smiled slowly and raised her hand to kiss the back of it. "Actually, I was hoping to send them to their grandparents for the weekend."

Her eyes widened and her cheeks flushed. "Oh," she whispered.

"Is that okay? I don't want to presume." His expression turned vulnerable.

She nodded quickly. "Yeah, that's okay. I mean, you're pretty hot so it wouldn't be a chore or anything."

He burst out laughing, and she grinned wider. Movement to her left drew her attention, and Hunter strode over.

She sat up straighter and squeezed Scott's hand. He looked up and smiled.

"Hey, Hunter, I didn't know you'd gotten back together with Jewel. Congratulations, man."

Hunter glanced at Scott and nodded, then his eyes shifted to Taylor. She felt like a bug under a microscope, but she tilted her chin up. She had no reason to feel like a kid caught with her hand in the candy jar.

"Taylor," he said, his voice deep and growly. It sent a

shiver along her spine and made the hair on the back of her neck stand up.

"Hunter," she said softly.

An awkward pause had Scott looking from Hunter to her and back again, but she couldn't look away from Hunter. He drew her in like a moth to a flame.

"We're not back together," Jewel said, stepping up beside Hunter. "Hey, Scott. It's good to see you again."

"You too," he said with a smile. "I need you to come out and look at one of our steers next week. Or Gemma or Henry. Whoever is free."

"Sure thing. I'll call you when I get back to the office and see what our schedules look like."

Another pause and she could feel Jewel's stare now too, yet still she didn't look away. She maintained eye contact, locked in a battle of wills with him.

He was the one who hadn't texted her back. He was the one who said he didn't date locals. He was the one who acted like they had barely met at church last week.

And now he was staring at her with heavy lidded eyes and a clenched jaw? No, he didn't get to act jealous anymore.

Jewel put her hand on Hunter's forearm, and Taylor flinched, squeezing Scott's hand.

"I need to use the restroom before we head out," Jewel told Hunter. He nodded once, and Scott released her hand and pushed his chair back.

"I'm going to go pay. Is that alright?" he asked, his voice cordial but his eyes frowning with hesitation.

Taylor nodded and smiled, but still didn't look away from Hunter. "That's fine. I'm not going anywhere."

Scott stepped through the door behind Jewel into the

restaurant. Hunter looked down at her, his hands fisting at his sides.

Calmly, she asked, "What are you doing?"

His brows rose. "What am I doing? What the hell are you doing?"

She arched a brow and crossed her arms. "Going on a second date. What's it look like?"

"I thought I told you I didn't like seeing his hands on you."

She snorted and narrowed her eyes, grabbing her purse and standing up. "What did you expect me to do? Just not date Scott because you don't like it?"

He swallowed hard but didn't say anything.

She sighed. "I texted you, but you didn't reply. You acted like you didn't know me after church. Like I meant nothing to you."

"But you do mean something."

"Do I?" She leaned closer, stepping into his personal space. "You said you don't date locals, but here you are with Jewel. Your ex-girlfriend. A local."

"We're not dating in town. I took her out of town, just like I did with you."

"Fort Worth, Denton, it's all the same, as long as you don't get your mom's hopes up, right?" She shook her head sadly and stepped away.

"I hope you and Jewel have a great night, Hunter. A great life, actually. Obviously, you don't want to pursue anything with me further, since I haven't heard a word from you. And I get it. I'm not really the type of girl you're looking for. You and Jewel are perfect together. She's a veterinarian, for fuck's sake."

She turned to walk around him, but he grabbed her

wrist and leaned in. "But you're a fucking librarian. You're my kryptonite, princess."

She looked over her shoulder and met his gaze. "Don't toy with me, Hunter. If you wanted anything other than a fuck buddy, you could've said something, but it's been nothing but silence, as if I don't exist or matter to you at all. I got the message loud and clear. I won't humiliate myself or beg for your attention."

"But you beg so prettily," he growled, tugging her flush with his body.

She gasped, her other hand settling flat on his chest. She couldn't push him away. Her mind warred with the tingles through her body.

Her mind won, though, and she finally pushed gently on his chest to give them a few precious inches of space. "No, Hunter. I want something more. I'm trying to be a better person, remember?"

She had to make him see reason. They couldn't keep doing this, whatever this was.

"You don't have to be better, princess. You're already perfect."

She melted at his words. What was it with this man and the way he talked that had her ready to bend over and take everything he had to give? Her eyes prickled with tears.

Chapter Twenty-Eight

"No one's perfect," Taylor said, her voice a soft whisper on his cheek.

Hunter felt some tension leave him at having her so close after going so long without her. Her palm stroked his chest, but he didn't think she realized she was even doing it. She stared up at him with her big eyes, and he tugged on the end of her braid.

He'd been trying to focus on the ranch all week, but he'd been puzzling over Taylor instead. What did she mean to him? What did he really want?

And now that she was here in his arms, it was like he just knew.

He shifted, drawing her closer with a groan. "You're perfect *for me*." His heart raced at the admission, but it was true.

Her eyes flashed, and she pushed him away. "Liar. If I was so perfect, why didn't you want me?"

"I do want you." He reached for her, but she stepped back, causing his hands to fall to his sides.

She shook her head, her eyes full of sadness. "No, you want my body. Not me."

She looked behind him and smiled with wobbly lips. "Scott's back. We're going now. Enjoy your date, Hunter. I wish you nothing but the best, I hope you know that."

Scott met her halfway and put his hand on the small of her back, making Hunter's hands fist at his sides. "Ready?" Scott asked.

She nodded, and Scott looked at Hunter suspiciously. "Hunter, it was good to see you. Tell Jewel I'll talk to her next week."

Hunter nodded and watched them walk through the outdoor gate and to an extended cab truck. Every step that took her farther away made his skin crawl.

His anger went higher as he held the door for her, and she climbed inside. He saw Scott staring at her ass as she stepped into the truck. He clenched his jaw.

That ass was his, not Scott's.

Jewel stepped beside him, watching with him as Scott went around the cab and opened his own door. "Well, now I know why you're not really interested in me anymore."

Hunter frowned. "What?"

Jewel nodded to Scott and Taylor as they drove away. "She's the reason you're so distracted all the time?"

He shrugged. "No more distracted than usual, I think. But I have tried, Jewel, for Destini's sake."

He'd asked Jewel on the date tonight to see if he could make it work. His mom had a point. They'd needed to try for Destini's sake.

She smiled sadly. "Ouch, that's not exactly what a girl wants to hear, is it? I don't want to date you just because everyone thinks it'll be better for us as a family."

He raked a hand through his hair and sighed. He didn't

have the words to explain it or help. Jewel knew him, though. She put a hand on his arm and together they walked inside to pay for dinner.

She leaned closer. "It's been good hanging out with you this week. Not because of the chemistry but because it's like when we were friends as kids again. Honestly, my heart's not here anymore, either. Being with you… it's like my favorite pair of jeans. They're comfortable, and I love them, but I can't keep them forever."

He smiled at the hostess and handed over his card before turning to Jewel. "At least we're not fighting anymore."

Jewel nudged his shoulder with hers. "It's good having you as a friend again, Hunter. I've missed this."

He sighed and wrapped an arm around her shoulders as they walked out the gate and to his Jeep. "Same, babe. You were my first best friend. It's been good having you back."

"Can you take me to our spot? I'm not ready to go home yet."

He nodded and opened the door for her. They drove in silence, the radio playing Kryptonite and making his chest feel heavy. When they got to Crimson Creek, he turned to drive to the Old Mill.

"Did you know that the Old Mill is a bed and breakfast now?"

She shook her head as they drove past it. "No, but that's great for the town. I always thought it could be so cute with a bit more time and effort."

He nodded and drove along the creek. "Yeah, Parker actually owns it."

She frowned and fidgeted with her hands. "I thought he was coaching at the school."

"He is, but he's managed his soccer money really well.

He owns the gym in town and the mill and hired a girl to run it for him. It's doing pretty well. I can take you if you'd like. The restaurant is pretty good."

She shrugged. "Maybe some other time."

They drove past the turn off and to the public park next to the creek. When they got out of the truck, they walked through the park, stopping on the bridge over the creek. She leaned her arms on the railing and looked up at the sky.

He stared at the water, enjoying the night sounds of nature around him. He'd always found this spot peaceful.

"There's something I haven't told you," she said.

He shoved his hands in his pockets and waited, his stomach in knots. She'd been nervous since leaving the restaurant, but he couldn't make her talk about it.

He wondered if it was thoughts of Taylor that troubled her or if it was Destini. Lord knew it was troubling him.

"I'm sick," she said with a sigh. "It's why I moved back to town after all these years, actually. I was perfectly happy in north Houston, but after a lot of doctor's visits, they finally settled on Lyme disease. Probably picked up from a tick bite while working on some farm somewhere."

Hunter frowned. "How bad is it?"

She shrugged. "It was pretty bad for a while. Painful with lots of fatigue, but I'm slowly learning some lifestyle changes to manage it better. Things are looking up, so I should be fine."

Hunter listened to the water and waited for her to continue.

"It made me think more long-term about Destini. If I had gotten something more serious or if something were to happen to me, then Destini would move in with Dad or Gemma. That's why I want her to know her dad now.

That's why I stopped ignoring her asking about you and actually made the move back home."

Hunter nodded. It made sense. "If she's mine and something were to happen to you, I'd want her to come live with us."

"Us? Hunter, you don't even have a place of your own. What are you talking about? Your parents?"

Hunter shifted on his feet, feeling frustrated with his stagnant life for the first time. Hadn't he told himself something similar last weekend with Taylor?

"Your parents aren't going to give up the house, and trust me when I say it's hard moving back into the house with your parents. I'm hoping it's only temporary because I cannot handle living with Dad for long."

She chuckled, and he smiled. She'd mentioned earlier this week how hard sharing a kitchen with her dad was.

"Maybe I'll build a house on the ranch," he said. He'd had the idea for a few years now. "Landry can be the general contractor, and we can do a lot of it ourselves. Ma and Dad will give me whatever land I want, I know that. They've said it for years."

An easy silence settled between them. The warm breeze blew through her hair, tugging at her messy bun.

She sighed. "You're lucky in that regard. I've been searching for houses but none of them are really fitting right with my budget. I hope you don't think I'm fishing for you to build a house or anything, though. I don't want to live with you."

He grinned. "I've always appreciated your bluntness."

She laughed and nudged his shoulder with hers again. "Thanks."

He nudged her shoulder right back. "Hm, maybe a better question would be—do you want to live with Chase?"

She gasped and reared back. "What? No, I can't do that. Why? Did he say something?"

Now he laughed and turned to lean against the railing. "If it were light enough, I bet I'd see you blushing so hard right now. Am I right?"

She cupped her cheeks with her palms and shook her head. "No, absolutely not."

He chuckled and shook his head. "Liar. What's going on with you two? I know you've been at the ranch every day this week, and we've had fun hanging out but within an hour or so, Chase will show up and BAM—you're all gaga eyes for him."

She wrapped her arms around her waist and turned back to the water. "I am not—I don't gaga. Geez, grow up."

"You grow up," he responded automatically.

She laughed and shook her head. "Good to see not much has changed."

"Except for you and Chase…"

The silence was broken only by the cicadas before she sighed again. "I don't know what there, to be honest. It's—it's a strange situation. I can't believe you even want to talk about it."

He looked up, tracing the stars and picking out constellations. "I can't really believe it either, but here we are. Maybe we should've stayed friends all those years ago. It's definitely easier being your friend than it was being your boyfriend."

She sighed. "That's what they all say. All the guys I've dated since we actually broke up, anyway. I'm always better as the girl next door. Never the romantic lead."

"But you want to be that with Chase?" He wasn't jealous at all, not the way he was over Scott spending time with Taylor. He didn't want to analyze why that difference existed.

She shrugged and looked into the small trickle of water. The summer had scorched the earth, and the fact there was any water in the creek at all was a miracle.

"Maybe. I don't know. He's younger than us. We didn't really hang out with him when we were kids, although I'm not sure why."

Hunter knew why. Chase had always marched to the beat of his own drum. He was the opposite of their entire family until Parker came along. Chase had been nerdy, had wanted to stay inside, hadn't wanted much to do with the ranch or horses.

"Are you really alright with me talking to Chase?" Her voice was hesitant.

Hunter nodded. "Yep, I'm fine. My only concern is I don't want to see him get hurt. The way we broke up that Christmas… I don't want him to have to go through something like that, Jewel."

"I won't," she rushed, pushing her hair back.

He crossed his arms. "I know that's what you say, but no one can predict the future. He's tough. He had to be to survive prison, but don't hurt him, Jewel."

"I said I won't, for fuck's sake," she mumbled.

Hunter let the sounds of the night sweep over them once more, both of them lost in their own thoughts. Jewel was probably thinking about Chase. He'd seen the way they talked with each other, the way he looked at her when Chase thought no one was watching… The way she looked at his brother was the same.

He'd been so wrapped up in working full time on the ranch back then, trying to prove himself as more than just the owner's son, that he'd never really paid attention to how they interacted before. He couldn't say whether that was new or not.

"I'm ready to go home now," she said softly with a yawn. Together they turned and walked through the path to the Jeep. It was a good date, even if it wasn't a real date.

He didn't know what it was with him and the ladies lately. First Taylor and a practice date, and now Jewel and a friendship date.

He pulled up to Jewel and Henry's house and parked. She threw her door open and hopped out, turning to grin at him under the faint light of the Jeep.

"The good thing about us not dating is that you don't have to hold open the door or any of the other gentlemanly things you do."

He already had his door open and turned to frown. "Are you sure? It seems like a trap."

She laughed and grabbed her purse. "I'm sure. This is fine. We're friends now, remember?"

He nodded, shutting his door and putting his wrist on the steering wheel. "Right."

She grabbed the door and held it open, tilting her head and staring at him. "As your friend, I should point out that Taylor is really beautiful."

His brows rose as his guard went up. "I know."

"And you should date her."

He frowned, his heart aching to do just that. "That, I'm not so sure about."

Jewel rolled her eyes. "Oh please, you both feel strongly for each other. You could cut the chemistry with a knife."

He gripped the steering wheel tightly. "Yeah, but she's with Scott now."

Jewel's voice was soft as she said, "You can still tell her how you feel. If you don't take a chance to tell her now, you're definitely going to lose her to Scott. Just think about it, Hunter. You deserve someone who'll make you happy."

Hunter frowned and nodded slowly but didn't say anything as she shut the door and walked up the drive to the front door. He waited until she was inside before driving home.

She was right, but he had to figure out this Destini thing first. He couldn't start a relationship with Taylor without knowing if he was a dad, but if he waited too long, she'd be head over heels in love with Scott. He had to tell Taylor how he felt about marriage and family.

Whoa, slow down, Hunter. Who said anything about marriage? They had only been talking about dating.

Still, the unbidden image of Taylor pregnant with his baby came to his mind. She would glow, and her smile would be relaxed and happy.

The glow of her cheeks would be brighter than the sun, and her laughter would warm him the same. She'd be a force of nature, his woman, a goddess divine.

She would be even more beautiful than she already was. Tonight, she'd worn that little mini-skirt, pencil style to show off her juicy ass, and it had driven him crazy.

He hadn't seen her at the library yet. He wondered if she dressed like the standard librarian with the sexy tight skirt. He wondered if he could fuck her against the librarian's desk, bent over and taking his dick.

He looked around and did a u-turn in the road, heading back to Denton and the sex toy store. He needed to get a few things and make a plan to talk with her about this thing between them, and the best way to get through to his wild princess was through her weakness in bed.

Chapter Twenty-Nine

Taylor sat in the truck as Scott hummed to the radio. Before she realized it, they were pulling up to her apartment complex. She looked around and unbuckled.

He opened her door and put his hand on the small of her back as they walked. "You were quiet on the drive back. It's because of Hunter, isn't it. What's going on between you two?"

His question made her stumble on the stairs, and he grabbed her elbow to help steady her.

She sighed and grabbed the railing. "It's complicated."

He snorted. "You just arrived in town. You've been here for like three weeks, and it's already complicated?"

She shrugged and unlocked her door, turning to look at him. She raised her chin, refusing to let Hunter dictate her life.

"Do you want to come in? I have some ice cream and peach cobbler if you'd like some."

He nodded, "Yes, I want to continue this conversation.

Communication is key with me. Elaina didn't really believe in it."

She held the door open and shut it behind him as he talked about his wife. She dropped her purse and keys beside the door and kicked off her shoes. Then she went to the fridge to get out the desserts.

"So?" He paused, sitting on the couch and watching her. "What's up with Hunter?"

She sighed, turning her back to put the peach cobbler in the microwave. "When I first came to town, he took me home from the Electric Cowboy. I was drunk, and he was a perfect gentleman. However, we've run into each other a few times since then."

"Do you get drunk often?"

She shook her head and took the food out of the microwave before scooping ice cream into the bowls. "Not anymore. Back in college, yes. But not really in the past year… that night was a special circumstance."

"That's good. I'm not sure I'd want the girls around someone who drinks too much, you know?"

She winced and walked toward him, handing him a bowl before sitting on the opposite side of the couch with her own.

"I don't blame you at all for thinking that way. If I had kids, I'd probably say the same thing. I love how great of a dad you are. The kind of girl I used to be—well, I'm a work in progress, but I *am* changing, with the help of a good therapist. Being an adult is hard, but like I said before, I want a family, kids, marriage, the whole deal. That's not something Hunter's interested in, so here we are."

He ducked his head and frowned, and they ate in silence for a few minutes. When he finished, he put the bowl on the coffee table and half turned to face her, putting his arm along the back of the couch.

"Speaking of open communication, I want you to know that I really like you. I'd like to kiss you again if that's okay."

She flushed and sat her bowl on the coffee table. Her stomach twisted as she slid closer to him. She'd known they'd kiss again when she started this second date, but somehow she didn't quite think it'd feel this weird, like she was betraying Hunter.

Except Hunter didn't want her. Scott did.

And Scott was a great dad, a good man, the whole package. He placed his palm on the side of her face, and she tilted her lips up to his.

In time, some of the pain of rejection from Hunter would ease. She knew that logically and kept telling herself all week to let it go. She had to get over him.

Kissing Scott was a great way to practice getting over him, and maybe it would lead to all her dreams coming true. Dreams of a stable, loving family and a peaceful life without drama.

His lips melded to hers, a little too wet but that was fine. He tasted like peaches and ice cream and smelled clean, like fresh laundered clothes. It instantly put her at ease.

His tongue teased the seam of her lips, and she opened up. The kiss was good. He'd sweep his tongue inside her mouth, then she'd dive into his mouth. It was a give and take, a back and forth built on mutual respect and curious exploration.

His hands on her face made her melt. He was just so sweet as he drew her closer. She sat across his lap, one hand behind her back and the other on her hip.

She wiggled closer, feeling the evidence of his arousal

under her ass. His hand on her hip crept up to cup her breast, and she felt like all her breath left her body.

She gasped for breath and broke the kiss. He immediately moved his hand back to her hip and gave a nervous smile. He was disheveled and had a mischievous twinkle in his eyes that made some of the uneasiness inside her fade.

"Sorry," he said with a sheepish grin. "Too fast? That's alright. I can go slow. I like it slow."

She grinned and flushed, feeling her cheeks heat in embarrassment. She wasn't the jittery sort, so why was she acting all nervous? She wiggled on his lap again, making his brows rise.

"Thanks," she said, kissing up his jaw to his ear. "I like it slow too, slow and deep."

He groaned and buried his head in her neck, nuzzling and making her gasp.

"God, yes," he said, nipping her slightly on the neck.

She moaned, digging her hand into the back of his head to press him closer. It was similar to how Hunter kissed her, that same spot that he just somehow knew drove her crazy.

And thinking of Hunter brought on the panic again. She gasped and pulled his head away. He sat up, holding her neither too tight nor too loose as they both got their breathing back under control.

She smiled and felt her lips wobble. "Sorry, maybe we *should* slow down. As in, maybe we should try again next weekend?"

He nodded and placed a chaste, soft kiss on her lips. She wanted to want him more. He felt good, was a good kisser, and with all her experience, she knew sleeping with him would be good.

Not Hunter mind-blowing good, but still good.

She could do this. She could forget Hunter and move on

into a real adult relationship. It would be fine. Eventually she'd fall in love with Scott and not even think about Hunter.

He broke the kiss and leaned back, so she slid off his lap and grabbed the bowls. She walked to the kitchen and placed them in the sink. When she turned around, Scott was standing between the kitchen table and the door with a small smile on his face.

"I'll talk to you tomorrow?"

She flushed and nodded, walking toward him to let him out. He kissed her one more time on the front doorstep, then he was walking down the stairs. She watched him until he disappeared on the landing, then she shut and locked the door behind her, leaning on it with a sigh.

This night was so weird. She walked to her bedroom and grabbed some clothes, then went to the bathroom.

She felt like she needed another shower but didn't want to put forth the effort. If she was going to make a serious attempt at dating Scott, she'd need to get used to his scent. She just washed her face and thought about Scott.

When she'd first dated Hunter, he'd been the easy one. Things had just happened. It was easy talking with Hunter. Easy to fuck him. She loved his wicked streak, loved how he kept his thoughts to himself, yet she could somehow look at him and know what he was thinking. It was like a secret just between the two of them.

It had been harder with Scott. He'd not really opened up at first, but the attraction had been there. Sure, it wasn't as intense and chemically charged as with Hunter, but the more she'd gotten to know Scott, the more she could see herself settling down with him.

The tables had turned. Hunter was complicated, and

Scott was easy. But there wasn't really anything she could do about Hunter. He was a lost cause.

A message appeared on her phone, and she looked down. Her heart raced to see that Hunter had finally texted her back.

God, why now? What could he possibly have to say that wouldn't break her heart.

Either way, she had to know. She swiped on her phone and read.

Chapter Thirty

Hunter's stomach was roiling with worry and excitement as he drove to her apartment complex from the store. He pulled into the parking lot but didn't see Scott's truck.

He let out a breath of relief and some of the tension in his stomach eased. He thought, tapping his hands on the steering wheel. Then he pulled out his phone and scrolled to the unknown number that had texted him on Monday.

I had a great time Saturday night. Are we fuck buddies now or what?

He'd known it was her, but he'd been at the ranch working. He'd thought about what to reply all day, but ultimately hadn't.

Then on Tuesday, he'd gotten another text.

Want to hang out today or tomorrow? I'm off work.

He'd been with Jewel when he'd gotten her message and

had told himself he needed to ignore Taylor and try to make things work with Jewel.

So that's what he'd done, even though he couldn't stop thinking of Taylor all week. He saved her number as Princess and clicked the microphone icon.

He said, "Are you fucking Scott right now?" The phone typed his words out, and he hit send.

He waited for her to reply, hoping she wasn't already asleep, praying that she was alone. Seeing her hold Scott's hand had gutted him. Watching her smile at him, talk with such ease and flirt—he knew her flirting look.

He'd paused mid-sentence when she'd made that little smirk, her eyes twinkling in the faint light as she batted her eyes at Scott.

He wanted her to look at him like that. She *had* looked at him with that look on their practice date.

Three dots appeared, and he took a deep breath as he waited.

No, we're not fucking. We made out on the couch, then he went home.

What's it to you? Why are you asking?

He told himself it didn't matter, but he breathed a sigh of relief. He wasn't sure how to answer, though. It didn't matter to him. It shouldn't matter to him.

He bounced his fingers on the steering wheel and thought, his heart racing as he stared up at her apartment. If he answered her, he'd end up going inside. He wanted to claim her body and remind her who she belonged to.

But he didn't own her, no matter what his heart said, no matter how much he wished it was otherwise.

He needed to let her go. But something inside of him just couldn't. He clicked on the microphone icon and spoke.

"Because I'm downstairs and need to know. I need to know if you're with him. The idea of you with him is driving me fucking crazy because some part of me thinks you're mine. All mine."

He hit send before he could talk himself out of it, his heart in his throat. Three dots appeared again, then she replied.

I can't be yours if you're Jewel's. It doesn't work like that.

The confusion, frustration, and rage bubbled within him. Fuck it, he had to go up there. He frowned and opened his door. He wasn't going to keep dragging out this text conversation when he could solve it easier and faster in person. He bounded up the stairs, the bag from the store swinging in one hand as he knocked on her door with the other.

She opened it wearing her short booty shorts and a crop top tank top. Her hair was still braided from her date, but her face was clean, makeup wiped off.

And yet, she was so beautiful. The sharp angles of her face and the curve of her cheek drew him in.

She scowled and crossed her arms, cocking a hip. "What—"

"I'm not Jewel's. You're mine, and I'm yours."

She frowned and rubbed her forehead. "For how long, Hunter? I'm tired of being fuck buddies. I need more than this."

"And Scott is willing to give you that?"

She nodded, her eyes flashing with fire. "Yes, he is. He's

willing to go the distance. Marriage, babies, the whole nine yards. Are you?"

He frowned, his head and his heart warring with each other as his frustration rose. He needed to feel her in his arms, but she seemed so tense and vulnerable, bristling like a porcupine with its quills up to keep from being hurt. He was afraid to act and afraid to not. If he reached for her, they'd both be lost forever.

He couldn't really answer her. He didn't want to make a rash decision based on his gut response. No, he needed to think and process. Except he'd been thinking all week, and it had gotten him nowhere. He hadn't dated anyone local in so long.

Was it worth it? Was it worth getting his hopes up, his mom's hopes up? Was it worth the risk of heartache like what he'd gone through when Jewel had left and they'd had that huge fight?

She smiled sadly and sighed. "That's what I thought. Go home, Hunter. If you ever change your mind, let me know."

She closed the door softly in his face. He stared at the wood, blinking. He frowned, anger threatening to drown him. He saw red and pounded on the door again.

She threw it open, one hand on her hip. "I said—"

"I know what you fucking said." He stormed inside, slamming the door behind him and dropping the grocery bag on the kitchen table.

She turned on her heel, her braid flipping over her shoulder at the movement. "Get out, Hunter. This isn't going to end well."

He stepped closer, and she froze, her eyes widening. He reached for her wrist, giving her enough time to pull away. She swallowed hard as he slowly tugged her closer, finally into his arms where she belonged.

"I'll leave if you can honestly tell me you don't want me to stay."

She stumbled into his arms, her mouth opening and closing silently as she tried to think. He gave her time, burying his head in her neck. "Tell me you don't want me, and I'll leave."

"I—I can't tell you that, Hunter. It's not about me not wanting you."

He breathed in with relief, then froze. He smelled her neck and pulled back, his nostrils flaring. "You smell like him."

Her eyes narrowed as she pushed on his chest and waved her hands wide. "I told you, we made out on the couch. Of course, I smell like him. What was I supposed to do when you ignored me all week?"

"I don't know, how about *not* jump into a relationship with someone else?"

She rolled her eyes and crossed her arms, and it was sexy as hell. He wanted to spank the sass out of her.

"For fuck's sake, Hunter, I'm not jumping into anything. But what did you expect? Did you want me to stop living? Mope around and wait for you when you don't even have the decency to text me back?"

Guilt ate at him and twisted his stomach. He was losing her, but he had to fix this. He had to do something to make her see how much she meant to him.

She spun on her heels and walked away, pacing in front of the door. "Well, if you want to pretend like we never happened, like we weren't anything, here ya go."

She came closer and waved to her neck as if to push the scent to him. Her eyes flashed with anger.

"Sniff up, buttercup. Then get the hell out."

He saw red and picked her up. "Don't you talk to me like that, princess."

"What are you going to do? Toss me over your shoulder like a heathen?" She snorted and turned to the door.

He saw red, seething at the challenge, and tossed her over his shoulder. She squealed and gripped his back, his shirt fisting in her hands. The sound came out more like a chuckle, but her voice was all righteous indignation.

"What the fuck? Put me down, Hunter!" She hit him on the back, but he walked steadily through her bedroom to the bathroom and spanked her ass. She jerked and moaned, so he rubbed the spot, his thumb sliding underneath her shorts. She wiggled on his shoulder, her hands fisting at his back as she tried to get more.

"Put me down," she panted again, her voice needy and sending a thrill up his spine.

"I will not. We need to settle this right here and right now, but I can't fucking think with you smelling like *him*."

He turned on the water to the shower and stood her on her feet. Her eyes were wild, and she blinked. In the time it took her to steady on her feet, he'd stripped her shorts off and pushed them to the floor.

Then he grabbed her crop top and ripped it down the front. She gasped, grabbing at the pieces, and trying to cover her breasts. He didn't waste a moment. Instead, he picked her up by her hips and set her in the shower.

Water poured over her head, and she sputtered out a shriek at the cold water. She jerked to the side, and he adjusted the water temperature as he kicked off his boots.

She hissed, her eyes wide with righteous fury. "What the hell are you doing, Hunter? Is this supposed to make me happy? Convince me to sleep with you again?"

He pulled his clothes off as he replied. "Oh, come on,

admit it. You liked the manhandling a little. After all, you're my little slut, aren't you?"

He stood in front of her, feet wide, buck naked, and fist wrapped around his dick. Her eyes were no longer spitting fire but staring at him like a snake in a trance.

"Admit it," he said softly, waiting her out.

She bit her lip and shifted on her feet. Then she sniffed and tilted her head up, pulling her elastic band, freeing her braid.

"No, I don't think I will." The stubborn tilt of the head matched her peeved tone.

He grinned and stepped into the shower with her, pressing her against the cold tile.

"Come on, admit it. You're my little cum princess, my little slut who liked being tossed around by a big brute cowboy like me," he said, caging her in with his forearms on the tile on either side of her head.

He didn't move, keeping their bodies flush and still. She panted, her eyes wild as she stared up at him.

"I—I'm not. I mean, I don't."

He shifted slightly, and her eyes fluttered as she moaned. Their bodies rubbed together in a promise of more.

"I'm the Hunter, and you're the prey. You have his scent on you like a filthy little slut, but I'm the beast here. I'll tell you whether you can kiss him or not."

She glared, "That's shit, Hunter. You don't own me."

"Oh, but I do, little slut. You just don't realize it yet," he nuzzled her neck, breathing deep and frowning. Then he pulled back and grabbed the loofah and body wash.

"You're being unreasonable, Hunter. I—"

He glared at her. "You called me a beast, slut, so I'm going to act like one. You're mine."

She rolled her eyes, and he slapped his hand to the tile

by her head, making her jump. Before she could do anything else, he was scrubbing her body with the loofah.

She stood straight, her head held high, and her fists clenched to her sides. Her eyes burned with fire, but she swayed toward him as he swiped gently over her breasts.

It made excitement flow through him to see her war with her body. It gave him hope that maybe he hadn't already lost her to a better man.

He washed her neck gently, scrubbing away his scent and making strawberries flood his nose.

"This neck is mine. No one else's, not even yours. I say who gets to kiss it, and I'm fucking tired of your dates with Scott."

She glared and tried to pull back from him, hitting her head on the tile. "It's not your decision to make. I'll date him if I want."

He cradled her head in his hand, feeling for a bump and watching for a wince. She only glared at him though, so he let his hands caress down to her breasts.

"You will not date him anymore," he growled, scrubbing her breasts. "These breasts are mine. Did he touch you?"

She narrowed her eyes. "He did."

"Where?"

"My breasts, duh. Have you seen them? No man can resist." She gave a little shimmy, making them sway as she glared at him with an arched brow.

The attitude made him go wild. He squeezed her nipples and twisted, making her gasp and arch her back. "These are my fucking tits, not his. Got it?"

She whimpered and nodded, her body seeming to melt in his hands. She really did love this and was putty in his hands. He had to show her that they were the perfect match, and if that meant being a little bestial with her, then so be it.

He moved the loofah in circles over her breasts and palmed her pussy with her other hand. She jumped with a gasp.

"This is my pussy. I say who gets to fuck it, and that will only be me, princess. My pussy, not yours. Not fucking Scott's."

She shook her head, but her hand wrapped around his forearm and pulled him closer. He dipped his fingers to her clit, and she squeezed his arm, coming up on her tiptoes as he plunged two fingers into her pussy.

"Feel this? I'm the only one who can make you feel like this, princess. Say it. Who does this pussy belong to?"

She whimpered as he pumped his fingers in and out, her eyes fluttering. She opened and closed her mouth, shaking her head. The need to see her come undone in his hands swept through him like a wild fire.

He leaned over and hooked her knee over his other arm. He slowly stood, lifting her knee up and spreading her wider for his steady fingers.

She banged her head back on the tile again, closing her eyes as she gasped. Her hips rose to meet his hand as she teetered on one foot. The angle changed once more, and he teased her asshole with a finger.

"Tell me you love this as much as I do, princess."

She tensed, her nails digging into his arms as he plunged a finger deep in her ass. She gasped and shook her head even as she moaned.

His hand pumped into her, and her balance on one leg wobbled. He pressed his free hand to the wall to give her something to balance on.

"Say it," he ground out, digging into her deeper. Her

head went back with a gasp, her mouth opening and her eyes fluttering closed. Her nails dug into his arm as her hips bucked, and his cock wept for her.

"Who does this pussy belong to?" He murmured in her ear, coaxing her with his words, his hands, his body. "You're so close. Don't you want to come?"

She moaned and nodded. He eased his fingers out, and her hips chased his hand. "Then who does this pussy belong to?"

"You," she gasped. He plunged his fingers back in, and she jerked with a moan.

"And who owns this ass?" He twisted his fingers and stretched her wide as he plunged in.

"You, fucking you!"

"Then come for me, princess. Come like the dirty little slut you are."

She screamed as she came on his hand. Her legs buckled, and he held her up, pausing with his fingers buried deep inside.

Triumph swept through him along with hope, peace, and another emotion that he didn't want to identify.

"That's right," he whispered into her temple. "You're fucking mine. This ass, this pussy, this body. Your heart, mind, and soul. It's all mine."

He panted, the words reverberating through his mind with a finality and rightness that scared him. He swallowed hard and kissed her cheek softly, desperate for a distraction from the intensity of his feelings.

"I'm about to show you just how good I can make you feel, princess."

And then I'm going to keep you forever.

His thoughts shook him from his trance. He eased his

The Cowboy Gets His Girl

hand out, holding her up against his body. He reached over and turned the water off.

She picked up her head. "What—"

"Sh," he said, picking her up by the ass. She wrapped her arms around his neck and her legs around his waist. "I've got you, and I won't let anything happen to you, princess."

He swallowed hard as he walked them dripping into the bedroom, the certainty and rightness of his words settling in his soul. This was exactly where he needed to be. He laid her down gently, and she sighed, not even opening her eyes.

He spun on his heels and went for the bag he'd dropped in the kitchen. He would give her a short rest, a power nap.

But they were just getting started. It would take hours to show her how much she meant to him. He had to make her see the truth of what they were together before it was too late.

Chapter Thirty-One

Taylor's head swam as she settled on the bed. The past few minutes had been a whirlwind. Hunter really was a jealous beast.

But there was a softness underneath that made her want to dig deeper.

He came back into the room, but she kept her eyes closed and focused on her breathing. She tried to get it under control, but then she felt her eye mask slip onto her head, his hands gentle at her temples.

She lifted her head, and Hunter set it in place. She laid there as he moved her arms over her head and wrapped something around her wrists.

She didn't have the energy to even try to tug them apart, but he still said, "I guess you don't need a nap after all? Such a good little slut, ready for more."

She moaned, clasping her legs together at her aching core.

"Now now, don't move unless I tell you to move. You

need to learn to listen. Yes, sir?" He pushed her legs apart gently.

She bit her lip, then nodded, her heart racing in anticipation. "Yes sir," she said softly.

He traced his hand softly up her stomach and over to her breasts. Her nipples pebbled as he said, "Good little slut."

He twisted her nipples and tugged, making her gasp. Then something cold clamped on them. She arched her back at the sensation, whimpering as pain and pleasure speared her. "What—"

"You'll love this, slut. You're going to lose count of how many times you come. You're my cum princess, and you're going to lay there and take this dick until I say it's time to stop. Do you understand?"

She whimpered and nodded.

He twisted her nipple even more and she cried out.

"Yes sir," he demanded.

"Yes sir," she gasped, pain making spots behind her eyes. "But it hurts."

He stopped immediately, releasing her nipple. Then she felt his tongue swirling around it, soothing the pain. She felt her body relax and her legs spread wider. He didn't touch her where she really needed him, though.

Her pussy ached for him, then he pulled away and added the nipple clamp again. She gasped, tensing in anticipation of the pain. Pain that never came. This time it was pure pleasure and the cold chain connecting the two clamps settled between her breasts.

"Tell me if they hurt too much, princess. I adjusted it to the lowest setting. Do you want me to take it back off?"

She shook her head quickly. "No—it's fine." Her voice

was soft with anticipation, need coursing through her. The shower had done nothing but make her want him more.

He licked her nipple again. "This might be my favorite jewelry on you. You look so good, princess, and I'm going to take such good care of you, you'll never want another man."

She whimpered and nodded, shifting her hips to bring him closer. Her reply choked in her throat, and she simply couldn't tell him that she already only wanted him.

He kissed the chain and drew part of it into his mouth, tugging gently. "Does it hurt too much now?" His voice was soft and only slightly garbled as he tugged.

Her hips jerked, and she felt his breath on her stomach as he dropped the chain.

She shook her head. "No, it—it feels good." She spread her legs wider, trying to tell him without words what she wanted.

He kissed her stomach and moved lower, sliding a pillow under her hips. "Good, it is as it should be. I'm going to fuck you with a butt plug now. Tell me if it hurts."

Then his lips settled on her clit. Her hips bucked as she gasped. One of his arms settled on her lower stomach, holding her in place as he devoured her pussy.

Her pulse raced, just now processing his words. He was going to—oh God, the bag he'd brought inside. It had been toys. She bit her lip, hoping and praying it wouldn't be a giant one.

She couldn't—He sucked and licked, and her thoughts fractured. Her legs shook as her orgasm built.

She whimpered. "I'm going to—to come. I need to—"

"Yes, now," he growled before his mouth closed over her clit. Then she felt something tease her asshole. She gasped as something cold and wet slid inside, just the tip.

She screamed as a wave of pleasure and pain swept over her.

Spots burst behind her eyes, and her body spasmed. She jerked up, grinding on his mouth.

She clenched and shuddered, just the tip of the plug driving her wild along with his tongue. She wanted to come on his dick. Her pussy felt so empty as she came around nothing.

When her muscles relaxed and the tsunami had settled to a gentle wave, he began to ease the plug in and out, going deeper and deeper with each gentle thrust.

It stretched her wider than his finger had earlier, and she whimpered at a wave of pain. "Wait," she gasped, trying to force herself to relax.

He immediately paused his hand, the butt plug part way in even as his mouth continued to drive her wild. His mouth was magic because soon she was relaxing and pressing down onto his hand, trying to take it deeper.

He slowly eased more inside. Stars shot behind her eyes as her body raced to the edge. The volcano erupted again, and she screamed as he plunged it all the way inside.

Waves of pleasure and pain rippled through again. The force of it made her legs shake around his head, and her mouth gasped for air.

Her body shook, and his mouth never stopped. He lapped and licked, continuing his torture. Her shaking eased to faint tremors, then he slid up her body. She took one deep breath, then his dick slid inside, slow and steady.

She clenched around him, the aftershocks of her orgasms making her tighter. She groaned, unnaturally full and stretching beyond anything she'd ever felt before.

"My pussy," he groaned, easing out and plunging back in.

"Your pussy," she repeated, needing more. She'd do anything to keep this feeling going. She tilted her hips up, settling her feet on the bed.

One of his hands settled on her wrists, holding her down on the mattress. The other tugged on the chain connecting the nipple clamps.

She gasped, unable to see past the mask. His hips changed angles, and he plunged deeper, harder. His hips slammed into hers, making her groan.

The rhythm was steady and bruising, just the way she liked it. How he'd known, she didn't know. He'd been right all along though. Maybe he knew her better than she thought, or maybe their souls just knew each other on a different level. She loved how he'd tossed her around, how he was wringing orgasm after orgasm out of her.

His knees shifted on the bed, and her mind fractured and stopped thinking as the waves grew higher and higher with every thrust. She was so close, so stuffed with him. Then she plunged into darkness, star bursts shining behind her eyelids as she screamed.

He thrust deeper, too deep. The pain of it made all the orgasms before pale in comparison. She never wanted it to stop. Her legs wrapped around him, pulling him inside. Her body squirmed and jerked with each spasm.

"Oh God," he said, his head burying in her neck as he bowed and stilled. She felt him swelling even as she spasmed more, clenching and milking him for everything he had to give.

She ground onto him, making them both groan. When they were both spent, her legs fell shakily to the bed.

He pulled away, kissing her jaw and moving down her body again. The nipple clamps released, and she took a deep breath as he licked them.

Then he unwrapped her wrists, saying, "You can move your arms now, princess. You did so good."

His mouth on her nipples made the sensitive tips pulse, and her pussy drip with more need. Would she ever get enough of him?

She breathed deeply, her body Jello as she felt the bed dip when he eased away. The mask still covered her face, but she didn't want to look at him. She couldn't look him in the eyes right now. Not when she was so vulnerable.

Not when her heart begged him not to leave. Not when she was so worried that this was just about sex for him.

When he said she was his, her heart leapt with joy and excitement. But it was so new, so raw… she wasn't sure how to handle it. Did he mean they were more than fuck buddies? Did he want to date her for real?

The bed dipped again, and she felt a warm cloth wiping her pussy. She moaned, even that making her sensitive flesh pulse with need.

"Does that feel good, sugar?"

She whimpered. "Yes, sir."

"Oh, you *are* learning, aren't you? Good girl," he crooned softly. Then his mouth settled gently over her clit. Her hips jerked in surprise, then she groaned.

"You taste so good, princess. Such a good cum princess. I love to taste myself on your pussy."

His words made the breath catch in her throat. Two licks, a third, and then she was splintering apart again. Waves crashed, threatening to drown her as she gasped and bucked against his mouth.

It was a gentler orgasm than previously but still left her shaking.

When the aftershocks were soft, he slid up her body and spooned her. She wiggled against him, feeling the butt plug still in place. She frowned and reached back to remove it, but he grabbed her wrist and held her still.

"No, leave it in. Sleep with it, princess. I'm going to wake you up with my dick and leaving it in for as long as you can will help. Trust me."

She felt a thrill up her spine, then her body relaxed in his arms. The roller coaster of emotions with this man left her exhausted. She was falling more and more under his spell, but all she could think about was that he wasn't going to leave in the middle of the night.

When she woke up, her ass was on fire, and her stomach hurt. She shifted and winced at the feel of the plug still in her ass. She lifted her mask and rolled to the side of the bed, stumbling to the bathroom and removing it.

She sighed in relief and then used the toilet and washed her hands. When she stepped into her bedroom, she looked around, a stab of disappointment shooting through her.

He was gone. It was last weekend all over again. She'd fallen for the same trap as before.

She was nothing but a good fuck. He'd gotten what he wanted and was gone, just like every other guy she'd ever fucked.

Well, that was on him, and his loss. She looked at the clock and stretched. It was still early, but she might as well get ready for work. Today was Saturday, and she had some prepping to do for the afternoon story time.

She would go to work and ignore the crushing weight of sadness that threatened to pull her under. She didn't need him.

She needed someone to love her, someone to be there for her, someone she could count on. So what if that wasn't Hunter?

There was still hope for Scott. That would have to be enough.

Chapter Thirty-Two

Hunter wiped his eyes and twisted the wrench on the fence.

"I'm so sorry, Hunter, I don't know how he got in here. Is the mare going to be okay?" John asked, working on the bottom row of their shared fence.

Hunter nodded as the sun beat down on him. He'd left Taylor in the bed Saturday morning and hadn't made good on his promise to fuck her in the ass.

Even though the bull had rampaged through the field and scared one mare into early labor, he still couldn't focus on the problem at hand.

Not when he'd been so close with Taylor. They'd left things unsettled, and his mind wouldn't let him stop thinking about the problem.

He gripped the wrench and tried to focus. "Yeah, Jewel and Gemma are rotating shifts to stay with Clio. They're keeping her sedated for now to hope that stops the labor. If she has to deliver, the foal won't survive. It's too early."

"I hope the mare is okay either way," John said. "If the

foal doesn't survive, we'll pay a fair price to compensate for what you could've sold it for."

Clio's pregnancy had been accidental, which is why she still had at least two months left. Ma was worried and wouldn't leave her side, either.

That meant he and Dad had been stepping in to cook, rotating shifts too. He was exhausted, not having slept much since leaving Taylor.

He'd been so close to showing her all he had, all he was. He'd been about to wake her up real nice when his phone had rung.

He'd hurried to answer it, then had rushed to the ranch to help save Clio and the foal and get the bull back on John's side of the fence where he belonged.

"Do you think we need to invest in steel fencing along our property line?"

Hunter nodded. "I think it's long overdue. Ever since you brought in the bucking steers, I've known we'd need to eventually. Think we can split the cost right down the middle?"

John nodded. "Yeah, I'll get an invoice from the feed store and bring it by later this week to talk to your dad about it."

Hunter grunted, working on the next section of the fence. The sun was sapping his energy quick.

Yesterday had been spent trying to see what was going to happen with Clio and getting the bull back where he belonged. Today, they did damage control to fix the fence. It would probably take the next few days.

He sighed, wishing Taylor were here. If she were his girlfriend, she could bring him an iced sweet tea and take his mind off the heat. He thought about her all day, dreaming up different scenarios of her on the ranch with him.

When he was in the fields working on the fence line and later when he was cleaning out the barn, he thought about her. He wanted to take her riding around the ranch and show her the beauty of it. He wanted to bend her over the fence railing and fuck her hard in the ass. He wanted to have a quickie in the barn in an empty stall. He wanted to see her in the kitchen, helping Ma cook and laughing with a big baby belly.

"Hunter?" John asked.

Hunter looked up. "Huh?"

"Worried about the mare?"

Hunter kept thinking of Taylor and her sweet ass. He wanted to ride her so hard and plant that baby in her pussy so the entire world would know she was his.

Hunter cleared his throat as all the stress from the past few days piled on. He'd never had a breeding kink before, or an exhibitionist streak, but Taylor made him want to step out of his comfort zone. She was his shining light, the beacon of hope in all of it. He needed to see her but couldn't stop working. There was too much to do.

Even though his chest was tight from being away from her, from not talking with her. He couldn't focus, couldn't eat.

He knew it was inevitable, but his love for her had grown bigger and bigger since that first night at the Electric Cowboy.

"Hunter?"

He sighed and nodded again. "I think I love her."

"You think?" John asked.

Hunter nodded. It had to be love. If it wasn't love, it would be a psychotic obsession. Honestly, he was grateful she hadn't pressed charges for stalking the way he'd just shown up after her dates with Scott and pressed his advantage. So much for the gentleman he'd been when they'd first met.

But his princess loved to come, and he loved to make her lose control. The look on her face, the way her mouth opened in an o, the way she screamed and raked her nails down his back.

"How long have you had her?" John asked.

"Not even a month," Hunter said absently.

"And you love her?"

"I think so, yeah. It's the only thing that explains how frustrating this feels."

Hunter turned the wrench on the fence, tightening the barbed wire.

John chuckled and leaned on the fence post. "You're not talking about the mare, are you."

Hunter looked up. "Huh?"

John gave a full belly laugh at that and slapped his leg. "Fuck, you're in love, aren't you? Don't worry. It happens to the best of us. Want to tell me about her?"

Hunter felt heat creep under his collar, and he tugged on it, popping the pearl snaps and taking the entire shirt off. He tossed it to the ground on the toolbox and grunted.

John shrugged. "I remember how Dot first made me feel. I was so confused, and all the emotions were pure chaos."

Hunter worked beside him and eventually asked, "Does it get better?"

John grunted and twisted the wire. "Yeah, but only after you clear the air and tell her how you feel. She's a good woman. Been over to the ranch to help with some steers. She's got a good stomach for dirty work."

Hunter paused and glared at John. "It's not Jewel."

John stopped and looked at him with a blank expression. "Oh, it's not? Then who the hell are we talking about?"

Hunter sighed and shook his head. He hadn't wanted to date a local, but if he wanted to claim Taylor, he had to start somewhere.

"The new librarian in town."

John nodded. "Not sure I've met her yet, but it looks like I need to soon. I'll have Dot swing by the library sometime this week and scope her out."

Hunter groaned and shook his head. "No, don't do that. I don't want to be a creep."

They worked in silence for a little while, then Hunter asked, "How did you tell Dot you loved her? Was it a big deal?"

For the life of him, he couldn't remember how he'd first said it to Jewel. That had been half a lifetime ago.

John grunted and moved to the next section of the fence. "Everyone's different."

"How do you make it work with the ranch?"

"Everyone's different." John repeated with a chuckle. Hunter sighed, then John continued.

"As long as you're communicating every day, then things get easier. It's when you're not communicating that things are rough. Take, for example, when it's rodeo season. When I'm gone on the circuit for weeks at a time, it's hard on Dot and the kids. That's why they come with me as often as possible. And when they have to stay home, we call and FaceTime multiple times a day."

Hunter frowned. He'd not really texted Taylor at all. It was two days later, and he knew she would have tomorrow off work. He wanted to see her and tell her how much he loved her.

The Cowboy Gets His Girl

His phone rang, and he answered it.

"Hunter? Get to the house now. Your mom's been kicked." Bill sounded like he was running. "Ambulance is on the way. She should be okay, but I'm packing a bag now."

"I'm on my way," he said, but the line was already dead. He sucked in a breath and grabbed the toolbox and his shirt, quickly explaining to John.

His heart raced. A kick from a panicked horse was no joke. There could be a million things wrong, and his ma couldn't—she wouldn't...

Hunter forced his mind to blank as he jumped in the old farm truck and threw up dust as he peeled out. He left John racing to his own truck as he sped through the fields. It was a bumpy ride that felt like hours but was actually less than fifteen minutes.

When he finally slid to a stop in front of the house, the ambulance already waited with lights flashing, but thankfully not blaring a siren. He ran to the barn where they'd moved the mare and pushed open the door. A flurry of activity was on the right, and he strode over, his heart in his throat.

Ma laid on the gurney, pale and eyes closed. The paramedics lifted it and locked it in place, making her wince. She had a bloody gash on her forehead, and her hand held her side.

"Ma?" He grabbed her other hand, walking alongside her as the paramedics went down the aisle of the barn.

She blinked up at him, tears streaming down her face. She met his gaze and cursed. "Dang it, Hunter, I think I've broken a hip. You'll need to stay with the mare, and the feed in the two-year olds needs to be rotated out. They're too big for the baby stuff. And—"

"Ma, I'll handle it. Don't worry," he said, squeezing her

hand. "Is Dad going to the hospital with you? Do you want me to go with you?"

She shook her head and cried out as they pushed her through the door, making the wheels bounce on the dirt and gravel ground. "Ow, ow, ow, that hurts. Son of a bitch."

Hunter stopped the paramedics and raised his voice at the ranch hands standing in a group nearby. "Help me lift her into the ambulance, boys."

They leapt into action, and four or five guys each grabbed onto the side of the gurney, lifting her with ease. She gasped, and he kept hold of her hand, directing them slowly to the ambulance.

"That's it. We're almost there. Tip the front up a bit, there we go. Nice and easy." He jumped into the back of the ambulance as they rolled her forward gently, and the paramedic inside adjusted it.

"There we go, Mrs. Williams, you'll be alright now."

"Don't tell me it's alright. You've never broken a hip or been kicked in the stomach by a horse before. Oh," she moaned, closing her eyes and thrashing her head.

Hunter ignored the paramedic as his dad slid around the back of the ambulance, a bag in hand. He was winded as he said, "I got an overnight bag for us. Did you get some pain medicine?"

The paramedic shook his head, pulling out needles and vials from the wall. "Not yet. Working on it now, then we'll be on our way."

Hunter let go of her hand and stepped down to let Bill inside, his stomach in knots. Jewel stopped beside him and laced her fingers in his. He squeezed her hand tight.

They'd done this as kids. When his grandma had gotten sick, she'd been here to see the ambulance drive away. She might be younger than him, but she'd held his hand just like this.

He sighed, wishing Taylor were here. Then one of the ranch hands waved from the barn door.

Hunter leaned into the back of the ambulance and said, "Dad, call me when you hear something, okay? I'll take care of everything here. You just take care of Ma."

Bill nodded, not taking his eyes off Ava and hugging the bag on his lap in a deathly grip as he sat on the bench. Hunter sighed as they closed the doors, then he turned and strode to the barn, releasing Jewel's hand.

"How's Clio? What the fuck happened?"

Jewel shook her head. "It's not looking good. She kicked your mom in the side, and I had to drag her to the aisle. By the time I got your mom stable, called 911, and sent someone for your dad, the mare was out of control. I've given her another shot but we need to get her into a birthing stall to keep her still."

Hunter took a deep breath and nodded, looking around for his shirt. It was going to be a long fucking day.

"Hunter?"

He put his shirt on, leaving it unbuttoned as he looked up at her.

"The 911 lady on the phone asked about internal bleeding. If you need to be with your mom, Chase, Gemma, and I will handle this here."

His fingers froze and a chill ran down his spine. He took a deep breath and clenched his jaw. "There's no way of knowing what's going on right now. Let's focus on Clio. Dad will call when we need to know something. But I do appreciate you being here, Jewel."

She gave him a look and arched her brow. "Taylor should be here too."

He pulled out his phone and stared at it, then clicked over to messages. She hadn't texted him anymore, but he hadn't really expected her to.

He clicked over to call her, but before he could hit the button, Clio started to neigh and get kick the stall. He put his phone back in his pocket and rushed to her side.

Chapter Thirty-Three

It had been an entire week since she'd gone on her date with Scott, since she'd seen Hunter Friday night.

Sunday, she'd awoken with so much inner turmoil that she'd almost made herself sick. She hadn't wanted to go to church, but Lucy had told her she needed to.

Part of her had hoped he would've seen her, sat with her, and claimed her hand in front of the entire town. Hope had warred with dread of him walking with Jewel on his arm and acting like he didn't know her at all.

In the end, Hunter hadn't even been there.

Parker had said that there had been an emergency at the ranch, but everyone else in their family had gone to church except his parents. They'd had a prayer request for them, but she wasn't sure of the details.

Taylor knew an emergency would've explained why he'd snuck out at night, *again*, but she also suspected that he was just trying to avoid her.

True to her word, she wasn't going to beg for his attention. She didn't text him. The ball was in his court. If he wanted to talk to her, he knew where to find her.

Her stomach hurt all week from anxiety, waiting and hoping that he'd call. It was dumb, and she hated this feeling. She wasn't sure dating was worth this stress, honestly. Maybe it would've been better to just stay the slut she used to be.

Taylor sighed and drove to the address on her map.

She'd gone to work, gotten groceries, made food and babysat Harry on her two days off. Hunter hadn't texted her, but Scott had. When the girls and he had come in on Monday to exchange their books, they'd brought lunch and flowers with them.

They'd all had a picnic in the library and had talked about their favorite books and hobbies. The girls had told her about their rooms and their farm.

It had been wholesome and fun, low key and comfortable. Lucy swore it counted as a third date, but Taylor wasn't sure.

Monday had been a much needed, a balm to her soul. The girls had brought her light and joy and all good things. Then the Harry snuggles on Tuesday and Wednesday had left her emotional but ready to move on.

It wasn't worth all the stress to find out what Hunter meant by being the master of her body. By the end of Wednesday, she felt like no communication gave her the answer. He didn't want her for anything other than sex.

It hurt more than the butt plug had.

She pulled onto a long driveway and bit her lip. She had packed a small bag, just in case she ended up staying the night at Scott's. She was done waiting around for Hunter, done with being left high and dry. What did they say in her smut books? The best way to get over a guy is to get under another?

Hunter may fuck like a princess, but he ignored her like she wasn't even worth the muck on his boots. So fuck him.

She pursed her lips and parked in front of a cute little farmhouse. It reminded her of Lucy's, but it was bigger. The wraparound porch had a swing on one corner and two kid swings hung from a large tree in the front yard.

Tears pricked her eyes. This could be her home someday. If she and Scott fell in love and got married, she could have a real family.

She took a deep breath as Scott pushed open the screen door and stepped onto the porch. His megawatt smile shone in the setting sun. He slid his hands in his pockets and waited as she opened her door and got out.

"You made it. Did you find the place okay?"

She nodded, walking up the three stairs to the porch. "Yeah, it's a close enough drive. Not too bad."

He grinned and opened the screen door, touching her wrist and kissing her cheek as she stepped inside.

"That's good. What do you think of the house? Here, let me give you a tour."

He didn't wait for her to answer. Instead, he launched into an explanation of each room on the main level. He talked faster than normal, and she realized he was nervous.

Her heart melted at the realization. A buzzer went off, and he bounced into the kitchen. He opened the oven and pulled out a casserole. The smell of herb chicken and veggies flooded her nose, and she smiled.

"Can I help with anything?"

He shook his head and nodded to the kitchen table. It was set for two with candles already lit on top and fancy China organized neatly. Even the napkins were real cloth napkins, pressed and at perfect angles with the place settings.

"No, it's ready to eat. I hope you like it. Have a seat."

She pulled out the chair at the end of the table, and he shook his head. "No, your chair is the other one. Sorry, I hope you don't mind."

She chuckled and shook her head, pulling out the chair beside it. "Not at all. It's your house, after all."

He placed the casserole on the table as she sat. Then he came back with a bottle of wine and poured her glass half full.

"I hope you like red wine. I wasn't sure, so I have white too. But the red goes better with the meal."

She grinned and teased him. "This is perfect, Scott. I'm really impressed with how much effort you've put into all this."

He finally sat, his cheeks tinging pink as he scooped some of the casserole onto his plate. "What can I say? I'm a romantic without someone to share it with. It's been a lonely four years."

She touched his arm, and he finally stopped fidgeting and looked at her. "I appreciate it. You're so sweet, and this is all so perfect, Scott. You have no idea how much it means to me."

His lips stretched into a big grin. "Want to show me how much later?"

She burst into laughter and sat back.

"Sorry!" He said with a wince. "Sometimes my baseball experience comes back at the weirdest times. They're a horny bunch."

She waved a hand as he spooned a portion onto her plate too. "Don't even worry about it. I have quite the naughty sense of humor too. Tell me about your baseball days?"

He nodded. "I told you the gist of it on our first date."

"I know, but which team did you like playing for the most and why?"

He looked up, tilting his head as he thought. Then he launched into an animated discussion of the pros and cons of each of the teams.

She listened and ate, asking questions throughout. When the topic finally exhausted itself, she asked, "Do you still play?"

He nodded. "Yeah, Crimson Creek has a church league that plays softball every September and October. It ends before Thanksgiving, usually in time for harvest for most folks around here."

"I'd love to play, if you'll have me."

He grinned, his eyes lighting in excitement. "I'd love that. We can always use a good third baseman."

She took a drink. "Tell me about your farm. What do you do here? I didn't see any livestock."

He nodded and began discussing the steers he raised. "They're meat steers—burger cows, as Paige likes to say. Originally Elaina's parents wanted to get into the orchard business, but Vonda has a lockdown on that market."

She looked at him in confusion, but he waved his hand.

"Sorry, the neighbors down the road. You might have met Lola around town? She's the tall redhead married to the town doctor."

Taylor shrugged. "Maybe I met her at yoga. I'm not sure."

They talked about people she had met in town, which church organized the softball, and other various fall events he and the girls were looking forward to this year.

He filled up her wine glass again, then asked, "Do you want to sit on the porch swing? It's a gorgeous night."

She nodded and followed him outside, leaving her glass of wine behind. She was feeling relaxed but not buzzed and didn't want to make any drunk or tipsy decisions.

She took a deep breath and sat beside him. He put his arm along the back of the swing, and she snuggled into his arm as he pushed them gently.

They rocked and the night sounds made her relax even more. It reminded her of being in Hunter's barn. The crickets set up music that made her sad.

Scott tugged on her hair, moving it to the other side and exposing her neck. She shivered at his touch, even as her stomach roiled. She had to get over this feeling of guilt. Hunter wasn't interested, but Scott was.

Scott was offering her everything she'd ever wanted. He leaned forward and kissed her cheek, moving his mouth to her ear.

"I don't know if I can keep my hands off you tonight. If you don't want to move this upstairs, then I will escort you to your car so you can go home."

She chuckled, smiling at the open communication and the way his words were like a gently swaying ocean tickling her feet. "I actually brought a bag just in case I stayed over."

"Hallelujah," he breathed, kissing her neck and sucking.

She giggled, twisting in his arms as his five o'clock shadow scratched her. He pulled back and met her lips with his own. She was still smiling as they kissed, enjoying the gentle joy that his attention brought her.

It was uncomplicated and easy. Sure, the passion wasn't there much, but that would come. The more she started to love him, the more she'd appreciate their time together.

Her heart beat a steady rhythm as their tongues dueled. Part of her mind was detached, unable to stay in the moment. She kept forcing herself to focus on him, especially as the kisses grew deeper.

He finally broke the kiss and leaned back, a smile on his lips. "Do you want to go inside?"

She nodded, and he grabbed her hand and led her up the stairs. He hadn't given her a tour upstairs but didn't stop now. He led them straight to his bedroom and opened the door.

Chapter Thirty-Four

She stepped inside, her nerves shooting up at the sight of the giant bed covered in silk sheets. This was really going to happen, and it wasn't just a one-night stand or a random stranger at a party.

This was someone she was developing a relationship with. Someone she might marry. Dare she say it, her first boyfriend?

He shut the door behind them and put his hands on her shoulders, turning her around. "Are you sure? We don't have to do anything if you don't want to."

She smiled up at him and settled her hands on his lean hips. "No, it's fine. I want to, but maybe we can go slow?"

He grinned, his hands moving from her shoulders down her back. "Slow and deep, right?"

She grinned and nodded as he pulled her into his arms. Their lips met again, this time with more passion and heat. It was still nothing like what Hunter made her feel.

Thinking of him made her heart stutter, but she forced him out of her mind. When Scott's hands slid up her waist to her breasts, she arched into him, determined to do this and leave Hunter behind for good.

Then a phone rang. His head popped up even as he groaned and reached for his back pocket. He broke the kiss and answered it.

"Hello?"

She couldn't hear the other side of the conversation, but he frowned and half-turned away from her.

"Are you sure? Did you try—" He paused, listening. Then he sighed and nodded, raking a hand through his hair. "Yeah, I'll be there in twenty minutes. Thanks."

He ended the call and looked at her. "Paige is throwing up, so I'm going to go pick them up."

She frowned, worry hitting her stomach and making it twist. "Oh, I'm so sorry. Is she going to be okay?"

He nodded, opening the bedroom door. "Yeah, I'll bring both girls back here."

"Do you want me to stay and help?"

He shook his head as they went back down the stairs, clearly distracted. "No, you don't have to put yourself through the chaos of a sick kid. You can go home."

"Are you sure? I've helped Lucy before—"

He stopped at the bottom of the stairs and grabbed his keys. "No, I'll be fine. This happens pretty regularly when she goes over to her grandparents. I think she's allergic to Elaina's mom's cooking."

He chuckled mirthlessly, and she smiled as they walked out the door.

"I'm really disappointed that you're not staying though," he said, opening her car door.

She paused and covered his hand with hers. "Me too, but there will be other nights. This is just slower than I expected."

He chuckled with real mirth this time. "Me too, babe. Me too. I'll call you tomorrow?"

She nodded and kissed him on the cheek. Then she slid into her seat, and he shut the door.

Driving back to her apartment, she knew she wouldn't be able to sleep. She changed from her date clothes and went for a late-night run. If she were still living in the city, she wouldn't feel safe enough to run at night.

Crimson Creek was practically all shut down. No one wandered the streets. She ran to the gym and tested the door. Finding it open, she went in and saw Parker.

He looked up and set his free weights down. "Hey, Taylor. What are you doing out so late?"

She panted and looked around. "Had a date go south, so I'm burning off some energy. Can I work out?"

He nodded. "Of course. Do you want to talk about it? Do I need to beat anyone up?"

She laughed and shook her head. "No, Scott's daughter's just sick, so we had to cut the date short. That's all."

Parker nodded. "Ah, gotcha. Hope she's okay."

"She will be. According to Scott, it's nothing to worry about," Taylor said as she settled on the leg press. She bit her lip and asked what was burning in her brain. "How's the emergency going at the ranch?"

"What?" He frowned in confusion.

"At church on Sunday, there was an emergency at the ranch that we prayed for. Is it better now?"

She really hated that she needed to know the answer, but it was eating at her. Perhaps there was a legitimate reason that he didn't leave her a note or text her or anything.

Parker nodded. "Oh yeah, that. Yeah, the fence between our property and the next got taken out by an angry bull who chased one of our pregnant mares. It was a pretty dicey situation, especially with Ma getting so banged up."

Worry hit her again, and she frowned. "What happened with your mom?"

"Broke a hip while Hunter was fixing the fence. Hunter had to stay with the mare and Jewel had to help with the delivery while Ma was in the hospital."

"Ah, Jewel. I see," she said, hope dying in her chest. She moved on to the row machine, wondering why she'd gotten her hopes up.

"It's a shame about them," he said. "It would be so much better for the kid if they would've worked out."

The row machine slipped out of her hand, banging down with a clatter. "What kid?" Her head spun. What was he talking about?

"Well, it'd just be better if the parents were together, you know? Instead, they've decided to just be friends, which is still better than what they used to be."

He laughed but must've seen the confusion on her face. He tried to explain, but it didn't really help.

"Oh, the way they broke up fifteen years ago was something else. It was so public, Hunter didn't go to church for a good six months. Mom was furious."

She nodded, not quite understanding what he was saying. She hoped by staying quiet, he'd keep going.

"It's good that she's back, though. I can't wait to meet Destini."

"Destini?"

He nodded. "Yeah, my niece. She's almost fifteen and will be coming back from NASA camp in a few weeks, right before school starts. Can you believe it? She's some kind of genius."

"And you've never met her?"

He shook his head. "Nope, we had no idea she even existed until Jewel came back to town. I don't blame Mom for trying to get Jewel and Hunter back together, but that ship has sailed. Mom will realize it eventually. The important thing is that both Hunter and Jewel are good people who will do what's right with Destini. Mom's going to have a field day with her too."

Parker laughed again, and his phone dinged. "Hey, speak of the devil."

He answered it, saying, "Hey, what's up?... Yeah, I can do that. Just let me get Taylor settled... yeah, Taylor from church... she's working out because her date went bad. Why... alright."

He held the phone out to her with a frown. "Hunter wants to talk to you."

She swallowed and stepped over, taking the phone and holding it to her ear. "Hello?"

"What the hell does he mean, your date went bad? What the hell happened? Are you alright?" Hunter's voice was harsh and made her wince.

"I'm alright. Scott's daughter got sick. That's all. Nothing to do with me."

Hunter paused on the other line. Then he said, "So he didn't touch you?"

She arched a brow, turning away from Parker who appeared to be listening too intently. "I didn't say that."

"I swear to God, princess, if he touched you—"

"You have nothing to say about it, remember? You left and haven't talked to me all week, so I moved on. Fuck you, Hunter. I'm done."

She clicked the end call button, then took a deep breath. Her stomach rolled, but she pasted on a bright smile and turned back to Parker, handing him his phone back.

"Here you go. Sorry about that."

"What the hell was that?" His eyebrows were sky high in surprise, but she just shrugged and walked to the door.

"Nothing," she said, pushing it open. "It's all in the past now. Thanks for letting me in. I'll come by to do all the registration for a membership at some point."

He nodded, but she let the door shut behind her before he could say anything. She didn't have the energy to answer his questions right now.

She ran back home, enjoying the burn in her muscles and the way she'd mouthed off to Hunter. She stomped up the stairs, sweat dripping down her spine as she unlocked her door and checked her phone.

Don't forget to call me and tell me all about your date.

Taylor smiled and sank onto her couch to call Lucy.

"I didn't mean you had to call me right this minute," Lucy said with a chuckle.

Taylor winced. "Is it a bad time?"

"No," Lucy said. "It's good. Harry's already in bed, and I was just working on my novel. How did the date go?"

Taylor told her all about it, what they talked about, what they ate. "It wasn't a boring quick date like the first one. It was better than the second one, that's for sure."

"Wait, what happened with the second one? I thought it was a great date at a cute little restaurant in Denton?"

Taylor sighed and leaned her head back on the couch. "It was, but then Hunter showed up with Jewel at the same restaurant."

Lucy gasped. "Damn it, Tay, I thought you were going to keep me up to date on your life from now on? Ugh, whatever. Are they back together?"

Taylor winced as guilt flooded her. She could've talked to Lucy about all this when she watched Harry this week, but she was hurting too much and didn't want to rip her heart open again.

She curled onto her side on the couch. "I don't know if they are or not. He said they weren't, but the way they acted so familiar with each other, I think so. And tonight, Parker said they're just friends because—get this—they have a fucking *teenage daughter* together."

"Oh my God," Lucy whispered.

Taylor nodded. "I know. I just have no idea if they're together or not. It doesn't really matter though because even when I called him out about only wanting me as a fuck buddy, he still only used me as a fuck buddy."

"What does that mean?"

"He said that I meant something to him, that I was his kryptonite, but kryptonite killed Superman, right? His actions show that he wants to avoid me at all costs. Like, he came over after my date with Scott and fucked me senseless last weekend too. Then when I woke up, he was gone *again*."

Lucy gasped, but Taylor kept going. "If he cared about me at all, he would've texted or called or hell, he could've shown up at the library anytime. But no, he ignored me and broke my heart."

Lucy gasped again. "What? What do you mean, he broke your heart? Tay, do you love him?"

Taylor groaned, tears pricking her eyes. "I—I love his dick. That's what I'm telling myself, that it's not real love. It's just the love of his dick."

Lucy laughed. "Oh Tay, how many dicks have you had?"

Taylor winced. "I don't want to answer that."

Lucy laughed again. "And how many of those dicks have you loved like this?"

Taylor frowned, her heart stuttering as the truth glared her in the face. "I—I don't want to answer that either."

A knock sounded at the front door, and she stood with a groan. "Actually, there's someone at the door. I'm going to go answer that instead."

"Maybe it'll be Hunter again. He showed up after your first and second dates with Scott after all."

"It better not be," Taylor grumbled as she stretched and yawned. "I'll call you tomorrow?"

"Oh my God, Tay, don't go until you look in the peep hole. I need to know if it's him."

Taylor sighed and walked to the door. She gasped and peered through the peephole. Hunter stood on the doorstep, shifting nervously and frowning.

She pulled away from the door, her heart racing. "Shit, it really is him."

Her voice was barely a whisper, but Lucy squealed into the phone. Taylor held it away from her head as Hunter knocked on the door again. Her heart raced, and she wanted to throw it open. She was desperate to hold him, see him, just talk to him about anything.

But a part of her dreaded what would come next. Was she doomed to repeat this vicious cycle? Why couldn't she bring herself to say no to him?

"Oh my God, Tay, open the door. See what he wants. Maybe he's decided he loves you too?"

Tay snorted and shook her head, her stomach roiling as she stared at the door. She bit her lip and nerves shot down her spine.

"I don't know. I feel like this is just beating a dead horse.

I talked to him on the phone earlier at the gym. I told him to fuck off."

Lucy groaned. "Well, no wonder he showed up. He's not going to let you go now."

Taylor snorted. "As if."

But maybe Lucy was right. Hadn't she told him to get out last weekend? And instead, it had just driven him mad with lust. Maybe he had a power trip and got off on her telling him to fuck off?

She just didn't know him well enough to figure out that answer, and that was the crux of the problem. She didn't know him, despite what her heart and body said.

"You'll never know if you don't answer it."

She bit her lip and sighed. "Okay, wish me luck. I'll call you in the morning?"

"You better," Lucy said. They both laughed and said goodbye. Then she took a deep breath and opened the door.

Chapter Thirty-Five

Taylor opened the door, crossed her arms, and narrowed her eyes. "What are you doing here?"

Her tone was scathing, but Hunter frowned and stepped inside. He didn't push, but when he stepped forward, she danced out of his reach, eyeing him warily as he shut the door behind him.

"I wanted to talk to you," he said. His stomach was in knots just being in her presence.

She snorted. "No, you wanted to fuck me. That's all I am to you. Just a little fuck toy to use whenever you get jealous or hear that I'm out with Scott. Well, it ends now, Hunter. You can't keep doing this to me."

Her voice wobbled on the last word, and she turned away, her eyes glistening. She wrapped her arms around her waist and took a few steps toward the couch.

His hands ached to hold her, and he wanted to pull her into his arms and tell her it was going to be alright. He raked a hand through his hair and went behind her couch to the other side, giving her plenty of room.

He knew how to break wild horses. He settled on the couch to let her get used to his presence, then he changed his tone of voice to be smooth, soft, deep, and low.

"Taylor, all I want to do is talk."

The vulnerable look on her face gutted him even as she eyed him suspiciously. He wanted to protect her and love her the way she deserved to be loved.

He frowned, his heart racing. That's what this was. He'd thought about it all week. It was love, plain and simple. It was more powerful than anything he'd ever felt with Jewel.

"You're not just a fuck toy. You're—"

Her eyes glistened from the other side of the couch as she burst out, "Yes, I am. That's all I've ever been. I don't know why I thought I could change. I just need to go back to being the town whore that I used to be. You already treat me like one, so why not? I should just give in already."

She stood in a defensive protective stance, her arms wrapped around herself but her feet wide and ready to fight.

He sat forward, aching to jump up and wrap his arms around her, but she scampered to the other side of the coffee table even further away from him, so he stayed seated on the edge of the couch.

He clasped his hands together. "You're my slut, princess, but you're not a whore. Let's get that straight right now."

Her eyes brightened at his words, and she watched him warily. She shook her head and wiped a tear from her eye. "You're just saying that, even though it makes no sense when all you do is use me and fuck me then leave."

She sobbed, burying her face in her hands.

Fuck it. He jumped up and wrapped her in his arms. He ignored the smell of another man and just held her and rocked her gently where they stood.

He kissed the side of her head. "I'm so sorry, sugar. I don't text well. I'd rather call, but every time I wanted to call it was another emergency at the ranch, the early hours of the morning, or you were at work—"

"Excuses," she said into his chest, her face still covered with her hands.

He shook his head, rubbing his cheek against her hair. "Never. I don't text unless I can do audio to text because I have dyslexia. I hate reading because it doesn't make any sense, but if you text me, I promise I'll respond from now on."

"Bullshit," she mumbled into her hands. "We talked about poetry and Greek mythology and astronomy on our date, remember? I know you read."

He shook his head. "It's all audio books and picture books, sugar."

She sighed, her body sinking into his and giving him hope. "I've heard all these same excuses from my dad. He always calls, says he'll change, and then he never does."

"I'm not your dad," he said softly, his hands gripping her back. It didn't escape his notice that she'd not talked about her family on their date or any of their time together.

She laughed bitterly and spun out of his arms. She flung her arms wide. "You'd think not, but you act just like him. When we talk, it's all sunshine and rainbows, but then he disappears and only comes to me when he wants something. You do the same fucking thing."

He frowned, not liking the comparison. "I meant what I said last weekend. You're mine. I don't just want you as a fuck buddy, I want to date you."

Her jaw dropped and her eyes widened. "You never fucking said that."

He frowned and nodded. "I did."

She shook her head. "No, you said I was yours and you were mine, not Jewel's. That was it. I texted you to ask if we were fuck buddies, but you never responded. You never said anything about wanting to date. Are you—are you serious? Don't joke about this, Hunter."

"I'm not joking."

She raised a finger and pointed it at him. "For the love of God, if you say you want to date and then disappear again and don't talk to me—"

He shook his head and dropped to his knees, opening his hands wide. "I'm not going to leave you. I can't even if I wanted to because I love you, Taylor."

Tears flooded her eyes, and she froze like a deer in the headlights. His heart pounded at the silence, and his stomach knotted up. He stared up at her, his knees aching and hands wide.

She sniffed and shook her head, backing up toward the kitchen. "I don't fucking believe you."

He frowned, his hands dropping to his side. "What do I have to do to prove it to you?"

She wrapped her arms around her waist, and her eyes pleaded with him. "Just talk to me! We never talk and being in love means knowing someone more than in a physical sense. For fuck's sake, Hunter. You're a *dad*. Why didn't you tell me? That's a major deal, but you never said a word."

He sighed and got to his feet, sinking back onto the couch. He closed his eyes and rubbed his temples. "That's because we don't know if she's my daughter."

Taylor didn't say anything for a few seconds, so he opened his eyes. Her forehead was drawn in a frown, and she shook her head. "I'm sorry, say that again? Didn't you and Jewel date for like five years before she went to college?"

He nodded. "Yeah, but she fucked my brother too."

Taylor gasped and drew closer. Hope bloomed in his chest, and it made him want to keep talking. He wanted to tell her everything.

"Parker?"

He shook his head. "No, Chase, the one who went to prison."

Taylor crossed her arms and frowned, so he told her the entire story of Jewel coming home, him and Chase getting into the fight, and the daughter he'd never met. As he talked, she moved closer, eventually sitting on the opposite end of the couch.

"So that's why you and Chase fought, and you had that black eye," she said softly.

He nodded and rubbed his temples. He hadn't slept much this week, too stressed about the ranch and his mom.

"Are you okay?" She shifted closer, now almost in arm's reach.

He shook his head and sighed. "Got a headache is all. It's been a long week, and I didn't eat today."

She frowned and jumped up, turning back to the kitchen. "Tell me about your week. What happened with the mare and the bull and your mom? Parker wasn't that great at explaining it earlier."

She went around the kitchen, pulling things out of the fridge while he talked. He probably hadn't spoken this much in years, probably not since a public speaking class in high school.

It just poured out of him. "Thankfully, there wasn't any internal bleeding, just the broken hip. Ma should get out of the hospital on Monday. She's getting antsy at being there for so long."

"When did all this happen?"

"Sunday afternoon."

She glared at him and pointed a spatula at him. "Why didn't you call me? I have Tuesday and Wednesdays off, remember? I could've come and helped."

He flushed and raked a hand through his hair. "I was afraid you wouldn't talk to me."

Her face softened, then she turned back to the stove.

"The mare and foal didn't make it," he sighed. Her shoulders tensed, but she didn't turn around again, so he continued. "It was gruesome. We haven't had that hard of a birth in a long time. We were all crying."

She finally spooned something onto a plate and set it on the table, pulling out the chair and pointing. "Come eat. I'll get you a drink."

He stood and dizziness washed over him. When it passed, he walked to the table and sank onto the chair.

Rotisserie chicken and pancakes sat on the plate, and his mouth watered. He looked up as she set a cup of water and a fork down, but she still danced out of arms' length warily. She took the chair beside him though and fiddled with a coffee cup.

He swallowed past the lump in his throat to say, "You cooked for me?"

She arched a brow and nodded, just barely meeting his gaze before looking away. "The chicken is from the store, but the pancakes are fresh. Eat."

He cut in and savored the first bite with a moan. He looked up at her, his eyes wide. "You can cook?"

She shrugged. "Girl's gotta survive somehow, and eating out was typically too expensive while in college."

"This is fucking delicious," he said.

Her cheeks tinged pink at the praise, and she glanced down still avoiding his gaze. "My mom worked at a cafe in the evenings, after her first job at the factory. All my spare time growing up was in that cafe, helping out when I got too hyper."

He smiled softly. "I bet you were the cutest kid."

She shrugged, pulling her knee up and leaning her face on it. Then she asked softly, "Was Jewel there? This week when the mare and your mom got hurt?"

He swallowed some water, then he nodded. "Yes, she and Gemma rotated when dealing with the mare before she died."

She nodded and wiped a tear. "She was there for you when you needed her, but I didn't even get a chance, Hunter. Don't you see?"

He frowned and finished the last bite. "See what?"

Taylor shrugged, her face fallen in defeat. "She gets you. She's the perfect woman for you. She can help on the ranch, she was there when you needed her, you might have a daughter together."

He reached across the table and took her hand. Finally, she looked at him. "She's not you, princess."

Taylor blinked, and her lower lip started to quiver. He moved his chair over, gently taking her other hand too.

"She's not you. She doesn't hold a candle to you. We might have a daughter together, but we're just friends. That date we went on last weekend? We decided then to just be friends, and both of us were relieved when we stopped trying to force something that's not there anymore."

Taylor blinked and tears rolled down her eyes. "Are you sure?"

He cupped her face with one hand and wiped the tear away. "Oh sugar, there's only one you, and you're the only one for me."

She shook her head and choked back a sob, saying, "But—but love doesn't leave."

He kissed the side of her face, shying away from saying the actual words and baring his heart again, but he could tell her the rest of the truth. "I won't ever leave again, I swear."

She cried, "No more leaving in the middle of the night?"

He kissed her cheek, tasting the tears. "No more."

"You're going to date me?" Her tone was accusatory, like a challenge.

It made him smile as he kissed her again. "Yes, I'm going to date you so hard you're not going to want to let me go."

She sobbed and leaned back. "I already don't want to let you go. Don't you get that? God, you're such an idiot."

"An idiot in love," he said, pulling her to her feet and setting her on the table. It was dangerously close to saying those three powerful words.

She wiped her eyes and shook her head. "I don't believe it."

He kissed her cheek and grabbed her tank top, pulling it up and off. Her sports bra zipped in the front, and he quickly got rid of it too.

"Do you love me?" His voice was as soft as her breasts in his hand, and he held his breath as he waited for her answer.

She sighed, leaned back on her palms on the table, and closed her eyes. "Of course I do. That's why this has been so hard."

He grinned and tugged on her nipples. "I'll show you what's been so hard."

She choked on a laugh, a half-laugh half-sob hybrid that both broke his heart and gave him hope.

Then he twisted her nipples, and her eyes flew open. Her mouth dropped into that *o* that drove him crazy, and her eyes went glassy with desire.

He gently pressed her back on the table until she was spread out, her legs dangling off the edge. He tugged her shorts and underwear down, then moved her feet to rest on chairs on either side of him.

Then he pulled up another chair and leaned forward, breathing in the sweet smell of her delicious pussy.

"Hunter?" Her voice was needy, barely a whisper as she sat up on her elbows and looked down at him with those bright green eyes.

He met her gaze and smiled. "When we're alone, call me a beast. Call me papa bear, master, a fucking idiot. I don't care. As long as we're alone every day."

Her expression melted, and she shook her head. "We can't be alone every day, Hunter. We're not married, and we don't live together."

"Yet," he said. Her eyes widened, and he grinned. "Now sit back and let the beast eat his dessert."

Then he leaned forward and sucked on her clit. She gasped, falling onto her back on the table.

He teased and tugged on her little bud, tasting the sweetness and smelling the salty sweat from her run earlier. It was a heady combination that made him want to plunge inside and never leave.

And that's exactly what he promised her he'd do, wasn't it? He wasn't going to leave ever again.

Chapter Thirty-Six

Taylor gasped as Hunter's fingers probed her pussy and her ass. She groaned and squirmed on the table, his plate, fork, and cup crashing to the ground, shattering, not that either of them stopped.

Instead, his mouth drove her higher and higher as he added another finger and then another.

She ground down on him, desperate for him, needing him with every cell in her body as he reached down and pressed his face to her pussy. She screamed, feeling his whiskers rake her bare flesh.

The waves built higher and higher, threatening to drown her as she raced toward the edge. "Oh, yes, almost—" she gasped.

Then he pulled away and stood up. "What the fuck?" she demanded, glaring.

He smirked, his eyes dark as he pulled his shirt over his head. "I want to feel you come on my dick, princess. After the shittiest week of my life, I need you."

Her heart skipped a beat at the raw beauty of his words,

The Cowboy Gets His Girl

the stark need on his face. She widened her legs and played with her clit while he kicked his boots off.

His eyes dipped down, watching every movement. She felt desired and wanted, but the feeling went deeper than that. There was more to this than she'd realized. It was more than sexual, more than physical, and she now realized it was only with him. The thought of depending on him terrified her, but there was no stopping this raging wildfire of love. It had swept over her until there was nothing left but the two of them.

He grabbed her thigh and stepped between her legs, staring down at her with a possessive gaze. His hand traced down her breasts lightly, and she sucked in a breath. He palmed his dick, stroking it slowly as she tweaked her clit with her own fingers.

"You went on another date with Scott." It was a statement full of hurt, but she responded anyway.

"Yes." Her voice didn't sound like her. It was a breathy apology wrapped in one word.

He stroked his dick and frowned. "I don't like it."

She nodded, feeling the flames stroke higher with her fingers. "I know."

He pressed forward, the head of his cock teasing her molten core. "Did you kiss him again?"

His dick gave the lightest touch to her clit, and it sent her in a tailspin. He leaned over the table, his fingers caressing her neck again. He slid two fingers inside her pussy even as her own fingers still played with her clit.

She whimpered, jerking under his hand. "We kissed on the front porch."

"And that's it?"

She shook her head, feeling his hand caressing her neck and his mere presence holding her down to wait in anticipation. She wanted his hand to wrap around her neck while he took her like the savage beast he was.

She taunted him with the truth. "We—we went up to his room and made out."

His eyes flashed. "No more. Tell me you're mine. I need you, Taylor. I need you to need only me, no one else. Break up with him. Don't date him again. Be mine and mine only."

He teased her folds with each word, and she gasped, "No fair. You're using your dick to persuade me."

He arched a brow and moved his hand from her neck, leaning on the table beside her, the tip easing inside just a little. "I'll use anything I can to my advantage. I'll do whatever it takes to keep you."

She sucked in a breath, her heart racing at his words. Did he mean for now or forever? Before she could ask, he stretched her wider, easing inside inch by slow inch. She whimpered and closed her eyes, soaking up the pleasure of it.

"Don't make out with him again, princess. Tell me you won't."

"I won't," she gasped as he eased in again, too slowly. Every inch was the best kind of torture.

"Swear it."

"I swear."

"Your lips are mine."

"Yours," she gasped.

"My pussy. My ass." He lifted her leg, easing her ankle on his shoulder as his fingers teased her ass. She jerked at the new angle, the double penetration making her breathing ragged.

He slid inside with a groan, slow and steady. "You're mine, my cum princess, my sugar tits, mine, mine, mine."

He leaned over her, pinning her to the table with his body, and she gasped as he slowed his thrusts.

"Say you're mine, princess." He peppered soft kisses along her jaw, but with him bent over, it drove him deeper.

She licked her lips, trying to hold out longer. "But I'm scared."

"Of what?"

"That you'll leave me again," she whispered, meeting his gaze as he held himself still and deep.

He shifted, releasing her leg and cupping her face in his palm, their faces just inches apart. His strong jaw and sharp features made her ache at his beauty, but it was his touch that made her pulse race.

"I can't leave you," he said softly, raking her hair away from her face. "I want to be with you all day every day. I can't live without you, Taylor, not anymore. If this week has taught me anything, it's that this is it for me. You're all I want at the end of the day and everything I need in my life. Say you feel the same."

He kissed her softly, coaxing the words from her even as tears seeped down her temples and into her hair. The table creaked as he rocked against her, going impossibly deeper as he started their dance once more. She closed off the emotional turmoil of their relationship and gave into his kiss, wrapping her legs around him.

He swooped in to take advantage, and his tongue met hers in an electric shock that rocked her core. She squeezed him in reaction, and he groaned into her mouth.

His words settled deep within her, nagging at the back of her mind. She wanted to trust him, wanted to believe that he would follow through on the words, but a part of her worried that it was just empty promises.

She tangled her tongue with his, her need ratcheting up

as he rocked his hips slowly. Even if he wasn't sincere, even if tonight was all they had, she would enjoy it. If he was gone in the morning, she would probably cry and her heart would break, but it wasn't the worst thing in the world. She would survive this.

Just one more night with him.

She wrapped her arms around his back and raked her nails into his skin. He pulled back and looked down at her.

"You're mine," she said softly.

His eyes flashed in victory, his jaw firm and unrelenting as he thrust deeper. "Whose pussy is this?"

She whimpered at his dirty talk. "Yours."

"Whose ass is this?"

"Yours."

"Whose heart is this?"

She hesitated just a half-second, then gasped, "Yours."

He thrust deeper, the rhythm changing from slow and deep to hard and rough. His hips slammed into hers and the table shifted under them.

He thrust again, the scrape against the tile floor mixing with their panting and groaning. It felt like he was trying to bang her into the table with the power of his thrusts, and she was so here for it. Her eyes rolled back in her head as they closed, gripping his back with a gasp.

"Fuck yes," he groaned. "You're so tight. I dream about this pussy. Your eyes. Your hair wrapped in my fist as I fuck you hard. Your scream as you lose it. Come for me, princess."

She whimpered as he buried his hands in her hair, pulling hard. The pain shot through her, driving up her pleasure. She gasped, feeling her body careening closer to the edge.

His dick stretched her wider with every thrust. The table

shifted and his hips hit her clit just right. She broke apart on the waves with a scream.

"That's it, princess. Come on that dick." He groaned, driving deeper once, twice, then holding still.

Each word was a spear that went into her soul. Her mind splintered, and she screamed, flashes of light shooting behind her eyes as she spasmed under him.

Her body thrashed, but his arms caged her in. She couldn't control it, but she milked him for all she was worth. The throbbing heat of his dick swelled as he spilled inside, and she whimpered with every pulse.

He groaned and grabbed her breast, kneading it. With a twist of her nipple, she gasped and squeezed. He paused, buried to the hilt and spilling hot lava inside.

She whimpered and soaked up the sensations of him. She could get used to this undivided attention from a good man who thought she hung the moon. Shivering with aftershocks, she was afraid to hope that this would last, afraid that she'd get hurt like every phone call and visit with her dad.

Hunter held her, safe and secure as he kissed her temple tenderly, and she felt loved for the first time in a long time. This moment meant more than any other encounter in her life. It was everything she'd been searching for. Safety, love, a joining that defied words.

Hadn't she thought the same thing with every sexual encounter they had thus far? Somehow each one was better than the last, each one reaching further into her soul to brand her as his.

He kissed her cheek, then her lips, his tongue dueling slowly and softly with hers. He broke the kiss and sighed, "I love you, Taylor."

She felt tears prick her eyes once more, and her heart

ached. "I love you too, Hunter." Damn her heart, but she did.

He leaned back and slowly helped her to sit up. "Come on. Let's go to bed. I need to hold you."

Without dislodging each other, she wrapped her legs around him, her heart full and heavy as he walked them to the bedroom.

He laid her on the bed and turned them on their sides, cradling her head to kiss her forehead. "Sh, let's sleep. I'll wake you up for the next round."

She melted into his arms, finally relaxing. She didn't know if it'd last. Only time would tell if he was still here in the morning, and she refused to worry about it.

She had wet dreams of sex in a field, the crickets singing to them with the stars overhead. It was smooth and gentle and made her want to cry. Then he'd flipped her over and probed her ass.

The dream turned into more, into things she'd never even tell Lucy, they were too embarrassing. She throbbed, aching and pushing back on him, feeling her ass stretch and her clit throb.

"That's it, princess. You're almost there." His voice broke through the haze of sleep.

She came slowly awake to a feeling of tightness in her ass. Her fingers stretched over the smooth, cool sheets, and she found herself on her stomach with some pillows under her hips.

She turned her head. His arms settled beside her, caging her under him.

"Good morning, princess. Do you feel that?" His voice was deep and rough, from sleep or desire she didn't know. He pulsed behind her, and she gasped.

His dick was buried in her ass. She felt it throbbing inside, and she automatically squeezed in surprise.

He groaned, his head resting between her shoulder blades. "Fuck, that feels so good. Please tell me you love it as much as I do, princess. Or does it hurt? Do you want me to stop?"

He held still, and she wiggled a little, testing the feel and weight of him. She gasped again and widened her hips, pulling her knees under her more.

"Oh god, that feels so good. How did you—oh god," she groaned as he pulsed inside. She whimpered, pushing back against him.

He eased out slowly, making her gasp at the sensation, the stretching. It was unreal. She'd read about it, dreamed about it, had never admitted her secret fantasies, but nothing could've prepared her for the real deal.

He pressed back in, the slickness of it making her wonder. How had she missed him moving on the bed or getting the lube from her bedside table?

He pulsed and pulled out, not quite leaving her empty before gently rocking forward. He groaned, "God, this was worth the wait. This ass is all I've dreamed of since I took you home from the bar."

He withdrew and set up a slow and steady rhythm. She kept waiting for the pain, but it never came. Instead, the pleasure built with each thrust until she was moaning louder and louder.

When the orgasm crested, she screamed into the pillow and thrashed under him. He pinned her ass to the bed, the pillows not enough as she throbbed.

He groaned, his head on her back as she felt him swell within her. "Oh fuck," he growled, biting her shoulder as he spilled inside. She gasped at the fullness, his orgasm triggering her own to keep going.

Sparks shot off behind her eyes, their combined pulsing and throbbing making her whimper as the aftershocks eased. He held himself on his hands and knees, caging her body under his as he waited. Random pulses made her squirm and moan.

He kissed her shoulder again and pushed off her. She gasped a breath as he slowly pulled out of her ass. The tugging was odd, mildly uncomfortable, but coming so close after a softer orgasm, she didn't care. She fell onto her side and hugged the pillows to her stomach.

He slid his hands along her sides, pushing her hair from her face. "Are you alright? Was that okay? Did I hurt you?"

She shook her head and sighed. "No, that was fucking amazing. I woke up, and you're still here."

She sniffed and opened her eyes, finally meeting him in the faint light of the morning. He smiled and leaned over, kissing her softly with lips that were made for hers.

"I'll always be here for you. For as long as you'll have me, and maybe even after you tell me to hit the curb."

She chuckled as he stood with a grin and walked to the bathroom. He'd already done that, since she's thought they were over every time she woke up alone and he ignored her texts. Dread and worry began to seep into her mind, and she tried to shut it down, she really did. The water turned on, and she looked at the clock. She groaned to see seven and light through the curtains.

He chuckled, leaning on the bathroom doorway. "Not used to waking up this early?"

She nodded and stretched with a yawn. "Not used to being fucked in the ass, either."

He arched his brow and turned back into the bathroom.

The Cowboy Gets His Girl

"You better get used to it, princess, if we're going to make this work. Want to shower?"

She nodded and followed him under the water on wobbly legs, her body aching with a delicious stretch from good lovin'. As her body adjusted to his, so too did her soul. She just hoped her soul didn't end up bruised in the process.

He reached for the loofah and asked softly, "Are you sure you're alright?"

She leaned her head back against the tile and sighed. "Yeah, just tired."

His hands slowly rubbed against her skin, the bubbles lathering on her body. His hand and the loofah raked over her breasts, making her groan and arch into his touch, her body too sensitive yet still aching for more.

"What do you see happening today?"

She frowned, not opening her eyes. "What do you mean?"

He paused, then said, "I'm still here this morning, but what about today? How do we make a relationship work? It's been so long since I've had a girlfriend, I'm not sure I remember how."

"First of all, I love the idea of having a real relationship with you. Second of all, I have to work today, so I need to be there by nine. What do you need to do today?"

He rubbed the loofah lower, the scrubbing of her clit making her gasp.

"I need to go to the hospital to see if Ma needs anything before they release her, then I need to make sure the ranch is running smoothly. I don't want her worrying about anything when she gets home."

"She cooks for the ranch hands every day?" Taylor frowned, remembering the conversation from their date and opening her eyes to step under the water. The movement dislodged his hands, but she wanted to talk. Her pussy needed a break.

He nodded and lathered his own body. "Yeah, breakfast and lunch. Dinner is just family, though."

She frowned and nodded. "Who's been cooking since she's been in the hospital?"

He shrugged. "I have mostly. Gemma brought over some breakfast sandwiches one morning, and Jewel brought over pastries from Maryanne's bakery. Chase was supposed to do something this morning."

Taylor shook her head. "I can help. I'll stop by and take inventory. Then I'll bring stuff to make breakfast and be there—what time do y'all usually eat breakfast?"

He arched his brow. "Six o'clock. We actually slept in today."

She winced. "Shit, that's early. Okay, it'll be fine. I can do that."

He put a palm on the tile, caging her in and looking down at her with hooded eyes. "It'd be easier if you just stayed the night."

She tilted her chin up. "And stay where? In the stinky bunk house with twenty other guys? In your parents' house when I've only met them twice? Yeah, neither is a good idea."

He leaned into her, kissed her cheek, and drew his lips to her ear. His breath sent a shiver down her spine as he said, "You could stay at the barn with me."

She sucked in a breath, frowning as she tried to think through the possibilities. His hips thrust into hers, and she groaned.

"Yeah, I suppose I could do that."

"Then it's settled," he said. "You'll come stay at the barn with me tonight. Indefinitely."

Her eyes flew open, and she pulled away to stare at him. "What? Are you serious?"

He shrugged and reached for the shampoo, giving her some much needed space. "I don't see why not. We need to talk more so I can show you I'm serious about this being a relationship. I'll try to be better about video calling you and voice texts, but it'd be way easier to manage all this chaos at the ranch if you're there with me."

He rinsed his hair as he talked, then he raked the water away and cupped her face. "Please Taylor. Come stay with me while we try to figure this out."

Her chest tightened at the vulnerability in his face, the challenge and hesitation. She smiled and nodded, and the grin that broke out on his face made it seem worth it.

Some of her fears fled as she washed her own hair, and he talked about their typical schedule at the ranch, his parents and how they did things. The excitement in his voice was infectious. It was sweet how he wanted to share his life with her.

They shut off the water, and he handed her a dry towel. "How long is the library open today?"

"Nine to three. It's a short day, but we have story time at noon, so it'll be busy."

He nodded and asked, "Do you have a spare toothbrush?"

She dug one out from under the sink and left him to it, going to get some clean clothes from the closet. She tugged her pencil skirt and silk blouse on, then followed his towel covered ass to the kitchen.

He paused from gathering his clothes to stare and whistle, "Hot damn, I've dreamed of you in exactly that outfit, but you're even better in person, princess."

She blushed and opened her mouth to reply but was interrupted by a knock on the door.

She sighed and walked to it, expecting a complaint about the sex noise from the neighbors again. "It's probably the neighbor. I think he's senile."

Hunter spanked her ass as she walked by, making her yelp and grin. He tucked the towel around his waist and bent to pick up his clothes.

She opened the door, but it wasn't the neighbor. It was Scott.

Chapter Thirty-Seven

Scott looked behind her, his eyes taking in Hunter standing in a towel with hair dripping, holding his clothes in his arms. They all froze for a moment, then Scott looked at her.

"Well, I'm glad I let the girls go to the playground downstairs instead of coming up here."

His words were hurt, his face hard and sad at the same time. He thrust a box of donuts to her. "I brought you breakfast. Y'all enjoy. I guess I'll leave you to it."

Her hands automatically took the box, then he turned and strode to the stairs.

Taylor snapped out of her shock and stepped out of the apartment. "Scott, it's not what it looks like—"

"The hell it's not," Hunter said, grabbing her wrist and tugging her back into the apartment. "Sorry, Scott. Nothing personal," he called.

Scott waved a hand over his shoulder but didn't look back. Taylor winced, feeling a stab of guilt shoot through her.

Hunter closed the door behind them, and she sighed. "This sucks," she grumbled.

Hunter's spine straightened, and he crossed his arms. His clothes sat on the kitchen table now, and he still stood in just a towel.

"Does it?" His voice was soft, but his face was closed and wary. She sighed and rubbed her temples, clicking the coffee pot on and sitting at the kitchen table.

"Yeah, it does because I didn't have time to break up with him first. We weren't exclusive, but he's going to think I'm such a whore to almost sleep with him last night and instead sleep with you."

He swaggered over in his towel and knelt in front of her. He grabbed her hands and stared up at her with those bright hazel eyes that made her melt.

"Let's get one thing clear right now, sugar. You're not a whore. You might be my slut, but never a whore. Everyone makes mistakes. Scott will understand. Just give him time to cool off."

She shrugged and bit her lip with a sigh. "I know, but I feel terrible. We were starting this beautiful relationship. All our goals and dreams were laid out on the table, and we were on the same page. Mostly."

He arched a brow and stood up, his lips tensing as he jerked on his clothes. "What goals? Had you two talked marriage?"

She shrugged, her cheeks heating as she got up to get her coffee. "Maybe. I mean, he has two girls to think about. Of course they need a mother."

The shuffling sounds behind her stopped, and she turned her head, spoon stirring in her cup.

He frowned. "You'll only be marrying me, Taylor."

Her brows rose at his tone, at the surprise of it, but the

thrill down her spine told her she was excited by his high-handed behavior. "Slow down, cowboy. We just admitted we loved each other last night. Don't go proposing to me now."

He quirked a grin, jerking his shirt over his head. "When I propose, you'll know it. But back to Scott. Do you want me to talk to him man to man? I mean, the past few weeks, I've been the one showing up here. You didn't come looking for me, and I can explain that."

She sighed, nodding as she took her coffee to the table and sat again. He was right. She wasn't the whore she thought she was. This time last year, she probably would've already slept with Scott and forgotten both him and Hunter.

Seeing all Lucy went through had changed her. She was ready for the next stage of life, but maybe not marriage just yet. The cereal and milk on the counter drew her eye, and she remembered what she'd been doing before Scott knocked.

"Do you like strawberry flakes?" she asked.

He nodded as he pulled on his socks. She got up and poured milk and cereal into a bowl. There was nothing she could do about Scott right now. She'd call him on her way to work, and hopefully they could talk it out. He was such a great guy, but not the guy for her. She turned back to the man that made her heart race, stress over hurting Scott making her nervous and chatty.

"They're my favorite. I like the raisin ones too, but don't worry, I'll make real breakfast for your ranch hands. What do they typically eat?"

He grunted and tipped the bowl, already finished and drinking the leftover milk. She blinked and ate her own as he responded.

"Big breakfast is about three times a week. Biscuits, gravy, sausage, eggs, the works. Then it rotates between pastries once a week, pancakes, cinnamon rolls, and stuff like that. Never the same thing two days in a row. But darlin', we'll be perfectly fine with breakfast casseroles or burritos if we want to make those at night, just to be reheated in the morning. That's mostly what I've been doing. Nothing fancy."

She nodded, her anxiety skyrocketing as she worried about whether she'd be able to do this, but she wanted to try. At least she had her experience helping Mom at the café to fall back on. She wanted to help him out and show him that she could fit into his life.

He glanced at the clock and leaned over to kiss her. "I need to run to the hospital. The doctors will be making their rounds, and I want to be there to hear the discharge instructions."

She nodded as he shifted and put on his boots.

"I'll be at the ranch after I get off work. I already have an overnight bag packed from last night."

His hands paused, then he slowly sat up, staring at her with a frown. "You're not going to see him again, right?"

She nodded, feeling the weight of this moment with him. "Right, because I'm yours."

Some of the tension around his lips eased, and he nodded as he smiled. Then he kissed her again, a deep and bruising kiss that left her head spinning.

"I'm sorry if I get a bit possessive, it's just—Jewel and I broke up because I thought she was banging some guy down in college. Since then, I've always been scared to get close to anyone else, but the way I love you, Taylor?" His eyes held promises. Promises she was afraid to trust in. "I'm ten times more afraid I'll lose you. There's no escaping this feeling, and I don't want to, but I'll try to tone down the jealousy, so I don't scare you away."

She smiled with wobbly lips. "I'm not going anywhere, Hunter. I love you too, and there's nothing to be jealous about. Just trust me, alright?"

He smiled softly and nodded, kissing her cheek swiftly before walking out the door. Had there still been a hesitation in his eyes, or had she imagined it? The door clicked softly behind him, and she sat at the kitchen table.

The past twenty-four hours had left her wheels spinning. She had no idea what would happen next, but still worry plagued her.

Her phone rang, and she went to the bedroom to grab it.

"Hello?"

"Would you like to accept a collect call from Chris Grimes? Select one for yes, two for no."

She winced and sighed. She hesitated, then clicked one. The phone took a few seconds, and she breathed deeply to collect her thoughts.

If Hunter could be something more, if he could change and not leave her like he'd done before, maybe her dad could change too.

"Baby girl, are you there?"

Her dad's voice was rough and to the point, but it still brought a tear to her eye.

"Hey Dad," she sighed. Her chest ached, hoping that for once it'd be a good conversation.

"There you are. Did you get your first paycheck? I still need bailed out."

She bit her lip and rubbed her chest, disappointment spearing her. "I did, yes. I have two hundred dollars left over after bills. How much is bail money?"

"Five hundred? I'm not sure. Call the bail bondsman. Maybe you can put the other half on a credit card?"

She blinked and fisted her hand in anger. "I don't *have* any more credit cards, Dad. I can't do that."

"Baby girl, if you can get me out of here, I can pay you back. I have a plan in place and can get to it when I get out. I can have it back to you in less than a week."

She felt a tear roll down her cheek. People couldn't change. Why had she thought differently?

"This is the same conversation as always, Dad. You say you'll pay me back. You tell me to use a card and don't care what that does to my finances or credit. You don't care about me *at all*. I'm just a cash cow to you."

"Baby girl, don't talk like that. You're my one and only daughter."

"And I'll always be your daughter, but I can't kill myself to take care of you. I love you, Dad, even if you don't love me."

He sputtered, but she hung up. The line went dead, and she laid on her bed, curling into a ball and squeezing her eyes.

She prayed that Hunter was different. She prayed that this was the start of a new life with him, and not another heartbreak waiting to happen.

She couldn't take it that her dad only wanted her money, and for once, she was glad she didn't fucking have any.

Her phone rang again, and she looked at the caller ID. She smiled and rolled to her back.

"Hey, Luce."

"Morning, Tay. What happened with Hunter? Is he still there? Should I call back?"

She sighed and shoved off the bed to get ready for work. "No, he just left. After Scott showed up with breakfast."

The line went silent, and Taylor asked, "Uh, Lucy? You still there?"

"Yeah," she said, and Taylor could just picture her frown. "Just trying to unpack what you said."

She snorted. "Right? Kinda crazy. You should've seen Scott's face. I feel absolutely terrible."

"I'm sure you can explain things to him. If there's anything to explain, that is?"

Taylor nodded and wiped a tear. "Yeah, it was actually good, Luce. We talked before we did the sexy times, probably more talking than since our first date. He—he says he loves me."

Lucy gasped. "Seriously? What'd you say?"

"I told him I'd believe it when I see it, that the way he's been ignoring me doesn't show me that he loves me."

"That's good. Words are cheap. Actions speak louder than words."

"Exactly. He was still here when I woke up though, so that's a step in the right direction. He asked me to move in with him too."

Lucy gasped and fired off question after question. Taylor laughed and filled her in on the details as she did her makeup for work.

Then she said, "Also, I just got off the phone with my dad, who was asking for bail money again."

"Ugh, I'm so sorry, Tay. What did you tell him?"

She shrugged and put it on speaker so she could re-pack her bag. "The truth. I still can't afford it. Nothing I can do about it."

"Do you want me to help?"

Taylor winced and grabbed the toys from the bedside table, throwing them into her overnight bag. She wanted to be prepared for anything. She never knew what Hunter would want to do.

"No, I need to break the cycle. It's time. Maybe you can help me with something else though. Do you know how to cook for a lot of people?"

"Um, not really. Why?"

"Well, his mom's in the hospital and gets released today. I'm going to stay with Hunter so I can make breakfast for the ranch hands before going to work. I'll make lunch on my days off too. Then I'll see what else I can help with while she's recovering."

"Oh, I wonder if the church is doing a meal train."

"That's what I wanted to ask you. Can you find out? That way I don't worry about dinners for his parents and him or whoever else eats with them?"

"Yeah, I'm on it."

They chatted about Harry, and Taylor told her she'd still babysit him on Tuesday and Wednesday, but Lucy would bring him to the ranch instead.

Taylor hoped that would be fine with his parents, but she would know more by tonight. Her nerves made her stomach flip as they hung up. She brushed her teeth and did the dishes, then she grabbed her overnight bag and went to work.

Chapter Thirty-Eight

Hunter sat in the hospital and listened to Kendall that Saturday morning.

Kendall was their friend, but he was also the best doctor in town. He shook his head. "I'm sorry, but I think you should stay at least seventy-two hours. You just had surgery, and we need to make sure there's no infection before you go home."

Ma clenched her fists in the hospital bed. "No, I'm going home today. You said I could be home by the weekend, doc."

Kendall nodded. "I know, and I'm sorry about that. I talked with the infectious disease doctor, and he'd rather wait on lab samples to come back first."

"Well, fuck him. I want to go home," she glared. Hunter's lips twitched at her attitude, but he didn't interfere yet.

Kendall frowned, "I agree with him."

Hunter crossed his feet at the ankles and put his thumbs in the pockets of his jeans. "Ma, this will be a good thing."

"Don't talk to me like that, son, or I'll whip your butt all the way home. I've done it before."

"Ma, breathe," he said firmly, giving her the look. "This will give us a chance to turn the downstairs den into a bedroom for you. Doc says you're not going to go up the stairs for a few weeks."

Kendall nodded, "That's right, after physical therapy clears you."

Hunter continued, "Exactly, so now Landry and I can make some adjustments to the den. Give us a few days to make this as comfortable of a recovery as possible, okay?"

She frowned but finally leaned her head back and closed her eyes as she sighed. "Fine, whatever. But turn it into a proper bedroom with a door. I'm going to dress myself and don't want to worry about any of you yay-hoos glimpsing my lily-white butt."

Dad rolled his eyes. "Enough, Ava. You're acting like a child."

"Well, you would too if you were hyped up on painkillers and still hurting from surgery."

Kendall frowned and checked her IV bags. "You're still hurting? Hm, looks like you have some decent pain meds, but no muscle relaxers. Let's try that and see if it helps, okay? I'll be here all weekend, so if you need me, just push the button."

She nodded, and Hunter followed him out the door.

"She'll be alright?"

Kendall typed onto the computer by the door. "Yeah, the hardest part will probably be keeping her down for the recovery time. She's going to need to stay in bed for at least two weeks, getting up only to use the bathroom and bathe. After that, we'll start physical therapy at home."

"What do we need to do downstairs?" Hunter asked.

"An elevated toilet is a must. And if you have one of the electric recliners, she'll like that. She shouldn't lean forward or bend too much at first, so having the electric recliner help her move from sitting or lying down to standing will be ideal."

Hunter thanked him, then called Landry. They talked through the details, then he went back into Ma's room.

"I talked to Landry. We'll get the den set up for you, Ma. Don't worry."

She frowned. "I can't help worrying. There's so much I have to do."

Hunter rubbed the back of his neck. "I'm working on all that, Ma. I've got someone coming in to make breakfasts, and I'll take care of lunches. I have the lists on the computer that Dad and I have been making. We handled everything fine this week, and it went well."

"Except for putting down Clio and her foal," Ava mumbled.

Bill frowned, scolding her. "Ava, that couldn't be helped."

Hunter felt the guilt begin to mount. He didn't feel like he was handling this week well, despite the calm front he showed them. He had barely kept his head above water, which might be why he'd broken down after talking to Taylor on the phone last night and finally went to see her.

He shoved his hands in his pockets and blurted out, "I have a girlfriend."

Ava and Bill both stared at him with wide eyes.

"What did you say?" Bill asked softly.

"Is it Jewel? Did the stress of this week bring you together?" Ava asked.

Hunter frowned, afraid to disappoint them, but then he saw Taylor in his mind's eye, her mischievous smile as she looked up at him expectantly. She was counting on him, and he needed to be a better person.

"No, it's not Jewel," he said quietly. "It's Taylor actually."

Ava frowned, asking, "Who?"

Bill replied, "The girl who just moved here a few weeks ago? The one we helped with the couch and table?"

Hunter nodded, and Ava said, "Oh. Well, what about Destini and Jewel?"

Hunter shrugged, not willing to spill that secret about Chase's part in it yet. It wasn't really his secret to tell, and it might amount to nothing.

So he just said, "We'll cross that bridge when she comes home. For now, Taylor is going to take care of breakfasts. She'll be at the ranch a lot in the next few weeks, so make her feel welcome, okay?"

Ava narrowed her eyes suspiciously. "I don't want some stranger cooking in my house."

Hunter shrugged. "Sorry, but that's what's going to happen, Ma. It would be too much on anyone to make a big breakfast then drive it to the ranch before going to work. It'll be better for her to just cook it at home."

"But it's *my* kitchen. Why does she need to come into the house anyway?" Ava asked, her jaw clenching.

He stared down at her with crossed arms, refusing to back down and break eye contact. Finally, she sighed and nodded.

Hunter sighed. "Thanks, Ma. There are so many people that are going to come in to help you. We're all here for you."

Kendall came back in, a nurse on his heels with another bag for the IV.

"I have the muscle relaxer here. Edna is going to put it

in, but I'll be back around after lunch to see how it's helping, okay?"

They chatted about what else might be needed for discharge on Monday, then Hunter kissed his mom goodbye. He took her hand and leaned over her.

"I'll take care of the ranch, Ma. Don't worry."

She just frowned and nodded, a line of worry creasing her forehead. She'd built up the ranch with her steely will and iron fist. Everyone respected her, and she wasn't to be crossed.

Hunter nodded to Bill and left in the Jeep. It was almost lunch, but Taylor had said she would be busy today at work.

He'd also said that he would be better about texting and calling her. He tapped the steering wheel as he drove, then he called the flower shop and placed an order to be delivered to the library. The same order as last time, as their first practice date.

He smiled, hoping that this time they'd start their relationship off right. He stopped at a stoplight and pushed the audio icon.

He said, "I'm leaving the hospital now. Ma won't be going home tonight, but will you still come over after work? I want you to stay with me."

He hit send and the light changed. As he drove to the ranch, he thought about the future. It was brighter with Taylor in it, but he wasn't sure how she'd get along with Ma. They'd been fine when they'd met at Taylor's apartment, but this was completely different.

He parked and checked his phone messages. An audio message blinked at him, and he pressed play.

"I'd love to. Do audio messages work better for you?"

He sighed in relief and hit reply. "Yes, this is much better. I love the sound of your voice."

Three dots appeared, then her reply came through. "Haha, I like your voice too. And your face. And your dick."

He grinned and got out of the truck just as Landry pulled up. He hit reply and said, "I have to go now. We're going to remodel the downstairs den for Ma to stay in when she comes home. I'll see you later, princess."

Her reply was almost instant. "I can't wait."

He slid his phone into his back pocket as he met Landry at the stairs to the house. They walked in together, talking about the plan with the den.

They worked to move the couch into the front living room. It was crowded but it worked.

"Ma's not going to like all this change," Landry said.

Hunter grunted, then looked around the den. "How long does it take to install a bathroom, if there's already plumbing?"

Landry shrugged. "To remodel the downstairs half-bath down here into one that she'll use comfortably? I think we should put in one of those walk-in baths. They're not getting any younger and will need it eventually anyway. What do you think?"

Hunter nodded. "Yeah, I think that'll work, but I was also wondering about remodeling the sale barn."

Landry's brows rose. "What do you mean?"

Hunter shrugged. "Remember the attic that Pops remodeled with me before he passed? I'd like to add another few rooms up there. It's just rafters now, but could you add another room or two? An actual living room and kitchen and a real bathroom with a shower or tub?"

Landry rubbed his chin and pursed his lips. "I'm not sure. I'll swing by there and check it out on my way home. Are you thinking of moving out there permanently?"

Hunter nodded, feeling a flush rise in his cheeks.

Landry arched a brow. "Why now? With Ma getting hurt, I'd assume you'd move back into the house to help her out. Not move out of the bunk house and into your own place."

Hunter swallowed hard and avoided his eyes as they moved more furniture.

"Just thinking long-term. It's not the best living arrangement, and I'd like more comfort there. I don't really want to take the time to build a whole new barndominium though."

"You might have to, depending on the state of the barn. It's pretty solid with all that steel, but I'll check."

"Just let me know," Hunter said.

"Does this have anything to do with Jewel?"

Hunter gripped the lamp and sighed. He was getting fucking tired of everyone assuming it was about Jewel.

"No, it's not fucking Jewel. I'm in love with Taylor. Taylor." He sounded out her name like a extra slowly, and it made him wince.

Landry just laughed. "Well, that's a surprise. I didn't even know you were dating. Wasn't she dating Scott?"

Hunter's teeth clenched, and he ground out, "Yes, but not anymore. She's with me now."

Landry slapped him on the back. "Well, I'm happy for you, brother. I can't wait to get to know her better."

Landry looked around and didn't dwell on it, which made him Hunter's favorite brother today. "Now about this house. You know Mom's going to throw a fit at how filthy it is, right?"

Hunter winced and nodded. "Think Holly and Maryanne and y'all can come over after church tomorrow for a cleaning party? Taylor will be here too."

Landry grinned, and Hunter wanted to sock him in the

jaw. "If that's what it takes to get the dirt on you two, then yes. I can almost guarantee the girls will want to come over, just to get to the bottom of it."

Hunter sighed in relief. He'd have to prepare Taylor for the interrogation, but she could handle it. If she could handle his dick in her ass, she could handle anything.

He smiled at the memory, and Landry led the way through the house.

"Do you have any pictures or anything of what you'd like the barn to look like? Do you want to go now and show me what you're thinking?"

Hunter nodded, and they hopped in his Jeep to drive across the ranch to the barn.

Chapter Thirty-Nine

Taylor frowned as she parked in front of Hunter's parents' house after work. There were several vehicles, but Hunter's Jeep wasn't there. She looked around while she turned off the engine.

She stepped out, her heels sinking into the hard packed dirt drive. She tucked her silk tank top into her skirt and walked to the front door, her nerves making her jittery. She hadn't really heard from Hunter the rest of the day, except for one message that said to meet him here.

She walked up the steps and knocked on the front door. It opened to reveal the petite blond from yoga holding a toddler boy on her hip.

She pushed open the screen with a wide smile. "Taylor, how good to see you again. Come in, come in."

"Hello. Holly, right?" Taylor asked, looking around. She hadn't been inside before, but it was all she'd imagined a working ranch house to be. Wood paneling wrapped every wall. To the left was the living room and to the right was the dining room and kitchen.

"Right, sorry to spring this on you. We're just all so excited to meet you we couldn't wait until Sunday."

Taylor frowned, seeing Maryanne from the bakery step out of the kitchen. What was she talking about? A toddler shrieked and ran through the kitchen and around the wall that separated it from the living room. Maryanne smiled and pointed.

"I'm Gunner's wife—another Williams brother—and that's our daughter, Connie. She's two and a half."

Another little girl chased after her, and the boy in Holly's arms squirmed to join them. Holly set him down and said, "This is Eddi and that was Freddi. They're almost eighteen months."

Taylor nodded but didn't know what to say. Finally, she cleared her throat, "Um, is Hunter here?"

Holly waved a hand. "Yeah, he's at the barn with Landry. They'll be here any minute. They had to haul some of the furniture from the den out there."

Cursing came from the stairs, then a man appeared carrying the corner of a mattress.

Holly said, "Watch out for the kids."

The kids had disappeared down the hall, and another man helped haul it down the hall. They were familiar, and the last one finally turned and gave her the head nod.

She waved, recognizing Chase. The other must be Gunner? Holly stepped back into the kitchen and grabbed a plate out of the dishwasher to put into the cabinet.

Maryanne turned back into the kitchen as well, wiping down the counters.

"So, you're dating Hunter now? What happened with Scott? He was so excited to pick up donuts and bring them to you this morning," Maryanne said.

Taylor winced and twisted her hands at the end of the

kitchen. "Um, yeah that didn't work out. Scott's a great guy, and I was really enjoying getting to know him, though."

Holly glanced over. "But?"

Taylor shrugged. She couldn't really hide the truth, could she? She might as well face it the same way she'd always faced her reputation at college, with head held high and chin up.

"Well, he showed up with the donuts, but Hunter had spent the night. Scott saw him in my apartment this morning."

"But you've been dating Scott? Were you dating Hunter too?"

Taylor frowned and straightened her back, rocking on her heels as she held her hands behind her back.

"No, I wasn't dating them both. I actually went on a date with Hunter first, but we agreed it was just a one-time thing. The date with Hunter was a practice date so I wouldn't blow it with Scott. But one thing led to another with Hunter."

"I'm confused. Why would you then date Scott if you were already sleeping with Hunter?" Holly asked.

"Hunter didn't want anything to do with me. When I'd go on a date with Scott, somehow Hunter would hear about it and show up. I couldn't tell him no."

Maryanne snorted. "I know how that feels. But it's kind of weird, knowing all the backstory. I'm not sure if you were cheating on Scott with Hunter or if you were cheating on Hunter with Scott."

Taylor bit her lip. "Hunter never talked with me after that first practice date. Scott was pretty good at texting and calling, though. I tried to forget about Hunter and focus on Scott, but then Hunter kept coming over."

Holly grinned, "He can be pretty persistent."

Maryanne smirked, "I'd say that stubbornness runs in the family. Gunner did something similar. He just couldn't stay away."

Holly laughed and nodded. "Same with us."

Taylor felt some of the tension in her stomach release. "And y'all worked through it?"

Holly nodded. "Yep, we did. It was pretty rough in the beginning, but then it all worked out."

"But we didn't have to deal with cheating," Maryanne pointed out.

Taylor winced. "I didn't cheat. Scott and I only went on three dates, and while we talked a lot, we didn't talk about being exclusive. I've tried calling him to talk it out, but he's not answering. Should I take him an apology present? Maybe some of your pastries, Maryanne?"

Maryanne shrugged, but it was Holly who said, "I think you should talk to him, but wait a few days. Right now, he's probably hurt, and anything you say will just make it worse."

Taylor nodded with a frown, her stomach twisting. "I never wanted to hurt him. He'll bring the girls to the library on Monday. I'll talk to him then and try to settle the air. At the very least, I'll apologize."

She hadn't wanted to hurt Scott. He was such a good man, and the look on his face that morning had been devastating. She'd texted him before work, but his reply had been short and to the point.

I need time to process.
We won't be at story time but will see you on Monday.

She didn't know what to say to make it better, but at least she had a few days to figure it out.

"What exactly will you apologize for?" Maryanne asked.

Taylor hesitated, and Maryanne turned, meeting her gaze with a direct and open one of her own.

"Are you apologizing for sleeping with Hunter or for getting caught?"

Taylor shook her head and sighed, sinking into a kitchen chair. "For all of it, but mostly for hurting Scott. He was caught in the crossfire."

"You might want to work on that apology," Holly winced.

Maryanne snorted and nodded, which just made Taylor feel even worse. She rubbed her forehead.

"So, Hunter wouldn't just leave you alone, huh? And now you're going to be cooking breakfast for the ranch?" Holly asked, shutting the now empty dishwasher.

Taylor nodded and looked around. "Yeah, he—he says he wants to date for real, and I do want to help where I can. Is Mrs. Williams going to be okay?"

Maryanne nodded and leaned around the kitchen wall to yell down the hall, "Dinner's ready."

Then she turned and said, "Come get a plate. And yes, she'll be alright. She's a cranky bitch at the moment. I went to visit her today, and she's spitting angry and ready to get out of there."

"The surgery went well, but now it's the hard part. Keeping her still long enough to recover," Holly said as she scooped two small bowls of the chicken and rice.

The front door opened, and Landry and Hunter strode in. Hunter's eyes settled on her, and he paused, causing Landry to run into him.

"You're here," he said softly, striding to her side.

She nodded up at him, and he leaned over to kiss her cheek. "I didn't know your whole family would be here."

He winced, sitting in the chair next to hers, his hand sliding from her shoulder down her bare arm. Tingles shot down her spine as the hair on her arm stood up.

"Yeah, sorry about that. Landry and I had decided the house needed to be cleaned, so I asked the girls to come over after church tomorrow. But when Landry told them I'd invited you over to stay for a while, they swarmed immediately."

Maryanne slapped him playfully on the arm as she set a small bowl on the table. "Hey, you make us sound like a pack of wolves or something."

He shrugged and grinned. "If the shoe fits…"

She wrinkled her nose, but Gunner just chuckled and said, "He's got a point, M."

She stuck her tongue out at him, but he just arched a brow.

"There wasn't any time to send a text and warn me?" Taylor asked with narrowed eyes.

Landry snorted. "Y'all must not know each other well. Hunter doesn't text." There was a flurry of activity as Landry pulled highchairs over and kids were caught and strapped in.

Conversation mostly centered on the changes that needed to happen to the house, the progress they'd made today, and what they needed to do tomorrow.

Then Landry said, "So Taylor, Hunter says you're going to be staying with him for a few weeks while Mom is recovering."

"Thanks for doing that," Gunner said stoically.

Landry continued, "But what's the plan? You're taking care of breakfasts?"

Taylor wiped her mouth and nodded. "Yes, I'll be here

all day Tuesdays and Wednesdays too, as those are my days off, so I can do lunches and whatever else is needed."

Chase put his drink down and said, "That's perfect. Someone will need to be in the house with Mom all day in case she needs a drink or something."

Holly volunteered to stay with her on Mondays and Fridays, and Maryanne said, "I'll stay Thursdays and Saturdays. When I visited this afternoon, they were discussing home health and physical therapy."

Taylor's phone buzzed, and she checked the message.

I've organized the meal train at church, but it won't start until Tuesday.
Can you let the family know?

Taylor cleared her throat. "Lucy says the meal train from church will start on Tuesday."

Everyone started talking over each other and then broke into multiple conversations. Taylor vaguely listened as one end talked about things Mrs. Williams would be picky about and the other end talked about the to-do list for tomorrow after church.

Hunter put his fork down and then slid his hand over, lacing their fingers together under the table. She felt her shoulders relax at his touch.

He kept her grounded when all the chaos broke out around her, when it became too loud. There was a reason she loved the library so much. It was quiet and peaceful and ordered.

This family was anything but.

The others finished eating, then Holly, Landry, and Maryanne each took a kid up the stairs to the bath. Gunner and Chase went back to moving things around the back room.

Hunter stood and took her empty bowl. "I usually do the dishes around here. Do you want to give me a hand?"

She shrugged and started collecting the bowls and silverware from the table. "Sure, I can do that."

She put the dishes in the sink and reached for the soap. "I'll wash if you'll dry and put up, since I don't know where anything is yet?"

He nodded and wrapped his arms around her from behind, sliding his hands along hers and into the soapy water. He whispered in her ear, "Or I can help you wash too."

Her breath shuddered as he nuzzled under her ear. Desire seeped under her skin, but it was how her shoulders relaxed at his touch that made her sigh.

"They're not coming home until Monday so tonight and tomorrow night, we'll stay here in the house. I want to fuck you in my old room."

She panted, her mind struggling to make sense of his words. "I—okay, whatever you say."

He grinned and rinsed his hands and a bowl, stepping away to the side. "That's what I like to hear."

She rolled her eyes and bit her lip. "We need to talk though."

He gave her a side eye as he dried the bowl and frowned. "Uh oh. This can't be good."

"It's not that kind of talk. Landry had a point earlier. We don't know each other that well. Sure, we've known each other for a month, but we've spent most of our time together not talking."

He wiggled his brows, and she grinned, handing him another clean bowl.

"It's going to take time to get to know each other, you know," he said.

She nodded, scrubbing the next dish. "I know."

He rinsed and dried another, then said, "If I don't talk enough, you need to just point-blank call me on it, okay? Because the only other girlfriend I've had was Jewel and when we started dating, we'd already known each other for ten or fifteen years."

She winced and nodded, hating being compared to Jewel, but there was no helping it. "Yeah, I guess I can understand that."

"What things does a boyfriend normally know about a girlfriend?"

She shrugged. "How the fuck should I know? I've never had a boyfriend before. Well, that guy in middle school, but he doesn't count."

He smirked. "Fair enough. Well, there's always twenty questions again."

She nodded and handed him another dish. "Did we cover favorite colors last time?"

Chapter Forty

After the dishes were done and all the kids left, Parker and Chase went to the barn to check on the new foals. Finally, they were alone in the house.

Hunter smiled at Taylor as she came back inside with her duffle bag. He took it from her and grabbed her hand, anticipation and nerves flooding him.

"Let me show you to my room upstairs."

Her cheeks flushed so prettily. He led her up the stairs, trying to puzzle out why this felt so much more intimate than what they'd done so far together. Was it because this was his home?

He opened doors on either side of the hallway.

"This was Landry and Parker's room growing up. Now it's the office and computer room. And this was mine and Gunner's room."

She stepped inside and looked around. "What about Chase?"

"He slept in Landry and Parker's room until he was

bigger, then he moved into the big kid room with Gunner and me."

He looked around, trying to see it from her perspective. It was cramped and dirty, but had potential. His twin bed had been taken down the stairs earlier. Gunner and Chase had set it up in the den for Ma. The room was emptier and would need vacuumed where the bed had been.

Across the room was the bunk bed, twin on top and full on bottom. He nodded to the bed. "We can sleep there until the folks get home. I figured it'd be easier for you to sleep here with plumbing down the hall."

She snorted. "Yeah, I'd rather not have to stumble down a ladder to use the bathroom. Although I do love that skylight."

He reached for her and drew her into his arms, the feeling of rightness making him sigh. "I can't wait to get you back there and hear you scream my name."

She tilted her face up and smiled, a ray of sunshine in his heart. "I can do that here, tonight. No need to wait for the barn."

He grinned and kissed her softly on the lips, a gentle and quick kiss. "I'm looking forward to it."

"Hunter? I'm coming up," Chase called as boots echoed on the stairs. When he appeared in the doorway, Hunter still hadn't let go of Taylor. He just held her as Chase asked, "Can I talk to you about the computer stuff?"

Hunter nodded and turned to tug her into the office with them. She stopped him and leaned closer. "I'll let y'all talk. I want to get out of these work clothes."

He pointed down the hallway. "The bathroom is across the hall, and Ma and Dad's room is on this side of the hall right next door."

She nodded and stepped past him. "Thanks."

He watched her grab her bag from where he'd dropped it by the bedroom doorway and walk down the hallway, her ass shaking so prettily in that pencil skirt from her work. This was the right thing to do, having her here, but he wasn't sure how it would all fit with Ma and Dad when they got home.

When she finally disappeared, he stepped into the office to join his brother.

Chase sat in a chair, leaning back and smirking at him. "You've got it bad, don't ya?"

Hunter nodded and smiled. "Sure do. Now what's up?"

Chase spun around and clicked on the computer, bringing up one of Dad's spreadsheets.

"I was going over this spreadsheet on the sales for the year and found the files for the last four years. I've created this sheet and pulled the data. Do you see this column? This shows what type of horse we're selling the most of but we don't have enough to meet the demand."

Hunter sat down on another chair and shook his head. "I see the column, but I don't understand it. It's all gibberish to me."

Chase clicked and a different page pulled up with pie charts and line graphs. He pointed to one. "I thought you might say that, so I made this. See this graph? It shows the three types of horses we sold, each year in a different color. See how the purple line is going down but the orange one is going up?"

Hunter nodded, hearing Taylor turn on the shower. He tried to stay focused on the computer, but he just wanted to be with her. He hated this computer work.

"What it means is we need to breed more of the quarter horses next year. That's a consistent trend over the past five years. Can we make that change?"

Hunter sat back and rubbed the back of his neck, thinking through the horses they already had. "I think so. We won't be able to sell them for two years, though. You know Ma's rule."

Chase nodded. "I know, but that's alright. We can do some advertising which will drive up the price since we'll have low inventory."

Hunter chuckled. "They're horses, not inventory."

Chase grinned and shook his head. "You know what I mean. But actually, speaking of inventory, look at this."

He clicked on the computer and another spreadsheet popped up. "This column here? This is lost inventory."

"What do you mean lost?"

"It's feed that we buy that doesn't get used. And this column here? This is hay that we store that doesn't get used either. We have a surplus of both, but if we could sell the extra half-way through the year well before it goes bad, we'd cut the costs by a third. It'd save money."

Hunter looked at his brother in a new light. Then he smiled and put his hands on his knees.

"I always knew you were a genius, but I think we just found your place on the ranch, brother."

Chase didn't look at him, instead clicking away on the laptop. "What do you mean?"

Hunter stood and slapped Chase's shoulders, squeezing softly. "I think you should run the business side of the ranch. I'll handle the outdoor stuff, the day-to-day operations, but if you can run the computer stuff? Dude, I would fucking love you forever."

Chase laughed and looked over his shoulder. "You already love me forever. Right?"

A look of vulnerability passed over his face, and Hunter

was reminded of when they were kids. Chase looked up at him, and at some point, he'd forgotten that.

Hunter squeezed his shoulders and nodded. "Right. Bros forever."

Footsteps echoed down the hall, then Parker stepped into the office. "I checked on the white barn, and I can't get the door closed. Do you want the foals to run around outside at night? Or do you want them shut inside?"

Hunter turned and frowned. "Yeah, they need to be inside. The coyotes have sounded closer the past few weeks. I think they know it's foaling season."

Parker nodded, and Hunter led him down the stairs, leaving Chase to click away on the computer.

As they walked through the dark along the fence line, Parker cleared his throat. "So, Taylor huh?"

Hunter sighed, "God, not you too."

Parker held his hands out. "I didn't say anything."

Hunter scowled. "You didn't have to. Yes, we went on a date a few weeks ago, but I haven't really talked to her since. Now we're a thing."

Parker paused, then said, "So when you talked to her last night, she told you to fuck off. But this morning, you were in her apartment?"

Hunter grunted. "Yeah, I went to talk to her about it. We worked it out."

"And she's moving in? Isn't that kind of rushing it?"

Hunter shrugged. "I love her. It's as simple as that."

Parker shook his head as they came to the barn. "I don't think it's simple at all, but I wish you both all the best. You looked happy at dinner, and that's the most important thing."

Hunter thought about it as he jiggled the door and got it back on the track. Thankfully, the foals were all still inside with their mamas. It only took a few minutes and some solid kicks to the door before they were turning back to the house.

Parker went to his Corvette and waved. "I'm heading home now. Call if you need me? Otherwise, I'll see you at church tomorrow."

Hunter waved. "See ya." He went inside, but Taylor still wasn't downstairs. He went up the stairs and was halfway up when Chase yelled.

He took the remaining stairs two at a time, nearly stumbling on the last step as Taylor walked down the hall with a wad of clothes pressed to her naked chest. She wore a black silky thong, her glorious breasts covered by the clothes she'd changed out of. She walked calmly down the hall, head held high even as a flush crossed her cheeks.

Chase stood with his back pressed to the wall, his eyes wide as he stared at her nearly naked form.

She glared at Hunter and ducked into his old room, keeping her body turned so that Chase didn't see her ass. She slammed the door, leaving them both speechless in the hall.

Chase shook his head, walking toward him and the stairs with brows raised. "Hot damn. You're one lucky son of a bitch, you know that?"

Hunter sucked in a deep breath, his mind shooting back to nearly sixteen years ago. "Is that how you felt about Jewel when I was dating her?"

Chase paused beside him and frowned, his back stiffening. "Yes, but I told you I was sorry about that."

Hunter frowned, his hands fisting, jealousy making his stomach roll. Flashbacks and memories flooded him, but one stuck out. Hunter waved at the closed door. "Was it like that? She came out of the bathroom and didn't make a move. It was just a misunderstanding, but you pounced?"

Chase's brows rose, and he crossed his arms, widening his stance.

"Hell no, I'm not that kind of guy. With Jewel, I came out of the bathroom at the barn, but it was dark. She pushed me against the wall and jumped into my arms. I caught her on reflex, and she was naked. Then she started kissing me, and honestly? I didn't even realize it was Jewel until she started talking. By then I was already balls deep."

Hunter held up a hand. He didn't want to listen to this. And honestly, it had no bearing on the present. Right? He tried to convince himself to let it go, but the pressure increased on his chest.

"It doesn't matter. Jewel is in the past, and you're welcome to her. But Taylor is off-limits. She's different. This isn't some puppy love. She's mine." The last word was practically a growl that made his brother wince, but he didn't back down.

He'd finally admitted the truth of his feelings. She'd questioned it, but he knew down to his soul that she was the one for him. Now he just had to convince her it was real.

Chase held his hands out. "Absolutely, I wouldn't do that to you. Not again and certainly not deliberately."

Hunter snorted and rubbed a hand on the back of his neck. "Well, let's not have any other accidents like Jewel, alright? I love you, Chase. I've forgiven both you and Jewel, but Taylor is mine. If you go near her, our wrestling match from a few weeks ago will look like child's play compared to what I will do. Do I make myself clear?"

Chase's hands fisted at his side. "Don't threaten me, big brother. As much as I appreciate the forgiveness," he sneered the word and added air quotes. "I don't appreciate you automatically assuming I'll jump all over Taylor. Who do you think I am?"

Hunter shrugged and crossed his arms. "I thought I knew who you were fifteen years ago, but then again, I never would've thought you'd have slept with my girlfriend, either. I don't really know you at all, do I?"

Chase stared at him, his jaw clenching.

Taylor opened the bedroom door, now dressed in a pair of loose shorts and a crop top. She tucked her wet hair behind her ear and looked between them. Her cheeks were flushed in embarrassment, but she held her head high.

"Sorry," she said breathlessly. "I thought you'd left."

Chase glared at him, making him feel slightly guilty about their conversation. "Don't worry about it. I was just leaving. See y'all at church tomorrow."

Chase slid past him toward the stairs, careful to avoid touching him. Hunter stared at Taylor, his hands fisted and his spine tingling, confused by all the different emotions.

"Aren't I making breakfast in the morning?" Taylor asked as he stomped down the stairs.

Hunter nodded and stared at her, arms crossed. "Forget him. He'll do what he wants. Always has."

She bit her lip and frowned. "Are you alright? I'm sorry I came out in my underwear."

Hunter swallowed hard, and his nostrils flared. She'd said they needed to talk more and get to know each other, so he had to explain what he was feeling.

"When Jewel came home at Christmas after her first semester away, she brought a guy with her. Apparently, they were just friends, but I didn't know that. It was the first time I've gotten so jealous that I raged out."

Her brows rose. "Raged out."

He nodded curtly. "I had some anger issues growing up.

I keep a tight control on myself these days but seeing you nearly naked with someone else nearby—it triggered that side of me."

Her eyes sharpened. "The beast," she whispered.

A slow smile spread across his face as he stalked toward her. She backed up into the bedroom, her eyes wide as he shut the bedroom door.

"Precisely." He pulled his shirt over his head and growled, "Strip, slut. Let's sate the beast, shall we?"

Her cheeks flushed deeper, but she raced to take her clothes off. By the time he got his jeans and boots tossed aside, she stood next to the bunk bed naked.

She licked her lips but didn't appear phased at her nakedness. He loved that about her, that she didn't give a fuck who saw her.

He prowled to her, getting as close to her as possible without touching. They stood naked, neither moving, just enjoying the anticipation.

He let his breath tease her ear. "I love that you don't give a fuck who sees your fucking hot body, but this body is mine, princess. I don't know how you did it in college, but from now on, you're mine."

She sucked in a breath, holding still otherwise as he lifted a finger and traced it over her collarbone and down her breasts. He didn't touch her nipples, even though they beaded into hard little nubs that demanded his attention.

"You're not my fuck toy or my fuck buddy. This isn't a fling for me. You're mine forever, my girlfriend, my future, my obsession, my love."

She arched her back slightly, trying to get his hand to her nipples. "Yes sir. I'm yours, I get it. But maybe I should show you that I understand."

She sat on the edge of the bed and ran her hands up his

thighs. She looked up with those wide green eyes, her hand wrapping around his dick.

He sucked in a breath and wrapped her wet hair in his fist. "Fuck," he hissed as her hand tugged on his throbbing hard cock.

"Does this show you that I'm yours?" Her voice was a husky siren's song as she rubbed the tip over her lips. "Don't you want to face fuck me like the slut I am?"

She blinked up at him, and he groaned, thrusting his hips slightly to get her to take him. She licked the tip and hummed in pleasure. God, he couldn't remember the last blow job he'd gotten. He couldn't really remember any other girl.

Only Taylor remained. Only she took up all his thoughts and feelings, filling his soul with joy, laughter, and love.

He pulled back, and she licked her lips, pulling her hand along his shaft.

"You're my slut, no one else's. You're not going to show your hot body off to anyone else, do you understand, princess?"

She nodded, licking her lips and opening wide as he slowly pressed the tip into her tight, wet mouth. She opened wider, and he slid into the hot cavern with a groan.

He closed his eyes at the feel of her wrapped around him. She only took him about three-fourths of the way in, but it was fucking heaven.

He eased out and pressed back in, slow and steady. "You're my slut. Rub yourself as I fuck your face, princess."

Her hand went to her clit, and he leaned down to grab one of her breasts with his free hand. He twisted her nipple, and she moaned, taking him a little bit deeper. He fucked her mouth harder.

"That's it. Take all my dick, you dirty little slut. I want to taste your pretty little pussy, but first, I'm going to—oh God."

She gagged, the sound sending him closer to the edge. She moaned, burying her hand in her pussy and the other holding onto his thigh, drawing him closer or holding him at bay, he wasn't sure.

Eyes fluttering, he slammed into the back of her throat, the sensation making his balls tense. Tighter and tighter, deeper and deeper, then he was shooting a hot load into her waiting mouth.

He pumped and gasped, staring down at her. Her big eyes looked up at him, and he knew he'd remember this moment all of his life.

She was so beautiful and his other half. He couldn't imagine a life without her in it. He needed her and knew he wouldn't be able to go a day without her.

It was the first day of them living together and already he knew he needed to keep her forever at his side. Or forever on her knees in front of him. This was fucking heaven on earth.

He slid out of her mouth, and she opened wide, showing him the load. Then she swallowed and opened her mouth again, sliding her empty tongue out.

He cupped her cheek and smiled, palming her heavy breast. "That's a good little slut. Now lay back and let me devour that pussy."

She smirked, a triumphant cat who ate the canary twist of the lips. "Whatever you say, beast. I'm yours, after all."

He grinned and knelt, spreading her legs wide. "That's what I like to hear, my love." Then he lowered his head.

Chapter Forty-One

The next morning, Hunter drove them to church half an hour before services were to start. He said he needed to practice with his brothers and make sure they were ready for the worship service.

Taylor fidgeted with her skirt, nervous to walk into church with him. They arrived so early, not a lot of people saw them together.

She sat on the pew and listened to them practice. It was so much different than when she'd first met them. Parker had been as drunk as she had been, and Hunter had been the strong, silent bad boy at the bar. Chase wasn't up there, though.

Now she sat in church watching them practice worship songs. Someone stopped beside her, and she looked up.

Jewel stepped past her and sat down. Taylor tensed but tried to be logical about it. She'd liked Jewel when they'd first met, before learning about her past. Maybe they could be friends? Would that be weird?

She supposed weirder things had happened. They sat shoulder to shoulder watching the guys.

"Why isn't Chase here?" Taylor asked, deciding to make the first move.

Jewel shifted and said, "He was in prison when the guys were doing their brother band phase. He missed when they formed the band and started playing at the bar and in church."

"That's not really a reason he can't play with them now, is it?"

Jewel shrugged. "No, but it's been a long time since he played an instrument, and he doesn't really want to sing because then the attention would be completely on him. He's not one for the limelight."

Taylor snorted, watching as Landry sang into the mic as if to a crowd of thousands. "He's definitely no Parker or Landry."

Jewel grinned, and their eyes met as they both giggled. Perhaps they could be friends after all. They turned back to watch the guys.

She needed to address the elephant in the room. Her stomach twisted in knots.

"So, you have a daughter?" Taylor asked, not knowing how else to broach the subject.

Jewel nodded and sighed. "Yeah, did Hunter tell you he's the dad?"

She shook her head and leaned in closer. "No, he said he *might* be the dad."

Jewel's eyes widened, and she looked around them but most of the early people were still talking in the foyer. "Um, yeah, but that's not common knowledge. If you could keep that quiet for now, I'd really appreciate it. Destini doesn't know either. She just knows her dad lives in this town."

Taylor nodded. "That's what Hunter said, and I get it. It's hard enough moving, but for a teenager to have that kind of rumor following her would be hard. Trust me, I know how that feels. I won't tell anyone, not even Lucy."

"Lucy?"

"My best friend."

"Ah, ok, thanks. Destini gets back to town next week. Then we'll do the DNA test and figure this out. Until then, we all three decided to just let the town think Hunter's the dad."

"Do you want Hunter to be the dad?" Taylor asked, unsure of how he thought about it. Did he hope for it or dread it?

Jewel shrugged. "It'd be way easier, but I don't know. I actually stopped by to see if you and I would be okay. Me as the ex-girlfriend and potential baby mama, and you as the new girlfriend and potential step-mama."

Taylor's heart raced, her mind stuttering. "He—we haven't talked long term."

Jewel's brows rose. "It's early in your relationship, but Hunter hasn't changed that much in the past few decades. He's a one-woman man, a long-term kind of guy. I saw how he looked at you at the restaurant. I knew he was smitten. It's only a matter of time before he makes it official."

She flushed, her heart hoping for a future with him. They'd said they loved each other at her apartment, but they hadn't said it much since then.

Thoughts of Jewel and Destini warred with images of a wedding and life with Hunter. If Hunter was a dad and they worked this out... dear Lord, she would be a stepmom. To a teenage girl.

"Fuck," Taylor whispered, nerves gripping her.

Jewel's head whipped to her, and she frowned. "Please

don't tell me you're only looking for a fling with him. I don't want to see him hurt."

Taylor took a deep breath and shook her head. "No, it's not that. I love him and don't plan on hurting him. I just hadn't realized that if Hunter is the dad, and he and I—well, the dots just connected in my brain. Sorry for cursing in church. Now you know what kind of person I am, I guess. Are you sure you're okay with me being a potential stepmom?"

Jewel nodded. "Yeah, you're a librarian. Destini will love that. Somehow, we'll all make it work, right?"

Taylor shifted on the pew. "I don't know. Hunter and I have been mostly just physical the past few weeks. I'm not sure we'll go the distance. I mean, we haven't really talked about marriage."

Jewel patted her leg. "After you left the restaurant, we talked about you. I didn't just see his face. I heard it in his voice too. I've known him since we were babies, and I wouldn't be surprised if he popped the question."

Taylor's eyes couldn't leave Hunter as his hands flew over the drum set. He kept his eyes on Landry mostly, watching for changes in the music and rhythm. His face was focused but peaceful, and he obviously enjoyed playing.

And he was damn good at it too. She was proud of him, and her heart swelled. She wanted to watch him play for years, even when they were old and gray. She could picture him now, hair turned white with deep laugh lines beside his eyes.

She wanted that. Wanted to be with him long term.

"That's good, since I kind of love him," Taylor said.

Jewel sighed and looked behind them as more people arrived. "I'm glad to hear it. I'll stop by tomorrow evening when Ava and Bill get home, alright? If you need anything before then, let me know. I heard you're doing breakfasts at the ranch, which is a lot to handle, especially for a city girl. Do you want some help?"

Taylor wrinkled her nose. "I'll keep you in mind. It went alright this morning though, except I don't think they liked the coffee I made."

Jewel chuckled and stood to walk back to join her family. "Well, they're cowboys. They typically like their coffee black and strong."

Taylor grinned up at her. "And my mind immediately went to the gutter with a very naughty joke at that comment. See? Not so sure I should be anyone's stepmom, much less a real mom."

Jewel grinned and winked. "Actually, I think you're the perfect choice for Hunter and will do fine."

Taylor pursed her lips and shrugged as Jewel walked away. Soon Maryanne and Holly were filling in the pew beside her, having dropped the kids off at the nursery. They chatted until church services began.

After worship, Hunter walked down the aisle and took the seat next to her, picking up her hand and lacing their fingers together. His thigh pressed against hers, distracting her from the sermon.

Her heart filled with joy and love. He didn't just claim her body at night in private, but publicly in front of everyone. Maybe he really did love her. It was still too early to tell if this was real or would last.

She was afraid to hope, but she couldn't stop herself. She wanted a forever with him.

The next day, Taylor woke up to Hunter's dick inside her. His arms caged her head, and she moaned as she came awake with such an intense fullness in her pussy.

"Good morning, princess. Rise and shine," he murmured as he kissed her jaw and captured her mouth. His kiss was long and deep. He lazily dueled his tongue with hers and rocked his hips.

She gasped, her eyes flying open, but her eye mask preventing her from seeing anything. She twisted under him and squeezed, making him groan.

He rocked his hips again, and she felt him grow inside her, flexing, pumping, stretching. He set up a slow and steady rhythm, but it was his pelvis hitting her clit that drove her to the edge in just a few short minutes.

He kissed her the entire time, his lips never leaving hers even as she whimpered and moaned. Finally, his rhythm broke along with their kiss.

He began to pump harder, saying, "That's it, princess. Come for the beast. Squeeze that dick."

She was almost there, then he changed the angle of his hips. Her vision swam with white spots as she gasped and raked his back with her nails. Her orgasm swept over her with a ferocity that took her breath away.

He groaned and stilled, pumping into her even as she spasmed and thrashed underneath him. Their release together felt good, better than the last time, but every time with him seemed better than the last.

Eventually their breathing slowed, and he rolled away. He grabbed a dirty t-shirt from the laundry basket, wiped himself off, and handed it to her.

She cleaned up as he pulled clothes out of a backpack in the corner and walked out the bedroom bare ass naked.

She frowned and narrowed her eyes. With no clothes,

she followed him to the bathroom and shut the door behind him.

"What the fuck, Hunter? You can walk to the bathroom naked, but I can't?"

He looked over his shoulder and turned on the water, pointing to the clothes on the counter. "I brought clothes with me. By the time I get out, the ranch hands might be downstairs for coffee. I don't mind you walking around naked, sugar. I do mind you walking around naked with other people around."

She frowned and washed her face, scrubbing it as he stepped into the shower. "You're so weird," she mumbled.

But maybe she just needed some caffeine and to acclimate to the early hour. It was barely five o'clock, but she had to admit. The wake-up sex the past two days had been way better than any alarm clock.

She walked back to the bedroom in his t-shirt and pulled on some shorts.

She wasn't sure what Mrs. Williams wore to breakfast, but she was damned if she was going to get dressed for work only to have bacon grease pop on her work clothes. She'd normally wear a crop top at home, but she didn't think Hunter would be okay with her dressing like that in front of all the other guys.

She smirked. Although it might drive him to fuck her hard like the beast he really was. She might test it out someday, but not today.

Today, his mom came home, and nerves already made her stomach twist. She was only going into work for a few hours this morning. Helen was going to cover her for the afternoon so she could make sure the house was spotless.

Maybe if she had supper ready when Mrs. Williams got home tonight, she'd make a good impression. Plus, the rest of the family wanted to be there too, so it was a lot of mouths to feed. It'd take a while to cook.

She fixed a pot of coffee, using double the amount of coffee grounds as yesterday, and started making pancakes, bacon, and eggs. They could make pancake breakfast sandwiches if they wanted, but it was the fastest and most filling breakfast.

Soon there were a dozen or more big, tough cowboys tromping inside. She felt a little out of her element, but it didn't drive up her anxiety as much today as it did yesterday. They talked and flirted, and she laughed as Hunter came down the stairs, her phone in his hand.

He set it on the counter and kissed her cheek as he walked to the coffee pot.

"Hunter, you better be glad you scooped her up as soon as she came to town. The way she cooks, I wish I'd seen her first," one hand said. She thought his name was Tom, but she couldn't remember.

Another said, "No shit. Honey, if Hunter doesn't treat you right, just let me know. I'll gladly take his place."

She felt a blush tinge her cheeks, but she grinned and cocked a hip, waving a spatula at him. "Don't tempt me with a good time, mister."

Hunter slid his hands around her waist and looked down at her with an arched brow. "Don't even think about it, guys. She's mine."

"Yeah, but for how long," someone asked.

Hunter never let go or looked away. "For forever," he said.

She sucked in a breath as he dipped his head and kissed her. The others hooted and hollered, and she blushed. This was the first time he'd mentioned forever since that night in her apartment.

He broke the kiss, and she turned back to the griddle to flip the pancakes.

Hunter spanked her on the ass, making her yelp and the guys laugh. Then he grabbed his mug and sat at the table. When they all trickled out of the kitchen and only two or three were left, Hunter gathered the dishes.

She touched his arm at the sink and said, "I know you have morning chores, and some animals can't wait. I can take care of this."

He frowned and asked, "Are you sure?"

She nodded, and he kissed her cheek. "Okay, what time do you need to leave for work?"

"Between eight and eight-thirty, probably."

He nodded and hugged her. "Alright, I'll be back here by eight. I want to kiss you again before you go to work."

She grinned as he released her and headed out the door with the last ranch hand. She turned back to the dishes and watched as the sun rose higher on the horizon. The yard was a flurry of activity as different people went this way and that, but the peace of the sunrise made the dishes a more enjoyable chore. For the first time, she felt like maybe, just maybe, this could be her future.

This morning had gone pretty well. Yesterday the guys had been a little bit quieter, but they were slowly opening up to her. The food definitely helped.

True to his word, Hunter came by and kissed her before she went to work. Actually, they did more than that. He locked the front door and bent her over the kitchen table.

It was hard and fast and rough. His hand settled between her shoulder blades, pressing her breasts to the table. His hand had pushed her pencil skirt to her hips, revealing her white thong.

He'd unzipped and slid home, making her gasp. Then

he'd been off to the races, riding her like a man possessed. She'd come twice before he pulled out and spun her around, pushing her to her knees and shoving his dick in her mouth.

She'd swallowed every drop, throbbing as he'd gripped her ponytail and said, "That's it, princess. Take it all. Swallow every drop, you dirty little slut."

She'd showed him his load, then swallowed. He'd caressed her cheek and smiled, the sated look in his eyes filling her with pride.

"Good girl, such a good little cum princess. Now go to work with my taste in your mouth and come home as soon as you can."

He'd helped her to her feet and then pulled her into a hug. She didn't care that her ass was still hanging out and her skirt was still pushed up to her waist. Her shoulders relaxed as he held her.

They were finding a new normal. Maybe they could make this work long term. She settled her skirt and left Hunter on the front porch as she drove to work.

Her anxiety left her frowning by the time she parked though, the sated after-glow fading as she thought of facing Scott and the girls.

She tidied up and organized the shelves like she needed to, trying to keep herself busy. Sure enough, Scott came in before lunch.

The girls bounced inside, saying, "Good morning, Miss Taylor."

She smiled as they put their stacks of books in the return bin. "Good morning, girls. Are you feeling better, Paige?"

Paige nodded and smiled. "Yep, it happens sometimes, but I'm okay."

The Cowboy Gets His Girl

They skipped to the children's section, leaving her to face Scott alone. She looked up, catching the guarded look in his eyes, and sighed.

She leaned against the librarian's desk and crossed her ankles, but didn't look away. "I'm sorry, Scott," she said softly. "I didn't mean to hurt you. I didn't plan any of this."

His lips flattened into a thin line, and he nodded before taking a few steps toward the children's section.

"Scott, we need to talk this out. I—I value your friendship and don't want to end like this," she said, her voice soft so the girls wouldn't hear.

He stopped and looked down at his feet, shoving his hands in his pockets. "There's not really anything to talk about. Unless you still want me? If you still want me, I'll fight for you. We don't have to be exclusive. You can date us both until you decide who you love."

She felt her chest tighten. "I—actually, I already love him. I didn't realize until—"

"Friday night? After you left?" His voice was flat, but his face was hopeful, she nodded.

He sighed and raked a hand through his hair, causing a strand to fall toward his eyebrow. "I thought so. We weren't exclusive before, but it does feel a bit like Elaina cheating all over again."

"I'm so sorry, Scott. I didn't mean—"

"I know," he said. He took a deep breath and smiled ruefully. "But the heart wants what the heart wants. Isn't that what they say? And if you really do love him, who am I to stand in the way?"

She straightened and stepped toward him but didn't reach out. "You're a good man, Scott, and a great dad. Given time, I could've loved you too."

"But you don't," he said.

She shook her head slowly. "No, but you'll find someone to love soon, I just know it."

He shrugged as Paige came running over with her arms stacked high with books. "I hope so," he murmured, turning his attention to his daughter.

She took the stack and talked with Paige as he went to check on Paisley. This conversation wasn't the worst, but she hated that she'd hurt him. It wasn't fair, but he was right. She loved Hunter, and that was all that mattered, in the end.

Chapter Forty-Two

"Ma, you can't do that. The doctors told you to take it easy, remember?"

"They said limited weight bearing, not no weight. I know what I can and can't do," Ava grumbled, using the crutches to get out of the Jeep.

Hunter had picked her and Bill up half an hour ago, and she'd been tired and cranky the entire drive late Monday afternoon. The morning errands in Fort Worth had been stressful, and he wasn't sure how Taylor would react to his news. His mom's release had overshadowed it, pushing it to the back of his mind.

Bill hovered beside Ava, so Hunter grabbed her bag from the back and shut the door behind her. He bounded around them to open the front door. She was panting by the time she made it to the stairs at the bottom of the porch.

He stayed behind her just in case she fell. She was very spry and not even sixty yet, but he'd never really been apart from her for long. Gunner had joined the Marines. Chase had gone to prison. Landry was on tour with his music a lot, and Parker had played professional soccer.

But Hunter had always stayed home. Aside from a few weeks here and there for camping, he'd always preferred the peace of the ranch, of being there to make sure all was well.

He opened the screen door, and Ava went through.

"Surprise," people shouted inside.

Ava's jaw dropped. "What's all this?"

Hunter stepped inside after them. His brothers and their wives stood around the living room and kitchen. His nieces and nephew chased each other down the hall, laughing and squealing like only toddlers can.

Taylor stood in the kitchen, and he met her soft smile. She'd taken the afternoon off to be here, and his heart swelled at her thoughtfulness. She'd fed a dozen men for two mornings in a row without a complaint. Yesterday morning, she'd made the coffee too weak, but it was perfect this morning.

Not that he'd had the heart to tell her, but she'd overheard some comments from the ranch hands and had adjusted without a word. She was resilient.

Ava sniffled, pulling him away from staring at Taylor. Bill gently guided her through the crowd of people talking one over the other until they reached the den, Hunter following the crowd.

She gasped and looked around, and he breathed a sigh of relief at her joy. His old twin bed now sat against the bookshelf on one wall. Across from it was the fireplace with the TV over the mantle. The couch had been removed and, in its place, sat two brand new electric recliners that they'd picked up yesterday afternoon.

They'd decided to get one for Bill too, as he would probably spend a lot of his time with Ava. He'd not left the hospital the entire time.

The kids ran into the den just as Ava sat in the electric recliner, and Hunter ran interference, making sure they didn't get too close and jostle her.

"Careful," he said, turning Connie around to run the other direction. She squealed and took off back down the hall.

Maryanne and Holly grabbed pillows and settled them around Ava, talking about the bedside toilet and how they were going to take care of her. Hunter looked around, not seeing Taylor.

Gunner came in to help, so Hunter left, the room already too crowded. He found Taylor in the kitchen pulling grilled chicken off the stove. She looked up at him with a soft smile, but there was a twitch under one eye.

He kissed her on the cheek and leaned against the counter, grabbing a small piece of chicken and popping it into his mouth.

"How was the drive?" She turned back to the stove, and he smiled at the easy domestication of this moment.

She looked good in the kitchen, not that he'd ever tell her that. She was an independent woman who could do what she wanted. She didn't need to be in the kitchen, but there was something about how inviting she looked with that soft, relaxed smile on her face that made him happy.

"It was good, but she's pretty tired and cranky. Whatever happens, just know that she's not always like this."

Taylor rolled her eyes and turned the chicken. "Thanks, that really helps my nerves."

He chuckled and pulled her into a hug. She seemed to relax in his arms before she pulled away to fiddle with the food.

She pointed to the dining table. "Do you want to set up the highchairs for the kids? Dinner'll be ready in about fifteen minutes."

It was still early for food, not quite five, but with the kids and the transition home, they'd all decided that it was best for his mom. She'd tire out quickly.

He nodded and kissed her cheek again. "Sure thing, sugar. How was work?"

She frowned and hesitated, then said, "It was fine. I'll talk to you about it later. Let's just enjoy your family for now, alright?"

He nodded, his stomach churning as he set the table for dinner. That tone didn't bode well, but he tried to let it go during the chaos of the family. He and his brothers ended up eating in the den. They sat on the fireplace while their parents sat in their recliners.

The girls fed the kids at the kitchen table, and he hoped Taylor was bonding with his sisters-in-law. But it was good for him and his brothers to spend this time together as a family. There was a time when he was the only brother eating with his parents. He knew how lonely they had been, and having all five of them here tonight was important.

Ava turned her sharp eyes on him. "Taylor's been doing breakfast?"

Hunter nodded. "Two days so far, yeah. She made dinner tonight too, so you can thank her when you see her."

Ava harrumphed and took another bite. His lips twisted into a smile as he kept his mouth shut and ate. There was a knock on the door. He leaned to have a clear view to the front door as Jewel arrived.

He looked back at his mother but before he could say anything, she smiled and said brightly, "Is that Henry and the girls?"

The Cowboy Gets His Girl

He knew it'd take time for her to warm up to Taylor—she'd done this with Maryanne and Holly too—but inviting his ex-girlfriend to dinner was unacceptable. He'd have to have a chat with her about this, but he refused to ruin their family night. His jaw clenched as he nodded, and he forced a smile as he rose to greet their unexpected guests.

Chase followed, which didn't surprise him, even if no one else in the family realized what was going on with his brother.

Jewel was smiling and talking animatedly with Taylor when he got to the room. He slipped his hand along Taylor's lower back and smiled at her. She looked up at him, her eyes soft and relaxed before turning back to Jewel who was talking about the library.

Gemma put her sweater on the hook by the door next to him. He leaned over and said, "Ma's in the den. Have y'all eaten? Grab a plate if you'd like."

Taylor laughed at something Jewel said then Jewel and Gemma went to the kitchen with Chase hot on their heels. Taylor sat back at the table, and Holly handed her a baby food jar.

"Can you feed him for a second?"

Taylor nodded so Hunter sat at the table, taking Holly's seat and watching her feed him. Normally Landry and Holly tag teamed the twins, but Landry was visiting their mom in the den.

It made him smile, and he wanted to have their own baby someday. She met his gaze and blinked. "What? Do I have food on my face?"

He shook his head. "No, just imagining you feeding our own kid someday."

Maryanne's jaw dropped, and Taylor's cheeks turned red.

She fed him another bite and asked, "You want kids? I thought you said that life isn't for you."

He nodded. "That was before I found out about Destini, so I might as well embrace it. It'd be nice to have a few of them, actually. These three running around like three peas in a pod—now that's a great childhood. I wouldn't mind having some of our own running around."

"I would've loved having all these cousins running around to play with."

He nodded, remembering their conversation about being an only child. She'd moved here to be closer to Lucy, who was more like a sister to her. That's how he felt about his brothers and their kids. To be honest, that's part of what had been bothering him the past few months. They were all moving on with their lives, but he'd been stuck in the same old, same old.

Holly cleared her throat and gave Eddi the sippy cup again.

"Um, can you two handle the three kids for a few minutes? They should be occupied with the food for a bit. Maryanne, let's go see if Ava needs a refill."

Maryanne grinned, glancing from Taylor to Hunter as she stood up and handed over Connie's bowl.

"Sure thing," Taylor said. "Take your time. They'll be fine."

Holly went to the diaper bag by the door and took out an envelope, then went to the den with Maryanne. Taylor turned to feed Freddi, so Hunter took a spoonful of mashed potatoes to feed his nephew. He watched as most of the others went into the den to see his mom.

When they were mostly alone, he asked, "Are you okay with Jewel being here?"

Taylor made a funny face to his niece as she put the spoon in her mouth. "Why wouldn't I be? You said you're nothing but friends, right? Has that changed?"

Her eyes widened and turned wary as she spoke, but he shook his head. "Nope, we're just friends, but she probably will be here a lot."

"Because she might be the mom of your first born?"

Hunter nodded his head toward the kitchen where Jewel and Chase stood close, not touching but talking quietly. He jerked a thumb to them and leaned close to whisper, "And because of that."

Taylor turned to the kitchen and her eyes widened at how close they were standing. "Are you sure no one else in the family knows?"

He shook his head. "Not yet anyway. Secrets have a way of blowing up in this town."

She snorted and bit her lip. "Got that right. Speaking of secrets blowing up, I saw Scott at the library today."

Hunter's head whipped to her, and his stomach tightened. "What happened? Why?"

She fed Eddi and wiped Freddi's mouth. "He brings the girls in every Monday morning to return their books. We talked things out. It was super awkward, but an important conversation to have."

"Did he touch you?"

"Of course not, Hunter, he's not you." She scowled at him. "He's just a regular guy, a dad whose primary interest at the moment is finding a mom for his girls. Don't worry about him anymore. He knows we're together now, and I apologized for how it all went down."

He frowned, trying to tamp down the jealousy that ripped through him. He knew logically that he couldn't protect her from everyone or everything. As much as he'd love to tie her up and keep her from running around town, it wasn't practical.

But maybe he needed to stake his claim publicly.

Chapter Forty-Three

He swallowed hard to push past the jealousy and fed Connie a bite. A squeal and shouts echoed from the den. The kids got startled and began banging their fists and baby spoons on the highchairs, yelling, "Down, down, down."

Taylor grabbed the sippy cups for the twins, and he wiped Connie's face.

Jewel and Chase went to the den, but he and Taylor unhooked the trays and set the kids down on the floor. They immediately raced to the den to see what was going on.

Taylor didn't seem curious at all. She just started cleaning the trays and highchairs, so he grabbed a rag and wiped them down with her. It was an easy silence, but he strained to hear what was going on down the hall.

Parker came through to the kitchen carrying a stack of used plates, a huge grin on his face. "Guess what? Holly's pregnant!"

Taylor's eyes got huge and said, "Oh, that's so exciting."

Hunter grinned. "That explains the dark circles under her eyes."

Taylor scowled at him. "Don't you dare tell her that."

He raised his hands, palms out. "I won't, don't worry. I'm smarter than that."

She sniffed and began wiping down the table as Parker put the dirty dishes in the sink and went back to the den. Hunter started on the dishes and soon Taylor joined him.

"How soon do you want kids?" He couldn't stop the question from coming. He had to know. His brain was already thinking up ways to keep her with him forever, and a baby wouldn't be the worst way to do it.

She shook her head. "I want to do things in the right order. After so many years of being wild in college, I want to date, then have an engagement, then a wedding, then babies."

He suddenly frowned and scrubbed the plates. "What about your dad?"

She stiffened beside him and asked, "What about him?"

"If you want to do things the right way, I need his permission." Why hadn't he thought of that this morning when he'd been in Fort Worth? He could've asked then.

But she shook her head. "No, he's not really in the picture."

"What does that mean?" He tried to remember all their past conversations. That night in her apartment, she'd cried because he'd acted like her dad. What else had she said about him?

She sighed and rinsed the dishes. "It means he's currently in jail down in Fort Worth with no way to pay bail. Who knows how long he'll be there? No, the less I see him the better it is."

He opened and closed his mouth, uncertainty making his head hurt. What he'd wanted to tell her had to wait until he got more answers. Perhaps he shouldn't have assumed and jumped to problem solve today. No wonder she said they needed to get to know each other more.

"That must hurt a lot," he said softly.

She nodded and her shoulders seemed to sag. "Yeah, it sucks to have a deadbeat dad, but I've given up on trying to change him. There's nothing I can do. I've already paid his rent multiple times and maxed out my credit cards trying to take care of him. He has to figure this out for himself now. He got himself into jail, he can get himself out."

He winced, not realizing that her dad had maxed her out financially. It shed a different light on this morning's events.

He scrubbed another plate as Gunner and Maryanne came in with more dishes. Maryanne was grinning and she'd obviously been crying.

"Can you believe it? They're pregnant," she sighed wistfully, but Gunner frowned.

"No," his brother said with narrowed eyes, his tone almost exactly like Connie's when she was about to throw a tantrum.

Maryanne glared at him but didn't say anything. They had a staring contest, which he and Taylor ignored as they did the dishes. Apparently, his brother was being stubborn again, which didn't really surprise him.

Either Gunner couldn't believe Holly was pregnant or he was saying no to he and Maryanne having another kid. Hunter suddenly wondered if Holly's pregnancy would interfere with finishing the barn renovations.

He glanced at Taylor. They had so much to learn about each other. Did she even want to live in the barn with him or did she want a house of her own? He should probably ask.

Soon everyone was leaving. Taylor and he stood on the

porch waving. Then Taylor sighed. "I guess I should introduce myself to your mom, huh?"

He frowned and linked their fingers together. "What are you talking about? You've already met."

She rolled her eyes and pushed the screen door open. He followed, not releasing her hand. "I know, but it's different to meet them as your girlfriend."

He gave her a quick hug, the smell of strawberries flooding his nostrils. "It'll be fine, eventually."

She grumbled into his shirt. "I know, let's just get this over with."

He led her into the den. His parents were in their recliners, the TV turned down low with some farming show on.

"Ma, do you remember Taylor? We helped her move into her apartment a few weeks ago."

Ava eyed Taylor and said with a tight smile, "It's nice to see you again, Taylor. Thanks for helping with breakfasts and for dinner tonight. That's a huge weight off my shoulders."

"Happy to help, ma'am," Taylor said, sitting on the fireplace edge primly. He wasn't nervous to see how the two most important women in his life got along, but the way Taylor fidgeted with the hem of her shirt just showed how nervous *she* really was. He sat beside her and squeezed her hand.

"Oh, none of that ma'am stuff. Call me Ava. Hunter tells me y'all are dating. Did he tell you he has a fifteen-year-old daughter?"

Taylor nodded, not even looking at him as she replied. "He did. That's really exciting for him."

"Where do you see this going long term?"

"Ma," he said sternly.

She waved a hand at him. "You hush. This is between us women. Well?"

Taylor grinned and sat up straighter. "A no-nonsense woman. How refreshing. I see this going as far as Hunter wants to take it. I'm not looking to trap him into marriage, but if that's what he wants, I'm down for it."

Hunter sucked in a breath and pulled her hand to his knee. She looked at him and winked, and a weight eased from his chest. As much as she'd seemed nervous, when it came right down to it, he was the one who was on edge.

"Of course you're open to marriage. Hunter's quite the catch."

"Ma," Hunter said with a scowl.

Ava shrugged, her eyes piercing. "It's the truth. I just want to get it all out in the open instead of having some gold digger come in trying to take over the ranch."

Taylor stiffened beside him, and Hunter squeezed her hand. "She's not a gold digger, Ma. Cut it out."

Ava raised a brow and crossed her arms. "We'll see what the next few weeks bring. It'll be good to finally meet Destini, won't it? I can't wait for her to finish camp and move up here for good."

Taylor gave a tight smile to Ava. "It's going to be a transition, that's for sure. Since I'm new to town, we'll have that to bond over."

Ava harrumphed. "She won't need to spend time with *you*, dear. She needs to spend time with her real family, with Hunter."

Taylor stiffened next to him. Hunter narrowed his eyes on his mom. "I love Taylor, Ma, so Destini will need to spend time with her too. She'll eventually be Destini's stepmom."

Taylor's cheeks flushed, but she tipped her chin up as they stared at his mom.

Ava shifted with a wince on the recliner. "Are you prepared to have a daughter not even half your age? Deal with teenage attitude?"

Bill frowned at Ava. "There's plenty of time for everyone to get to know each other. The next few weeks will test us all. We're glad you're here, Taylor, and welcome the help. Running a ranch is hard work, and we're grateful."

Ava pursed her lips. "We'll see if you have what it takes to survive the ranch *and* a teenager. What do you say about that, Taylor? Do you even love him enough to stick it out through thick and thin?"

Taylor squeezed his hand. "I love him, yes," she said steadily.

Ava glanced from Hunter to Taylor and back again. "And you've talked about marriage and raising a teenager?"

Hunter nodded, but Taylor gave a nervous laugh.

"This seems a lot like saying wedding vows at the moment. That's not what this is, is it? I heard about that surprise wedding thing a while back, and I'm actually down for something like that, within reason."

Bill chuckled, and Ava's lips softened into a smile at the memory. Hunter's brows rose in surprise. How'd she hear about the fiasco at Landry's wedding?

Ava grimaced, "No, no. This isn't an exchange of vows or anything. I just don't have time to be messing around, not with this damn hip and the ranch to run. I just need to know if I can rely on you for the next few weeks with breakfasts and light cleaning."

Taylor nodded, and he noticed her picking at the hem of her shorts with her other hand. "I'm not going anywhere. Whatever you need, just let me know."

Ava sat back and closed her eyes with a sigh. "Fantastic."

Ava talked quietly with Bill so Hunter half turned to face Taylor, leaning in close to speak low.

"So you heard about the surprise marriage? What do you mean within reason?"

Taylor shrugged. "I don't want my dad to walk me down the aisle. I'd rather not get married in the church. That way I don't think about him not being there and get sad."

Hunter squeezed her hand, but she just smiled sadly and leaned her head on his shoulder. He frowned, thinking to what he'd done that morning. She might not be pleased by it after all, but what's done was done. He'd tell her after they were alone.

He kissed her hair and said, "I've always wanted an outdoor wedding myself. Under a tree or on the bank of the creek or something."

She nodded. "That could work. I want a dress, flowers, and a cake. As long as I have those, little else matters. Oh, and a party with all our friends to celebrate. Definitely need a party."

He grinned. "As long as you don't get as drunk as when we met."

She laughed. "Make sure there are no eighties heavy metal songs, and I should be good. Those trigger me."

He nodded. That was good to know. They had so much to learn about each other, but it would take a lifetime to learn everything. He filed the note into his mind to ask her why she was triggered when they were alone.

Ava looked over and smiled tightly. "I'm going to go to bed for the night. Can you help me get ready for bed, dear?"

Bill jumped up, ready to help, but Ava shooed him away. "Not you. I meant Taylor. You two men, out of the room. Shut the new den door behind you."

Hunter's nerves came back with a vengeance, but he did as she asked and followed Bill out the door. Bill stared at the door looking lost, and Hunter knew exactly how he felt.

Then his dad rubbed the back of his neck and sighed. "I —I guess I can go check on the computer and try to get caught up on things."

Hunter followed him up the stairs, saying, "Actually, Chase handled it."

"What? What do you mean, Chase handled it?"

Hunter followed him into the office. "Exactly what I said. Chase has been in here every day poring over your files. He's made some suggestions that I think you're going to like."

"Did he change anything?" Bill asked, sitting down and waking the computer up.

"No, of course not. We wouldn't do that without talking to you and Ma, you know that. But you should talk to him tomorrow about it. He can show you all the things he's found. He's great at all this computer business stuff."

Bill frowned and clicked around. "I don't know, Hunter. I don't think he's ready for something this big. He's still getting used to being free."

Hunter sat, propping his head in his hand. "Neither of you give him enough credit. He's always been a genius, and he's worked hard the past year to finish his computer certifications."

Bill sighed. "I know, I should probably trust him."

Hunter nodded, thinking the same thing. He felt guilty with how he'd talked to Chase on Saturday. They'd mostly ignored each other today, barely talking. These emotions didn't need to fester, but he didn't know how to fix it yet.

Chapter Forty-Four

Taylor hopped to her feet to help Ava with the chair. She held her elbow and moved the portable toilet chair beside the electric recliner.

"How's this? Close enough?" Taylor asked.

Ava nodded. "That's great," she said through gritted teeth.

Taylor looked around and brought her toilet paper. She carefully avoided looking, giving the woman some privacy. When she was done, she helped her back to the recliner, moved the toilet chair back, then took the bucket to empty in the actual bathroom.

She returned with it washed and cleaned, bringing a bottle of hand sanitizer too. Ava sighed gratefully and washed her hands.

"Thanks, dear. While I wait for these pills to kick in, I'll be frank with you about Destini and Jewel. Hunter belongs with them."

Ava popped her pills and took a drink of water, and Taylor's stomach twisted at the words.

Taylor shrugged. "Jewel's pretty cool, but that decision is up to both of them, not you."

Ava eyed her. "We'll see. We need Jewel's help around the ranch. Hunter says we wouldn't have managed last week without her and Gemma, so if being around Jewel is going to be a problem for you—"

Taylor shook her head, finding a toiletry bag and handing Ava the toothbrush and toothpaste. "No, it won't be. I'm fine with Jewel. We've had a few conversations, and I think we could be friends."

"And Destini?" Ava pressed.

Taylor watched, seeing if she needed help with the toothpaste. "It'll be interesting to see how Hunter handles a teenager, but he seemed fine with the toddlers tonight at dinner. He's a good man, and I know he'll make an excellent father."

Ava nodded and looked around. Taylor handed her someone's empty cup from dinner, and Ava spat into it.

Ava said, "If you're going to break his heart, you should just leave."

Taylor twisted her lips and took the cup from her. "Why would I break his heart? I love him."

Ava shrugged and handed over the rest of the toiletries. Taylor went to the kitchen and dropped the cup into the sink. She didn't see Hunter but heard voices upstairs.

She went to the downstairs bathroom and found a hand towel. She wet it, then went into the den and handed it to Ava.

Ava wiped her face with it and asked, "Who are your people? If you love him, I think we should meet your parents too."

Taylor sucked in a breath. "Mom died a few years back."

Ava paused and looked at her. "Oh, I'm so sorry, dear. What about your dad?"

"Currently in jail." Taylor pursed her lips and watched, waiting for Ava's eyes to turn judgmental or for her to say something negative.

But all she did was frown and sigh. "I'm sorry about that too."

Taylor shrugged, feeling some of the nervous weight shifting from her chest at her easy acceptance. She thought Ava would be more... well, not this. She reminded Taylor of her own mother, but oddly it didn't hurt or make her angry.

"Don't worry about it. Actually, I had to help my mom through something like this before she died. She was an invalid for a few months."

Ava scowled and washed her face with the rag. "I'm not an invalid."

Taylor quirked an eyebrow. "Not for long, you won't be. What else can I help you with?"

Ava handed the wash rag over and sighed. "Actually, can you go upstairs and find some walkie talkies? The boys had some years ago, but I know they're still around somewhere. A fresh set of batteries, and then I can call for you in the middle of the night if I need help."

Taylor frowned. "I think we're going to the barn, not staying here."

Ava arched a brow, her eyes calculating as she observed Taylor's reactions.

"Would you *mind* staying here? I love Bill to the moon and back, but that man would sleep through a tornado. If I need to get up and use the bathroom, he'll be no help. I'd rather he go sleep in our bed and get a good night's rest. Lord knows none of us slept well in the hospital."

Taylor grinned and nodded. "Ah, I see. Yes, that's not a problem. The bunk bed upstairs is actually pretty comfortable."

Ava hit the button on the electric recliner and moved it back to a sleeping position, so Taylor tidied up the room and took the wet rag and trash out. Then she went upstairs to find Hunter.

Voices drew her in, but she paused outside the door when she heard Bill ask, "Do you really love her?"

"Yeah, I really do."

"And she's staying with you in the barn?"

Hunter must have nodded because Bill continued.

"Ok, well, the house is yours if you want it. Your mom and I can build something smaller on the ranch. That'll give y'all space together and won't force Taylor to live without a bathroom or kitchen of her own. You know how territorial your mom is."

She peeked around the doorway and saw Hunter leaning back in a computer chair, his fingers linked behind his head. "Actually, I've talked to Landry about remodeling the attic at the sale barn to be full living quarters for us."

Bill sat at the computer desk, clicking away. "I know you love that barn and the attic, but I don't know if the plumbing or support beams will handle a full remodel."

Hunter sighed. "I know. I had Landry go over there Saturday and look at it. We're still coming up with a solution. Now that he's expecting a baby, I think the faster we can get something done, the better."

Bill nodded, and Taylor cleared her throat as she came through the doorway. Hunter spun the chair to face her, and his face softened. She smiled when she saw him. He was already planning their future, and her heart was so full.

She'd questioned whether she'd be able to find someone

to treat her the way Mason treated Lucy. She always assumed she'd find someone like her dad, a deadbeat who wouldn't stick around and would break his promises.

She'd thought Hunter was like that last week, but the past few days being around him and his family more had shown her a different side of him. When they'd first met, she hadn't expected him to be the one she'd find her future with.

She was still hesitant about Hunter following through on the communication thing, but with such a big family, perhaps he would be better at it than she originally thought. Besides, someone around here would know what was going on, even if he didn't tell her about it.

"Everything alright?" Hunter asked.

She nodded, smiling as she was brought back to the present. "Change of plans about staying in the barn. We're going to stay here in the house instead. She says you have walkie talkies up here somewhere? She wants a way to call for help in the middle of the night."

Bill scowled. "I told her I'd help. I'm right here."

Taylor shrugged. "I think it makes her feel better about having a girl there. Lord knows there are some things I wouldn't want Hunter to see."

Bill laughed. "Fair enough," he said, turning back to the computer.

Hunter stood and smiled. "Let's find those walkie talkies, then."

They went across the hall to the bunk bed, and Hunter opened a large toy chest.

"You're really thinking of remodeling the barn?" Her voice was quiet and vulnerable, and she straightened her spine.

He nodded with barely a glance over his shoulder. "Is

that alright? Do you want something else? A regular house or a farmhouse or this house?"

She shook her head. "I've only ever lived in an apartment, so I can't say I have a preference. I think it'd be fun to raise kids in a barn though."

He found the walkie talkies and stood up, taking the batteries out. "I'm not sure yet how long a remodel will take, and with Holly pregnant, I know Landry is going to want to spend most of his time with her."

He stopped in front of her. His gaze was clear and open, and it felt like they had no secrets.

She loved it, and she loved him. She took the walkie talkies as he held the batteries. "Do you have any fresh batteries?"

He nodded. "Downstairs in the junk drawer."

She followed him down the stairs, listening as he talked softly.

"I never thought about moving. I've been here all my life. First in this house then in the bunkhouse. It doesn't matter to me if we live in the barn or here in the house or even somewhere else that's all ours. Either way, I want more than a place to live. I want to build a home, a life with you, Taylor. I meant what I said earlier. I love you, and I'm here for the long haul. Marriage, kids, everything."

Taylor felt her heart squeeze, and she knew that everything was going to be alright between them. They went to the kitchen where he tossed the old batteries and opened a drawer to rummage for new ones.

She stopped him, wrapping her arms around his waist.

"Me too," she said softly. "I'm in it to win it, Hunter. You're my one true love. I know you said you don't believe in finding true love—"

He pulled back, and she looked up.

"I was wrong," he said, holding her tightly and staring down at her with those gorgeous hazel eyes. "I found you. You were right under my nose, and I'm so glad I took you home from the bar that night."

She grinned and tilted her lips to kiss him. "Me too."

Their lips met in a soft kiss full of promises. It was the start of more than just her new job. It was the start of the rest of her life with this man.

He pulled back and held out the batteries. "Take these to Ma and see if they work? I need to grab something."

She nodded, and he disappeared up the stairs.

Taylor went to the den and tried not to wake Ava, but she blinked slowly at her anyway.

She handed Ava the walkie talkies. "These work now. I'll take one upstairs with me. Do you need anything else? Do you have enough water?"

She shook her head. "No, dear, I'm fine. I'll see you at breakfast at five am sharp."

"Yes ma'am," Taylor said, her stomach twisting. It was almost like living a constant job interview. She had to impress his mom and win her over, and it was going to be a long, hard few weeks.

Chapter Forty-Five

Taylor woke up the next day and groaned at her alarm, silencing it quickly. Ava had called her on the walkie talkies at one and again at three. She'd been cranky and had been hurting, but Taylor had convinced her to take the actual pain medication she'd been prescribed.

If she was going to maintain these five a.m. mornings, she'd need to go to bed earlier. She was determined to excel in her new role and prove to Ava and Bill that she was a valuable member of the ranch team. This meant rescheduling her appointments with Tasha on Tuesdays since she would be out at the ranch all day. Tasha would probably say something about seeking parental approval and relying too heavily on them as surrogate parents. But the truth was, she desperately wanted their acceptance.

Hunter's side of the bed was still warm, but the bathroom door down the hall was shut, so she grabbed the walkie talkie and her phone and went to the downstairs bathroom. After washing her face, she checked that her pajama shorts and Hunter's t-shirt were covering everything they needed to before she tiptoed into the hall. The door to the den was still closed, so she didn't go check on Ava.

The menu board on the fridge said it was sausage and cheese biscuit day with two types of gravy, regular and chocolate. She'd brought that with her from her own apartment because she could not function without a meal plan. She put in headphones while she worked, trying to use the music to help her wake up.

She put the biscuits in the oven, then felt a hand grab her ass. She yelped and jumped, spinning around. Hunter pulled her into his arms, laughing as she took out her headphones.

"Don't do that! You scared me. I could've burned myself," she scolded.

He grinned and kissed her hard on the lips. "And good morning to you too, princess. How'd you sleep?"

She shrugged and snuggled her head on his chest. "Not enough sleep, but okay overall."

"You have the entire day off today?"

She nodded, and he released her so she could continue making breakfast. "Yes, I was supposed to watch Harry but Lucy is going to keep him this week so I can acclimate to the ranch. I'm all yours."

His grin spread and his eyes turned mischievous. "I have you to myself all day? Very interesting," he rubbed his hands together in anticipation, and she chuckled.

Some of the ranch hands came in for coffee, and they changed the subject to their favorite breakfasts. Apparently, she'd be able to sleep in on Fridays because that was donut day.

After breakfast was done, Taylor made Ava a plate and took it to her. Hunter followed her and sat on the fireplace to talk to his mom, who was already awake and watching the morning news.

"Would you like some coffee?"

Ava nodded, "Yes, with two sugars. Thank you, dear."

When Taylor returned with the coffee, Hunter had his arms crossed and a thoughtful look on his face.

"I just don't know if she'll be up for it, Hunter. She's a city girl."

Hunter rolled his eyes. "I think you underestimate her. Taylor, how do you feel about a tour of the ranch? I'd like to show you what all we do, and it's the best way to get around."

Taylor bit her lip and nodded. "I'd love that. I want to see what all is involved here so I know how I can help the most."

Hunter nodded approvingly, but Ava arched a brow. "You'll be on horses most of the day. Do you even ride?"

Taylor shrugged. "I've ridden a half dozen times at Girl Scout camp back in the day. Other than that, no."

Ava's lips pursed, and Taylor had a sinking feeling that she'd just proved Ava's point.

Hunter didn't seem to pick up on it though. He slapped his thighs and stood. "See? She may be a city girl, but she's got a good head on her shoulders and will learn. Do you have jeans?"

She shook her head, a smile on her lips at his compliment. Ava might be trouble, but Hunter believed in her. That was all that mattered in the long run. "At my apartment, yes. I didn't pack any, though."

"Alright, do you want to run to your apartment for some more clothes while I do the morning chores?"

"Am I not supposed to sit with Ava today and tomorrow?"

Ava waved a hand. "Psh, off with you. I have a full schedule of visitors, and Bill can stay with me until they arrive."

Taylor smiled, and soon she was parking in front of her building, taking the steps two at a time. She stumbled on the landing, her dad sitting on the front step flipping through a magazine.

Heart racing, her chest tight with emotion. "What are you doing here?" Her voice was soft and child-like, and she winced as she continued up the last few stairs.

Chris smiled and lumbered to his feet. He was tall and lanky with stringy black hair that hung to his shoulders and a full salt and pepper beard. He wore dirty, baggy jeans and a faded Guns N' Roses shirt.

"Baby girl," he said, holding his arms wide. She hugged him and closed her eyes, too weak to deny him this one simple thing. He was still her dad. He smelled of musty old cigarettes and stale beer.

"Hey Dad," she said, pulling away and unlocking the door. "How'd you find me? How'd you get out?"

Chris walked in behind her, and she shut the door. "Your cowboy boyfriend bailed me out yesterday morning. He even paid my phone bill and gave me a prepaid visa gift card for a hundred bucks. We grabbed an early lunch, and then he dropped me off at my apartment."

Taylor sucked in a breath and blinked. "Hunter?"

"Yeah, that's him. He's a pretty decent guy. I like him."

He'd gotten her dad out of jail? Without asking her? He hadn't even told her he'd gone down to Fort Worth after she'd gone to work yesterday morning. He must've dropped her dad off then gone to the hospital to get his mom.

Why hadn't he told her?

Chris pulled open the fridge and found leftovers,

popping them into the microwave without a word. Taylor shuffled on her feet, resentment bubbling up at the way he just made himself at home.

"What's your plan now? Why are you here in Crimson Creek?"

"Dave kicked me out. Apparently, I was gone too long, and he'd already replaced me in the apartment. Same with my job. I was fired for too many missed days, so I used the gift card to get up here. Gotta get a new job and will stay here while I get back on my feet."

Taylor blinked, her anger rising. "I see," she said, walking to the bedroom and pulling out some jeans and other clothes with jerky movements.

Chris followed her, a fork in the leftovers as he chewed. "What's that mean? I thought you'd fight me on it."

He talked with an open mouth, spitting food particles that she could see all the way across the room. She turned her back, her chest cold and tight.

"Doesn't matter to me. Stay here as long as you like. *I* won't be here, but you're welcome for as long as you need. I signed a one-year lease."

Chris blinked, then he grinned and gave her a side hug, holding his plate of food high. She pulled back as soon as she could.

"Thanks, baby girl. I knew I could count on you. Now where's your boyfriend?"

She sighed and continued packing. "At the ranch working. I have to get back and help out."

Chris' eyebrows rose. "I thought he had money, the way he bailed me out. But he's just a ranch hand?"

Taylor nodded slowly as he turned to go back into the kitchen. She wouldn't correct him about mostly running the ranch. He would try to milk Hunter for money, and that wouldn't help any of them.

Taylor's brain worked overtime as she thought of all the valuables she had in the apartment. She went room by room and threw what she could into her two big luggage bags. Jewelry, clothes, and even two photo albums.

When she was done, she rolled the first one to the front door. "Can you grab my other bag?"

He had the remote pointed to the TV and sat on the couch with his dirty sneakers on the coffee table. He barely looked at her, saying, "Huh? Oh yeah, just a second."

She sighed and opened the front door, taking the first bag down on her own. Some things never changed. That was what he'd done her entire childhood. He'd come home from the factory and plop in front of the TV, ignoring her mother and her and everything else until dinner was ready.

That was when the drinking and fighting would kick in. Then she'd run to her room and escape into a good book. She wrangled her bag into the car, then went back upstairs.

Dear old Dad was asleep on the couch, his head thrown back as he snored. She felt numb, her entire body cold as she dragged the other bag to the front door. She took it to the car and returned, looking around the apartment, a feeling of finality about it.

Fists clenching, she grabbed all the boxes along the wall. She refused to leave the things she'd saved from her childhood for him to pawn.

It was like watching the start of an avalanche. She knew how this was going to go with her dad. She'd been there, done that, over and over again.

Hunter had bailed him out, but at least she wouldn't have to live with her dad. She still wanted to live with Hunter and marry him. They just needed to talk this out.

The Cowboy Gets His Girl

He had to know that him bailing out her dad was not what she wanted.

She sighed and locked the door behind her, wiping sweat from her forehead. She drove to Tasha's to talk and change her appointment days to Mondays, then she went back to the ranch, her car loaded with luggage and boxes and everything she held dear.

By that time, it was nearly lunch, so she unloaded one of her bags and changed into jeans. She checked on Ava, then began chopping the chicken and throwing it in the skillet to grill. She set the rice to boil and chopped garlic and onions.

The front door opened, and she glanced over, then looked back down at her task at hand. Hunter's hands slid over her shoulders, and she stiffened.

He kissed the side of her neck. "Welcome home, princess."

She took a deep breath and didn't say anything, conflicting emotions warring within her. She loved hearing that she was home now. This was the start of a whole new chapter of her life. Anger still made her stiff in his arms, but he stepped away and popped a piece of chicken in his mouth.

"I found the perfect horse for you to ride. Minerva is older and settled. She's not a brood mare anymore, so she's just been in the pasture for about two years now. You'll love her."

The front door opened, and some ranchers came inside. She sucked in a deep breath, pushing her emotions aside and adding the veggies to the chicken. She smiled at them and talked with false animation. If any of them noticed, they didn't say anything.

They laughed and carried on like they did at breakfast

as they ate chicken and rice. She made Ava a plate and took it into the den, setting it on the side table before grabbing her water to refill.

Hunter stood in the doorway of the den, a frown on his face. "What is it?"

She glared and strode past him. "We'll discuss it later."

She filled the cup from the fridge, and he followed her back to the den, his voice lowering so as not to be heard from the rest of the guys.

"What's going on? You're upset. Did I do something?"

She ignored him, pushing into the den and handing Ava the water with a smile. "Do you need anything else?"

Ava shook her head as Bill came in. Taylor looked at Hunter and smiled tightly. "Alright then, how about that tour of the ranch?"

Hunter's face lit up. "Great, Dad, can you stay with Ma for a while? We'll be back in a couple of hours."

Bill sat down in the other chair and nodded, so Hunter tugged her out the front door. The screen door slammed shut, and she strode across the yard toward the barn.

"Now what's wrong?" he asked again.

She turned and faced him, finally meeting his hazel eyes. "Did you go to Fort Worth yesterday morning and bail my dad out of jail?"

His eyes widened. "Yes, I thought you'd be pleased. I answered your phone yesterday morning when you went downstairs. We chatted, I got the details, and I took care of it."

It was a question, and she sighed as he opened the barn door. "This isn't cool, Hunter, it's not good at all." She waved to her car. "I packed up everything important to me, but I won't be surprised if he starts pawning the rest of my stuff."

"What do you mean? Why are you upset about your dad? What's going on?" He led them into the barn where two horses stood with bridles already on.

"I don't want to talk about it," she said, crossing her arms as he worked. He grabbed blankets and strapped the saddles in place.

"You can't tell me we need to talk and then not talk to me. This is how we get to know each other, right?"

She gritted her teeth together and took the reins to the black one. She followed him as he led the bigger brown one out of the barn.

The horse nudged her shoulder, and she turned to walk backward, rubbing the old girl's forehead. She frowned. Did horses have foreheads?

When they got to the front yard, Hunter turned to help her into the saddle. Taylor bounced a few steps, trying to reach the too high stirrup.

Hunter steadied the stirrup as she struggled to get her foot in. She grabbed onto the pommel and grunted, swinging her leg over the saddle. For a moment, it seemed like she might fall off the other side, but she managed to settle herself in place.

Once she was somewhat comfortable, Hunter mounted his own horse and she reached for her reins as he gave her a quick rundown on riding.

She had always loved working with horses during her time at the Girl Scout Camp. She didn't mention that she had also volunteered as a counselor at the day camp throughout high school, hoping to earn a scholarship through her volunteer hours.

Though she had fond memories of horses, she wasn't sure how long she'd last on one after so many years not riding.

Hunter turned and led them between the house and the bunk house to a well-traveled track that looped behind the bunk house to the west. She followed behind him, and the wide-open space made her big feelings seem so small and insignificant.

When Hunter pulled his horse to walk beside hers, he said, "Now about your dad."

Taylor sighed and tipped her head back. The sun beat down on her, driving away some of the coldness in her chest.

"I've never been able to tell him no. My therapists say it's because I crave parental approval, but I had just stood up for myself for the first time ever. For weeks when he's called, I've told him no more bailouts, no more rent money. I was proud of myself because I actually stuck to it too. I didn't let him talk me into it like normal. I started ignoring his calls because he'll keep asking until he gets what he wants. Give an inch, and he'll take a mile."

"But he's family," Hunter said.

Taylor's grip on the reins tightened along with her chest, tears pricking her eyes. "I know that, but as much as I want to help him, I can't keep enabling him."

"Enabling?" Hunter asked.

Taylor swallowed hard and nodded, anger burning in her chest. "He's an addict who can't keep a job. There's no way he's going to hang around Crimson Creek long enough to get a job, much less keep it."

Hunter frowned. "He's in Crimson Creek? I left him in Fort Worth yesterday with his roommate."

"Well, his roommate kicked him out, and he lost his job while in jail. Now he's at my apartment, and I'm fully prepared for what's going to happen next."

"*The future's an uncertain ride, it's path twisting with dreams weeping, none know what lies around the bend, whether life or life's end."*

Taylor rolled her eyes, not that he could see them behind the sunglasses. "Life's not explained so easily in a poem, Hunter. He's manipulative and hasn't changed since he got into drugs. He'll get a job that'll last about one to three months. Then he's going to get in trouble, blame the boss, get some drugs, and sell all my shit to pay for them. Then he'll disappear for a while before he calls me asking for money, either under the guise for rent, groceries, phone bill, or bail. It's always some excuse that he uses to buy more drugs."

Hunter frowned. "You don't know that. If he's been in jail, he's probably clean by now."

She glared but he didn't look at her. "I know my own dad, Hunter. It's what he did in high school to both Mom and me. Hell, he even did it after she died. Thankfully, I was in college by then with most of the stuff I'd rescued from him."

He turned to follow a fence line. "Wow, that's a really tough upbringing. It's hard for me to comprehend it because mine was so... normal, I guess, even with Chase going to prison. You mentioned not wanting him at your wedding, but I didn't fully understand until now."

She breathed in the hay and let the peace of nature calm her. "There was no way you could've known. We haven't really talked about him. What did you think when you met him?"

"We had some good conversations about when you were in elementary school, but knowing what I know now, his questions about my money and job make more sense."

She snorted. "Yeah, he was scoping you out to see how much money he can get from you. I told him today you're just a ranch hand. Hopefully that keeps him from asking for more."

They rode in silence, the birds chirping as they drew closer to the trees.

Hunter's voice was soft as he said, "I'm sorry he's not the dad you should've had, but why did you compare him to me?"

Her anger spiked. She waved her arm wide, the other still holding her horse's reins steady as they stood in the field. "Because you're both high-handed, just doing whatever you think without talking to me. Both of you manipulate me into what *you* want."

"Do you not want me? This? A future together?" The accusatory tone made her frustration rise higher.

She rubbed her temple and ground out, "Ugh, no, that's not what I'm saying. The similarities stop there, Hunter. Living together the past few days has shown me a different side of you. We're both trying to communicate better, and you actually want to learn how to have a relationship. That's more than my dad ever did."

They followed the fence line to the trees, and the shade immediately made it feel almost ten degrees cooler. She sighed and wiped her forehead. "We're both going to need to compromise to make this work, but one thing I can't compromise on is talking through shit."

"That's why I asked you to move in, so we could talk more. I'm shit at texting, sugar."

Fields stretched on either side of them as they crested a small ridge. He came to a stop under an old oak tree, and she pulled her horse around so she faced him. "I get that, and we are doing better, but I won't have you making decisions for me, especially on things dealing with my dad and my life. I know you have good intentions, but last night, you were talking to your dad about remodeling the barn, or living in the house, or doing something else. Yet *we* haven't had that conversation. You've talked to Landry, had him inspect the barn, but I had to *overhear* that to learn about it? Not cool."

Hunter breathed a sigh of relief. "I'm sorry, I was just trying to figure it all out before presenting it to you."

"Like on some kind of fucking silver platter?" She laughed. "Hunter, you may call me a princess, but don't fucking treat me like one by keeping me in the dark. Talk to me, for fuck's sake."

He chuckled and reached for her hand. He rubbed the back of wrist with his thumb. "I'm sorry, you're right. I shouldn't have bailed him out without talking with you first, and I'm sorry he's landed in Crimson Creek."

She sighed and squeezed his hand. "Me too."

He paused then said, "I know you probably don't want to hear this, but... you gave me a chance after I fucked up multiple times the past few weeks. Maybe your dad needs another chance too."

She frowned. "What the fuck do you mean by that?"

He winced, then said, "We should have dinner with him one night this week."

She sighed, her shoulders rolling against the tension, and he let go of her hand. "I guess that'd be the decent thing to do. It might help you to see what kind of man he is too, but for the love of God, do *not* invite him to your parent's place. Do not tell him your parents own this ranch or are well-off. We'll meet him in town somewhere. If he comes here, he might try to swipe something and pawn it."

Hunter nodded and sighed. "Deal."

She wagged her finger. "Don't tell him you're practically

running this place either, or he'll start begging you for money too."

He reached over and laid his hand on her thigh. "Alright, I get the message. I'll watch my words around him. But if he's in Crimson Creek for any amount of time, he'll hear the small-town rumor mill. Not sure we can keep this stuff from him."

She sighed and patted his hand on her thigh. "I know, but a girl can hope, right?"

He chuckled and nodded, releasing her hand. "I really did think you'd be happy with bailing him out."

She put her other hand on top of his. "Some surprises are good. Some aren't. It's just life. Nothing you can really do about it now."

He reached up and caressed her cheek, drawing their horses closer together. Their knees touched, but it was the soft touch of his hand on her cheek that made her sigh.

"I love you, sugar. All I want to do is make you happy."

She leaned into his touch, her eyes fluttering. "You make me happy. You're all I need."

"I want to give you the world, princess. I want to give you everything you've ever wanted. Just tell me what that is, and I'll make it happen."

She smiled, some of the frustration easing in her chest, softening under the light of his love. "I want a family. I want a house full of kids, a career that fulfills me, a husband that will love me all the days of our lives."

He grinned, squeezing her hand. "I think I can make that happen. Want me to show you your new home?"

She nodded, some of the excitement in his voice infecting her. He was right. This wasn't just his parents' ranch. It was their home.

Chapter Forty-Six

Hunter waved his hand to the land around them. "All of this is ours. It's been in our family for four generations now and over a hundred years. This ranch is one of the most important things to me, second only to my family."

She nodded, still distant from their conversation. He didn't like it, wanted her close always, not just physically but emotionally too.

"All of my brothers left the ranch, have their own lives, but not me. This ranch *is* my life." He linked their fingers and let their hands dangle between the horses. "You're my life now. You're my number one, then my family, then the ranch," he said softly.

She turned to face him, and he saw some of the tightness around her lips ease as she smiled softly. "You're my number one too."

"I... don't know how to explain how important this is to me." He paused then looked around at the field, the way the light streaked through the clouds, the wind on his skin. Then he took a deep breath and said,

"Saddle sores and calluses on my hands,
Weathered face—my badges from these lands.
A field of murals, painted by God's grace,
A masterpiece I call my dwelling place.
A man who loves the whispering of trees,
Where others flee, I stand in peace.
My boots are muddy, hat torn and gray,
This ranch, like me, is worn in every way.
With steady hands, I work the soil each day,
And God provides in His eternal way.
Together we have triumphed, the land and I,
Through trials faced beneath an open sky.
This ground I tread is sacred, tried, and true,
No path will lead me far from this view.
My cowboy's heart unbridled and free,
This ranch is my world, my destiny."

The scent of grass and earth filled Hunter's nostrils, mixing with the wildflowers and the horse beneath him. They rode in silence a few moments, Hunter feeling vulnerable and on edge at sharing his poetry with her.

He shook his shoulders and snorted. "Well, Jewel's daughter Destini might be my destiny too, if the DNA test shows she's mine."

She reached over, taking his hand and pulling them to a stop once more. "Hunter, that was beautiful. Did you just come up with that?"

He shrugged. "Yeah, sometimes when I'm riding out here, checking fences or training horses, my thoughts just flow into poetry for some reason. I—I've never shared any of them though. That's a first."

She sniffed and pulled his hand to her heart, bringing their horses closer together. "I'm honored, Hunter, but you need to share these with the world too. That was amazing."

He shook his head, pulling back and placing their laced fingers onto his thigh. "Share them how? You know how I feel about writing."

Her jaw dropped and her brows rose. "Speak it into a note's app on your phone, or hell, send me a voice message with your poems anytime. If you want, we can compile them into a book of poetry or even a children's book or something."

The awe and admiration in her gaze made his cheeks flush in the hot late summer sun. Her strength and support flowed through their connection to his soul as she squeezed his hand.

"I—I don't know about that. They're not that good." He breathed a sigh of relief. "But you—like it though? That's all that matters, really. You don't think it's lame or girly?"

She rolled her eyes, that too-wide smile flashing across her face. "I don't just like it, I *love* it. The idea of something being girly is a societal construct that's a bunch of shit. But if it makes you feel better, no, it's not girly. You're Hunter, a predator, the beast, remember? Everything you do screams manly man. You're my beastie."

He laughed, and her grin widened. He flushed more, feeling truly seen for the first time in his life. It was like a vise around his heart released, and he realized how important her happiness and acceptance were to him.

"I like that," he said.

"It totally fits, right?"

"Yep, I want to go beast mode on your ass, but first, let's finish the tour."

She licked her mischievous lips. "I can't wait. Carry on, good sir."

He chuckled and pointed with his other hand. "The

river is that way. It's our property line on the west side. To the south is John and Dot's place. They raise bucking bulls for the rodeos. You know Trent, the ranch hand?"

She nodded, and he continued. "John's his dad, so he's here and there, back and forth all the time. To the north we have the Delaney's place, and at the northeast corner by the Delaney's is Andy and Cindy's place. My folks have a hunting cabin in that corner, and Chase spends half his time there, when he gets tired of being around people. To the east we have the road to town and the big sale barn. Hundreds of acres, and I never get tired of this view."

She sighed. "It's beautiful, Hunter. I don't blame you for not wanting to move away."

He nodded and turned his horse to continue on the well-worn path. "I want to show you my favorite place on the ranch."

He led her to the river and stopped at the ridge above the bank, looking down at the shallow water. With the heat of summer, the water was down. Hunter's horse shifted, and he slid off Prancer's back to lead him to the trees and shade. Taylor followed and slid off her horse easily enough, and he took her hand as they stretched their legs.

She pointed. "Is that where you went fishing and I watched Harry?"

"Where you wore that itty bitty bikini and drove me wild? Yeah."

She snorted but seemed to relax more. He wanted to bring her back to being the fun, vivacious, smiling woman he loved. He needed to see her happy. It was a deeper ache than the one that told him to fuck her all day and all night.

He looked around and nodded to the trees that came up the bank and stretched well into the field. "If we have to build a place of our own, I'd like to build here. Far enough from the river that we won't need to worry about flooding, but close enough that we can just go fishing in the backyard whenever we want."

She looked around. "Closer to the trees for shade? Yeah, that could work. Maybe a big red barn but when you get inside, it's got a cozy modern farmhouse vibe?"

He nodded, excitement running through him. "Yeah, we could put in skylights and open them to look at the stars on clear nights."

She smiled and nodded. "Perfect. I'd love that. I—I've always lived in an apartment, but there's something so freeing about being out here."

"Yes," he sighed, relief going through him. "That's it exactly. I want to point out that it was *your* suggestion to live in a barn, not mine."

She laughed, "I think it'd be cute for people to ask our kids *what, were you raised in a barn* and then they'd sass back at them *yeah, actually, we were.*"

A thrill went through him to know that she really was thinking about their kids, their future together. The easy conversation made some of the changes of the past month feel less overwhelming. With her at his side, he could handle his aging parents, the ranch, a possible daughter—

His cell phone rang, breaking the moment, and he answered it without looking.

"Hunter, it's Jewel. I have a situation."

He frowned. "What's up?"

"Destini has decided she's done with high school, and she's going to stay in Houston."

He frowned. "What?"

Jewel sighed, and he looked over at Taylor. She was frowning, and on impulse, he put it on speaker. He didn't want to keep anything from Taylor again. Not with the way she'd responded to the surprise with her dad.

He didn't want to fuck up twice in a row.

Jewel said, "You know how I went down to Houston today to pick her up from space camp? Well, she wants to stay in Houston. She even wrote a five-page persuasive essay on how she should go back to her regular high school for another semester."

"And live with who?"

"With my cousins. They're alright with it, but that's not even the worst part."

He rubbed his forehead. "What's the worst part?"

"She has a letter from a tech company whose main contract is NASA. They've offered her a one semester internship here in Houston. It starts next week. She wants to stay in Houston with my cousins, go to her normal high school, and do the internship. It would literally be her only extra-curricular, what with the hours they want her to work."

The birds chirped in the trees broke the silence, and Hunter swallowed hard. "What about the DNA test? I need to know, Jewel."

"She says that she can do it when she comes in for Thanksgiving break."

Hunter frowned and paced under the trees. "Chase and I can both go down there next weekend and do the DNA test, then. That way we will all know for sure, and we can all move forward without this huge question mark looming over our heads."

"No, I don't think you need to do that. She's being moody and defensive about this opportunity. I need to walk a fine line here because she's so excited. She's going on and on about how good this will be for her career."

"Jesus, she's only fifteen. What fucking career?" He practically growled into the phone, and then Taylor was touching his back. He turned to face her, and she rubbed a soothing circle.

"Hey Jewel," Taylor said, and he held the phone so they could both talk into it.

"Hey Taylor. Sorry to interrupt y'all with this."

"Not a problem," Taylor said. "I think this is an amazing opportunity for Destini, and you should be excited with her. It will show her that you're still on her side, just like always. Ask her if the guys can do the DNA test from here or if they can go to Houston to get it done. That way we have the results when she comes in for Thanksgiving. It might take them a few weeks to get it figured out, but it's a good bargaining chip with her. If you're thinking of letting her stay and take the opportunity, my suggestion would be to agree on the condition that she does the DNA test. That's just my two cents though."

Hunter nodded and sighed, wrapping his other free arm around her. She helped his frustration settle as if she was his anchor in the storm. The smell of her strawberry shampoo mixed with the grass and earth around them, soothing him.

He said, "I like that idea. I was really looking forward to meeting her this weekend. Are you sure she can't come up for just a few days and see everyone?"

"No," Jewel said softly. "I think a part of her is using this as an opportunity to run away from finding out who her dad is. I think she's scared that you won't live up to the image in her head. She's built you up to be this great hero."

Hunter squeezed his arm around Taylor, briefly closing his eyes against the pressure in his chest. "But we don't even know that she's mine."

There was a pause on the other line, then Jewel said, "I know."

She sounded so weary and beat down. Taylor must've picked up on it too because she said, "Whatever she decides, it'll be alright. We'll be here regardless, ready to meet her when she's ready. You're doing a great job handling a genius teenager, Jewel."

A sniff came through the line, then Jewel said, "Thanks. To both of you. I gotta go now. I should probably fill Chase in."

She sighed, and they said their goodbyes. Hunter put his phone in his back pocket and pulled Taylor closer. They stood there for long minutes, listening to the crickets and cicadas.

Eventually the heat drove them apart, and she found a broken old fence row on the edge of the trees. She leaned against the top railing, testing its strength first.

"I'm sorry about Destini. I know you were ready to get answers," Taylor said softly as she messed with the fence.

He sighed and raked a hand through his hair. "One of the main reasons I didn't want to date you was because I didn't have answers for the Destini question. It's not fair to ask you to be part of all this."

She put her elbows on the fence and propped her face in her hand. "Falling in love isn't about being fair. Being in a relationship is a give and take. You have Destini, I have my dad—everyone has baggage, Hunter."

Her words soothed some unknown tension within his chest. He sighed, "I know there's time. Seems like she's not in a rush to do the DNA test or meet any of us. If it were me, I'd want to know. Hell, I *do* want to know. I want this figured out now."

She chuckled. "More like, you want this figured out yesterday."

He laughed and nodded. "That too."

He breathed deeply, then leaned over the fence to kiss her. He needed the distraction, didn't want to think about Destini and Jewel anymore. He didn't like the not knowing, the unsettled feeling of it.

The kiss grounded him, though. It was a long, deep, tender kiss that worked its magic and brought his attention back to Taylor. Back to their future, their lives, their love. Tongues dueled lazily as he stretched the moment between them.

When they finally parted, her eyes were shining bright in the filtered light through the trees, her sunglasses now on top of her head.

"I love you, Taylor. I don't know what you see in me or why you put up with my baggage, but I thank my lucky stars that you're here."

He couldn't wait to claim her in front of everyone. Her lips parted in desire, and he caressed her cheek, tracing a finger down her neck to the tank top strap.

"I'm glad I'm here too." Her voice was husky as she looked around the shaded fence row. She leaned back and wiggled the old wooden fence.

He raised his brows. "What are you doing?"

"Just testing the strength of it."

He snorted and adjusted his cowboy hat. "It's solid. I built the damn thing myself and check it every week."

She grinned and stepped back, pulling her tank top over her head. "Good, because I have plans. Didn't you say once something about fucking me over a fence post?"

His mouth watered as her breasts spilled out, bare in the

soft sunlight. His head began to buzz with the familiar heat, the need to brand her and make her scream his name.

"Hell yes," he said, taking off his hat and pulling his shirt up and over his head. Her tinkling laugh distracted him almost as much as her breasts.

He reached for the button on his pants as he bent his head and took her pebbled nipple into his mouth. He sucked gently, and her hands wrapped around the back of his head, pressing him closer.

"God, yes, that's exactly what I need."

Her voice caused a shiver to race up his spine. He moved to her other nipple as he freed his dick to the gentle breeze.

He pulled one of her wrists down, and her hand wrapped around him. He shuttered a breath, moving his own hands to her jeans. He shoved them down, his hand sliding over her ass.

God, had she been wearing a thong? She drove him wild, and she was all his. His to spoil. His to love. His to claim.

He pulled back and looked down at her, moving one hand to her clit. Her back arched, offering her breasts up like a delicacy. He wanted to feast on her, but there was something he needed to do more.

"I've been wanting to bend you over this fence and fuck you hard for weeks. I've been dreaming of it, princess."

She gasped, her eyes heavy lidded with desire as her hips thrust onto his fingers between her legs.

"Then do it, you beast."

His eyes flared, and he spun her around. She stumbled, her pants around her ankles.

"The top fence row is too high. Put your waist on the

second one and bend over." It wasn't a request, and it pleased him that she was so quick to comply.

His fingers found her wet slit from behind, and he teased her. She moaned, settling her knees on the lower fence row, her ankles bound by her pants.

He teased her entrance with his dick, and she moaned.

"Is this what you want?"

"God yes. Please, Hunter, fuck me like the slut I am."

He speared her, slamming inside with one smooth thrust. She squealed at the intrusion, tightening around him like a vise, and he groaned.

His eyes closed, bursts of light swarming his senses. She made low, throaty sounds of pleasure, and it made him pound her faster, harder, deeper.

No woman had ever felt so good, so perfect. It was like they were made for each other.

Relentless thrusts rammed into her. He was chasing more than just a simple orgasm. He was chasing a future with her, securing their future together with every surge inside. She took all of him, caging the most animal part of him and making it hers.

He lost himself in her wet warmth. His fingers gripped her hips tight enough to leave bruises, and he grew even more excited to see evidence of his claim.

Her moans changed, growing shallower as she tensed. They were hungry slaves of love, primitive in their desire, rutting in the open air like animals. He knew she was almost to the edge and thank fuck for that. He couldn't hold out much longer.

"That's it, slut. Come on that dick like the dirty little slut you are."

She cried out, her entire body shuddering. Head tilted

back, her voice echoed through the field. A raw, rippling wave swept through her pussy, clamping down on his cock over and over.

He was trapped between torment and ecstasy as she gripped him in a velvet prison. His spine tingled as she spasmed around him, jerking her ass back against his hips.

He stiffened, holding her deep. A fireball of pure bliss raged inside him, every muscle tensing as he flooded her. The hot pulsing heat exploded, violent and virile, leaving him gasping.

He stayed inside as long as he could, her body milking him. He leaned his head on the top fence post, waiting for his breathing to slow.

She hummed, and he bent over to kiss her spine.

"That was incredible," she panted. He nipped her shoulder blade, and she squeezed him in response. He grinned even though the action pushed him out.

He stepped back, smacking her ass and making her jump with a squeal. "It was incredible because you're incredible, princess. The things you do to me…"

He trailed off as she dipped her hand between her legs and began to lick her sticky fingers. His throat closed, his head shaking side to side in disbelief.

He wasn't sure he'd ever get used to her brazen sexuality, but he didn't want her to change. He loved everything about her.

Her eyes twinkled in the sunlight, her sunglasses missing. "Aww, say more nice things like that, beastie."

He laughed and grabbed his dripping dick. "Why don't you clean me off too, slut?"

She grinned and bent at the waist. "Happy to oblige."

She sucked him so hard he hissed, his toes curling in his boots.

"Hot damn," he gasped, gently pushing her off him. "Your mouth is a weapon of mass destruction, princess."

She laughed, the sound tinkering through the field and lighting his heart.

Chapter Forty-Seven

The next few days were a whirlwind of activity. Ava slept a lot and Maryanne and Holly came over while Taylor went to work. She was tired from waking up so early to cook every day, then working a full day at the library. She'd get back to the ranch around five-thirty and scramble to get dinner on the table for Hunter, Chase, Bill, and Ava.

Friday night, Hunter and Taylor met her dad at the Diner. Taylor fidgeted with her purse and hid a yawn while they waited in the booth in the corner.

Hunter slid his arm behind her shoulder, and she rested her head on him. "Tired?"

She nodded, breathing in the scents from the Diner mixed with the leather, sweat, and outdoors that was Hunter. "Yeah, I can't wait for my days off so I can take a nap and catch up on sleep. I'm not used to these early mornings."

He kissed the side of her head. "I know, but I appreciate it so much. You're my princess, and I want to spoil you."

She snorted and sat up as her dad pushed open the door

and looked around. "Don't let him hear you say that," she murmured.

Hunter stood up and offered her father, Chris, a hand to shake. She glanced from one to the other. They were both tall but dear old Dad was still gaunt and shaggy from being in jail.

Chris slid into the booth opposite, and Hunter sank onto the bench beside her. "This is a cute little place. Is the food any good?"

Taylor nodded. "Yeah, it's delicious. Down home cooking but there's some healthy options too."

Hunter slid his hand along Taylor's knee under the table, stopping her bouncing foot. He smiled as the waitress came to take their order. When she walked away, Taylor looked down at the twisted napkin in her hand.

"Since you've moved in with Hunter, I guess you two are pretty serious, huh?" Chris asked.

Taylor looked at Hunter, and some of her tension eased as he smiled. He nodded, "I'm crazy in love with her, yes. I'd like to ask your permission to marry her."

Taylor felt her face flame, but neither of them looked at her.

Chris' bushy brows rose then he grinned, eying Hunter with a calculating stare that she didn't like. "Well, that's great! Of course you have it, of course. My baby girl deserves the best, and you're a decent sort, Hunter. I appreciate you bailing me out."

Hunter's lips twitched as he linked his fingers with Taylor's. "No problem, but Taylor and I have agreed that we can't bail you out anymore."

Taylor bit her lip, watching her dad warily. They'd talked and talked about what to do about her dad.

Chris' eyes narrowed as his brow arched. "Oh really?"

Hunter nodded and stared him down. "Yes, you see, Taylor and I have to save up for a house of our own. We'd like to get into a new place within the next few months so we can start a family. Kids are expensive, Mr. Grimes. I'm sure you understand."

Chris crossed his arms as the waitress brought their food. "And where exactly are you living now? All I know is on some ranch."

Hunter met the waitress' gaze and shook his head slightly before he jumped in to stop her from joining the conversation. "We're living with my parents right now. It's hard because Ma's laid up from a broken hip. There's no way we could've managed this week without Taylor's help."

Chris snorted and picked up his fork. "I see. You don't want me to take up any time and attention because she's already so busy being at your beck and call."

Taylor frowned. "It's not like that, Dad."

"Isn't it? Those dark circles under your eyes don't lie."

Hunter shook his head. "Absolutely not. Taylor has a big heart and just wants to help. My work is at the ranch and being with my parents gives me more time to spend with her and take care of her."

Taylor pushed her French fries around in the ketchup but couldn't bring herself to eat. Her stomach was too on edge.

"How are you taking care of her?"

Hunter glanced at Taylor, his eyes twinkling as he winked. "Oh, a little of this and a little of that. We're still working out our partnership and how we want our lives to be. But rest assured, I only want the best for your daughter. Just like you, right?"

Hunter stared at Chris. The men seemed to measure each other with some ancient ritual staring contest. But

The Cowboy Gets His Girl

eventually Chris harrumphed and bit into his cheeseburger. The rest of dinner, they talked about sports teams, the holidays, and family traditions. Slowly Taylor relaxed, sipping a milkshake for dessert.

"Do you remember when I surprised your mom at the cafe on Christmas?" Chris asked with a laugh.

Taylor's lips twisted. "You mean when you almost cost her the job at the cafe? Yeah, I remember."

Chris tossed his napkin onto his empty plate in mock outrage. "What? I did no such thing. All I did was surprise her with her Christmas present."

Taylor rolled her eyes and sat back in the booth. "Yeah, with an angry, wet, homeless kitten who was spitting mad you put her in that box."

Chris leaned his head back and laughed. "The look on your mom's face when that cat took off through the cafe like lightning!"

Taylor chuckled at the memory.

Hunter looked at her and smiled. "Are you a cat person or a dog person?"

She shrugged. "I like them both but never had a chance to find out. That kitten was the closest we ever got to having a pet, and when the cafe owner finally kicked it out with the broom, it was gone. We never saw it again."

"I spent hours roaming the streets looking for that cat," Chris said with a sigh.

Taylor looked at him, tilting her head. "You did?"

He nodded, his weary eyes heavy with sadness. "Yeah, I did," he said softly.

She felt her lips softening as Hunter stood up. "Well, we need to get on home. Ranch life means rising before dawn. I'll be right back." He walked toward the counter and handed his card over to the waitress.

Chris cleared his throat and stood. "He seems like an upstanding young man, baby girl. I'm glad you've found someone to spend your life with."

"Me too, Dad. Me too." She took one last drink then followed them out the door.

They walked out into the setting sun, Hunter's hand on her back. His other hand reached out to shake.

"Sir, thank you for meeting us for dinner tonight. We'll need to make this a weekly thing. Maybe once Ma is healed up, you can come to their house for dinner and meet my folks."

They shook but her dad just looked at her with a thoughtful expression on his face. "Perhaps. I'm glad she has you to take care of her, Hunter."

He held out his arms, and Taylor hugged him. He still smelled like stale beer and old cigarettes, but instead of making her gag, it made her smile from nostalgia.

"I'll drop by next week and check on you. Let me know if you get a job or need help looking."

Chris rubbed the back of his neck and looked away. Her heart sank as he avoided her eyes. "Yes, well, I'll let you know. I didn't have much luck this week, but tomorrow's a new day."

He waved as he walked back toward the apartment a few blocks to the east. Hunter slipped his fingers into hers and squeezed.

"You alright?" he asked softly.

She sighed and leaned her head against his bicep. "Yeah, I'll be fine. It's just so hard knowing that he's throwing his life away. I just wish—well, if wishes were horses, all men would ride. Isn't that what you cowboys say?"

Hunter laughed and escorted her to the Jeep. "Yeah,

The Cowboy Gets His Girl

how can I help though? Do you want to take your mind off it?"

She jumped into the passenger seat, and he leaned close. She kissed him softly, knowing him well enough to read his body language. It was a kiss of promise, of tenderness and love. It made her ache with comfort.

When he pulled back, he tipped his cowboy hat up on his forehead. "How about we go to the Electric Cowboy? Some of the other ranch hands are going, plus Parker and Chase."

She nodded and looked down. "Sure, but I'm still in my work clothes."

He slid his hand up her knee to tease her inner thighs. "Oh, I know, and it's the sexiest thing I've ever seen. I love you in your work clothes."

She grinned and reached up to pop the top button of her black silk blouse. It gaped in the center, barely revealing a black and red laced bra. "I guess I can make do like this."

He licked his lips, his eyes darkening. "Oh yes, that'll work nicely."

He shut the door and went to the driver's side. The drive to the bar was barely twenty minutes, but he'd rolled down the windows. The warm air blowing through her fingers helped relax her from the stress of seeing her dad.

There wasn't any point in worrying about him. He was going to do whatever he wanted. She just hoped she wouldn't have to pick up the pieces again.

They got out of the Jeep to the sound of music thumping. After paying the cover charge, Hunter walked inside with his hand on Taylor's back. She wore a red pencil skirt with that black silk shirt and red heels. Her hair was a little windblown but still up in a bun from work, and she'd kept the reading glasses on.

Damn, she drove him crazy. He leaned close to be heard over the music. "Can you believe just a few weeks ago, we met right here?"

She looked up at him through the lenses. "Are you looking to score, cowboy? Because I'm a sure thing."

He grinned and swept her onto the dance floor, pulling her close. "*With you in my arms, I am never alone. I don't care if we score or screw, as long as I'm with you.*"

She leaned her head back and laughed, the sound blending with the music and making his chest heat. "That wasn't your best work, beastie."

He grinned as he spun her around. "Oh? I guess I need more inspiration, sugar tits."

Her eyes twinkled under the dim lights of the bar. "I can probably help with that, but first, will you get me a drink while I use the bathroom?"

The song ended as he nodded, his hand on her back as long as he could. When she disappeared in the crowd, he walked to the bar and nodded to Katie.

"Well, hey there, handsome. Aren't you a sight for sore eyes?" she said with a smile, sliding his favorite bottle of beer across the counter.

He smiled and picked it up, tipping it toward her in thanks. "Appreciate it, but can I get something fruity too?"

Katie's eyebrows rose. "Ah, for that girl who's staying with you this week? What's her name?"

"Taylor, the one I took home from the bar who was too drunk to drive?"

Katie's mouth dropped open a little as she mixed a

drink. "Really? Congratulations, Hunter. I bet your mom was so excited to hear about that."

A familiar woman leaned against the bar next to him. "I don't think so," Jewel said with a scowl. "I think his mom still has hopes *we'll* work out."

He winced. "You're probably right."

Jewel nodded. "Yeah, when I came by yesterday to check on the foals, she was talking about nothing but how amazing you are. She even had Holly pull out the high school photo albums to show us both what a good couple we made."

Hunter frowned and took a drink of his beer.

"Well, that's moms for you," Katie said, handing Jewel two beers.

Jewel must've seen the look on his face because she held one up sheepishly and said, "Um, Chase is playing pool if you want to join the rest of us?"

He nodded, unable to stop his grin. "Sure, I'll wait for Taylor here, then we'll both be in."

"Great," she said, leaning forward. She put her hand on his chest and said into his ear, "By the way, do you want to go to Denton tomorrow for a DNA test? Destini agreed and my cousin took her to the lab today. So now we just need yours and…"

Hunter sucked in a breath, covering her hand with his as he leaned back and met her gaze. It felt like he'd been kicked in the nuts, so he just nodded.

A throat cleared next to them, and Hunter looked over to see Taylor with a frown on her face. She looked from him to Jewel and back again. He dropped Jewel's hand, and she stepped back, picking her beers back up.

"Taylor, how great to see you. We're playing pool. Do you want to join us?"

Hunter handed Taylor her drink, but Jewel took her arm and practically dragged her toward the back room. He didn't have a chance to talk to her and explain that it wasn't what she'd probably been thinking.

Chase leaned against the wall, separated from the rest of their poker buddies and the ranch hands. He was at least in the same room and would occasionally participate in a conversation.

Hunter followed Jewel over as she handed Chase the beer, then she and Taylor went to a booth in the corner to sit across from Kendall and Lola.

"Jewel told you about tomorrow?" Chase asked.

Hunter nodded, leaning against the wall next to his brother. "Yeah, do you know how long it'll take to get the results back?"

"Up to a week, I think."

Hunter sighed and sipped his beer. It was going to be a long week, but maybe Taylor could go with them tomorrow. He talked logistics with Chase before *Everybody Wants to Rule the World* started playing. He was watching Taylor and saw her spine snap straight.

She took a deep breath and refocused on her conversation, but he could see she was on edge now. He spoke to Chase, then walked over to her.

He offered a hand. "Hey, have you seen the outside of this place? It's pretty cool."

She took his hand and nodded to Lola, Kendall, and Jewel. "No, I haven't seen it. I thought this door led to the kitchens or something."

He pushed the door open. There were low outdoor couches and chairs around a firepit. The music could still be heard but it was fainter here.

They sat on one of the love seats, and he pulled her into

his arms. He kissed the side of her head as she relaxed into him.

"You alright now?"

She frowned and looked up at him. "What do you mean? I was fine before."

He shook his head. "You don't have to lie to me, Taylor, or pretend it's okay. You said last week that 80s songs trigger you. I saw the way you reacted to that one. Want to talk about it?"

She blinked up at him, tears in her eyes. "You–you really do love me, don't you?"

He tilted his head. "What do you mean? Of course I love you."

She pushed off him and turned to face him better, leaning forward and placing her hand on his knee. "No, I mean, you love me for real. You pay attention to me, you remember the little things. Hunter, I–I can't tell you how much that means to me."

He pulled on her arm slowly, and she fell against his chest. She was almost straddling his leg as he crushed their mouths together. She tasted like strawberries and liquor, of hope and sex.

She moaned into his mouth as the song changed to something more recent. His tongue tangled with hers, one hand on her ass and the other on the back of her head.

"Oh god, get a room, you two," Jewel said with a laugh.

Taylor jerked back, straightening her clothes. "Oh, sorry, I just got carried away there."

Jewel sat across from them, her jeans tight and her plaid shirt tied in a knot at her stomach. She grinned and raised her beer to them. "Oh, I don't blame you. Don't worry."

Chase joined them, sitting next to Jewel. They didn't

touch, both of them seemingly careful to keep their distance on the loveseat.

"The band tonight won't play anymore 80s songs," Chase said.

Taylor sucked in a breath and looked at Hunter, her eyes wide with emotion before turning back to Chase. "Thank you."

Chase nodded, and Jewel waved her hand. "According to Destini, the 80s are so cringe anyway."

Taylor chuckled, and they all relaxed, talking about teenagers and comparing when they were teens to today's kids. It wasn't long before the conversation turned to the plans for tomorrow. Hunter felt his stomach tighten in knots. A few more days, and he'd know if he was a father or not.

Chapter Forty-Eight

Taylor laughed with Hunter as they stepped into the house Saturday night. He'd picked her up from the library at lunch after story time was over. Scott and the girls hadn't shown up, but Helen was kind enough to work the rest of the afternoon so she could go to Denton with Hunter, Chase, and Jewel.

It had actually been rather fun. She'd gotten to know Jewel and even Chase had come out of his shell a few times, especially when they got to talking about finances. He'd offered a few tips to help her knock out her credit card debt from bailing her dad out so many times.

It had led to some much-needed conversations with Hunter on how money would work between them. They'd also stopped by a tiny house and bardominium center on the edge of town and explored a few.

Landry had called Hunter that morning and told him the barn wouldn't be able to be remodeled into a full home. Hunter had surprised her with the detour, but Chase and Jewel had disappeared while they'd walked the lot.

The last little, tiny home was actually really cute. It had white farmhouse vibes with a split floor plan and two bedrooms. She'd fallen in love with it, and she and Hunter had taken the salesman's card to think about it.

"We could move into the tiny house while we figure out a larger barndominium build. This way we have our own space and can live together. We can build the barndo when we have kids."

She pushed open the front door and held the screen open for him. "Exactly, just imagine all the things we can do in a little house of our own," she said, wiggling her eyebrows as he walked by, arms laden with the packages and groceries they'd bought.

He chuckled, and she dropped her own grocery bags on the dining table, kicking off her shoes. A noise from the hallway drew her attention.

Ava stood, leaning on a walker and frowning at them. "What have y'all been up to?"

Taylor gasped, rushing to her side. "Ava, what are you doing up? Where's Bill?"

"He's asleep in the recliner, and I had to pee. I'm going crazy from inactivity."

"Let me help you," Taylor said, hovering as Ava turned around slowly.

"I'll just take these upstairs," Hunter said, his footsteps echoing up the stairs.

"What did y'all go shopping for? Were those Target bags?"

"Yeah, we got a few things for the house and stopped to get groceries on our way back from Denton. We're all stocked up for the week's food. How does a loaded hash-brown casserole sound for dinner tonight?"

"That sounds fine, but I want to see the receipts if you're using the ranch card."

She settled Ava back into her chair. "That's understandable, but I don't have the ranch card. Hunter does."

Ava patted the side table next to her. "Hand me that photo album, dear."

Taylor handed her the book and reached for a throw blanket to place over Bill on the other recliner. The evening news played on mute on the television, but he must not have his hearing aids in since he didn't stir at their voices. She grabbed Ava's cup and turned to go get a refill when Ava stopped her.

"They were such a beautiful couple. Look. See this? This was at prom her senior year."

Taylor leaned over and smiled, even as an ache grew in her chest. "Aw, they're adorable. I bet Jewel hates that big hair now, doesn't she?"

Ava chuckled. "She might've mentioned how Destini would get a kick out of these pictures. I think Destini's pictures look like the perfect combination of them, don't you?"

Taylor nodded, pointing to another picture of Jewel and Hunter with some horses. "Is that the summer she went to college?"

Ava nodded and sighed. "If she would've just gone to the university in Denton like Gemma, she and Hunter never would've split up. We never would've lost all this time with Destini. I can't wait to meet her and for them to be a real family. It's all I've ever wanted for Hunter."

Taylor frowned and stood straighter. What did she mean about them being a real family? They already were a family, although not a traditional one. She didn't want to point that out to Ava again though. She'd come around eventually.

She shook her head and focused on the Destini issue. "I—he's very nervous to meet her."

They'd decided not to tell anyone about the DNA test, not until the results come back anyway. No sense in spreading drama if there wasn't a cause for it.

"He's going to make such a great dad. You're stopping that sweet girl from having a proper family, you know. If you weren't here, Jewel and Hunter would've made up by now."

Taylor felt a stab of pain in her chest at Ava's matter-of-fact tone of voice. The heartache of rejection ripped through her. It made her question herself. Wouldn't his mom know him better since she'd known him longer?

She took a deep breath and shook her head, warring with herself. Hunter loved her. "I don't think so. What they had is all in the past."

Ava harrumphed. "And you believe that? Don't get me wrong. I love Bill with everything I have. But I tell you what, I've never forgotten my first love. If we'd had a child together, you better believe I would've done everything in my power to stay with that man. A kid should have a real family, don't you think?"

Taylor hummed and lifted her cup with a shaky hand. "I—I'm going to get you a refill. I'll be right back."

Unease twisted her stomach. Was Ava right? She'd often wondered if she and Mom would've been better off without Dad and all his drama. He'd been in and out of jail during high school, and Mom had held onto all hope that he'd turn things around.

But Jewel and Hunter weren't like her parents. They were both good people with good hearts and good heads on their shoulders. If they had a chance to be a family, they should take it. Right?

Taylor came back with the water, lips pursed in thought.

"Aw, look at this one of Hunter holding—is that Gunner? Gosh, it must be. Hunter was almost three then. I wonder if Destini looked like him at that age. Oh, these are the menu notes I made. This is the kind of thing our people are used to. I know your food is good, but maybe stick to more familiar foods, eh?"

Ava handed her a scribbled piece of paper and turned back to the photo album, ignoring her. Taylor took the paper and left, pressure on her chest building as she walked away and read the list.

Had some of the guys complained about her spinach chicken quiches? She'd taken a chance on it, but that was because they'd run out of bacon and sausage. She'd made sure to buy double that amount on the grocery run earlier.

She sighed and went back to the kitchen to put away the groceries, her shoulders curled inward. No matter how hard she tried, it wouldn't make a difference. She'd never be good enough for Ava. Her throat threatened to close in frustration as she worked.

The next week was busy putting the final touches on the fall camp out with the teenagers from school. Hunter focused on that because worrying about the DNA results was driving him mad.

There was nothing he could do about it. The facility had warned them that it might take more than the normal three to five days because they were siblings. They'd have to do more extensive tests on their DNA than normal.

He still hadn't talked to Destini on the phone or by FaceTime, even though he'd offered. Jewel had said to not push it because she was being a typical teenager about it and ignoring the problem.

He got it. He really did, but it didn't stop him from worrying.

Then there was Taylor and the adjustment to the ranch life. She seemed to be getting along just fine, but she was crankier than last week. Her dad had been right about the bags under her eyes, even though she'd slept in that Friday. On Tuesday and Wednesday, he'd bribed her with a bookstore shopping trip to take a nap, since she was off work.

He had the sinking feeling that something was bothering her. He didn't want to make a mountain of a molehill and bug her about it. When she was ready, she'd tell him.

In the meantime, he just had to focus on the kids and the camp out. Friday had dawned a bit chilly, and after he'd come back home with the donuts and pastries, he'd gotten started on the morning chores.

It had warmed up significantly, but it might rain on Sunday. Hopefully they'd be home by the time it broke.

He worked on the last of the chores and checked in with the ranch hands, making sure each one knew what the expectations were for the weekend. At this point, the ranch operated like a well-oiled machine, but it still needed oil and oversight consistently.

A few hours later, he finished loading up his Jeep as Taylor came outside with a duffle bag. She smiled at him, and he just stared at her, taking in her presence. She was like his princess, the stuff of all his dreams. *How I got to be so lucky as to find a woman to love me, a woman with curves like a switchback road, a woman with a heart of gold...*

"What? Do I have lunch on my face?" She wiped her lips with the back of her hand.

The Cowboy Gets His Girl

He just shook his head. "No, you're just so beautiful, that's all."

She grinned, a little dimple popping out. "Is that so? Tell me more, tell me more."

He couldn't see her eyes with the sunglasses, but he knew they'd be sparkling with joy. He pulled her in close, and she dropped her bag to wrap her arms around him.

"I was just making up some poems about you, going on and on about your swaying hips and booty that I want to plunder like a pirate."

She laughed, rubbing her hands along his biceps. "Oh yeah? Well, anytime you get inspired by me, feel free to tell me. Girls are typically insecure, and I may come off pretty confident—"

"I'll make sure you come, princess."

Her grin widened as she squeezed his arms. "Anytime, cowboy. But as I was saying, a girl likes to be told nice things about her, so share all the poems when you get inspired."

He kissed the tip of her nose. "If I told you all the poems I came up with that were just about you, you'd get tired of hearing it. I'd bore you. You'd wince at the cheesiness."

She cupped his face, her eyes soft. "Hunter, I admire and love you so much, but don't you dare talk like that again."

He tilted his head. "Like what?"

"Don't sell yourself short. You're very talented, and you're too humble for your own good. Promise me you'll share your poems with me?"

He sighed and kissed her softly on the lips. When they parted, he said, "Fine, if it's what pleases the princess, so be it."

She gave a breathy chuckle and nodded. "Great, now

either share your poem with me or let's get this show on the road. Do we have everything we need?"

He nodded. "Yeah, I have all the tents here. You and I will get the camp mostly set up so by the time the kids get there, they'll just have to pop the tents up and eat dinner. Is this all you need for two nights in the woods?"

She nodded. "Yep, we're all set."

"Great, you can go ahead and load up. I'm going to go tell Ma bye, then we'll be on the road."

After a few minutes, he was back in the Jeep and off they went.

Chapter Forty-Nine

The drive to the Grasslands only took thirty minutes, and Taylor filled the time with excited chatter about her plans to get the kids interested in reading. Hunter enjoyed talking books with her, explaining which books he enjoyed because of the good narrator and which ones he hadn't.

They turned onto a bumpy dirt path, but the Jeep handled it like a pro. Parker would bring the kids in a small school bus in about an hour and park it at the trailhead. Then, they'd walk down the path through the trees to reach the lakeside.

Hunter's Jeep bounced along the barely visible tracks to stop at the small clearing near the water. Taylor stretched, her grin wide and excited as she looked around.

"Oh, this is gorgeous. I love it!"

He chuckled but didn't stop to chat. They had to get all the things set up and had a limited amount of time. Taylor followed his instructions without complaint, asking questions on why they were doing different things. He answered as they finished setting up the pop-up canopies, the hand-washing station, kitchen tables, and coolers. Next came the pop-up tents, which they left in their bags where the kids would set them up, and the fire-pit prep.

Finally, they completed everything, and Hunter set up a hammock between two trees. He motioned for her to join him, and when she settled into his arms, her back plastered to his front, he wrapped his arms around her and sighed. Together they swayed peacefully while gazing out at the water and listening to birds chirping above them.

He kissed the side of her head. "Thank you for doing this."

"What do you mean?"

"I didn't expect you to want to go camping. I mean, I know we'd talked about it before, but you're a city girl."

She stiffened in his arms, and he hugged her tighter, kicking his foot on the tree to start swinging again.

"No, no, I don't mean that as a bad thing."

"Then why did you say it?" She was testy about it, but he wasn't sure why. "I used to do day camps every summer for Girl Scouts, remember?"

"I know, but you're my princess, and I always picture you as such, not outside roughing it."

She chuckled, "I didn't mind being outside roughing it when we went to our spot by the river yesterday."

His arms tightened as he remembered the evening. Sunset had been beautiful, but he hadn't been paying attention since they'd been rolling around in the dirt naked together.

He kissed her temple. "That was a wonderful night, but with how tired you've been the past few weeks, I'd have thought you'd jump at the opportunity to stay home and catch up on more sleep. Why are you so upset about being called a city girl?"

She sighed but stayed relaxed in his arms. "I'm not upset. Well, not really. It's just—I don't know. I still feel like an outsider at the ranch, like I'm not doing things right or in the right way, like I'm not welcome."

He frowned and shifted them, tipping her chin up to stare into her eyes. "I'm sorry you feel like that, but the past two weeks of living with you have been everything I've ever wanted. Except for all the quiet sex and sharing a house with my parents, that is."

She softened and chuckled, turning slightly so she could kiss his chin. "Yeah, that puts a damper in our style, doesn't it? But the outdoor sex has been fun."

The hammock swayed gently as he kissed her softly. "Speaking of, how would you feel about a little outdoor sex now?"

She moaned into his mouth, their lips barely grazing in the softest of kisses.

"God, yes, but what if the kids arrive early?"

He shook his head, his lips rubbing gently back and forth over hers. "Not likely. Have you ever tried to wrangle a group of kids to go anywhere? It normally takes twice as long as anticipated. They'll probably not be here for another hour."

He felt a vibration in his pocket and reached for his phone, the hammock swaying gently. He looked at the message and showed her.

"See? That's Parker now saying they're just now leaving the school's parking lot."

She grinned and looked around. "Well, let's go, then, beastie. How do you want to do this?"

He snorted as they tried to get out of the hammock without falling onto the ground. "Maybe we should get out of here first."

She giggled then it turned into a full belly laugh. It was awkward and not graceful at all. He finally stood up and dusted his hands off. She was nearly bent over double in laughter.

He spun her around and pushed her against a tree, nuzzling her neck. "Don't you laugh at me, sugar tits."

She giggled, wiggling in his arms as his stubble scratched the sensitive place under her ear. "Whatcha gonna do about it, beastie?"

He nipped and her laughs turned breathy and shallow. "I'm going to make you feel good, princess, just like always. Does this feel good?"

She hummed. "Ohh, yes, it does. Oh, right there."

He bit her neck harder, his hands fondling her breasts. She wore a sports bra, and he couldn't get a good handful until he leaned back and shoved his hands under her bra, exposing her breasts to the air.

They pebbled immediately, and he bent to lick, suck, worship. Her hands in his hair pressed him closer as she squirmed in his arms. He slid his hands inside her leggings to push them down to her knees.

Soon they were both panting. "Lay back on the hammock, knees on the side."

He helped maneuver her until she was laying sideways on the hammock, her head dangling off one side and her knees off the other. Then he knelt on the grass and lifted her legs.

With her shoes still on and leggings around her ankles, he pushed her thighs wide, settling her ankles on his back. Then he feasted on her sweet nectar.

At the first kiss to her clit, her hips bucked, sending the hammock swinging.

"Ah, Hunter," she panted. God, he loved the sounds she

made. He had to push harder to get the tiny home set up for her near the creek because he wanted to get her in their own bed and hear her scream for hours.

He pushed a finger inside her wet, warm heat. She clenched him, still so tight, as he sucked on her clit in a rhythm as old as time. She pressed her heels into his back, pushing her hips up into his mouth. He used one hand to set the hammock into a swaying motion, using it along with his mouth to drive her closer and closer to the edge.

Too soon, she cried out, her hands in his hair as she spasmed around his fingers.

His voice was a soft whisper on the wind as the poetry sprang to his mind. She'd wanted to hear it earlier, so he didn't stop it. He teased her with his fingers, saying, *"The cries of passion raised in prayer, a song of praise, hands in his hair. His love lay panting and replete, but he had promises to keep."*

He stood up, shifting so that her feet dangled to the ground as he unzipped his jeans.

She gasped, "Fuck, I love it when you talk like that."

He grabbed her hands and pulled her up, her eyes still blank and pleasure dazed. He kissed her roughly, his hand sliding between her legs to rub her clit. She jerked in his hand until he felt her knees start to buckle.

Then he spun her around and said roughly, "Face down on the hammock, ass in the air."

She gasped, practically falling onto the hammock with her hands on the opposite edge. "I love it when you talk like that too."

He reached down and pulled off one of her sneakers then slipped her leggings off that ankle.

Leaving the other shoe and pants on the other foot, he lifted her hips high, her feet coming off the ground. He twisted her around until her knees were on the hammock, then he pulled her back until she was at the height he needed.

She cried out as her hands landed on the ground, the hammock the only thing keeping her from falling on her face, but he would never let his princess fall.

He lined up the head then teased her entrance until she begged.

She panted again, "Hunter, God, yes."

He slid inside, slow and steady, throwing his head back and breathing deeply through his nose. "Fuck, yes. You feel so good, princess."

Every touch, every movement, every breath shared between them was a testament to their deep and unbreakable connection. It caught him by surprise every time he slid home, reminding him in this moment of pure bliss that nothing else in the world mattered except for the two of them entwined in each other's arms.

She whimpered as he slid out then rammed back home, hard and deep, staking his claim and reminding her of his love. She jerked, crying out with a sound that ripped straight to his soul. The need of the beast inside him swept through like wildfire.

"Ah yes, that's the sound I want to hear. Scream for me, slut."

He set up a bruising rhythm, using the hammock to swing her back on his dick like a spear hitting the heart of its prey. He drove deep with an animal fierceness, branding her soul. Every time he slid deep, she cried out, and her thighs began to quiver.

He lost himself in her wet, wild warmth, his shaft slicking in and out. Together, they chased the pure rush of need like nothing else existed. The urge to explode built inside, like a tidal wave rising higher and higher.

Eyes closing, he refused to plunge over the edge without her. The scent of moss, pine, and cedar mixed with the faint smell of sweat and body heat. Senses heightened, and he reached a hand around to her clit, strumming like a guitar until her back arched and she cried out, spasming around him. She squeezed him like a glove as he relentlessly thrust into her.

Her back arched as she screamed, her body growing taught as she squirmed on his dick. Her entire body shuddered, her pussy milking him and clenching wildly. Their bodies moved in perfect rhythm, a dance of pure intimacy and connection that transcended physical sensations.

His balls tensed up, and he groaned as he pounded furiously. Only a few thrusts, then he stilled in an explosion of hot lava. Violent and virile, it left him gasping. He saw spots behind his eyelids as she squeezed him like a vise, pouring inside her in spurts of hot liquid love. In that moment, they were truly one, united in love and desire.

As their bodies shook and quivered together, she let out a soft whimper of pleasure. He slowly withdrew from her, his body still pulsing with release. She lay there, completely exposed to the cool breeze coming off the nearby lake, as he got up and walked around the tree. He pushed her hair back from her face and checked on her. "You alright, princess?"

She grunted in response, shifting to look up at him and moving her hands from the ground to his thighs.

He chuckled, knowing what she usually wanted after. She swung closer to him, and when she looked up, he held out his dripping dick.

"There's my dessert. Come to mama." He chuckled at her words, a slow grin spreading across her face as she gazed up at him, her eyes still dazed with satisfaction.

Without hesitation, she took him into her mouth and cleaned every last remnant of their passionate encounter.

He stared across the lake, a boat in the distance driving on the clear blue surface. His eyes fluttered at the sensation, and he jerked at the sensitivity of it, pulling back.

She tried to follow him, but he grunted. "That was amazing, sugar. Do you want me to clean you up now too? I can lick that pussy clean and get you off again."

She sighed and shifted, standing on one shoe as she hiked the other and set her bare foot on the edge of the hammock. She tilted her head back, her eyes slits of desire, a soft smile on her face that beckoned him like a sex goddess come to life.

"That's alright. I got it." Then she dipped her hands inside and raised her fingers, licking them clean like a popsicle.

"Hot damn," he whispered, tucking himself back into his pants. "If you keep that up, we'll have another round, and *then* the kids might catch us."

She finished cleaning herself, the satisfied smile on her face making him proud.

"Well, we can't have that, but you do realize that we'll be sleeping in different tents, right?"

He frowned as she pulled her pants back up and tied her shoe. "What do you mean? We have the adult tents, and we have the kids' tents."

She shook her head. "No, Tasha and I will share a tent, and you and Parker will share a tent. We can't share a tent because we're not married. This is a school sanctioned field trip, so we have to follow their rules."

An emptiness spread from his chest as her words sank into his soul. They hadn't slept apart for weeks, and his frustration mounted that he hadn't thought of that before now.

He put his hands on his hips. "You mean I can't sleep with you until we get home on Sunday?"

She smirked and dusted her hands off on her hips. "Yep, we'll be on chaperone duty the rest of the time. We'll probably need to take shifts keeping watch at night to make sure none of the kids sneak out. Oh, and did you set up the portable toilet like I asked for?"

He rolled his eyes and sighed. "No, it's still in the back of the Jeep. I'll go get it."

She nodded. "Great, I'll make sure we're all set for walking tacos for dinner tonight then."

He started to walk away, but she grabbed his hand and pulled him into an embrace. Her cheek laid on his chest, her hands on his back. He relaxed in her arms, drawing her closer and smelling the delicious strawberries of her shampoo. It was as if they were two halves of a whole, fitting perfectly together even in this comforting hug.

"I love you, Hunter. I'm really glad to be camping with you and experiencing this first school camp out together." She tilted her head back and smiled. "Maybe next weekend we can go camping just the two of us?"

He perked up. "Really? You wouldn't mind? I mean, that's two weekends in a row."

"I'm sure. Then we can share a tent." She wiggled her eyebrows, and he laughed. She pulled out of his arms and waved him to the Jeep. "Go on, set up that toilet. I'm going to need to use it in a few minutes to finish cleaning up."

He hummed as he went to finish the last item of setting up camp. It was going to be a great weekend, even if he couldn't sleep with her in his arms at night, simply because they'd still be together.

Chapter Fifty

Taylor was tired, wet, and cold when they arrived back at the ranch on Sunday morning. They'd gotten the kids up and packed to a slight drizzle, but by the time they'd sent the kids, Parker, and Tasha hiking through the rain back to the bus, it had started pouring.

Hunter and Taylor had stayed another hour cleaning up camp, putting the muddy tents away, and packing the Jeep. Hunter had tried to get her to stay inside with the heated seats, but she'd refused. It'd go faster if they both worked. By the time they pulled up to the ranch house, they were still wet and bone tired. It felt like she'd barely slept a wink the past two nights on that cot.

Although it had been a lot of fun hanging out with Tasha and getting to know the middle schoolers, she wasn't sure that she'd made a difference in inspiring them to read more. They parked the Jeep, and Hunter leaned his head on the steering wheel with a sigh.

"Home sweet home," he said with relief.

She smiled but stared at the ranch house, loneliness

filling her. It still didn't feel like home. She was still just an outsider. Would she ever have the family she so desperately wanted?

He jerked a thumb to the cooler. "I'll get this out and take it to the front porch. If you can roll it inside and start unloading it, I'll get the rest of our bags. The tents and things I'll need to take to the sale barn and lay out to dry so they don't mold. Do you want to go with me?"

She nodded. "Yeah, but can we go later this afternoon? I'd like to take a hot shower first, then maybe nap until everyone arrives for lunch. If we go to the sale barn this afternoon, we can stay the night in the attic?"

He sat up, an excited smile on his face. "Yeah? That sounds like a great idea. I love it."

He grinned, his tiredness seemingly faded as he opened the door. She shook her head. He was like a kid at Christmas. She opened her door and ran for the front porch, hood pulled up against the rain.

She hauled the cooler inside, the screen door banging shut behind her. A squeal of laughter could be heard from the den, and she thought it might be Connie. Maryanne was supposed to stay with Ava last night.

While she put the food away, cleaning their pots and pans from the camping trip, Hunter hauled their bags upstairs then went down the hall to talk with his mom.

He walked into the kitchen, a weary smile on his face, and absently rubbed the back of his neck. "Ready to shower?"

She nodded, wiping her hands on her dirty leggings. "Yeah, I'm not sure what we're going to do for Sunday dinner. Are your brothers and everyone coming over after church or is it just us?"

He nodded as they went upstairs, updating her on the

conversation he had with his mom and Maryanne. They soaped together, then just held each other under the hot water, both of them too tired to make a move. When the water began to run cold, they got out and dressed in the bathroom barely big enough for both of them.

She glanced at the time on her phone and said, "It's already time to make lunch."

He sighed. "I need to go check on the horses and get reports from the ranch hands anyway. I'm sure Dad will want to update me on a few things too. I think he stayed home with Mom this morning too, but he's probably outside."

She followed him down to the den, where Connie now lay asleep on top of Maryanne, who laid sideways on the couch. Bill and Ava were both talking quietly in their recliners as the television played some evangelical preacher.

She whispered to Ava, "How are you feeling?"

Ava smiled tightly as Hunter went around to talk quietly to his dad. "I'm doing alright, dear. Thanks for asking. How was the camping trip? The big city girl survived?"

Taylor sighed and nodded, pursing her lips. "Yep, it went great. I think Tasha had a rougher time than I did. Poor thing got ate alive by the mosquitos, had an allergic reaction to some poison ivy, and was miserable."

Ava frowned. "Aw, poor dear. I'll have some of the church ladies give her a salve."

"Do you need any water, a snack? I'm going to get started on lunch so when the family gets here, it'll be ready."

Ava nodded, "That's fine. Maryanne set some deer meat to thaw. Do you know how to cook it?"

Taylor's spine straightened, frustrated at the snide remarks that reminded her she wasn't welcome. She fought to maintain the serene smile on her face. "Of course, I might've grown up in the city, but I *am* from Texas. I can cook it just fine. Let me just get you some more water, and I'll hop to it."

She turned on her heel and sighed as she walked to the kitchen. Why did she always feel on the defensive with Ava? She stretched, the familiar knot of tension between her shoulders again.

Lunch was a loud, chaotic affair. She was irritable because the first batch of deer meat was a little burned and the second batch was a little under-cooked. All of it was tough too.

Of course, Ava implied it was her cooking, but Taylor didn't say a word. No one else had heard her. When it was just the two of them, Ava said little things that made her feel excluded, but to everyone else, she acted like Taylor was just one of the family.

It was frustrating, but Taylor kept telling herself it'd just take time. She kept her head held high, smiled, and went to eat at the table with Landry, Holly, Maryanne, and the kids. They told funny stories of what their kids had done that week, and it made Taylor ache. She wanted to have those experiences for herself.

She couldn't wait to be a mom and have her own family, a family that would accept her for who she was, a family who wouldn't try to take advantage of her all the time.

Hunter brought the dishes from the den, and she hopped up to help with them. Side by side, she enjoyed working together toward a common goal.

The next morning, Taylor dragged herself out of bed and shuffled to the kitchen. Her muscles ached from a long day of farm work and her eyes burned from lack of sleep. As she cracked eggs into a bowl, she stifled a yawn and rubbed her gritty eyes. Suddenly, the hot grease from the bacon splattered onto her hand, causing her to wince in pain. She quickly ran cold water over the burn, trying to ignore the stinging pain, but the timer on the biscuits went off.

With a curse, she pulled them out of the oven and flipped the almost-burnt biscuits over. If she left them in the pan, they'd just keep cooking. She turned back to the stove and cursed. Now the bacon was too crispy.

She jerkily dumped it into the strainer and slammed the pan back onto the stove. As she stirred the eggs in the pan, tears threatened to spill down her cheeks. She wiped her cheek, trying to keep her mind off her exhaustion and emotional state.

Just as she finished scrambling the eggs, she heard the familiar sounds of ranch hands coming inside for breakfast. Taylor wiped away a stray tear and put on a fake smile as she greeted them with plates of food. It wasn't easy pretending everything was fine, but she didn't want anyone to worry about her.

Her throat was sore and scratchy, her ears were throbbing, and now this mishap with breakfast. She knew Ava would say something about the biscuits and bacon, and she wasn't sure if she could handle it today.

Hunter came through the front door and washed his hands at the sink.

"Morning, sugar," he said, kissing her cheek softly.

Ava called from the den, and Taylor winced. "Can you go see what she needs while I finish the hash browns and eggs?"

The Cowboy Gets His Girl

He nodded and went to help his mom. An hour later, everyone was full, and Taylor was cleaning up the kitchen. The guys must've sensed her mood because they were full of jokes. She'd laughed and was feeling much better after a hot breakfast.

She hummed quietly as she scraped the bottom of the glass pan to get the burnt biscuits off. Hunter had kissed her and said he had to check on a few things, but he'd see her after she got off work that afternoon.

With only an hour before work, she set the pan to soak in the sink. Just as she started up the stairs to get ready for work, Ava called her.

Taylor sighed and went into the den. Ava had hit the two-week recovery mark and was slowly shuffling to the downstairs bathroom and back to the den. She'd taken herself to the bathroom after breakfast.

"Did you need something, Ava?"

Ava waved a printed piece of paper at her. "I do. Gunner brought the mail from the mailbox after church yesterday, and I just opened it. Do you see this?"

Taylor shook her head. "No, I haven't seen it, as I don't read other people's mail. What is it? It looks like a bill."

Ava frowned and nodded. "It's the ranch credit card. It looks like there was a five-hundred-dollar charge to a bail bondsman in Fort Worth. Do you know anything about that?"

Taylor sighed and rubbed the back of her neck. "Ah, yes, that would be my dad's bail money."

"How dare you use our hard-earned money to bail your no-good dad out of jail," Ava said, her voice wavering with anger.

Taylor straightened, frowning as she opened her mouth to argue, but Ava kept going.

"I knew in the hospital that you were just after the money. The ranch is paid off, we're turning a handsome profit each year, and you somehow saw that when we came to help you move in. Well, the gravy train ends now. No more using the credit card, do you hear?"

"I hear," Taylor said. But it was all she was able to get in, as Ava pointed to another line.

"And what's this? Three hundred at Target? What could you have possibly bought at Target for that price? And that's not even the Sam's Club groceries you got. What in the world? That's nearly a thousand dollars you've cost the ranch in just two weeks. We can't keep doing this, Taylor."

Taylor rubbed her temples, but Ava just kept going.

"Not only are you a gold digger, but you're keeping my son away from the mother of his child. You're a homewrecker too."

Taylor's breath froze in her lungs like she'd been punched in the gut. She had flashbacks of her dad calling her mom those names, blaming Mom for spending all their money when it was really Dad's drug habit that was bleeding them dry every month.

Damn it, she'd worked too hard and come too far to be treated like this. She raised a finger at Ava. "You think I'm a gold digger and a homewrecker? Well, excuse me for doing what was necessary, for feeding your ranch hands and taking care of you. It's never going to be good enough, is it? *I'm* never going to be good enough."

The last sentence she whispered, backing up to the door. She turned on her heels and raced up the stairs, slamming the door to the bedroom through blurry eyes. She glanced around, jerking her work clothes out of the closet. Then she jerked more of them, throwing them into a bag.

Her duffle bag from the camping trip was still half

packed with her toiletries. She stuffed more clothes into it and then filled up one of her roller bags. How dare that woman treat her like shit? She had no idea how Taylor had bent over backwards to help not just the family but the entire ranch.

Furiously, she changed out of her pajamas and into her work clothes. After a quick trip to the bathroom, she threw her makeup and toothbrush and toothpaste into the bag.

She slung the duffle bag over her shoulder and slipped on her flats. Then she rolled the other bag down the hall and stairs and to the front door.

Ava called for her. "Taylor? Come here."

Taylor stopped at the front door and dropped her bags, indecision warring within her. She breathed deeply, trying to get her emotions under control. Finally, she sighed, hope blazing like a beacon in her chest as she walked back down the hall. Every step reminded her of hoping her dad had changed, hoping her mom would wake up and leave him. Perhaps Ava wanted to apologize and was ready to accept her as part of the family.

She stepped through the door. "Yes?"

Ava handed her the dirty dishes from breakfast and avoided eye-contact. "Here you go, dear."

Taylor blinked back tears. Hope was futile. She hadn't been part of a family in a long time, and this one wasn't meant for her. She'd never get out of Jewel's shadow in Ava's eyes. She looked at Ava, the realization settling in her stomach like a brick.

For the first time in her life, she actually felt connected to a few of those damn Disney princesses. She took the plate and fork and turned to walk slowly to the kitchen.

She was numb now. Glancing around the kitchen, there was nothing but work here. Nothing but slaving away in a kitchen with no gratitude, no help, no acknowledgement.

She wiped the tears and grabbed a few things from the freezer and pantry. Even though she'd never get a thank you from anyone but Hunter, she didn't want to leave them hungry tonight. She'd find a way to send dinner and breakfasts to the ranch.

But she didn't want to stay here anymore. She knew when she wasn't welcome.

She threw some chicken in the crock pot along with a few cans of corn, black beans, enchilada sauce, and cream of chicken. After turning it on, she walked woodenly to the front door and picked up her duffle and roller.

The heavy oak door shut behind her, slamming like a lid on her future. She'd never be welcomed like Holly or Maryanne. She took a deep breath and carefully walked around the mud puddles to her car.

At least it was a sunny day. She loaded her bags and started her car. Hunter was supposed to be along the back of the property today, near the creek. He'd been working there a lot last week.

She opened up the text app and sent Hunter a voice message. "I'm not staying at the house tonight. I'll either stay at my apartment or at Lucy's, but I need some space. I'll try calling you on my lunch break. Dinner is in the crock pot. Love you."

She took a deep breath and called Lucy, venting all the way to work about the incident.

"Do you want to stay with me for a few days?" Lucy asked.

Taylor shrugged. "I don't know. I'll probably go to my apartment and try to stay with my dad. Although, if he's been sleeping in my bed, I might come stay with you. Lord knows he's probably got lice from jail or something."

Lucy snorted. "Well, you just let me know what you want to do, and I'll make it happen, okay? I love you, girl."

"I love you too."

She hung up as she arrived in town, swinging by the grocery store to get some cough drops and medicine before going to work. Her head was pounding now, but could the day really get any worse?

Chapter Fifty-One

A few hours later, the bell above the library rang as the door opened. Two little girls sprinted inside, giggling as their dad came in behind them. Taylor blew her nose into her fiftieth napkin of the day and waved weakly.

"Morning," she croaked, picking up her warm lemon water.

Scott winced. "Looks like you got a cold. You alright?"

She shrugged. "I will be, once I get some medicine and catch up on some sleep. Thankfully I have tomorrow and Wednesday off work."

"Helen said on Saturday's story time that you were camping. How did that go?"

She smiled, leaning back in her chair as he leaned against the desk. "It was a lot of fun actually. I haven't been camping since my Girl Scout days, and it was a blast. I missed it."

"Do you miss playing softball too?" His head tilted, a thoughtful expression on his face.

She nodded and wrapped her sweater tighter. "You

know it. Once you play, it doesn't really leave your system, does it?"

He smiled. "No, it doesn't. The reason I ask is because we're short one third baseman this season. Feel like joining our church team?"

Her brows rose. "Oh, I didn't know you went to church."

He nodded. "The Baptist one on the edge of town."

"Ah, I've been going to the Church of God across from the town square."

He shrugged. "Doesn't matter which church. We'll welcome you no matter what."

Her eyes watered, and she sniffed, reaching for her napkin once more. She blew her nose. Stupid cold. Why couldn't the Williams family welcome her like that? Did he really mean it?

Suddenly Scott was kneeling in front of her behind the librarian's desk. He frowned up at her, his forehead wrinkled in concern as he put his hands on her knees.

"Hey, what's wrong? Are you okay?"

She shook her head, wiping her eyes. "No, I'm sick."

One eyebrow raised. "Besides that. Something else is wrong. What is it?"

She bit her lip and sighed, leaning back in her seat. "I—it's nothing. Just everything piling up on me."

The bell over the door jingled as it opened, and they glanced over. Hunter stood in the doorway, one hand on the handle as he looked from one to the other.

Scott stood up and stepped away from her as Piper came running around the corner.

"Daddy, Daddy, look! They have the new Geronimo Stilton book in!"

He nodded to Hunter then looked back at Taylor with a

frown as Piper began to tug on his hand back to the kid section.

"I'll be right around the corner. Yell if you need me," Scott said softly before he disappeared.

She turned back to look at Hunter, but he was still frozen in the doorway. She could see his jaw ticking from where she sat, and more tears pricked her eyes. With a cold hand, she reached for her coffee mug and sipped the now lukewarm water.

He strode to the librarian's desk and stared down at her, crossing his arms over his chest. "What the hell is the meaning of this, Taylor? What do you mean, you need space?"

She sighed, rubbing her throbbing forehead. "I just needed a break from it all, Hunter. Can't you understand?"

He put his palms on the desk and leaned forward to whisper furiously. "I don't understand. I thought we were happy together. Was it all a lie?"

Her eyes widened. "What? Was what a lie? I'm happy with you, but not your—"

"What? Is it the ranch? Is that it? Ma said you weren't cut out for ranch life, but you did fine camping this weekend. Hell, you've never once complained about riding around the ranch with me on your days off. Most people get bow legged and saddle sores if they do too much too fast, but you never said a word. But now you leave?"

Taylor blinked, her eyes and nose dripping. She reached for another tissue as he continued.

"I don't know how to please you, Taylor. I can't be the man you want me to be. I'm not a guy who spends a lot of time in libraries. I don't read a lot—"

"You do too. Audiobooks count, Hunter," she interrupted before blowing her nose loudly.

"Are you sure? If so, I can read more audiobooks. We can do book club crap together and talk about whatever books you want to read. Just please, Taylor, don't break us up."

She rubbed on sanitizer then slid her hand over his on the table and looked up at him, her nose sore and head pounding. "Hunter, I don't want to break up. I love you and want to be with you."

His jaw clenched, and he opened his mouth to speak. Scott and his girls came around the corner, causing Hunter to shut his mouth and step back. Taylor tossed her napkins in the trash at her feet and sanitized the desk with wipes as she looked at the girls.

"Did you find the books you were looking for?" She pasted on a rigid smile as Paige nodded, her ponytail swinging.

"I've finished all the Pete the Cat, but I found this animal crime fighting series. Are they good?"

Taylor turned them around and nodded, "Oh yes, these are really good. Very popular. Everyone's reading them. You're lucky they were in stock."

Paige beamed up at Scott as Piper set her stack of books on the desk.

"I'm ready to start the Thea Stilton books. Other than this new Geronimo one, I think I've read all the others."

Taylor nodded to her and smiled. "I'll see what I can do about getting more ordered, but you'll love the Thea books. Those girls are strong, fierce, and so smart, just like you."

Piper smiled shyly as Taylor checked the books into the system.

"There you go. You're all set. I'll see y'all next week?"

Scott looked at Hunter standing a few steps away with his arms crossed then looked back to Taylor with a frown.

"Do you want me to stay?" Scott eyed Hunter again.

Hunter just scowled and said, "We're fine, Scott. Hopefully it's just a misunderstanding."

Taylor smiled at Scott and picked up her coffee mug. "We'll be alright, but I appreciate the offer, Scott. You're a good friend."

Scott sighed and nodded, deflating a little as he opened the door for the girls. He looked over his shoulder and said, "Text me if you want to play ball. We'll start practicing next week."

She nodded. "Go ahead and count me in. I need the movement, and I'll be well enough to hit a few balls next week."

Scott smiled and nodded goodbye to them both, his gaze lingering a second longer on Hunter.

Hunter just waved and glared at him. Taylor rolled her eyes and stood to take her coffee mug through the swinging door into the employees only area. Helen had already put away the new shipment over the weekend, so there was little for her to do.

She rinsed her mug in the sink at the kitchenette and refilled it with hot water and lemon drops.

"We're not done talking about this," Hunter said, the door swinging behind him.

She blew her nose again and tossed the napkin into the sink. "I know. I just needed more water. I'm too cold."

He came closer and felt her forehead with the back of his hand. "You're burning up. Why didn't you say anything, Taylor? Call in sick and see if Helen can come in. Or just close up the library today and let's go home where I can take care of you."

She let him wrap his arms around her, soaking in his warmth. She blinked and sniffled. "That's just it, Hunter.

The Cowboy Gets His Girl

The ranch isn't home. I—I don't know where home is, but it's not there. I don't want to be at the ranch house anymore."

He stiffened, but he didn't pull away. "I have a surprise for you then, but it's not going to be ready until next week."

She groaned, rubbing her head on his chest. "I don't like surprises."

"You'll love this one, I promise," he said. "Now if you don't want to go back to the ranch, where do you want to stay? Because wherever you go, I go, sugar."

She felt the pressure in her head burst as tears poured down her cheeks. He tightened his arms, shushing her and rocking her slightly as she cried, which just made her cry harder. How could someone so sweet come from a woman so mean?

Avoiding Ava wasn't a long-term solution. Hunter's entire life was on the ranch. She couldn't just pick up and live in town. He needed to be there to take care of any emergencies.

But she didn't want him to leave her either. For once, she felt important, like she was worth the inconvenience, worth the effort. Her sobs slowed, and her entire body ached.

"Come on, let's call Helen and see if she can cover," he said softly, handing her a tissue.

She sniffed and reached for her phone. The call was quick, and Helen told her to just close up the library and put a sign on the door. She refused to leave her car at the library though, so Hunter went to the store to get her some medicine while she went to the apartment to take a hot shower.

She unlocked the door and flipped on the lights. She blinked, her shoulders weighing down with disappointment.

The table and chairs in the kitchen were gone. The couch, end tables, television, all the major furniture was gone. Even the refrigerator and stove were gone, which belonged to the apartment complex.

Papers were strewn over the floor, and cabinets were left open. She opened a few more. All her plates and dishes were gone too. She numbly walked to the bedroom. Nothing but some boxes of her clothes remained and the curtains over the windows.

"What the hell happened here?" Hunter asked. She turned to find him shutting the front door behind him.

She ignored the pressure in her chest. There were no more tears left to give. She was too worn out to care.

With a sigh, she said, "Dear old Dad probably took it all to the nearest pawn shop or sold it on Marketplace." She leaned on the door frame as Hunter walked briskly through the apartment, cursing under his breath.

He came back from the bathroom with a piece of paper and handed it to her with a frown.

"Here, you read it. I can't read his handwriting."

Taylor took the letter and read aloud.

Baby girl,
This probably won't come as a surprise to you, but considering none of this has sentimental value to you, I'm hoping you won't mind. I needed the money to get down to San Antonio. One of my old roommates has a job for me down there, and selling your stuff was the best way I knew to get the money for the bus ticket.
I'm also thinking you might not mind since I didn't come asking you for money. Hey, it's progress, right? I know I'm not the best dad around and you've got Hunter looking out for you now. So I feel good about moving down South and taking this opportunity to get back on my feet. Good luck and have fun, but not the type of fun I usually have. You

always were the smartest, best version of me and your mom. I'm proud of you.
Love ya,
Dad

She couldn't see through misty eyes, but Hunter pulled her into his arms again and just held her. Slowly they sank to the floor with her sitting sideways on his lap as he rocked her.

Chapter Fifty-Two

Taylor's phone buzzed in her sweater pocket, and Hunter reached for it.

"Hello," he whispered.

"Um, Hunter? This is Lucy. Is Taylor there?"

Hunter looked down at his sleeping princess and kept rocking her. "She's asleep right now and sick. I don't think I should wake her."

"Where are y'all? She'd never go to sleep on the job."

Hunter explained the situation, about the letter and all her things being gone.

Lucy sighed, "Damn it, we were afraid something like this was going to happen."

"You were?"

"Yeah, he does this kind of thing all the time. Well, she can't stay there now if there's not even a mattress. She can come stay with me for a while. Did she—um, did she talk to you about that situation?"

Hunter sighed and shifted slightly, his leg going numb.

"We talked a little. I just don't understand why she wants to take a break, but she still loves me? Am I smothering her?"

Lucy paused, then said, "I think you need to ask her that question. She's not the type to just run off, Hunter. Talk to her and find out *why* she needs a break. Also, don't just assume she needs a break from *you*. But if not you, then who or what does she need a break from?"

"I can do that," he said. "If you have room for Lucy, do you have room for me too? I don't want to leave her, especially with her being sick."

"How sick is she? I don't want Harry to catch anything," Lucy said.

Hunter shrugged. "I don't know. She's running a pretty high fever, but I bought her some medicine. That's a good point though. I don't want to put Harry in danger. The little guy was sick a few weeks ago, right?"

"Yeah, we all were."

"I'll find some other place then. Maybe the motel. Thanks, Lucy. You're a good friend." His own pocket vibrated.

She chuckled. "Thanks, Hunter. I'll reserve judgment on you until I see Taylor happy and healthy and settled."

He snorted. "Fair enough. I'll have her call you when she wakes up."

"Thanks, Hunter. Bye."

They hung up, and he switched phones.

"Hello?"

"Hey, I got a letter today. I think it's the results, but I don't want to open it by myself. Do you want me to come out to the ranch and all three of us can open it together?"

He leaned his head back against the wall and swallowed hard. His stomach clawed with hunger, and he was getting worried about Taylor's fever. She'd not taken any of the medicine before she'd cried herself to sleep.

"I don't think I can right now. I'm at Taylor's apartment, but we can't stay here. She's sick and burning up with a fever."

"Is she pale? What's her breathing sound like?" Jewel asked, instantly going into doctor mom mode.

Today had started like a normal day. His girl in his arms, a delicious hot breakfast, chores and ranching. It was a great morning. Then he'd gotten that text from her. He'd worked through the rest of his chores and assigned others to tasks so he could go track her down.

He wasn't any closer to a straight answer on what was going on. He could only hope that she was just tired and sick. Once she felt better, they could go back to normal.

Hunter listened to her breathing. "Her lungs sound clear enough, although she's breathing nasally. Her nose has been dripping and her eyes were red, but she's also been crying and emotional and worn out the past few days. She might just need some medicine and sleep, I'm not sure."

"Well, bring her to your ranch, and I'll make her some soup. Then once we get her settled, we can open the letter."

Hunter's frustration mounted as he thought back to the audio message from earlier and their fight at the library. "I don't think so. She doesn't want to be at the ranch right now. She said she wanted a break from the ranch. I can't take her to the barn. I'm afraid she'd become delirious and then be too difficult to get her down the ladder. Can't stay at her apartment or Lucy's. The hunting cabin is occupied. Do you want to meet us at the motel on the edge of town?"

"With all your brothers living in town, you want to go to a motel?"

"Lucy's got the baby, and I don't want to expose the

germs to him. Same goes for Landry and Gunner's families."

"And Parker? Doesn't he have a house in town now?"

Hunter blinked and breathed deeply as Taylor's eyes blinked open. She looked around, and he smiled down at her, "Good morning, princess. Did you have a good sleep?"

She moaned and buried her head in his chest.

"Sh, it's alright. Do you want to go stay at a motel or Parker's?"

Taylor looked up and frowned. "Lucy."

He shook his head. "Do you want to get your sick germs around Harry?"

She frowned and held her head as she sat forward.

Jewel echoed through the line. "Hunter? Once you figure out where you're going, let me know. I want to get this opened and done today. I'm tired of waiting."

"Me too," he said. "Okay, bye."

He hung up as Taylor stumbled to her feet and went to the bathroom. He tried to follow her, but she slammed the door on his face.

"Taylor? Are you alright?"

"Yeah," she said. "I just need to pee. And I'd rather not go to a motel. I don't want to spend my days off in a random motel. Would Parker really be alright with a sick guest? I don't want to put him out."

"He'll be at work during the day, so I'm sure it's fine. Plus, he's already exposed to all the germs from school. I'll ask him just in case."

"Okay, go away and let me do my business," she said through the muffled door.

He chuckled and walked back to the kitchen to call Parker.

Two hours later, Hunter had Taylor tucked into Parker's guest bedroom with a pile of blankets. He'd called in a soup and sandwich order from the Diner, then they'd gone to the house. He'd fed her soup and told her about Jewel and the results.

She'd insisted he go back to the ranch to find out with Chase. Once she'd taken her cold medicine and started to snore, he'd left for the ranch.

The entire way there, his mind flipped between worrying about Taylor, what he'd do if Destini was his, and what he'd do if she wasn't. She most likely was his. He'd always wrapped it, but they'd had sex that summer way more than Chase's three.

Images of Destini in pictures and Jewel's videos went through his head, and he smiled. She was a good kid, and he hoped she was his. He wanted a family like his brothers. People of his own to love and be loved by. He didn't want to stand on the sidelines while everyone else moved forward with their lives.

He parked in front of the house as the rain started again, and Jewel and Chase came out of the barn together. His stomach twisted with nerves, and he took a deep breath before jumping out of the Jeep and heading for the house. He met them on the front porch and opened the door.

None of them said a word. Chase was broody and stiff, and Jewel was pulling her sweater around her hunched shoulders, pushing off her hood. Together, they walked into the house and sat at the kitchen table, the smell of chicken filling the air. Jewel took the letter from her back pocket and set it on the table.

He stared across the table at Chase, but he just had his

arms crossed and looked stoic and defiant. He was starting to look more and more like Gunner with that attitude too. Gunner got his from the Marines, but Chase got his from prison. Gunner had relaxed a bit after getting married. Hopefully Chase would do the same when he found someone to love.

He looked from Chase to Jewel and wondered once again what was between them.

"Does anyone want to do the honors?" Jewel asked, fidgeting with the corner of the letter.

Chase didn't move, so Hunter leaned back in the chair and nodded to Jewel.

"You're her mom. You do it."

Jewel bit her lip and then sighed. She reached for the envelope and ripped the edge before pulling out the letter.

Her eyes flew across the paper, and her jaw dropped open. Her face grew pale, and her fingers shook. She looked at Hunter with shock on her face, and somehow, he knew.

Destini wasn't his daughter. A stab of pain pressed on his chest like a knife. He wanted to retreat to his room or run out the door and jump on a horse and just ride. He needed to process this and think about what it meant.

But it was raining, and he wouldn't just leave them here to pick up the pieces.

He reached for the letter as she turned to stare at Chase, needing to see exactly what it said. Perhaps she'd read it wrong. He licked his lips and took a deep breath to read slowly. He'd barely read the first line when a gasp behind him made him look over his shoulder.

Ma stood behind him, leaning on her walker and staring at the paper. "What does that say?" She reached over him with a wince and took it, pulling the letter closer and squinting. "No, it can't be. What's the meaning of this?"

Ava waved the paper at them, but Hunter looked from Jewel to Chase. They stared at each other, Jewel with horror on her face, and Chase revealing nothing.

Hunter cleared his throat and sighed, turning in his seat. "That is a paternity test, Ma, to see who Destini's real dad is. I didn't finish reading it, but I'm guessing from these reactions that it's not me?"

"What?" Ava screeched, the paper shaking.

Jewel's face was now blushing as she twisted her hands. She looked at Ava quickly, then Hunter before going back to Chase. "I—I made a mistake that summer after I graduated."

Chase jerked at the words, snapping back in his seat. "A mistake?" His voice was deadly quiet. "The first time, maybe, but you can't keep denying me, Jewel."

"What?" Ava screeched again, wavering on her feet. Hunter jumped up, taking her by the elbow.

"Ma, let's get you back to the den. You can't stay on your feet this long, remember?"

She scowled at him. "I've been doing physical therapy with Cindy. I'm supposed to walk around the house three times a day. I'm fine. Besides, this is more important. Now about Destini."

They turned to face Jewel and Chase. Jewel's shoulders were hunched over, and she looked like she was going to cry.

He reached for her hand and squeezed. "Hey, it's going to be alright. Everything happens for a reason, right? Dreams come and go, but family is forever. No matter who her dad is, you're both still family."

She gripped his hand in hers, squeezing like a drowning victim. "But everyone in town is going to talk, and that's going to hurt Destini when she decides to finally move here."

Ava snorted and sat slowly on a chair beside Hunter. "The town will talk, yeah. There's no way of getting out of that. You two made your bed, and now you have to lie in it."

Jewel winced, and Hunter tried to lighten the mood. "I guess this means your dad will lighten up about me not paying child support, huh?"

Jewel groaned and let go of his hand to bury her face in hers. "Oh god, what's Dad going to say?"

Chase crossed his arms again. "I'll pay child support. That's not a problem, and we'll deal with him when the time comes. Let's take a day or two to talk about what this means first."

"What this means?" Jewel asked, spreading her hands wide. "It means I'm going to be the town whore. Destini isn't going to fit in with anyone because her dad went to *prison*. And Dad's going to have a heart attack."

"Don't talk like that in my house, missy," Ava said sternly.

Jewel sighed. "Sorry, but you know it's true. This complicates everything."

Chase stiffened. "I'm sorry to be a complication, sweetheart, but we're not going to keep pretending like she's Hunter's. The fact is she's *my* daughter, and I want to get to know her. I want to be involved, Jewel. I won't be an absentee father. Not anymore."

Ava shook her head, the letter fluttering to the table. "Chase, you—how did this happen?"

The tone was the same disappointed tone she used when they were kids, the same one she'd used at the jail when Chase had been arrested.

Chase looked up at her and glared. "I know, Ma, I'm a big failure. The black sheep of the family. I knocked up my brother's girlfriend before going to prison for vehicular manslaughter. I'll be the talk of the town *again*. Surprise, surprise."

Hunter winced at the sneer in Chase's face and the sarcasm in his tone.

"You're not a failure, Chase," Hunter said gruffly. He waited for Ava to say something, but she just stared at the paper on the table, her hands still shaking with shock.

"Tell that to all the old busybodies at church. Tell that to everyone I see at the grocery store. Tell that to anyone in town actually. The only place I'm even semi-accepted is on this ranch, by everyone *except* Mom and Dad."

Chase's bitter tone left a heavy pall over the room, so Hunter went to the liquor cabinet and grabbed a bottle of whiskey. He couldn't escape this conversation and think about it, but he could help smooth things over for Chase and get them back on topic.

He found some glasses and poured them all drinks. Ava tossed hers back with a wince. Jewel played with her glass, and Chase just stared at Jewel.

"When does Destini come to town? When will we get to meet her?" Hunter asked before taking a drink. He'd been looking forward to being a dad, but now that she was his niece, he still wanted to meet her.

Jewel sighed. "Still Thanksgiving."

Hunter nodded as his phone vibrated. He glanced at a picture from one of the ranch hands. They'd long since realized he wasn't so good at texting, but if they sent him a picture, he either called or went to fix the problem.

He sighed and turned to Ava. "Come on, Ma. Let me

get you settled in the den. I need to help Trent with some of the foals who don't want to come in out of the rain."

She waved her hand. "You go on. I have a few things to say to these two."

Hunter frowned and looked from Ma to Chase and Jewel and back again. "No, Ma. This isn't about you. It's about them. They have things to discuss, not you."

Ava's jaw dropped, and her finger pointed at him. "Don't talk to me like that, young man. I brought you into this world, and I can take you out."

Hunter chuckled. "I know, and you go right ahead. But you'll leave Chase and Jewel to figure out how they want to parent and be a family."

Hunter turned to his brother. "Why don't you two go to the sale barn and have a nice, long talk. The attic is a good, warm private place away from prying eyes and ears. Figure out the logistics of parenting, maybe FaceTime Destini and let her know before anyone else finds out."

Jewel groaned, her hands on her cheeks once more. "Oh god, Destini's going to flip."

Chase stood and nodded. "That's a good plan. I'm open to a discussion if you are."

He offered Jewel his hand, and she looked up at him with her big doe eyes. She bit her lip then took it, letting him help her up.

She pushed in her chair and opened her mouth as she looked at Ava. Then she shook her head and turned away. Together they went out the front door.

He turned back to Ava and arched his brow. "Do you want to go back to the den now? I need to go help Trent."

She narrowed her eyes and grumbled. "Fine, but this conversation isn't over, son. Someone is going to explain what is going on before the end of the day, do you hear me?"

"Yes, ma'am, loud and clear," he said as he helped her to her feet.

She was quiet as she shuffled back to the den, quieter than normal. That was alright with him because he was thinking and processing. He settled her in the recliner, kissed her cheek, and left.

All that glitters is gold, and gold is fleeting. He had had it in his hands. He had the love of his life living in his home and a new daughter. Now he wasn't sure he even had Taylor.

He checked his phone, but he still didn't have any messages from her. He had one from Parker though. He'd taken a picture of Taylor sleeping from the door, the piles of blankets the only indication she was there.

He sent an audio message. "She's alright? I'll bring leftover dinner when I get done here."

Parker replied with a thumbs up and other emojis that made Hunter smile. His brother was already hungry. Hunter parked the Jeep and got out to help Trent.

A few months ago, he had envied Landry and Gunner their families. The unconditional love, the routines among the chaos, but he hadn't known if he'd wanted that for himself.

It had seemed unobtainable, like he'd missed his chance at happiness. Then it had all been within his grasp. He'd gotten used to the idea of having a family and raising a kid. He'd started to get excited about it.

He corralled the foals through the muddy fields to get them in from the rain. Sometimes they just wanted to play in the puddles like the children they were.

By the time he was done, he was an exhausted muddy mess. He went to the bunkhouse to clean up and take a

The Cowboy Gets His Girl

shower, since a lot of his clothes were still in his room there. It was almost dinner time, and he was hungry again.

He packed an overnight bag and went to the house to check on Ma. She was in the kitchen, and he scowled.

"Ma, what are you doing? You're supposed to be resting."

She waved her hand. "I can't sit still anymore. It's been almost three weeks. Physical therapy just left, and Cindy says I'm making great progress. Where's Taylor? I expected her to be off work by now."

He sniffed the crock pot and went to get a to-go container from the pantry. "She ended up leaving at lunch because she's sick, but she needs a break from the ranch for a few days. It's better this way, so she doesn't get anyone else sick. I'm going to go take care of her."

Ava sniffed. "I knew she wouldn't stick around, a city girl like that—"

"City girl?" Hunter asked, frowning as he filled the container for Taylor. "Are you the one who's been calling her that?"

Ava frowned. "What do you mean? I call them like I see them. Don't get me wrong, she's a great girl, she's just not meant for ranch life."

He turned and crossed his arms. "You mean like Jewel?"

She frowned and nodded slowly. "Exactly. She's not Jewel. Did you know about her and Chase back then?"

Hunter shook his head and finished gathering a second container for Parker. "No, I only found out about it a few weeks ago when Chase and I got into that fight."

"That's what it was about?" Ava asked, sitting at the kitchen table. "Get your dad and I bowls, will you? Your dad should be in any minute now."

He nodded and stirred the food in the crock pot as the

back door opened. Boots stomped as Ava yelled, "Don't make mud prints in this house! I can't mop, and Taylor's not here to do it."

Hunter plated two bowls of creamy chicken soup and put them on the table as Bill rounded the corner.

"Did I see Jewel's truck at the sale barn earlier?"

Hunter grabbed spoons as Ava nodded.

"Oh yes, she went with Chase to talk about how they're going to parent Destini because *Chase is her dad.*" Ava enunciated the last few words by pointing at Bill.

His brows rose, then he looked at Hunter. "Oh son, I'm so sorry. How are you holding up?"

Hunter shrugged as he put the waters on the table for them. "I'll be alright. I've had a few hours to process, and I'll talk with Taylor about it later. But this way, we can start a family of our own. We'll be fine."

Ava stopped blowing on her food and frowned at him. "What do you mean, a family of your own? I thought she was just a way to make Jewel jealous?"

Hunter's brows rose. "What made you think that? I told you I love her, that I'm going to marry her, if she'll have me. Don't you remember the day you came home?"

"Oh. Oh dear," she said softly, staring down at her soup as her spoon clattered in the bowl.

Hunter leaned on the counter as Bill said warningly, "Ava? What did you do?"

Ava sighed and glared at Bill. "Well, I did what any sane woman would've done when confronted with that credit card bill. She's just after the money, Hunter. I don't think she actually loves you, dear. I was just trying to get her to leave so you and Jewel could be together."

Hunter's hands fisted at his sides. "What. Did. You. Do."

Ava closed her eyes and pursed her lips. "Well, I might've called her a gold digger and some other things since she bailed her dad out of jail and then spent hundreds shopping. It was almost a thousand dollars in just the few weeks she was here! What was I supposed to do?"

Hunter slammed his hand on the counter, making her jump and wince. "*I'm* the one who bailed her dad out of jail! She didn't even know about it until her dad showed up at her apartment. He was supposedly trying to get a job, but do you know what happened when she tried to go to her apartment and rest after leaving the library today? Her dad stole all her stuff and pawned it."

Ava gasped, and Hunter waved his hands. "Exactly. All she's done the past few weeks is cook and clean and take care of every single one of us. She's worked herself to the bone, and it's made her sick. She's worn herself ragged trying to impress you. Can't you see that? And you called her a gold digger?"

"But the shopping—"

"That I forced her to do because her work flats were causing blisters. Do you know why? Because she hasn't bought new clothes in years because she's maxed out her own credit cards trying to help her dad. She's as selfless as the day is long, Ma."

"Hundreds of dollars for shoes?" Ava asked with raised brows.

Hunter shook his head. "Not just that. I wanted to buy some things for a place of our own. She needed a decent pillow because I knew she wasn't sleeping well, a new coat because hers was threadbare. The fact that she's stepped in to cook and clean for not just us but all these ranch hands and refused to take a paycheck for it? That little shopping trip was the only way I could thank her for her hard work. Jesus, Ma, did you really call her a gold digger?"

"Well, what was I supposed to think? I thought Jewel was a better fit for you, son."

Hunter slammed his hands on the counter again. "That's not your decision to make, Ma. I'm an adult in my thirties. I'm finally happy and found someone to build a life with, and you've been working on tearing it down this whole time?"

He shook his head and put the to-go containers in a grocery bag. "I can't believe you. Taylor's obviously not staying at her apartment since there's no furniture. We'll be at Parker's house if you need us. I'll be back tomorrow for work on the ranch, but this changes things, Ma. Where she goes, I go, and if she's not wanted on this ranch, then neither am I."

He stormed over to the front door as Bill said, "Wait, we can't run this ranch without you. Let's talk this over."

Hunter looked at his parents, the door open and the chilly, wet wind sweeping inside. "I love you both, but right now I need to leave before I say some things I might regret. Call me if you need me. Otherwise, I'll see you tomorrow morning, Dad."

He pointedly did not tell Ava he'd see her, and he saw her wince as she understood his intent. Then he went to the Jeep, pushing through the wind and drizzle.

Chapter Fifty-Three

Hunter pulled up in front of Parker's house and turned off the Jeep. He grabbed his overnight bag and dinner and went up the sidewalk to the front door. He didn't bother knocking but shut the door behind him.

Parker looked over the back of the couch and raised a beer. "Hey bro, what took you so long? I'm starving over here."

Hunter dropped his duffle bag and set the containers on the table. "Well, help yourself to one of them, but the other's for Taylor. How is she?"

Parker shrugged. "I heard her get up and take a shower in the guest bath, but I haven't seen her."

Hunter sat at the kitchen table and pulled off his boots to put them by the front door. "Thanks for putting us up. It might be a few days but could be up to a week or so. Is that alright?"

Parker came to the kitchen table and nodded. "That's fine, but who's going to take care of Ma?"

Hunter's fist clenched and he ground out, "She can fucking take care of herself now."

Parker's brows rose. "You sure?"

Hunter sighed and raked a hand through his hair, setting his cowboy hat on the corner of the chair. "Yeah, physical therapy cleared her to move around more today, so she can do light movement. Shit, I forgot about breakfast."

He leaned back in his chair and called Maryanne.

"Hello?"

"Hey, can you help with breakfasts at the ranch for a few days? Taylor's sick, I had a big fight with Ma, and Taylor and I are staying at Parker's for a while."

The other end of the line was quiet, and he looked at the phone. "Hello?"

"Sorry, was just trying to unpack all that. What's going on?" Maryanne asked with a yawn.

He frowned, his brain working overtime. "I don't want to get into it, but Taylor's dad stole and pawned all her stuff. Ma thinks Taylor's a gold digger, so Taylor doesn't feel welcome at the ranch anymore. Destini's not my daughter, she's Chase's. And we're staying at Parker's while Taylor's sick, so we need someone to help with breakfasts at the ranch."

Parker's jaw dropped, and he and Maryanne spoke at the same time.

"What the fuck?"

"What about Destini?"

Hunter sighed as Taylor walked down the hallway, her hair slicked back and wet. She wore a pair of sweatpants and a t-shirt. Her nose was red, and dark circles were under her eyes. But she went straight to him and put her hand on his shoulder.

He looked up at her with his throat full of emotions and choked out, "Destini's not mine."

His voice was soft, and Taylor stepped between his legs and pulled his head to her chest. She cradled him and wrapped her arms around him.

"Oh Hunter, I'm so sorry," she said softly, kissing him on the top of the head.

He felt the tension leave his shoulders as he sighed, breathing in the scent of the laundry detergent on her shirt. He squeezed her hips and wrapped his arms around her waist, holding her tight. In her embrace, it all melted away into a warm puddle. Her touch was like a soothing balm, easing all the aches and pains of the day, both physical and emotional.

"Well, that's unexpected," Maryanne said through the phone.

"Got that right," Parker said.

Taylor breathed deeply, then sneezed into her elbow. Hunter stood up. "Here, sit down. Let me heat up your dinner and get you some more medicine. Parker, do you have tissues?"

Parker pushed some from the center of the table to her while Hunter popped her dinner into the microwave. Maryanne and Taylor talked softly on the phone about breakfasts, and Parker came into the kitchen to grab another beer from the fridge. He handed it to Hunter.

"You look like you could use this. You okay, bro?"

Hunter nodded. "I will be, as long as I have her." He stared at Taylor and knew it was true. The shock of losing Destini wasn't as great as it could've been, probably because he was already planning a future with Taylor.

The microwave beeped, and he took the container to Taylor. He kissed her on the head and grabbed his phone.

"I'll send Gunner to the ranch tomorrow morning at five-thirty with breakfast. Do you want me to call Holly to see if she can make dinner?"

Taylor shook her head. "No, there's still some freezer meals from the church meal train."

Hunter nodded. "I'll make sure Dad and Ma know that's the plan for the next few days then. Actually, Parker can you text that to them? I need to call Landry and get Taylor back in bed. Her nose is already dripping into her dinner."

Taylor wiped her nose and winced. "Ew, gross, it is not."

Maryanne laughed on the phone and said goodbye. Then Hunter said, "I'm going to go grab your medicine. I'll be right back."

He stepped into the guest bedroom to find the medicine and quickly filled Landry in on what was going on. He asked him to text Chase and let him know the plan and see how he was taking the news about being a dad.

Then he stepped back into the dining room to take care of his girl. With all else that was going on, she was his priority now. One thing was clear to him now, and he couldn't wait any longer.

He needed her beside him every day and every night. The thought of her breaking up with him earlier—had that just been this morning? It felt like days ago—had left him dazed. Then he'd known deep in his soul that he had to secure her permanently at his side.

He set her pills on the table by her soup along with a ring. She grabbed the pills, but when she saw the ring, she paused. She looked up at him with those big green eyes, a frown on her face.

"What's this?"

The Cowboy Gets His Girl

He got down on one knee and rubbed his hands on her thighs. She gasped, and Parker groaned.

"Fuck, not another wedding," his brother mumbled. "Fine, I'll record this because Lord knows everyone will ask."

"Shut up," Hunter said, looking up at Taylor with all the love spilling out of him. He took a deep breath, ready to secure his future.

Taylor's brows rose and her heart stopped as she wiped her nose. Was this really happening?

Hunter's voice was steady and sure. "You're my family, princess. You're my one and only, the one I was waiting for all these years, and I didn't even know it. You blew into my life like a tornado, and I don't ever want to go a day without seeing your smiling face or a night without holding you in my arms. Will you marry me?"

His words were like a fairytale, but they felt too good to be true. She laughed nervously, her heart beating rapidly as she processed his proposal.

She wiped her nose with a tissue. "Holy shit, is this real?" Her head was spinning and groggy from the medicine. "Maybe I'm dreaming. Am I dreaming?"

She pinched her arm, and Hunter laughed, grabbing her hands and kissing each one. His touch felt real, and the love in his eyes was genuine.

"You're not dreaming. What we have is the real deal, the last-our-entire-lives kind of love. I don't want to go to bed at night without you in my arms. I want to wake up next to you every morning. Being without you this weekend in the tents? It was torture. The thought of you leaving me this morning? Soul crushing. Be mine, Taylor. Be my wife and my partner, the mother of our children. I want to make you mine, legally, because you already have my heart, my soul, my undivided attention forever. Say yes."

Now she was positive that she must be dreaming. This was beyond the realm of reality or any book she'd ever read. Taylor felt like her heart might beat its way out of her chest as she stared at the man she loved down on one knee, with a ring in his trembling hand.

She knew she loved him, knew she wanted to marry him. That's all that mattered in the end, but she couldn't shake the worry.

"Hunter, of course I love you, and I want to say yes, but what about your family?"

"They don't matter," he said.

"Hey," Parker whined.

He put his hands on her cheeks and peered into her eyes. "Ignore him. Everyone loves you, Taylor."

"Not your mom," she whispered, dread filling her chest and making her shiver.

He sighed and sat back on his knee. "She'll come around eventually. I got into it with her tonight actually and set her straight on a few things about the two of us."

"Oh Hunter, that's only going to make things worse." She twisted the napkin in her lap.

He shook his head. "I don't think so. She just needs some time to readjust her thinking. Are you hesitating to marry me because of my mom?"

Taylor snorted and rolled her eyes. "I'm not hesitating. I just want to make sure you're going to be okay if your mom and I don't see eye to eye about things. You're a bit of a mama's boy, you have to admit."

"Hey, I am not," Hunter said.

Parker snorted. "Dude, don't lie."

Hunter chuckled and shook his head. "Fine, but that doesn't matter because I'm not marrying my mom. I'm marrying *you*. If you'll say yes and have me?"

"I want to say yes, but how's that going to work when we have kids? I grew up with a lot of resentment between my parents. It's no way to raise a kid, and I don't want you to resent your mom or your mom to fill our kids heads with ideas that I'm not good enough for you or—"

He leaned forward and pressed his lips to hers. She sank into the kiss, her shoulders relaxing.

When he pulled away, he smiled. "It won't come to that. But if you want, I'll go to work for a different ranch. We can move wherever you want. I have a lot of rodeo connections. We can start over, just the two of us. Is that what you want?"

She shook her head, touching his chest and needing to be closer to him. "God no, I don't want you to leave your family. Family is important. But I don't know how to get on your mom's good side when she's constantly wanting me to be someone I'm not. I'm not Jewel, and I never will be."

He brushed the hair out of her face and wiped a tear off her cheek. "Sh, she won't be acting like that with you again. You let me know if she says something or calls you names, alright? Now that she knows Destini is Chase's daughter, not mine, I won't be surprised at all if she changes her tune. She was just trying to push Jewel and I together because of some outdated notion that parents should be married."

Taylor sniffed and blew her nose. "Do you really think she'll come around?"

He nodded. "I really do. I know we only met a few

months ago and there's drama with my mom, but love is the most important thing, right?

I love you more than words can show,
A depth of feeling you'll always know.
Through every challenge and every test,
We have our lives to figure out the rest.
Say yes, Taylor, my heart's desire,
Be my princess, my endless fire.
You're my everything, my dream, my feast,
Say yes, and tame this wild beast.
Forever yours, in love I stay,
Through every night, through every day.
With you, my world feels complete,
My soul bows humbly at your feet."

Tears pricked her eyes, her heart tightening with emotion as spoke. This wasn't how she pictured her proposal. In front of his brother at the kitchen table with a red, drippy and stopped up nose?

She hadn't thought about a proposal at all, really. She'd been so focused on the perfect first date that she hadn't stopped to think about everything that was supposed to come after. And then the past few weeks of trying to be everything for everyone at the ranch—well, it'd just been too chaotic to think about the future.

She leaned forward and kissed him, sniffing her nose and tears running down her cheeks. This felt right, like it was meant to be. All that really mattered was love. Everything else would fall into place eventually. Hopefully that included his mother.

She pulled back and he wiped the tears from her cheeks, hope shining in his hazel eyes. "Is that a yes?"

She glanced at the ring and back to him. His face, so open and hopeful, rugged and weather worn from all his days outside. If he knew what he was getting into, then there was only one thing left to do. Taylor took a deep breath and nodded.

"Like I could say no when you start spouting poetry at me."

He grinned, his brows rising. "Then I'll give you poetry every morning, noon, and night, princess, as long as it keeps you at my side."

She chuckled and nodded. "It's a deal then. Yes, I'll marry you, beastie." She grinned, her lips turning mischievous.

His eyes flashed and he grinned, slipping the ring on her finger. He crashed his lips to hers with a fierce, possessive kiss that took her breath away. The missing pieces of her life clicked into place. She'd found a family, a home.

Sure, that family was a little broken, and they didn't really have a roof of their own since they were bumming at his brother's. But as long as they were together, they could weather any storm.

When he pulled back, she looked down, breathless. It was an antique gold ring, but it shone bright with diamonds in a flower shape.

"This was my great-grandmother's ring. My great-grandfather bought it for her when they bought the ranch. It's stood the test of time, and so will we," he said, shifting to his feet with a flash of vulnerability on his face. "If you want something else, I can go tomorrow—"

"No," she said. "This is perfect, just like you."

She stood and threw her arms around his neck, kissing him with so much passion, she got light-headed. The world tilted, and he wrapped his arms around her.

"Whoa there, did the medicine hit you? Are you saying yes just because you're hyped up on NyQuil?"

She giggled and shook her head. "No, I'm saying yes because I love you, beastie."

He slid his arms under her knees and picked her up. He spun her around the room and shouted, making her cling to his neck as she laughed.

"God, get a room, you two," Parker said with a laugh.

Hunter stopped moving, and she kept her head buried in his chest as the world kept spinning. "Don't mind if we do. Good night, Parker."

He strode down the hall, and Taylor sighed, her eyes closed. They had moved so fast, she almost got whiplash from the start of their relationship. But perhaps being engaged would help things settle down. Either way she was going to jump into this new life with both feet and see where she landed. She just hoped he was right about Ava coming around.

Chapter Fifty-Four

The rest of the week was a blur. Taylor slept Tuesday, and when Hunter came back to Parker's house after working at the ranch all day, he'd looked awful. He caught her cold, so Wednesday they cuddled on the couch and watched old western comedies while eating soup.

She'd gone to work on Thursday like normal. Parker sent her the video of the proposal, but she waited until they were both feeling better before taking still-frame screenshots and texting them to Lucy on her lunch break.

By the end of the day, Holly, Maryanne, Helen, and Lucy had all stopped by the library to see the ring and hear all about the proposal. Taylor hadn't seen that much traffic at the library during the week before, and the constant talking and laughing was exhausting.

She hadn't wanted to, but Lucy had dragged her to the girl's yoga that night so all the gossiping people in the town could hear about the proposal... although several of them asked questions about Jewel and Chase and the fact that Destini was not Hunter's child.

Hunter must've still been under the weather because he was already asleep in the guest room when she came home that night. Now it was Sunday, and she walked up the steps of the church with her hand on Hunter's arm.

She nodded and chatted, but her stomach was twisted with knots. Parker had said that Ava and Bill were going to attend church today, so they could provide a united front to the town about supporting Chase and Jewel.

But this would be the first time Taylor would see Ava since Monday. She slid into the pew on the left while Hunter went to warm-up for worship service. Jewel and Lucy joined her, and they chatted about this and that.

Worship had already started when Ava rolled down the aisle on an electric scooter. Her head held high, she sat in the aisle and didn't look at anyone while they sang.

When worship was over, Hunter joined her in Lucy's row, not in his family's row like all the previous weeks. He slid his arm behind her on the pew, making her feel safe and loved.

When the service was over, people practically swarmed like vultures on Ava and Chase. A few came to chat with Hunter and asked probing questions about the baby daddy situation. Hunter just smiled and stood relaxed with his hands in his pockets as he talked about how excited he was for Chase.

Finally, Hunter put his hand on her back. "Are you ready to say hello?"

She bit her lip. "I guess she can't cuss me out in church, so let's see how it goes."

He chuckled as they walked over to join the thinning crowd. The toddlers were now crawling over the pew while the parents talked. Ava looked up at Taylor with her lips drawn in a thin line.

"Taylor," Ava said. "I hope you're feeling better."

Taylor nodded. "I am, yes. Thanks for asking."

"Good, I'm getting tired of pastries." Ava patted Maryanne's hand and arched a brow. "No offense, dear, your baking is delicious, but a ranch needs more meat and protein to start the day."

Taylor's spine straightened, and she cleared her throat. Pain twisted her insides. Ava hadn't said anything about the engagement or welcomed her to the family. All she cared about was the ranch and what Taylor could do for her.

That was fine. She couldn't change Ava. All she could control was herself.

She pulled her purse higher on her shoulder and smiled tightly. "Yes, well, I'll start sending breakfasts with Hunter in the morning then. Until you're well enough to take back over. It's good to see you out and about, but if you'll excuse me, I'm working this afternoon."

She nodded and bid her goodbyes, Hunter kissing her on the cheek as she walked out the church with her head held high, blinking back tears behind her sunglasses. She walked down the sidewalk, saying hello to various people that she'd come to know in the past few weeks.

Then she turned at the corner to walk the two blocks to the library. Hunter was supposed to join her after they finished lunch at the Diner as a family. Once more, she felt alone. Her purse vibrated, and she stopped to check her phone.

"Hello?"

"Will you stop for a minute and turn around?" Hunter said breathlessly.

She frowned and turned around, then her jaw dropped. Jewel and Parker stood in the street each stopping traffic with Parker holding one of the twins. The other four brothers were carrying Ava in her power scooter across the street like a queen.

Hunter caught her eye with a grin and a wink. Taylor stood frozen as all of the family surrounded Ava. Maryanne and Holly each held a toddler, and Bill led the charge, fussing around the boys.

"I thought that hospital stay would've had you lose weight, Mom," Landry said with a huff.

"Don't talk about a lady's weight. Geez, didn't you learn anything growing up on the ranch?" Gunner grumbled.

Ava looked around from her perch. "Stop chattering and focus because if you drop me, I swear—look out for the step to the sidewalk!"

The guys made the step easily, barely jarring Ava on the scooter as they turned onto the sidewalk.

"Don't drop her, for god's sake," Bill said. "Why couldn't this have waited, Ava?"

Ava gripped the armrest tightly, peering down at them all. "You saw her face. I upset her again, and I'm tired of it. So what if the scooter died? I need to—ah, there you are, my dear."

Taylor looked around and then back at Ava, completely bewildered.

"Yes, you. Taylor, come here before these giant oafs drop me. Careful, put me down now. Easy, boys, easy." Ava finally relaxed as her scooter settled on the sidewalk in front of Taylor.

"What in the world are y'all doing?" Taylor asked.

Ava grabbed her hand and tugged. "Girl, you didn't think you'd get away that easily, did you?"

Taylor frowned, leaning over to look her in the face. "What are you talking about?"

Ava sighed and let go of her hand, leaning back and

putting her hand to her fractured hip. "I'm talking about you and me. I owe you an apology, and I don't care if everyone in town hears it. I'm sorry for what I said last week."

Taylor felt her cheeks heat, and she shifted on her feet as Hunter slid his arm along her back, tucking her into his side. "Oh, it's alright, Ava."

"No, it's not," Ava said firmly. "Look, I know I'm difficult to get along with, and you've had the short end of the stick dealing with me as a cranky invalid, but you never complained and always took care of us. I never should've called you names or tried to run you off. To be honest, you're the best of all of us, child, and we're all very glad you're officially joining the family."

Taylor's hand rested on Hunter's chest, but her eyes remained on Ava as they misted. "Are—are you sure?"

Ava nodded and the rest of the family murmured agreements. "None of these fools told me about the engagement until you left the church. If I'd known, I would've had the pastor announce it to the congregation."

"Oh, that's not necessary."

"Yes, it is. We were so focused on showing the town how welcoming we are of Jewel and Destini and the Chase situation that we didn't get a chance to celebrate the love you two have found."

Taylor's chest tightened.

Ava continued, "I might not have been on board in the beginning, but that's because I didn't see what was so obvious to everyone else. You two were made for each other. You're like the sun and the rain. Together, you two make a beautiful rainbow of love and joy. I've never seen Hunter as happy as he was when you were around."

Taylor looked up at Hunter who was smiling softly, love

shining in his eyes. "It's true," he said. "You complete me. You're my better half, the goddess who hung the moon with stars in your eyes, the princess who fills my dreams with fairytales, the sugar in a life of bitterness."

"God, make him shut up already," Parker said with a groan. Landry punched him on the arm, then took his daughter from Parker when she lunged at him.

"Sh," Holly said, wiping an eye. "It's getting good."

Ava reached her hand out. "Will you forgive me, dear?"

Taylor took her hand and then knelt to hug her gently. "Of course," she whispered. "Consider it done."

Ava patted her on the back. "Good, because I'd like you to come home soon. You belong on the ranch with us."

Taylor blinked back the tears and sighed as she broke the hug. "We can probably arrange something."

Hunter cleared his throat. "Actually, we won't be moving back into the ranch house. I've spent the past two weeks setting up that tiny house we looked at in Denton near the creek. Surprise."

Taylor looked at him and gasped. "What? Really? But the money—"

"Isn't anything to worry about. Dad deeded me those ten acres years ago. I just never sectioned it off. And Chase has helped us all make investments for years, so once the well gets dug on Tuesday, we'll be able to move in."

She threw her arms around Hunter and kissed him as everyone began to talk about the tiny house, the location, and more. Jewel and Chase fielded a lot of the questions about the tiny house since they'd seen it on the lot all those weeks ago.

The kiss centered her. He was her rock, her anchor in the stormy chaos that was his family. When he pulled back

The Cowboy Gets His Girl

and tipped up his cowboy hat, he asked, "Is that alright? The house, that is?"

She nodded. "Yeah, I'd like to have our own space."

He grinned and kissed her quickly again. "Good, because I'm dying to hear you scream for me, sugar."

She chuckled and buried her head in his chest.

"Alright, let's go to the Diner. Boys, pick me up," Ava demanded.

Landry groaned. "But I have Freddi. Parker, it's your turn to help."

Bill shook his head. "No, this is getting too dangerous. The after-church traffic is picking up, and the kids are getting squirmy."

Taylor laughed and pecked Hunter on the cheek. "Good luck with lunch, beastie. I'm going to go open up the library now."

Ava shook her head and grabbed her hand. "No, I've already talked to Helen. She's going to do it. You're coming to lunch with us."

Taylor's breath froze in her chest. "Really?"

Ava nodded. "Yep, you're family, right? Let's go have a nice family dinner. Now, if you boys can get me to the door of the Diner, I'll hobble inside. Then one of y'all can go get the truck, toss this piece of garbage in the back, and get my walker. Can you believe we charged this thing all night and the batteries are already dead?"

Taylor shook her head as she released her hand and sat back, gripping the armrests as Gunner and Chase lifted her up. Hunter and Parker lunged forward to help. Holly and Maryanne flanked Taylor as they walked away from the library toward the Diner.

After a few steps, Landry handed the kid to her so he could help with his mom, and the girls followed behind them. Several cars slowed and people pointed and stared at them on the sidewalk.

But Taylor didn't care. She couldn't stop the smile on her face or the love in her heart. She was finally with a family who truly welcomed her, with a man who loved her despite all her quirks.

They set Ava down outside the Diner's door, and Hunter winked at her over his mom's head. She grinned, ready to step through the door to their future.

Next in the Crimson Creek Series

vinci-books.com/convict-gets-his-girl

Some secrets wait fifteen years to come home.

Jewel Jenkins swore she'd never return to Crimson Creek, until illness forces her home with a daughter and a truth she's kept hidden. Chase Williams, fresh out of prison, is rebuilding his life when a DNA test exposes a painful truth. Can forgiveness lead to a second chance at love?

Turn the page for a free preview…

The Convict Gets His Girl: Chapter One

Spring

Chase's brother, Hunter, laughed as he pushed the door open, not bothering to wait for a response. "Knock, knock, anyone home? Of course, you're home. Where else would you be?"

Chase tipped his head up in a nod, eyes still on his laptop. "Gimme a sec."

The numbers were lining up, forming the pattern he'd been searching for. With a few more keystrokes, it all clicked into place. A smile stole over his face as the final calculations confirmed what he suspected—the return was larger than expected. Enough for the client to send his kid to therapy. That thought settled something inside Chase, even as he pushed away from the computer.

The one-room cabin was warm from the fire roaring in the open hearth. Hunter stood close, rubbing his hands for warmth. The March rainstorm had dropped the tempera-

The Cowboy Gets His Girl

tures and caused flash floods, making the air damp and cool.

"What brings you out in this weather?" Chase asked, twisting his back from side to side to stretch.

"Ma wants you to come to Sunday dinner."

Chase snorted. "That's a given. Haven't been able to weasel out of it in six months. What else?"

Hunter grinned. "Thought you'd come to the Electric Cowboy with me this weekend. Feels like I haven't seen you all week."

He didn't say it, but his brother probably knew how he felt—being surrounded at a bar, pressed on all sides, too many moving bodies, too many variables—it reminded him of fights in prison. A bar full of strangers wasn't relaxing. It was a battlefield waiting to erupt.

Chase sighed, sinking onto the worn couch. "Aren't you getting tired of the bar scene?"

He expected Hunter to joke about it, but his brother just rubbed his hands together, looking down. "Maybe, but if I don't go, the itch won't leave me alone. It's constantly under my skin, just needing an outlet, you know?"

Recognition hit Chase like a gut punch. "Of all our family, I'm the only one who knows exactly what you mean. It's like needing to move, to do something, but you can't scratch the itch because it's buried so deep."

Hunter's eyes sharpened. "Why do you think we're like this?"

Chase leaned back, propping his feet on the wooden trunk he used as a coffee table. "I'm sure Landry could turn it into a song, but I don't have the words. It's been like this my whole life. Hell, it's why I pushed myself so hard that last year in school, why I… well, the things that take the edge off that itch have never been worth the price to me."

Hunter's lips pursed, and Chase looked into the fire, remembering the night that had changed everything for him, for his life, his plans, his dreams. His nostrils flared, refusing to give in to the darkness that threatened to pull him down. He jerked a thumb toward the computer and pasted on a tight smile.

"Numbers don't lie, cheat, or die. I stick to myself out here as much as possible and play with the only thing that makes sense."

"The numbers," Hunter said.

Chase nodded, even though it wasn't a question. "When I can analyze trends, make money work for people—that's when things click and the itch scratches in my mind."

Hunter studied him. "That's why you stay out here?"

Chase hesitated before nodding. "Partly. It's easier out here. Quieter."

With less people judging him, he could make atonement and help people at his own pace, doing a thorough job on the computer to get people a better deal with their investments, tax returns, whatever they needed.

"I just scratch the itch when there's a good woman in my arms," Hunter grumbled, making Chase snort a laugh. His oldest brother was a simple man of the earth, and sometimes Chase wished he could be more like him. Free to just ride the ranch and be himself.

Hunter turned back to the fire. "You can't let people keep you in a box, Chase. You've been away from the real world for too long. Maybe come work with me more? The ranch could use someone who understands the financial side of things."

Chase huffed a laugh, bitterness twisting in his gut. "Like Ma and Dad would trust me with that."

Hunter shoved his hands into his jeans and sighed.

"What did you expect when you refused to talk to them for fifteen years? They don't know you, Brother, which is why you should spend more time around the ranch. Show them who you are, if you won't talk with them."

Chase rubbed the back of his neck, his cheeks heating at the thought of how he'd treated his parents when he'd first gone to prison. By the time he took responsibility for his own actions and stopped blaming everyone else, it'd been years of refusing to talk to anyone but Landry and Hunter.

And each of Hunter's calls, he'd been waiting for the blow-up that he knew would come when Hunter realized how much Chase had betrayed him. Even now, he waited and watched.

Hunter launched into updates on the family—Landry's twins turning one, their niece Connie talking up a storm, their mom hosting weekly playdates. Chase nodded along, but the idea of all that noise made him shift uncomfortably on the couch. The chaos, the shrieking, the way conversations overlapped—it was overwhelming. At Sunday dinners, he kept to the edges, half-listening, half-enduring, half-hoping someday he'd feel welcomed and loved.

Hunter eventually left, making the short drive back to the ranch. Chase exhaled, relieved. He didn't hate his family. He loved them. But being around them, when they still saw him as the screw-up, the convict, was exhausting.

He turned back to his laptop, pulling up the financial statements again. Helping this client meant more than just a tax return. It meant a father could send his kid to therapy. Therapy mattered.

If Chase had gotten it as a teenager, maybe he wouldn't have been drunk behind the wheel that night. Maybe he wouldn't have made the mistake that cost a girl her life.

The black cloud of guilt settled on his shoulders, and he

clicked into the computer, diving back into the numbers and pushing the memories away. He'd deserved all he'd gotten. Hell, he deserved much, much more punishment, which is why he had to atone and help people with their finances.

If he could build an actual career in financial advising instead of just helping friends and family, maybe he'd be more than just an ex-con with baggage. Maybe someone would see past his record, past the mistakes, and take a chance on him.

Maybe he could be worth something to someone one day.

Half a year out of prison, and he was making a decent living—helping Lola with her bookkeeping part-time, working with the CPA in town to get through tax season, freelancing investment portfolios for Landry and his famous friends, even getting referrals from Parker's former teammates. His work was good. Most people trusted him with their money.

Except his parents.

They still saw him as the screw-up. Maybe that was why he still worked on the ranch part of the week. Hunter didn't really need him, didn't rely on him the way he did the other hands, but it kept him connected. Gave him a reason to be there.

Gave him a reason to hope, maybe, that one day they'd see him as something more. Maybe he'd finally be able to clear his conscience, of the accident, of his betrayal of Hunter, of his refusal to talk to his parents for so many years.

The friction and stilted relationship with his parents, the guilt he felt around Hunter, the turmoil over his actions that fateful night—those were the things that messed with his newfound peace and freedom.

Somehow, he landed on his feet, thanks to his brothers' support. They had believed in him and trusted him when they really shouldn't have. He frowned, ignoring the doubt that told him Hunter didn't actually know what had happened back then at all.

The Convict Gets His Girl: Chapter Two

Jewel's hand trembled as she reached for the syringe, her fingers grazing the cold metal of the tray. A wave of dizziness washed over her, blurring the edges of the stable into a hazy mirage. The expensive thoroughbred before her, worth more than most people's homes, nickered restlessly, sensing something amiss.

"Easy, boy," she murmured, fighting the vertigo that threatened to topple her. Her skin was clammy despite the Texas heat, and each joint in her body screamed with an invisible fire.

"Dr. Jenkins?" The ranch hand's voice sounded distant, but his hand on her arm was insistent. "You don't look so good."

"I'm fine," Jewel lied through gritted teeth. She couldn't afford to show weakness, not with her reputation for being one of the best equine veterinarians in the state. But her protest was cut short as a sharp pain lanced through her skull, sending spots dancing before her eyes.

"Oh my God, you cannot touch my precious baby like

The Cowboy Gets His Girl

that. Look at you! You're shaking worse than that dancer my ex ran off with. Step away from my baby."

The woman strode down the spacious, airy barn with golden highlights flying behind her like she was in some kind of damn hair commercial. Her eyes blazed with fire—part worry, part bitchiness—and Jewel struggled to rein her temper in.

Her shaking hand lowered as she stroked the horse's flank and met the woman's gaze with chin lifted and cheeks flushed. "I'm sorry, but do you or do you not want the cortisone shot today?"

The woman glared and came to a stop, crossing her arms and making her shirt sparkle in the late afternoon sunlight. "I do. It has to be today, or he won't be able to compete in the next race."

Jewel pasted on a bland expression and waved to the horse, silently asking if she could proceed. The woman's eyes narrowed at Jewel's hand, still shaking.

"Not you. Call in one of the other vets to come do it." The woman's hands went to her side, and Jewel recognized a tantrum boiling, but—like with her own daughter—was at a loss on how to stop it.

The ranch foreman stepped out from behind the other ranch hand, his sun-weathered face tipped in a severe frown. "I'll handle it, Mizz. Dr. Jenkinz? Will you come with me?"

He led the way behind the woman, who stepped up to the horse and crooned softly, ignoring Jewel now. Jewel put the cap back on the syringe and settled everything into her bag. Her shoulders shook as she walked weakly down the aisle, embarrassed like she hadn't been since vet school a decade ago.

She walked with head held high and exited the barn.

The foreman was lighting a cigarette and leaning against the outer wall. She stepped closer to him, the shade welcoming and cool.

"You can't argue with the mizzus, Dr. Jenkinz. She's too high-strung to be reasonable."

Jewel sighed, knowing this client's history with the clinic. She'd already gone through four other vets at their practice. "I understand that, but I'm just trying to do my job."

He looked up at her with a critical eye. "We both know that horse doesn't need more corazón shots. He's about done on the circuit."

She rubbed the back of her neck and stretched, the pops loud to her ears even as she smiled at his use of the wrong word. "I know. He needs stem cell therapy, rest, and a recovery time greater than she allows."

He nodded and took a drag on his cigarette. "You go on and leave like she said. Call for another doctor. It gives more time for the old horse to recover. And if there are no doctors available, zen it is better for the horse, yes?"

He walked toward her truck, his voice firm and brooking no argument. She knew the foreman had the complete trust of the owner, the woman's new husband.

Her legs threatened to buckle as she opened the truck door, chin high as she eased onto the leather seats with a grunt. Jewel closed her eyes against the light that seemed to pierce straight into her brain. Sweat beaded her brow as she slipped on her sunglasses and backed up.

As she drove away from the sprawling ranch, tears pricked her eyes. It felt like she'd been fired, but the way her whole body ached, she knew something was wrong. Maybe the sixth doctor's appointment tomorrow would provide the answers she needed.

She focused on regulating her breathing, trying to

muster the façade of normalcy she would need to maintain once home. She would tell Destini she had a migraine, a simple explanation that wouldn't worry the bright-eyed teenager too much.

Anxiety knotted her stomach at the thought of alarming her teenage daughter. Destini was currently obsessed with her science fair project and the prospect of glory at school. Jewel couldn't bear to puncture that bubble with her own health concerns.

She pulled up to her modest home, far removed from the opulence of the horses she treated. She dragged herself to lean heavily against the front door, the keys in her hand blurring together as she searched for the correct one, her body betraying her once more with a shudder.

"Mom?" Destini's voice called from inside, laced with excitement and anticipation as she threw open the door. "I've got so much to tell you about my project!"

"Can't wait to hear all about it, sweetheart," Jewel replied, her voice steady despite the turmoil roiling within her. "Just give me an hour to lie down, then you can tell me all about it while I make dinner."

"Sure, Mom. Rough day today?" Destini chirped, bouncing on her toes as she shut and locked the door behind her.

"A migraine."

"Another one? Geez, it's like a constant thing now."

Jewel mumbled under her breath, "Tell me about it." Destini didn't hear, going back into the dining room where the project supplies were strewn about, popping her earbuds back in and humming along.

Jewel slipped up the stairs, her heart heavy with secrets as she made her way to her bedroom, desperate for respite from the relentless assault of whatever was fucking up her body. It'd been almost a year, and it was getting worse, not better.

A few weeks later, Jewel clenched the steering wheel, her knuckles white as she navigated out of the bustling greater-Houston traffic. Each movement sent tremors of pain through her joints, but the weight of the diagnosis was heavier still. The doctor's words echoed in her mind: "I'm quite certain it's Lyme disease."

After months of uncertainty and visits to multiple doctors, the validation should have been a relief. It could be something way worse, but as she merged onto the highway leading north to Dallas, it felt like an anchor sinking her. Now she had to see a specialist hours away when she was already on thin ice with her bosses.

The drive was long, the landscape shifting from urban sprawl to open fields that reminded her of the ranch and the horses she cared for—creatures whose livelihoods depended on her expertise. She considered the irony that it was while working outdoors with these majestic animals that she had probably been bitten by the tiny tick responsible for her pain.

She didn't dare tell Destini, who was safely spending the night with her cousins, engrossed in the regional science fair preparations. She'd excitedly won the school's competition and now advanced.

Jewel didn't confide in her family in Crimson Creek, either. This journey was hers alone to navigate; she wasn't ready to reveal her vulnerability to them just yet.

Upon arriving in Dallas, she found herself in yet another sterile office, this one adorned with plaques boasting holistic approaches to healing. Dr. Marcus, the specialist, was a gentle man with a reassuring presence. He

The Cowboy Gets His Girl

spoke of major life changes with a calm certainty that made them seem possible, even hopeful.

"Your body is fighting a persistent invader," he explained. "We need to support it in every way we can. That means dietary changes, activity changes, even product changes in your home. We're going to load you up on anti-inflammatory foods—leafy greens, fatty fish, berries. And probiotics are key after so many rounds of antibiotics."

He handed her pamphlets filled with guidelines and recipes, then continued. "You'll also start a regimen of supplements and herbs known to support immune function and combat Lyme-related inflammation. Perhaps the most important ingredient to healing is stress management. Have you ever tried meditation or yoga?"

Jewel nodded automatically, though in truth, she didn't have time for any of this crap. The holistic side was the antithesis to everything she'd learned in medical school too. The stakes were too high not to embrace every potential solution, though. She noted everything down meticulously, aware that these changes were not mere suggestions but prescriptions for a new way of life.

Dr. Marcus added, "Regular visits here will be necessary so we can monitor your progress closely. I know it's a long drive, but your health must be your priority now. If you don't put in the work now, it could seriously affect your quality of life permanently."

His words echoed in the small room, reminiscent of the doctor in Houston who'd finally given her the diagnosis.

She agreed, knowing the truth in his words, even as a part of her rebelled against the upheaval looming on the horizon. Driving back to Houston later that same day after an extended break at Buc-ees, Jewel felt the gravity of the journey ahead—a path that would test her resolve, redefine her relationship with food, and force her to explore the unfamiliar terrain of holistic healing. But she was ready to fight for her health, for Destini, and for the chance to reclaim the life that Lyme disease threatened to steal away.

Months passed, and here she was again. Jewel's hands tightened around the steering wheel, knuckles whitening as Houston's skyline finally came into view. The sun was dipping low, casting a warm glow over the city—her home for the past decade—but now, it seemed less welcoming, more daunting.

She had returned from yet another trip to Dallas with a new arsenal: bottles of supplements, bags of organic produce, and a new yoga mat strapped to the backseat.

In the past few months, Jewel's life became a cadence of careful routines and self-discipline. She swapped coffee for green tea and CBD mushroom coffee, and her meals were now a colorful canvas of vegetables and lean proteins.

Her phone, once filled with veterinary journal articles, now had apps for meditation and reminders for yoga classes. Her favorite—and not so favorite—ranch clients saw less of her, as she spent more hours in the office, pouring over case files rather than tending to the horses she adored.

Yet another visit to Dr. Marcus in Dallas tipped the scales. With each trip, the familiarity of the city tugged at her more strongly, whispering promises of a community and a slower pace that could cradle her healing journey. "You're responding well," he said, his voice tinged with both approval and concern. "But you must consider your environment. Stress, exposure—it all plays a role, especially if you're going back to the same area you were exposed. Any infection must be treated quickly and without mercy."

The words echoed in her mind on the drive back, harmonizing with the hum of the tires against the highway.

As the landscape changed, so did her resolve. The vast Texas skies gave way to the closer buildings and tighter traffic, her stress and shoulders rising as she gripped the steering wheel.

The Woodlands were no longer her safe retreat, her home. These trips had allowed her to see beyond her current struggles and truly evaluate her life goals and plans. It wasn't just about proximity to medical care; it was about creating a sanctuary for herself, somewhere her body wouldn't constantly be on the defensive.

"Time for a new chapter," Jewel murmured to herself, her eyes tracing the horizon where city lights faded into the countryside. She envisioned the rolling hills near Crimson Creek, the gentle neighing of horses, and family dinners not confined to holiday gatherings.

She'd always planned to move back home after Destini moved out and went to college, but maybe they could both use a fresh start. In the past year, Destini had become so intensely obsessed with NASA that it bordered on the unhealthy. She'd stopped playing soccer and spending time with her friends. Perhaps she needed a change too, to remind her of what was truly important in life.

The decision settled over her like a gentle rain, refreshing and clear. Moving back to Crimson Creek wouldn't just bring her closer to Dr. Marcus; it would take her out of the Lyme-infected area that seemed to be a constant threat, lurking beneath every leaf and blade of grass.

Grab your copy…
vinci-books.com/convict-gets-his-girl

About the Author

Jane Poller always wanted to write romance. After years of back and forth, she finally took the plunge and never looked back. She still teaches online and homeschools her teenagers full-time. But with a commercial pilot and Army veteran for a hubby, she has a lot of free time in between his trips to write whatever stories the characters demand of her. She lives in Texas in a small town on four acres with her family of four, plus their two dogs. When she's not doing all the family things, she's reading in the hammock by the pond, writing in the treehouse, quilting and crafting, or arguing with her characters who refuse to do what she wants.

www.ingramcontent.com/pod-product-compliance
Ingram Content Group UK Ltd.
Pitfield, Milton Keynes, MK11 3LW, UK
UKHW040122190326
469155UK00004B/1303